WORLDLINES

A 'MANY WORLDS' NOVEL

ADAM GUEST

Many Worlds Novels Ltd

Worldlines

Acknowledgements

To my beautiful partner, Sarah, and our wonderful children, Jacob and Jessica, whom everything I do is for.

To Jenni Selvey, from Love Enca, for the amazing artwork and cover design.

To the original author of the article "The 10 Mind Bending Implications of the Many Worlds Theory", for initially piquing my interest in this subject; I owe you a beer.

For more information on the Many Worlds series, please visit our website at www.manyworldsnovels.net or follow us on Facebook and Twitter using the handle @manyworldsnovel.

Worldlines

In Loving Memory of my grandmother

Pauline Groves (1942-2020)

Whose long and courageous battle with vascular dementia inspired the characterisation of Mary O'Brien

Chapter One
The Blue Line

Death, the only thing in life that is guaranteed. That's what people say and that's what we all think. However, what if it isn't? What if, in fact, it is the only thing guaranteed not to happen to any of us, ever, and none of us realise because everyone else is busy dying all around us? Whilst we've all heard the phrase "Life's too short," we all have that feeling, that pre-programmed one, of thinking bad things will never happen to us; trying to live each day as if it were your last without ever really believing it will be. What if there's a reason for that? What if it isn't too short? What if it's infinite? My name is Gary Jackson, and I, like you, will probably live forever.

It was the summer of 2010, the middle of the GCSE exam season, but I was distracted. I'd attended Blackthorn Comprehensive School for the last five years and I'd sat all of my exams apart from one, English Literature, which was scheduled for that afternoon. It was the end of an era, although I didn't know it at the time. It was lunchtime, and I was walking to school with my two best mates, the twins, William and Henry. I say best mates, however, we all went separate ways after school finished, and I didn't see either of them for several years after this summer. However, right then we were still inseparable, and they were busy ribbing me over a girl I wanted to ask out, the beautiful Michelle Peyton.

"I always thought you'd end up with that Irish bird," William teased as we walked to school that lunchtime. "She's always fancied you."

"Sinead O'Brien? Don't be daft," I replied. "It was her idea for me to ask Michelle out."

"She'll turn you down," Henry chipped in.

"Shut up, the pair of you," I retorted.

In reality, I was really good friends with both Sinead and Michelle. I was probably closer to Sinead, but I fancied Michelle more. Sinead lived in the upper-class town of Badminton, whereas the rest of us resided in Barchester, its more industrialised neighbour. Our school was on the main

Barchester Road, between the Birchtree Estate where I lived, and the more middle-class area of Sycamore Village, where Henry, William, and Michelle resided.

On the one side of the road was the school and its vast playing fields, and on the other was the White Willow Industrial Estate, with its various factories and warehouses. There was a butchers' warehouse, a place where they made double-glazed windows, a bakery warehouse, an electrical wholesaler, and a used car dealership that was owned by Michelle's dad, to name but a few. Between the bakery and the electrical place, there was a burger van which got far more lunchtime custom from the kids than the school would like and, on our way to the exam, we crossed over to grab a bite to eat. Really, we should have eaten much earlier but, as we'd gotten carried away playing video games at my house on our free morning, we'd inevitably left it until now to grab lunch.

Having paid for our respective hot dogs and burgers, we turned to cross back over. I looked to my right and it was clear, although I did spot Sinead sitting with Michelle in the bus shelter outside the school gates; my ears started burning. Only half concentrating, I looked left and saw that there was a lorry approaching, but there was enough time to cross in front of it providing we were quick. I'd also noticed the long line of traffic behind it, so, being 16 and impatient, I called for the others to cross. Henry, being ever the smart one amongst us, stayed exactly where he was whilst Will and I darted for the other side. Will made it in plenty of time, but halfway across the road my biro bounced out of my pocket and landed in the road. Knowing the excuse "Miss, can I borrow a pen please as mine got run over by a lorry" was unlikely to sound feasible to our English Literature teacher, I instinctively bent down to pick it up.

"GAZ, MOVE!" came the scream, simultaneously from both Will and Henry. So, I did. I picked up the pen, dived for the footpath, and got there just in time to avoid being flattened by the 18-wheeler behind me. Will hit me on the back of the head (with the hand that wasn't holding his burger), while Henry, who had briefly had his view obscured by the lorry, meaning for a moment he didn't know if I was alive or dead, shouted, "Gaz, you could have been killed then, you bloody idiot!"

*****

"You probably were," said Professor Leyton Buzzard when I retold the story five years later in a university physics lecture, having left out the bit about Michelle and Sinead. Michelle was now my girlfriend; she had been ever since that day as I'd asked her out after the exam. Sinead, on the other hand, was now my best friend, and the only other student from my school, besides me, to decide to study physics at the University College of Southern England; my whole reason for omitting her from my story was that she was currently sitting next to me.

I looked at Professor Buzzard, confused. He was everything your stereotypical mad science professor should be. If you saw him in the street out of context, you'd just know he was a scientist. He was tall, thin, about 60, long grey hair, a small beard, thick-rimmed glasses, and he was wearing a white technician's coat.

"I think I survived," was the most intelligent thing I could think to say back to him.

"From your point of view, yes," he enthused. "But what about theirs?"

"I think they saw me survive too."

"From your point of view, yes," Buzzard repeated. "But what about theirs? You had to go through quite the sequence of events to get to that point. Let's discuss each one in turn. This road, was it a busy road?"

"Yeah, it was a main road."

"And do lorries use it regularly?"

"Yes, all the time."

"Is every vehicle that uses it a lorry?"

"No, of course not."

"How many of them are lorries?"

"I have no idea."

"You mentioned a line of traffic behind the lorry. How many vehicles?"

"I don't know, probably about ten."

"And were any of these vehicles also lorries?"

"Not that I can recall."

"Excellent, so we can estimate that one vehicle in ten is a lorry, correct?"

"Sounds about right," I said non-committally.

"And what about when you went to cross the road. Did you have to wait for a gap in front of the lorry or was it clear?"

"It was clear."

"Good, good," he said excitably. "What about the other side of the road?"

"What about it?" I asked, confused.

"I assume this isn't a one-way street, Mr Jackson. Was anything coming the other way?"

"I don't remember. All I remember is the lorry."

"Very good. So, we've already established a one in ten chance of the next vehicle being a lorry. We've established the other side of the road was clear, which in itself is unusual for a main road by a school. Why was there a long line of traffic behind it?"

"It's a narrow, single-carriageway road, lorries often go slowly down there."

"Ok, and it was far enough away for you to run across the road, but close enough that you didn't feel you could safely walk across at a normal speed."

"I'd go along with that," I confirmed.

"How fast were you running?"

"Quite fast."

"Were you sprinting? Jogging? Trotting?"

"Sprinting, I guess."

"Why not just jogging?"

"There wouldn't have been time."

"There wouldn't have been time merely to cross the road? Or there wouldn't have been time to half cross the road, drop your pen, bend down and pick it up, and then complete your trip to the other side?"

"It didn't seem there was time for that anyway, thinking about it."

"Precisely my point! And yet, from your point of view, there clearly was, otherwise you wouldn't be sitting here today telling us this remarkable tale."

I started to feel like he was patronising me, but yet he continued.

"Is it safe to assume then that had you looked to cross the road a second or two later, you'd have agreed with your friend Henry and decided against it?"

"Yes, I'd say so."

"And likewise, had you looked a few seconds earlier you'd have been able to safely walk across and there would have been no danger of your pen escaping from your pocket."

"Correct."

"It does seem like a series of increasingly unlikely events took place that day that put you in front of the lorry to begin with. Tell me about the pen. Why was it in your shirt pocket?"

"I always carried pens there."

"Loosely?

"It was a biro. I had the lid clipped over the top of the pocket."

"In order to try and prevent that very occurrence of the pen falling out when you walked?"

"Yes."

"But it still did, and what a time to do it. Not when you were walking, not when you were leaning on the counter of the hot dog stand, not even on the clear side of the road as you started running, but right in front of the lorry! It would seem, Mr Jackson, you were incredibly unlucky that circumstance had put you in that position to begin with, wouldn't you say?"

"That, and my own stupidity for running in front of a lorry," I said, acknowledging my mistake.

Buzzard smiled.

"We'll ignore that bit for now," he went on. "Now tell me, when the pen fell out of your pocket, why did you pick it up? You knew there was a lorry closing quickly on your position. Why didn't you just leave it?"

"It was just instinctive."

"And as you turned around to pick it up, did you see the lorry?"

"No, I never saw how close it was."

"How would you have reacted if you had seen it?"

"Dived out of the way, I guess."

"Panicked?"

"Possibly."

"You may even have been frozen to the spot."

"Unlikely."

"But not impossible. The fact remains you were spared from seeing the lorry and, as a result, calmly bent down, grabbed your pen, and made it safely to the pavement just in time."

"That's right."

"From your point of view. But I ask you again, what about theirs?"

I must confess I wasn't entirely sure where he was going with this. He was a man who would often go off on a tangent, speaking enthusiastically about a subject we had no idea we were meant to be discussing. Usually, you'd think you were following him, only to find you weren't when he revealed the real topic. It was his way of trying to get us to open our minds up to different scenarios and possibilities, many of which were often unfathomable. It felt like he was angling towards the subjects of probability, random chance, and our ability to recall events, but he probably wasn't.

"We'll discuss it in more detail in our next lecture on Monday," he continued. "In the meantime, does anyone else have an incident, a narrow escape they'd like to share?" Buzzard asked the class.

"I do, sir," said Sinead, raising her hand.

"Excellent, Miss O'Brien! Go ahead, please entertain us."

Sinead recounted her tale.

"I had a tyre blow out when I was driving down the motorway," she began.

"Ok, which tyre?" Buzzard enquired.

"The back left."

"So, how did it nearly kill you?"

"I was changing lanes at the time."

"Ahh."

"In the rain."

"Oh."

"Whilst..." She hesitated and looked down. "Whilst in the middle of a bout of road rage."

I grinned; I could remember her telling me about this incident at the time. Buzzard raised one eyebrow.

"Indeed," he commented. "Do explain to us how this came about."

"I hate lane hoggers," she said. "I was in the inside lane, and there was a white caddy van in the middle lane going slower than me. I thought he should have been in the inside lane with me, but now I had to cross two lanes to pass him. I moved out, and quite aggressively, to let the driver know he'd annoyed me, but as I was moving back to the inside lane my tyre gave up."

"Was the move to the inside lane as aggressive as the move out?" he asked.

"Yes," she replied. "You know what it's like."

"No, I confess I don't," replied Buzzard innocently. "Tell me, how close were you when you started to move across the lanes?"

"I was almost level with him."

"Really? So, you swerved violently across two lanes of traffic to show your annoyance to the driver in front?"

"Yes," Sinead replied reluctantly. She seemed embarrassed, and I got the impression she regretted starting this. Buzzard's tone had hardened; he seemed to be partly clarifying her story and partly telling her off for it.

"And, and I almost hesitate to ask this, but how far had you cleared him by before you moved back across?"

"Only just," she murmured.

"And, how far across the road were you when your tyre took exception to this manoeuvre?"

"In front of the van."

"Tell me, Miss O'Brien, do you still drive?"

Some of the students in the room sniggered, but Buzzard's face was serious.

"Yes, Professor."

"Any...accidents?"

"Not since then."

"Because you are wiser from this experience?"

"Yes, Professor."

"Excellent," Buzzard continued, returning to his more jocular manner. "So, your tyre has just exploded. What did you do next?"

"Took the car to the hard shoulder and stopped."

"Was it easy?"

"The car was already heading that way."

"Because the tyre gave up on the way back to lane number one, rather than on your journey to lane number three?"

"Correct."

"Tell me, how did you feel?"

"Scared."

"A bit silly, maybe?"

"Not at the time."

"Hmm."

"I do drive more sensibly now, professor."

"I'm pleased to hear it. But, being pragmatic for a moment, you could have had that blow out at any time. Either before you pulled out, or after you'd returned to the inside lane. What do you think the chances are of that happening at the worst possible time?"

"Quite low," Sinead offered.

"Precisely!" Buzzard went on. "The chances of you having that sort of incident happen at the specific moment you had just enough space to recover from it is quite remote in itself. Had it happened whilst you were venturing across lanes the other way, you may well have driven straight into the central barrier. Had you not been changing lanes at all, you may have inadvertently steered into the van in the other lane. In fact, it may even be possible to suggest that the manoeuvre you were in the middle of, as stupid as it may seem now, may actually be the thing that saved your life."

Sinead looked thoughtful but didn't actually comment.

"Does anyone else have a story they'd like to share?" he asked.

We repeated the process with about four other students, each one recounting a time in their lives where they felt that, given the circumstances at hand, they were fortunate to be able to stand there and tell the tale, and every time Buzzard would come in at the end and point out the series of events, how unlikely each one was, and how much more unlikely that made the subsequent event to follow it, right up until when the bell rang to signal the end of the lecture.

"Your task before our next lecture on Monday is simple," Buzzard called out as everyone got up to leave. "Try and work out what we're on about. Why are we talking about this, and what relevance does it have? You'll need to bring your brains with you for that on Monday morning, so don't go leaving them at home."

Sinead and I picked up our jackets and bags and made our way out of the lecture hall.

"What did you make of all that?" she asked, as we walked down the corridor.

"I think it would be really interesting, providing I had the first idea what he was on about."

"I guess that's why we study this stuff, to learn about it," she said. "I find it all fascinating. He's talking about parallel universes, isn't he?"

"It does sound like it. Are you heading back on the tube or are you going up to the library for a bit?"

"Actually, would you mind coming with me to The Oasis, just for a few minutes, please? I'm meant to be meeting someone, and I'd like it if you'd come with me."

"Yeah, of course, what's wrong?"

"There's nothing wrong, it's just…" she hesitated, then did an embarrassed little half-laugh before saying, "I've started seeing someone."

"Oh, wow," I responded, genuinely pleased for her. "That's brilliant. Anyone I know?"

"Actually, it is," she said. "That's what I'm worried about. You're not going to like it, but I'd like your blessing."

"You don't need my approval to go out with someone. Who is it?"

"Marcus Bray."

"Oh, Sinead!" I said, unable to hide the instinctive disappointment in my voice. Marcus Bray had been in our year at school, and he'd bullied me for a brief while. He thought he was a hard man and, whilst he was harder than me, he was still softer than he thought he was. He thought he had more brawn than I had brains, whereas it was clearly the opposite way around.

"How have you ended up doing something like that?" I asked her.

"I knew you wouldn't approve."

"No, I bloody don't! You're so much better than that, a million times better than him."

"He's really nice now, he's changed a lot since school."

"Sinead, he's just come out of prison!"

"Yeah, I know, but he says it's changed him. He's used his time in there to go a bit religious," she went on, as I felt my eyes roll automatically. "He's trying to live a more proper life now. He knows my family are Catholics, and I've been talking to him for the last few weeks about it. He's a different man now."

I thought for a moment. Sinead and I went back a long way; she would say our relationship was like brother and sister, but I have two sisters of my own, and it's nothing like what I have with either of them. It's also nothing like the one I have with Michelle, despite many people thinking we are, or should be, a couple. We talk about stuff that I would never tell Michelle, that my sisters would squirm at, and blokes just don't say to each other. We were each other's counsel; any trouble in either of our lives and the other was always the first place we turned. She was largely responsible for Michelle and I getting together, and she'd never really had a long-term boyfriend of her own. For her to be telling me this, he must mean something to her. It felt wrong of me to rain on her parade, even though I couldn't stand the bloke.

"How long have you been together?"

"Only about six weeks, but we're taking it slowly. I'm really nervous and he's agreed to go at my pace. This will be the first time we haven't met in secret, and I'd like you to see him first."

"Do your mum and dad know?"

"Yeah, he's been to the house a few times."

"Do they know about his past?"

"No, and I'd like it to stay that way for the time being. Not that Mum would remember from one time to the next. She barely remembers who I am now.

Sinead's mum, Mary O'Brien, had previously been one of the top solicitors in the country. However, she'd been forced to retire three years ago due to the onset of vascular dementia. It had been a couple of months since I'd last seen her, and even then, I noticed that she'd stopped referring to me by name. I was darling or sweetheart for my entire visit, something Sinead tells me is entirely normal for her. Her condition had seemed stable for some time, although only this morning Sinead had told me that they felt she was in decline again.

The main university campus that we were on kind of reminded me of a holiday park site you'd find by the seaside. There were buildings with halls of residence within them, there was a big reception office at the top of the site, an entertainment complex, an onsite mini market, and a laundrette, amongst a host of other things. There was even an old red phone box there, although I had no idea if it still functioned. The only thing it really felt like it was lacking was a path to the beach. We were heading to The Oasis, the student union bar.

I didn't tend to come in here very often; I don't stay in the halls of residence. Sinead and I still both live with our respective parents, so we tend to come to the campus just for the lectures and then go again. It had been decorated since I was last here, they'd had a new floor laid, and the walls were now much lighter in colour. The fluorescent daytime lights on the ceiling gave the place a bright and welcoming feel. There were also two new pool tables, an air hockey table, and a dartboard on the wall. I may start coming here more often.

I spotted Marcus as soon as we entered, and my dislike of him instantly came flooding back into me. I'd not seen him for nearly five years; Sinead, Michelle, and I had all stayed on at school after Year 11 to do our A-levels, whereas Marcus was far too manly and macho to do anything like that. I'm not a small man myself, I'm six foot two and about 12 stone, but

Marcus was a couple of inches taller and a good couple of stone heavier than I. He had short, dark ginger hair and an overwhelmingly punchable face.

"Hello, baby," he growled.

"Hiya," she said, leaning over to kiss him. "I'm glad you found us okay. You remember Gary from school, I assume?"

"Of course, how are you mate?" he said, standing up and offering a handshake.

"Surprised," I said, reluctantly returning it as firmly as I could.

"Yeah, Sinead warned me you might not like this initially."

"She just knows I wouldn't let anyone hurt her. We've been best friends for a long time."

"I know, I know all about it," he said. "Can I get you a drink?"

"No, I'm not staying," I said. "I need to go back into London and meet Michelle. She finishes work in an hour, and she's been on since six this morning. I don't want to make her wait around for me."

"I'll go and get the drinks," Sinead said to Marcus. "Are you having a cappuccino?"

"Yeah, extra wet please," he said, and Sinead and I left the table. The counter was right by the door, so we could talk as we crossed the floor.

"I always thought wet was standard when ordering a drink," I said, commenting on Marcus's order.

"Unless you're ordering a dry wine or a dry martini," Sinead said.

"True."

"Thank you," she said.

"I can't pretend that I like it," I said. "But, if you're happy, and he makes you happy, I'll give him a chance."

"I am happy, yes."

"But only one chance," I continued. "If he hurts you, he's going to have me to answer to."

We both smiled, and I leant forward and hugged her.

"Please be careful," I said.

"I will, I promise," she replied.

Chapter Two

The plan, as it usually was on a Thursday evening after university, was to pick up Michelle from work and then go out for dinner. She was an undergraduate student nurse, on placement at the University College Hospital, by Euston station. My journey home took me through Euston anyway, enabling us to take the train home together.

I exited the Northern Line and joined the queue for the escalators, a task made more difficult in recent weeks by the fact they'd closed one of them to refurbish it. There were signs all around the station telling us that, over the next two and a half years, they were going to refurbish each escalator in turn and that each one was going to take five months as they were tailor-made and had to be refurbished on-site, before apologising for the inconvenience caused. I was fascinated by, and loathed, the London Underground in equal measures. I hated it because it just seemed to be busy all the time, or at least whenever I was using it, which was usually during the peak periods. Trains are several hundred feet long and run pretty much on the minute every minute, and still you were sardined in. Signs in the carriages warned you to mind your hair and clothing in the doors, as there was usually no guarantee that, just because your legs had made it onto the train, there would be enough room for your head and your arms also. The shape of the carriages meant your legs could be onboard the train, but you still risked being decapitated by the doors if you were to stand up straight at the wrong moment. Driver announcements of "Please move right down inside the cars and use all available space" was a station-by-station occurrence, although where they expected you to go, I'd never quite worked out. Yet, at times I was mesmerised by it; who were all these people? Where had they all come from and where were they all going, all at the same time? It also amazed me that in this Health & Safety-driven world of 2015 the damned thing was still allowed to exist in the manner it does; although if it takes them five months to refurbish one escalator at one station, the chances of them doing anything about its more fundamental issues seem unlikely. It makes you wonder how, one hundred and fifty years ago, they ever managed to build it to begin with. The chaos when they eventually shut it down will be unimaginable.

I made it to the hospital in plenty of time; I generally got there around half an hour before Michelle was due to finish. Add on the extra twenty minutes it usually took her to do handover to the night staff, get changed out of her uniform, and actually make it to the main entrance, then I'd normally have been waiting nearly an hour by the time she eventually got out. I'm not a patient person and hate waiting around. However, tonight was date night, so I wanted to wait for her. Additionally, I didn't drive and Michelle did, so for me to get from the station at the other end, I then had to catch two buses to get home. So, on balance, I was better hanging around waiting for her. Michelle regularly suggested I should get off the tube at City Road instead of Euston and spend twenty minutes walking to make more productive use of the time, but I was too lazy. As much as I disliked the underground, I still preferred it to exercise.

Tonight, I was running a bit late myself after my brief trip to The Oasis caused me to end up on a later train. It was three minutes to six when I arrived and, unusually, Michelle was out by ten past. I stood in the foyer waiting for her to make her way down on the escalator, noticing, as I always did, that she was absolutely beautiful. As close and as intimate as my friendship with Sinead is, Michelle really was the girl of my dreams. Whereas Sinead was pretty in her own way, Michelle was stunning. She had bright blue eyes and curly blonde hair (when it wasn't tied up for work) and a physique that, even after five years together, still made me go wow when I saw it. I knew I was punching well above my weight, and I was proud of the fact. Not that I'm with her for purely aesthetical reasons, of course; she was also warm, clever, funny, caring, compassionate, and a million other things too. She had her quirks, as everyone does. I was very logical and would delay making decisions about stuff until I'd fully analysed all my data, whereas Michelle would quite happily make serious life choices seemingly on a whim. She was also easily stressed and very emotional, whereas I was neither. It did make nursing quite challenging for her sometimes though, as she was unable to easily detach herself from her patients. I like to think we complemented each other well, but you'd need to ask her about that too.

Michelle was usually very quiet when she first came out of work and tonight was no exception. She would claim that she'd spent all day rushing around being stressed, and that she needed the journey back to Barchester to allow herself to switch out of work mode and back into a more casual frame of mind. She'd sit on the train with her eyes closed and her earphones in and the two of us would barely say a word to each other, apart from the customary pleasantries when she first appeared. The alternative would have been to try and engage her in conversation before she was ready, which would generally result in her ranting about work and inevitably spending the evening in a far more agitated state than if I just left her alone for a while; I'd learned from experience that was in nobody's best interests. I didn't understand why it worked, but I accepted the fact that it did. We had a table booked at her local pub, The Loch & Quay, for 7:30. It was a regular reservation and I knew by the time she got there she'd be back to her normal self.

The pub itself used to have a country feel to it, the sort of place you'd find if you were on a caravanning holiday in the Cotswolds. However, it had recently been modernised and now had a much more contemporary feel about it. The main lounge area had fabric sofas dotted around to give it a comfortable, relaxed feel. The place used to have complete wooden flooring but they discovered when they put the sofas in that they would slide whenever anyone sat down on one, so they'd recently had a thin red patterned carpet fitted which I imagine was more expensive than it looked. To the left, there was a separate bar room which still had the old wooden floor as well as a pool table, a pinball machine, and a TV at either end that usually had a live sports channel on mute whilst background music, currently 'Hourglass' by Squeeze, played throughout.

We headed to the rear of the pub to the dining area, which had also been decked out with the same carpet and furniture that adorned the lounge. I preferred it to the wooden floor, as your feet didn't stick to it after someone had accidentally spilt a drink. There was only one table with a reserved sign on it, our regular booth against the side wall.

"How has your day been?" I asked her after we finally took our seats.

"Busy," she replied. "I can't wait for this placement to end."

"It's your last shift on Saturday, isn't it?"

"Yeah, but I've offered to pick up some HCA shifts over Easter."

"HCA?" I asked.

"Health Care Assistant, the people who work on the wards who aren't qualified nurses."

"Oh, wow, how come?"

"A lot of the carers have young kids, so they've got annual leave booked over the Easter holidays. With us saving to move, we could do with the extra money, so I thought I'd offer to pick up some shifts. My first one isn't until a week on Sunday, though."

"Good evening, Gary, Michelle, how are you both?" said the waitress as she arrived at our table.

"Hello, Mill, we're good thanks," I answered. "How are you?"

This was Mill Lane, or Milly to give her full name. She was short in height and had a very slim build with big, bushy brown hair and quite thick glasses, whilst her work uniform consisted of a plain black blouse and pencil skirt.

"Tired," she commented. "I'm so glad I'm off tomorrow."

"Does nobody work on a Friday these days?" I joked.

"Oh, are you both off too?" Mill asked.

"Yeah, but I've got to do a half-day on Saturday," Michelle answered.

"Some of us are having to work all weekend," I commented, but they both ignored me.

"Have you got any plans for the weekend?" Michelle asked Mill.

"Not really. I'm here on Saturday afternoon but I'm off on Sunday. Most people like a beer when they're not working but I'm sick of the sight of the stuff by the time I've finished here. What can I get you both?"

"I'll have a chicken Caesar salad please, and a Diet Coke," Michelle confirmed. This was because she had recently found a size twelve pair of jeans a fraction too tight, and now she'd decided she needed to lose weight because of it. I knew she'd be back on proper food once she could fit into them again.

"And I'll go for the T-bone steak, cooked medium-rare please, no mushrooms."

"And what do you want to drink?"

"I'll have a Birra Moretti," I said.

She went off to put our order through. I liked Mill; she was quite dizzy but managed to be cute with it. She was from my side of town and had been a couple of years below me at school, although I never really knew her until about six months ago when she started working in here.

"I had a really weird dream last night," Michelle said.

"Oh yeah, what about?"

"Do you know my friend, Jana?"

"Is she the one who works at the library with mum?"

"Yeah, that's her. Well, she's got this boyfriend called Robin. He's alright, I don't dislike him, but they're a bit of an odd couple. She's really loud and outgoing whereas he's a real introvert, wouldn't say boo to a goose. Anyway, I had a dream last night that I was working at the hospital, but I was working as a sonographer."

"What's a sonographer?" I asked.

"Someone who does the ultrasound scans, like those that pregnant women have to check their babies, they're done by a sonographer."

"Why are you dreaming about that?" I said with some alarm. "You're not pregnant, are you?"

"No, of course not. Anyway, I'm working there and I'm wearing a different uniform. My tunic was green in the dream whereas mine is blue."

"It's been so long since I saw you in it, I'd almost forgotten," I said. Michelle stuck her tongue out at me. She knew I had a thing for nurses, and I loved seeing her in her uniform. She hated wearing it outside of work, for obvious reasons, so rarely did so.

"Do sonographers wear green uniforms?" I asked her.

"They have a green trim, but they're mostly white. It's the assistant practitioners that wear green. Anyway, in the dream, I'd been asked to stay behind after work as we were having to do a scan unofficially. That's normally something that only happens if a woman had died and we were having to do a scan post-mortem to see if she was pregnant."

"Really?"

"No, not really, but that was what was happening in the dream. That's one of the reasons it was weird, as I knew the procedure, even though it doesn't exist really."

"That is a bit odd," I admitted.

"That wasn't all, though. So, I stayed behind, and this Indian lady walked in for the scan, and she was with Robin! I knew she was pregnant because I remembered scanning her before, but now it needed to be kept quiet because her and Robin were having an affair, and nobody was supposed to know. I had a go at him as, in the dream at least, it was the second time he'd cheated on Jana. I told him I was going to tell her."

"And did you?"

"No, my alarm went off and I woke up."

"You remembered scanning her before?" I said, backtracking slightly. "How can that happen in a dream?"

"I don't know, that's why it was so weird because it felt real. I was remembering things that, outside of the dream, hadn't happened. Same as I knew it was what we did on dead people, even though we don't as that would be proper weird. Anyway, I knew I'd scanned the woman before, and I knew it wasn't the first time Robin had done something like that. Do you reckon he could be cheating on her. Do you think that's why I was dreaming about it?"

"I don't know do I, I've never met the man, but probably not. You were just dreaming. I assume you're not going to say anything to her about it?"

"Oh God no, of course not," she answered.

I glanced up at the TV. The sports news was showing. The sound was off, but I could make out the pictures on the giant screen. It looked like a woman spectator had been injured at a golf event; they were showing her being treated for a head wound, and it seemed to be implying she'd been struck by a stray golf ball. Golf wasn't a sport I cared for, but I felt sympathy for the woman.

"What have you got to do next week?" Michelle asked me.

"Same as usual. Work on Saturday and Sunday, uni on Monday, Wednesday, and Thursday."

"You're not free for two straight days at any point?"

"No, I never am during term time. Why?"

"I was just hoping it might be possible for us to sneak away somewhere for a couple of days."

"Like where?"

"Well, mum texted me earlier, saying they'd got some last-minute deals on flights to Italy. I wondered if we could go skiing for a few days. I haven't been this winter and it's nearly the end of the season."

Michelle's mum, Denise, managed a travel agency in Barchester town centre.

"I thought we were supposed to be saving up to move in together," I reminded her.

"I know, and we are, but we're still allowed to have fun. We'll end up with our own place sometime in the next year, but it would be nice to have a last holiday before we're bogged down with rent and council tax payments. And it will give us some time on our own." She winked at me.

"We don't exactly struggle for that anyway," I admitted.

"Oh, come on, is there no way you could miss a couple of days of university to come with me? Please. I promise to pack my nurse's uniform," she said suggestively.

It genuinely would be a bit problematic. I didn't want to lose time from university, and I could also have done without losing the days' money from work. However, she knew I was going to end up saying yes to her. I always did.

"Fine," I said. "But I want to be back for work on Saturday morning. Also, we've got Sinead's 21st birthday party to go to next Saturday. I wouldn't want to let her down."

"I'd forgotten about that, actually," she said. "How is she?"

"She's got a new boyfriend."

"Really?" exclaimed Michelle. "That's great news."

"It's Marcus Bray."

"Oh, for goodness sake, it isn't?" she said.

"Sure is. He was even at the university today to meet her."

"Does she know he's only just come out of prison? He's probably still on parole."

"She claims to, although she's refusing to tell her mum and dad about it."

"About the relationship or his character?"

"The latter. She's claiming he's found God in prison, and this is what's changed him."

"Oh, the silly girl," Michelle said. "This is because of her party, isn't it? She's going to have all her family over, and they'll be asking her when she's getting married and having kids, and she's still not got a proper boyfriend."

"I don't know," I said. "But she does seem taken with him."

"She deserves better."

"I know."

"Here are your drinks," said Mill, returning to the table. "A Moretti for you, Gary, and your Coke, Michelle. There's about a twenty-minute wait for food, I hope that's ok."

"Yeah, it's fine," I said. "No rush."

"Thanks, I've opened you a tab up too, you're Tab 12."

"Cool, thanks Mill," I said, and off she went.

"So how was your day?" Michelle asked.

"It wasn't too bad," I replied. "We had Buzzard today. He had us telling stories about times we'd nearly died."

"What story did you have to tell?"

"I was nearly run over by a lorry once."

"Oh yeah, outside school before your English Literature exam."

"That's the one. But he was going into really fine detail with it, examining how we ended up in that situation, what the odds were of not only being in that position but surviving it having found ourselves there. He even implied that Will and Henry may have seen me die. He's given us homework for Monday, to try and work out why we were talking about it."

"What do you think?"

"I don't really know. Sinead thinks he's on about parallel universes, but it sounds more to me like he's on about random chance."

"Is that why you want to go to uni on Monday?"

"Yeah, I'd like to understand what he's on about."

"Well, why don't we go to the travel agent's tomorrow then and see if we can book something, say, going on Tuesday morning, coming back Friday?"

"As long as it's not too expensive. I don't want us using all our savings money up."

"We won't, and if it is too much, I'll just pick up a few extra shifts when we get home to earn it back again."

"Let's see what they've got available first," I said.

So, the next morning that's what we did; we got up, went into Barchester town centre, and into the travel agency where Denise worked. Ten years ago, Barchester town centre was quite nice, but in recent years it had started to suffer due to the decline of the high street. Many of the big-name stores had moved out of the town centre and onto the out-of-town shopping park in Badminton. Several of the shops had re-opened under different businesses, but the high street now was predominantly bookmakers, coffee bars, and charity shops. There were still a fair number of clothes shops and a couple of banks, however, Denise's travel agency was the last remaining one in the town centre. As a result of this, it seemed to do an excellent trade, particularly amongst the elderly who were still nervous about doing things like booking holidays online.

As I anticipated, the price was more expensive than I'd have ideally liked to pay. We were looking for the most basic accommodation; as long as it had a bed, a shower, and included breakfast, we were fine with just about anything, but even they were coming out at prices around a quarter more than I'd have wanted to pay. However, Michelle, being Michelle, managed to talk me into it, much to her mum's amusement. In my experience, ladies over a certain age always seemed to have quite short hair, and Denise was no exception; her dark brown hair, interspersed with a fair amount of grey, was cut into what I'd call a "boys'" hairstyle. I wouldn't say this to her, though. I got on well with my "in-laws," although Michelle also had a good relationship with my family too. Michelle looked nothing like her mum, and I was personally delighted by this.

"For the days you want to go," Denise advised, "Your best bet is probably something like Piancavallo, in the East Italian Alps. If you fly from Luton, you can fly direct to Venice in just over two hours, and then the transfer is about another two hours on top."

"What do you think?" Michelle asked me.

"When are the flights?"

"The outbound one is daily at 16:45," Denise advised, "Landing at 19:50 local time. Coming back, the flights are 14:25 daily local time, landing back in the UK at 15:40."

"So, we could go on Monday evening when you finish uni, and potentially not come back until Saturday," Michelle said excitedly.

"Babe, I've got work on Saturday morning. I can't just not turn up."

"Oh, can't you ask your boss to give you a day off? You'd only need the one day."

"Not at just a week's notice. And what about if we're delayed at the airport, we might end up missing Sinead's party."

Michelle pulled a puppy dog face at me, presumably because she knew how to win me round by now.

"I'll make it worth your while," she said.

"Michelle, I'm your mother," Denise commented. "I don't need to hear that."

"Mum! I meant I was going to pay for him."

"Of course you did," said Denise. "I think our Carl is meant to be off next Saturday, though. I'm sure he wouldn't mind covering for you for one shift."

Carl was Michelle's older brother with whom I worked. He was also a dickhead. Don't get me wrong, he is a nice enough bloke and I got on very well with him, but for someone I remember being very bright and intelligent at school, he'd somehow, on the eve of adulthood, managed to morph into an absolute moron. He was two years older than Michelle and me, and for a while, I looked up to him at school. He was a good-looking chap, very bright and a half-decent footballer. He got straight A grades at GCSE level (apart from the B he got in French which he was gutted about) and was tipped to do well at A-level before going on to one of the top universities. Unfortunately, that summer between school and sixth form, he suddenly appeared to lose interest in both living and learning. He hadn't been through a particularly traumatic event; none of his friends or family had died, and he hadn't suffered any problems with his health. Yet, one day he just seemed to change; he lost a load of weight to the point he looked gaunt, grew his hair and a stupid little beard, started smoking marijuana, and basically became a bum. It was as though he'd woken up one morning, shrugged his shoulders, and thought, "what's the point?"

At the time, it was all so out of character for him. Me and Michelle were both convinced he'd had a bad experience with a girl; he'd never really been able to hold down a long-term relationship as he was always getting bored and moving on to the next one. His mum and dad had tried to get him to sort his life out, but he always insisted he didn't have a problem. He said it was up to him how he lived his life, and he was happy the way he was which, to be fair, he always seemed to be. It was now seven years ago that all this had started, and he hadn't shown a single sign of fulfilling any of the massive potential he'd shown in his early teens ever since. He could drive, but both cars he'd owned he'd managed to crash and write off, meaning he was now carless, and he had been for a while. I did owe him for one thing; he'd managed to get me the job at Cables which I was quite grateful for. I still think he's a dickhead, though.

"I'd like to ask him first, or the boss," I protested. "I don't want to book something and then find we can't go, or we need to change the flight."

"This offer is only meant to be on until the end of today," Denise said in her best sales voice. "We have new offers at the weekend, so I can't guarantee you the price tomorrow."

I looked at Michelle, but I knew what was coming.

"We'll have it," she said, reaching for her bank card out of her purse.

"Gary, are you agreed?" Denise asked.

"Yeah, go on then," I sighed, before turning to Michelle. "But that's two days at uni and two evenings at work you owe me for."

"I know," Michelle said, as she winked and blew me a kiss.

Chapter Three

I spent that night at Michelle's, as I usually did on both Thursday and Friday nights. I actually spent more nights at Michelle's than I did at home these days. Her parents were quite liberal so were at ease with the two of us sharing a room. As long as we were quiet and didn't disturb anyone else, they left us to our own devices which I appreciated. It's why I stayed at Michelle's rather than her staying at my parents', who were much more traditional in their views.

I have two sisters, Donna, who was two years older than me, and Nicki, who was three years younger. Donna was a stylist in a hairdressing salon whereas Nicki was currently a gap year student. I was a gap year student once, which basically meant I spent a year off doing nothing whilst I decided what to study at university; Nicki was currently going through the same phase. My mum, Alexandra, was a librarian, whilst my dad, Gregor, was a mechanic who ran a garage on the Birchtree estate. He had a very close working relationship with Ed, Michelle's dad, who still ran Peyton's Automotives Ltd on the main road opposite the school. It was an arrangement born mostly out of the fact that Michelle and I were in a relationship.

Mum was quite open-minded, but Dad could be a bit holier than thou about things. Donna had always been allowed to have friends sleep over in her room, but boyfriends were not permitted overnight. The fact Donna had recently come out as gay was an irony not lost on me, but as she'd followed the "no overnight boyfriends" rule and they wanted Nicki to do the same, it unfortunately meant I couldn't have Michelle sleep in my room either.

"What do you think our house will be like when we get one?" Michelle asked me as we lay in bed that night. Michelle always slept to my left, mainly because her bedroom door was on the right and she liked me being closest to the door when we slept together. She was in a pink nightdress and was lying on her front facing me, resting herself on her elbows. I was in a black t-shirt and shorts, the same as I slept in every other night.

"I don't know, it'll depend what we can afford I guess."

"I have been looking," she said. "You can get a two-bedroom house in Birchtree for 160 grand or a three-bed for 180. We've got the thirty our parents have saved for us since we were kids to use as a deposit too."

"Yeah, but twenty-four of that is yours," I said.

"So, we're moving in together, I was always supposed to use it as a deposit. Thirty-thousand deposit, 150k mortgage, we'd only need a thirty grand income to get that. I'll get twenty-two as a starter salary when I qualify. If you work full time too, we'll make that easily."

"Maybe we shouldn't use it all on a deposit," I suggested.

"What else would you do with it?"

"Well, let's say we put down eighteen grand on a three-bed, so a ten per cent deposit. A 162k mortgage is an income around thirty-five k which we should still do. But there's going to be a lot of expense when we move in, legal fees and mortgage fees, not to mention stuff we'll need to buy. TV, sofa, bed, washing machine, stuff like that."

"I love that," Michelle laughed. "TV top of the list, washing machine down in fourth."

"You know what I mean," I grinned. "Would you really want to live on Birchtree, though?"

"Not for the rest of my life, no, but as a first step it's ok, and it's affordable. Besides, not everyone from Birchtree is bad, are they?" she said, leaning over to kiss me.

"We need to get some pictures of us together to hang on the wall when we move in," she continued. "We don't have many, do we, of us, I mean? When we're on holiday we take loads of scenic shots, and a few of each other, but there aren't many where we're together."

"We can try taking more selfies if you want."

"I was wondering if you wanted to get a selfie stick from work?"

"What, and have Carl take the piss out of me for it all day? No, thanks."

"Well, buy it at the end of the day then, before you finish. We could take it on holiday with us, make some memories."

"If you want, then yeah."

"Thank you," she said, kissing me again.

"I'll pick one up on Saturday."

As we were both working Saturday, but Michelle's shift started after mine, it meant I got a lift to the store. My job was a lot less serious than hers. I worked at a local electrical retailer called Cables. This meant that Carl got a lift in with us too, although only after Michelle had blackmailed him by telling him he had to cover my shift next Saturday, on what was supposed to be his day off, so we could go to Italy. However, she did make the mistake of reminding me about the selfie stick on the way there.

"What would you want to take pictures with you in them for, you ugly bastard?" Carl asked me in his dry, deadpan manner; it was difficult sometimes to tell if he was genuinely joking around or if he was actually being serious. He'd once addressed a customer in a similar manner, which hadn't gone down well with our store manager.

"Do you want to get out and walk?" Michelle snapped back at him, which was a much sharper put down than I'd have come up with. For some reason, he found this hilarious.

Carl's attitude towards life had, at times in the past, caused his relationship with Michelle to become quite strained; he was always more naturally talented than her and picked things up a lot quicker, meaning where he was able to see or hear something once and immediately understand it, she had had to work a lot harder for the successes in her life, a lot of the time for less reward. This had caused a lot of resentment during their childhoods, whereas now she'd gone past the stage of being jealous of him, straight through the being frustrated with him phase and by now mostly felt sorry for him for wasting his life. Michelle had, unfortunately, let slip our selfie stick plans, quite possibly on purpose, and Carl was behaving as predicted.

We arrived at Cables and I kissed Michelle as I got out of the car.

"Put her down," Carl interrupted. "You've had her the last two nights. I could hear you."

Me and Michelle just rolled our eyes at each other as I closed the car door; truth be told I hadn't 'had her' last night, so whatever he thought he was listening to, it wasn't that.

"You're such a moron sometimes," I informed him. "Are you going to serve me before we open?"

"Nope, can't serve family!"

"We're not family."

"Not yet we're not, but we soon will be if Michelle has her way," he continued, thinking he was some sort of comedy genius. "She'll have a ring on the one finger, and you wrapped around the little one with a massive thumb indent in your head."

I told you he was a dickhead.

*****

I wasn't due to see Michelle from then until Sunday afternoon when she came to my parents' for dinner. This was as long a period as we ever went without seeing each other, although we both openly admitted it was nice a couple of nights a week to actually sleep alone without either of us keeping the other awake through snoring, or accidental knees in the back, or just general fidgeting that people often did in the night to unintentionally irritate their co-sleeper. I'd bought the selfie stick, a black one obviously. Carl had tried to convince me that a nice pink one suited me better; I nearly poked him in the eye with it.

Once I'd finished my weekend shifts mid-afternoon on Sunday, it was back to my parents' for Sunday lunch with my family. This was a regular occurrence, and one I didn't appreciate anywhere near enough at the time. The "family" had gotten bigger in recent times as both me and my sisters brought our partners now. Donna was seeing a woman called Freya and had been since she came out two years ago. I wasn't keen on Freya, not that there was anything wrong with her personally, but I didn't like how Donna had changed since they'd met. She'd always been very prim and proper beforehand, whereas now she was more goth-like. She was always wearing black, she was always getting new piercings and tattoos, and today she was wearing a choker chain around her neck. Donna seemed happy, but I always thought she could do better. My other sister, Nicki, had recently started dating William Potts, my old friend from school and witness to my near-miss incident with the lorry. I confess I was originally furious about this; Nicki is my kid sister and she's still about twelve in my head. The idea of one of my old school mates sleeping with her made me want to smack him in the mouth. However, Nicki also seemed happy, Will seemed to treat her well, so what more could a big brother ask for? Mum and Dad were accepting of all our relationships, although they seemed most accepting of Nicki and Will. Donna and I have always felt Nicki was the favourite child. She got away with stuff we'd have been scolded for. They loved Michelle and Freya too, but it was something they developed over time, rather than the genuine affection they seemed to instantly have for Will. Maybe the fact they'd known him when he was a child helped matters.

"How has your week been?" Mum would usually ask of nobody in particular. I don't think she asked out of habit, she genuinely cared about our responses, she just didn't mind who answered first.

"Boring," Nicki responded, in the typical tone of a moody teenager.

"Have you still had no luck finding work?" Michelle asked her.

"Nope."

"Where have you been looking?" I asked.

"Just on the net, same as always." I used to give the same answer, and I took it to mean the same thing; no, she hadn't been looking.

"One of our girls is leaving the salon," Donna added. "I don't think it would be quite your thing, though."

"No, why would I want to spend my life cutting other people's hair? That's your job, I want my own."

"Who's leaving?" Mum asked Donna.

"Francesca, she handed her notice in last Thursday. She's been offered a job as a senior stylist at some hairdresser across town. I asked her where it was but she didn't say. I think she's worried our boss will scupper it for her if she does. He doesn't want her to leave."

"Why doesn't he make her a senior himself, then, if he wants her to stay so much?" Nicki asked.

"He says he doesn't have a vacancy for her to fill, and I think she's still a bit put out that I got the last senior job over her."

"He could always pay her more," Mum said. "There's not that much difference between the wages. You barely noticed the increase."

"He can't really. If he gives her a pay raise, all the other stylists will want one, and then the seniors will be complaining because they'll be getting the same money as the regular stylists, so he ends up having to lose her."

"Bosses are jerks," Nicki stated.

"How would you know? You've never had one!" Dad said, laughing. It was very rare for Dad to speak at the dinner table. Usually, he had his mouth too full of food. However, he'd make an exception when there was a chance to make what he thought was a witty one-liner.

"Funny!" she retorted sarcastically.

"How are you finding your new job, Will?" Mum asked. Will had recently started working as a barman in our local pub, The Red Chestnut. Historically, it wasn't a nice place. It had been closed down twice that I could remember because of trouble in there. Once it was for persistent fights and, most recently, because of a drug problem. However, it was now under new ownership and the proprietors seemed to be making a decent job of cleaning up its image. Personally, though, I'd still rather go to The Loch & Quay.

"Yeah, it's good," he said. "I enjoy it, more than I thought I would."

"Are you on set shifts?" Michelle asked him.

"No, I am full-time but it varies. I've got to go in later, I'm working from four until midnight. I'm off tomorrow, then I'm doing twelve until eight on Tuesday and Wednesday. I can't remember what I'm doing after that."

"Is it busy in there?" I asked.

"Steady. The bosses know it'll take them a while to improve its reputation, but there's always enough customers in. We rarely get to stand around doing nothing."

"How about you, Michelle, how has work been?" Mum asked, moving conversation around the table.

"It's been ok," Michelle said. "But I'm off for a week now. Looking forward to our holiday tomorrow."

"Holiday?" Dad and Nicki said together.

"Yeah, hasn't he told you?"

"He told me," Mum admitted. "But I didn't pass the message on."

"We're going to Italy, skiing, just until Saturday."

"You've broken up for Easter early," Donna commented.

"We haven't broken up yet," I admitted and told her about missing the two lectures and work. "Luckily, Michelle has managed to blackmail Carl into covering my shift next weekend."

"I love you, Shell," Nicki laughed. "You always manage to get your own way."

The different reactions this got around the table wasn't lost on me. Dad had a look of resignation, as though he knew how that felt. Mum looked mildly concerned, Donna gave Michelle a look of envy, whilst Nicki's was more admiration. I felt pride in her, thinking every woman at the table was wishing they were more like Michelle.

"Aren't you supposed to be saving for a house?" Mum asked.

"I'm going to start picking up extra shifts when I come back, try and ramp our savings up a bit."

"Yeah, I'm going to do the same," I said. "We'd like to be in our own place by the end of the year."

"How was university?" Mum asked.

"Yeah, it was alright. We had that mad professor lecturing us again on Thursday, which is always entertaining."

"Is that Professor Buzzard? I do think that's a funny name!" Mum remarked. "We had a customer in with a funny name this week. He came in to take out a membership at the library, a Mr Bacon. His name was Christopher but his middle name was Paul, meaning he was Chris P Bacon!" she said, bursting into a fit of giggles, whilst the rest of us grinned.

"I hadn't even noticed it," she continued. "It was only when Jana was going through typing up the forms that she asked if I'd seen his name. I hope I'm not there when he comes in next, as I don't know if I'll be able not to laugh at him."

"It is funny when customers have amusing names," Donna added. "We have a lady that comes in every eight weeks, and she's named Mrs Bates. She's pregnant, and she's having a little boy, so when he's born, he's going to be Master Bates isn't he."

"Oh, Donna stop being rude!" Mum said, laughing.

"I used to go to school with a Master Bates," Dad chimed in.

"Of course you did," Nicki said.

"I did!" Dad continued. "Simon Bates, he was called. Ironically, he was a complete…"

"Gregor!" Mum shouted, cutting him off and silencing us all. "Don't use language like that at the dinner table."

"Yeah, Dad!" Nicki said.

Dad knew to do as Mum said and returned to eating the final forkfuls of his dinner.

The conversation around the table continued for longer than I was able to listen or concentrate. Dad said he'd serviced nothing more interesting than a Jaguar X Type this week, a car he always described as "mutton dressed as lamb," as it was basically a Ford Mondeo with a Jaguar badge on it. Donna and Mum shared a couple more customer anecdotes whilst Freya, who worked in a tattoo parlour, seemed to enjoy mocking the fact a man in his fifties had come in to have the three lions England badge tattooed on his left thigh. It was Will standing up at half past three to leave for work that was the cue to bring this week's social gathering to an end.

"Are you two going to the pub later?" Nicki asked me and Michelle.

"Probably, yeah," I replied. "There's a quiz night tonight so we'll go there when we leave here and then go back to Michelle's later."

"Can I come too?" she asked. "To the pub, I mean? I like quizzes."

"I suppose it has nothing to do with the fact you know your brother and your sister-in-law will buy all your drinks?" Mum suggested.

"Well, maybe a bit," Nicki admitted, smiling.

*****

Mum was right about the fact that we would end up buying most of Nicki's drinks. We were back in The Loch & Quay, and I'd nabbed our favourite booth against the side wall; you know you spend too much time in the pub when you have a 'favourite' booth. The one advantage of taking your little sister to the pub for a free night out is you get to send her to the bar whilst you remain seated for the duration, although I'm sure she wasn't being entirely honest about the change from each round and was pocketing some of it herself. Nonetheless, I'd sent her up for our third round; she was drinking Bacardi and Coke, and I could almost guarantee she was treating herself to doubles. Michelle's diet was still in full swing so she was just on Diet Coke, whilst I was drinking San Miguel.

"Did you hear what your mum said earlier about 'brother and sister-in-law'?" Michelle asked.

"Yep," I replied. "Your Carl was making similar comments about us being like a married couple yesterday."

"I bet you wish people would just leave us to conduct our relationship at our own pace, don't you?"

Michelle would do this; give me what she thought was my opinion in the form of a question allowing me to either agree or not and then tailoring her response accordingly. I knew she'd thought about it a lot over the last year or so, and she knew I didn't consider getting married particularly important; this was just her way of testing the water again.

"The problem with it is," I began, trying not to sound too dismissive, "If we start spending all our money on planning a wedding, it's going to delay us being able to move in together. I think it's better for us to try and get our own place first."

"I hate that everything always comes down to money," she complained. "Nobody ever has enough of it."

"Probably doesn't help that we spend a small fortune every month in places like this."

Michelle grimaced. She knew I was right, but it would pain her to rein in our social life for financial reasons.

"What are you two chatting about?" Nicki asked, returning with our drinks. She handed me 80p back out of a £10 note; I'm sure she was ripping me off.

"Money," Michelle said, sounding bored.

"Can't you talk about it later?" she requested. "The quiz is about to start."

She was right. The quizmaster had just reached for his microphone as we looked up. The quiz followed its usual format with five questions on each of the six categories. Tonight's rounds were Sport, Geography, Music, History, Movies, and Food & Drink. I would usually cover off sport, me and Michelle would manage Geography and Music between us whilst she was also the historian amongst us, Nicki was the film buff, and we'd probably muddle through the last category together. We'd had to pick a team name, and Michelle had opted for The Jackson Three, which felt like another marriage hint.

The questions themselves were the usual mixed bag. I knew a few, Michelle knew some others, Nicki did well with the movie questions and then there were the couple we disagreed on; Michelle thought the maximum possible break in snooker was 147 when I knew it was 155, she insisted that Edinburgh was the furthest west capital of Great Britain whilst I said Cardiff (she was right on that one), and Nicki knew that the answer to '"I always get chocolate stains on my pants" is a line from which Thin Lizzy track?' as Dancing in the Moonlight. We didn't do badly, finishing 3rd of the 8 teams.

"Tomorrow, if you go to the airport straight from university, I can bring our bags. I'll get Dad to drop me off," Michelle said as we walked back to the car afterwards.

"Yeah, sounds good," I acknowledged.

"Why don't you try your new selfie stick, Gaz," Nicki suggested. "Get a picture of the three of us together."

It was a weird feeling, standing there taking photos of ourselves outside the local; it wasn't a very good picture either. Happily, Nicki was a dab hand at such things and soon got what she considered to be an acceptable shot.

"Ever considered studying photography at uni?" Michelle asked her, slightly tongue-in-cheek.

"Actually, that's not a bad idea," she said.

Chapter Four

So, just like that, the weekend was gone and, somehow, we were at Monday morning again. As I didn't spend Sunday night at Michelle's and given that I didn't yet drive, Sinead would regularly pick me up on a Monday morning as her route to the train station took her pretty much past my house.

"How are you?" I asked her as I got in her car. "Good weekend?"

"Not particularly," she admitted. "Mum has started to go downhill again. She had a fall yesterday afternoon."

"Is she ok?"

"Yeah, she's fine, just bruising. How was yours?"

"Yeah, it was good, apart from work of course. Me and Michelle have booked a holiday, though. We leave this afternoon."

"Where are you off to?"

"Skiing in Italy. It's only until Saturday."

"You are still coming to my party, aren't you?"

"Of course, we land around four o'clock, I think. We'll go home, get showered and changed, and then we'll be there."

"Good," she said. "I'd be gutted if you weren't there."

"Me too. How are things with Marcus?"

"It's going well. Dad has said he can stay at our place on Saturday night after the party."

"I bet he is pleased."

"Don't worry, he'll be in the spare room. Mum won't let us sleep in the same bed."

"How is she? I'm guessing the fall has shaken her."

"She's ok, but it's panicked Dad. He's thinking of getting a stair lift fitted, converting the garage into an en-suite bedroom and everything."

"It might not be a bad idea."

"Mum's not that bad yet."

"All the more reason to do it now before she is."

We went to the station where we caught the train into Euston and then took the tube towards the university. Afterwards, I'd have to go to King's Cross to get the train to Luton so I could meet Michelle at the airport. We'd decided to make our own separate ways there as I wouldn't have time to go home first; I was hoping she didn't forget my case.

*****

"Erwin Schrödinger!" Buzzard blurted out as the lecture began. "Who can tell me who he is?"

Being a keen pub quizzer, I knew he'd won a Nobel Prize for Physics back in the 1930s, but I couldn't remember what for. Sinead put her hand up.

"Yes, Miss O'Brien?"

"He was an Austrian physicist. He invented the Schrödinger's cat paradox, and he helped establish an institute for advanced studies in Dublin."

"I'm not sure invent is quite the right word," Buzzard said. "But yes, you are correct, he was the deviser of that paradox. Do you know why he devised it?"

Sinead shook her head, and nobody else raised a hand.

"He was attempting to illustrate what he saw as a flaw in the Copenhagen Interpretation of quantum mechanics," he continued. "The scenario presents a cat, a flask of poison, and a radioactive source being placed in a sealed box. If an internal monitor detects any radioactivity, as much as a single atom decaying, the flask is shattered, releasing the poison, and killing the cat. The Copenhagen Interpretation implies that after a while, the cat is simultaneously alive and dead, a state known as a quantum superposition. Yet, when one looks in the box, one sees the cat either alive or dead, not both. This poses the question of when exactly quantum superposition ends and reality collapses into one possibility or the other."

"Presumably when you open the box?" offered a fellow student on the front row.

"That is the suggestion, Mr Quinn," he concurred. "The prevailing theory is that a quantum system remained in this superposition until it interacted with, or was observed by, the external world, at which time the superposition collapses into one or another of the possible definite states. Schrödinger objected to the discontinuous jumps when there is an observation, the probabilistic element introduced upon observation, the subjectiveness of requiring an observer."

"Is that similar to the scenario of if a tree falls over in a forest and nobody is there to hear it, does it make a sound?" I asked, trying to confirm my understanding.

"Not quite," Buzzard corrected. "Whilst that paradox revolves around whether it made a sound, Schrödinger's view is more likely to revolve around whether the tree fell over at all. Until someone observes the tree, it is both still standing and felled, with the Copenhagen interpretation implying that the quantum superposition collapses into one state or the other at the point the tree is observed. Moving on slightly, back in the late 1950s another physicist by the name of Hugh Everett formulated something called the Many Worlds Interpretation, which does not single out observation as a special process. In the Many Worlds Interpretation, both alive and dead states of the cat persist after the box is opened but are decoherent from each other. In other words, when the box is opened, the observer and the possibly dead cat split into an observer looking at a box with a dead cat and an observer looking at a box with a live cat. But since the dead and alive states are decoherent, there is no effective communication or interaction between them."

"So, there'll be two of me?" I asked. "One seeing the cat alive and one seeing it dead?"

"Almost. When opening the box, the observer becomes entangled with the cat, so "observer states" corresponding to the cat's being alive and dead are formed. Each observer state is entangled or linked with the cat so that the 'observation of the cat's state' and the 'cat's state' correspond with each other. Quantum decoherence ensures that the different Worldlines have no interaction with one another. The same mechanism of quantum decoherence is also important for the interpretation in terms of consistent histories. Only the 'dead cat' or the 'alive cat' can be a part of a single Worldline in this interpretation."

This was heavy stuff for a Monday morning, but I think I was just about following it.

"Which brings us nicely back to your stories. Mr Jackson," he said, turning to me. "What do you imagine Mr Everett would hypothesise about your encounter with the lorry?"

"I guess," I began, without being at all sure what would follow next, "He'd propose that two Worldlines were formed at that moment, one where I died and one where I didn't."

"Excellent," he said, "But no. You're on the right lines but it's not quite that. You see, the Many Worlds Interpretation accounts for ALL possible scenarios. So, you are right in that, if the theory is correct, those two Worldlines would have formed, but it would have been two of an infinite amount. There would have been one where the lorry killed you outright, one where it hit you and you broke your leg, one where you broke both legs, and so on. There'd also be ones where you continued and the lorry crushed your pen, one where you continued and your pen also emerged unscathed, ones where you didn't drop the pen at all, and even ones where there wasn't even a lorry there to begin with. Each of them playing out in different Worldlines, with every single one ignorant to the existence of any of the others."

"So, we all died in different Worldlines but still survived from our own perspective," Sinead asked.

"Theoretically, yes," he said. "But it is only theory Miss O'Brien. None of this is factual or provable at this point."

"But it is believable, Professor," she added.

"Oh really?" he said, sounding almost amused. "Why is that?"

"Because of our stories the other day," she began. "We all nearly died, but none of us did, and for that to have happened and for us to all then be in this room talking about it in this one single linear world seems a bit far-fetched."

"Far-fetched?" he exclaimed. "You think the idea of multiple instances of you spawning up in other Worldlines as various scenarios play out is more likely to be true than the single instance of reality that we all perceive?"

"Yes, Professor."

"Why?"

"Because it sounds so two-dimensional," I added, trying to lend her some support. "Reality, I mean."

"Reality sounds two-dimensional to you?" he questioned.

"Yes."

"Why?"

"Because the world and the universe are so complex," Sinead picked up. "It would be disappointing if our role within it was so...singular."

"So, you'd like it to be true?"

"Yes," I confirmed. Sinead nodded in agreement while the rest of the class sat and observed this exchange.

"Because you believe it would give our lives more meaning?" Buzzard asked.

"Not just that," I answered. "But it would make everything possible, wouldn't it?"

"Everything?"

"Yes, think about it. People say it all the time, what will be will be, or anything is possible. This would prove that anything can happen, and does happen, all in different Worldlines."

"I was thinking about all this stuff a long time before you were." Buzzard smiled.

"Then you agree?"

"I didn't say that."

"Do you disagree?" Sinead asked.

"I didn't say that either."

"Then what do you believe?" asked Alan Quinn, who sat at the front. He was also one of the other students to have spoken up on this topic last week too.

"That quantum theory is a diverse subject. Many theories contradict each other and it's worth bearing in mind that nothing is provable at this point."

"But it's not disprovable, either," I suggested.

"No, it isn't. But we also are unable to disprove the existence of The Flying Spaghetti Monster, yet that doesn't mean it exists."

"It's a bit like religion though, isn't it?" Sinead added.

"How so?"

"Well, I go to church on a Sunday to pray. I can't prove God exists, but I still believe it to be true."

"And now you're applying the same logic to this scenario?"

"Yeah, I guess," she answered.

Professor Buzzard took a few seconds to absorb what Sinead had just said.

"Professor," I began, "If this were true and every scenario played out in different Worldlines, would there not continue to be a Worldline where we survived in every situation? And if that was the case, how would we ever die?"

"Are you suggesting you're some sort of immortal being?" Buzzard grinned.

"No sir, I'm suggesting we all are."

"I've seen enough death in my life to disprove that theory," Alan retorted.

"But it was only other people's deaths," I continued.

"My mother died of breast cancer last year," he said. "Trust me, she's definitely dead."

"I think what Mr Jackson is suggesting, Mr Quinn," said Buzzard, attempting to calm a situation that had suddenly gotten very tense, "Is another theory known as Quantum Immortality. It is another equally valid theory."

Alan sat back down but continued to glare at me.

"Is that an actual theory, sir?" Sinead asked.

"It is, it's a thought experiment. Everett believed this theory guaranteed him immortality as his consciousness, at every event, would always follow whichever path didn't result in his own death. Everett didn't come up with the experiment himself. There have been many independent instances of it published over the last years. However, the crux of the experiment is this; imagine you're sat in a room with a life terminating weapon positioned in front of you. Every ten seconds this weapon will measure some random event which has a fifty-fifty probability of being true or false, the spin value of a proton for example. Depending on the measurement, the device will either be triggered, killing you instantly, or else it will make an audible click and you survive for another iteration.

"The probability of surviving the first iteration of the experiment is fifty per cent. However, at the start of the second iteration, if the Copenhagen interpretation is true, the wave function has already collapsed, the experimenter could already be dead, meaning there'd be a nought per cent chance of survival. However, if the Many Worlds Interpretation is true, the experimenter will continue to experience survival regardless of the number of iterations or how improbable the outcome. It would not be possible for the experimenter to experience being killed so the only possible experience would be for them to have survived every iteration, no matter how improbable it became."

"But that would only be true from the experimenter's perspective, wouldn't it?" I asked.

"Well, it would also be true to every iteration of anyone living in the final Worldline where the experiment was concluded. Anyone observing the experiment in every other iteration would eventually experience the experimenter's death."

"But, would any observers not then think that the experimenter was the person who was immortal, not themselves?"

"Possibly, I suppose it depended on who was watching."

"Professor," Sinead interrupted. "Isn't the argument around whether consciousness can be terminated a moot point? I mean, it happens every night when we sleep."

"Not necessarily. What happens to our bodies and our consciousness when we sleep is also still a great scientific mystery, nobody really knows. Take dreaming, for example. We experience dreams from a point of view manner. If you dream you're sitting eating a meal, then you appear to experience that. However, what are you actually seeing? Nobody knows for sure. If these multiple Worldlines exist, your consciousness could potentially be drifting between them."

"Is that why dreams never make sense when you wake up and remember them but always do when you're in them?" I asked.

"Who knows?" Buzzard shrugged. "This is all fascinating conversation and I applaud the open-mindedness of your scientific minds. However, we are going off-topic and I actually do have a lecture to conduct. So, allow us to try and get back on track."

Buzzard returned to the front of the theatre and began the lecture we were now several minutes late starting. He spoke to us about several things on this topic, citing names and quotes from famous physicists. I struggled to concentrate for long periods; part of me kept going back and thinking about the dream state. I also thought back to the conversation I'd had with Michelle in the pub on Thursday night about her dream regarding her friend's boyfriend. If everything we'd spoken about happened to be true, then somewhere out there that really had happened. It had proved it was possible and, in theory, I guess that means it could have happened here too.

I must confess I was struggling to follow most of what he'd said even when I had been concentrating, and by glancing around the room, I could see that most of my classmates were too. But I did find myself fascinated by the idea that other Worldlines, as he put them, might play out different outcomes for the same event. It was an intriguing theory and one I wanted to learn more about. I hung back so I could ask him more about it, especially as I was now missing Thursday's lecture. Sinead was also doing the same thing.

"I thought this topic might interest the two of you," he said, looking pleased.

"Why?" I asked, both instinctively and more rudely than I'd intended.

"You're two of our more open-minded students, and this subject can go quite deep into the depths of quantum mechanics. We won't go as in-depth with it as a class as either of you would like, but I'm glad it's piqued your interest."

"Is it something we can do our dissertation on?" Sinead asked.

"You can do your dissertation on anything you want," Buzzard replied. "But it's a very difficult, complex, and in-depth topic to study. We probably won't cover it in the depth you need, so you'll have to put a lot of work into it outside of class time."

He paused.

"If it's something that interests the two of you, I'd suggest you work together on it."

"Aren't they supposed to be individual?" I asked.

"You can study the topic together and still produce different dissertations. Your views and opinions on the subject will still be your own. Personally, I take great enjoyment out of two science minds coming together to debate these theories. We're going to study it in slightly more detail on Thursday and then next week, but I suspect you'll discuss the topic in quite some depth privately between now and then."

"I won't be in on Thursday, Professor," I said.

"Why not?"

"My girlfriend is off work this week, and she's booked us a holiday."

"I hope you show more commitment to this course in some of those other Worldlines, Mr Jackson," which, given the topic we'd discussed, was quite a put-down. "I'm sure Miss O'Brien will take notes for you."

Sinead nodded, and the two of us left the lecture theatre.

"When are you going to the airport?" she asked.

"Straight from here. I'm going up to Luton to catch the plane. Michelle is bringing the luggage and meeting me there."

"I'm supposed to be meeting Marcus in The Oasis, so I'll see you on Saturday. Have a good holiday."

We hugged and I kissed her on the cheek, as I normally did before we went our separate ways.

The lecture had given me a lot to think about. It was going to take me some time to digest and process it all. It was still at the forefront of my mind when I got to the airport and met up with Michelle.

"Are you alright?" she asked, spotting the vacant expression on my face.

"Yeah, I'm fine," I replied. "Some of the stuff we were discussing in the lecture was quite deep, makes you think about stuff."

"Were you still talking about that parallel universes stuff?"

"Yeah. I've never been so fascinated by an area of study. Do you realise that, if it's true, it would mean everyone would actually live forever from their own viewpoint?"

"It would make old age boring and lonely," she said.

"What do you mean?"

"Well, if it was only you living forever, then everyone else would still die. I see it all the time at the hospital."

"No, everyone lives forever from their own viewpoint."

"Yes, but if I live forever, I still saw an old man die this morning and he's still dead to me. My parents will die, you will, our kids will, and I'll carry on living forever. Not sure I fancy that."

"Well, that's certainly put a dampener on the idea," I snorted. "I quite liked it up until then."

"No thanks, give me a proper death any day," she said emphatically.

"Well, maybe not any day," I said back. "I wouldn't be impressed if it happened any time soon."

"Well, no, me neither. But if it did, you wouldn't be able to think about us meeting again one day in heaven. You'd be stuck here without me, forever."

"It doesn't feel so appealing now," I admitted.

Chapter Five

It was nearly midnight by the time we reached our hotel in the Piancavallo resort. The flight was fine, as flights go, but the minibus transfer from the airport was deeply unpleasant. I can't remember ever feeling so disorientated as I did whilst we were driving up a winding mountain road, with its series of sudden turns, which allowed for two-way traffic but was only just over one vehicle wide, on icy roads, in the dark, with a driver who didn't speak English. It felt like it was pure good fortune that we didn't meet any other traffic on the sharp, tight bends. The driver, a scruffy-looking man in his forties' named Paulo, clearly knew the route well otherwise he'd surely have never driven as fast as he did. I was well aware skiing could be a dangerous activity, but surely nothing we did over the next four days was going to put our lives in jeopardy quite like that journey. Michelle, on the surface at least, appeared remarkably calm and relaxed about the whole thing, whereas I was terrified, so was delighted when we finally made it into the safety of our hotel room.

The room itself was even more basic than I imagined. There was a double bed with a wooden frame and no headboard, with just about enough room to walk around it. There was a bedside table and a chest of drawers at the end of the bed for us to put our clothes in for the next few days, but that was it. No wardrobe, no TV, no pictures on the plain white walls, nothing. The bathroom didn't have an actual bath, just a single shower cubicle. The bathroom door didn't open all the way as it hit the sink, and if anyone tried to open the door whilst you were in the bathroom it would whack you in the legs. Luckily, the cubicle had a sliding door, meaning space was at least saved that way. Still, we had said that as long as it had a bed and a shower that it was fine, and it ticked both boxes so we couldn't really complain.

One thing I did complain about was Michelle's insistence that I slept on the side of the bed nearest the door, which meant we were on opposite sides to literally every bed we'd ever slept in together. She couldn't explain why she didn't want to sleep nearest the door, just that she wasn't going to, and as a result, she slept to my right for the first time ever. It was surprisingly discombobulating.

Michelle was an accomplished skier. She'd been coming with her family since she was about eight years old, and she'd worked out on the way over that this was her tenth skiing holiday. It was only my second so, naturally, I wasn't as good at it as she was. My first trip had been to Austria with her two years ago, where I'd spent the first day sliding uncontrollably down the nursery slopes as soon as I stepped off the travellator. Once I'd learned that the best way to walk in skis is to side-on to the slope, it was on to the two most important pieces of information needed by rookie skiers; how to stop and how to fall over. Stopping was achieved using what my instructor had called the snowplough technique, which basically involved turning both skis inwards, causing the front of them to dig into the snow, thus creating a snowplough effect that would stop you from going further.

Falling over was also a skill in itself, as you had to remember to fall to the side. If you were to fall backwards with your skis still straight, there was a danger you'd just keep going. By falling sideways, it meant that the ski on the side you'd fallen would again dig into the snow and help bring you to a stop. The next step was learning to change direction which was easier than I expected once I'd mastered the basics, as you literally shifted your weight from one leg to the other depending on which direction you wanted to go. It all felt like slow progress, but by the middle of our third day, I was able to take the chairlift to the top of a medium complexity slope and make my way to the bottom under a reasonable amount of control and, more importantly, in one piece. Once you got your speed up and had your control it was a most exhilarating experience, one I was looking forward to repeating the next morning.

This will seem an obvious thing to say when you're in a snow-filled ski resort in the Alps in the middle of March, but it was bitterly cold that Tuesday morning. Michelle and I dressed ourselves so that there was no skin exposed at all. We both wore balaclavas with goggles and helmets, a couple of layers of clothing under our coats, including our salopettes which went over our shoulders and down our legs, as well as our gloves and ski boots.

Michelle had her own skis, but I hadn't bought any after our last trip so had to hire some, which was more expensive than the excess baggage fee Michelle had had to pay to check hers in on the flight over. I was in a plain black puffer jacket, whereas Michelle was in a sportier and distinctive-looking pink and purple coat.

All the ski slopes, of which there were over a dozen, were colour-coded into different categories, as was standard for European resorts. The green ones were the nursery slopes, a blue slope signified it was for beginners, red was for intermediate level skiers, and black showed the expert slopes. There was also an orange category which meant the slope was extremely difficult, but thankfully there were none of those here. By the end of our Austrian trip, I'd been quite confident on the red slopes but that was two years ago, so to build confidence, I went back to a blue slope for a run or two to make sure I could still do it.

One thing that I'd forgotten since my last trip was just how little skiing you seemed to do in any given period of time. By the time you'd traipsed to the bottom of the chair lifts, made your way back up to the top of the mountain slope, and then skied back down to the bottom, you were doing well if you managed more than a handful of runs in an hour. The higher up you went, and the more difficult the slope, the less skiing you actually got done.

Half an hour, or three runs, on the beginner slopes was sufficient to prove to myself that I hadn't forgotten everything, and we could move on to what Michelle termed the proper slopes. Despite the cold weather, our bodies were getting very warm under our various layers of clothing, and as we made our way round to the red routes, we both removed our helmets, balaclavas, and goggles to let some heat out. It was also ideal as it meant we could actually talk to each other, instead of communicating via hand gestures and muffled sounds.

"Oh, I've missed this," Michelle said, as she loosened her ski boots so we could walk around to the red run chairlifts. "Are you ok?"

"Yeah, I'm good, just hot."

"Did you bring the selfie stick?"

"No, of course not."

"Just thought it would be good to get some photos of us both skiing."

"It would. Let's get our confidence on these slopes today, though. . We've got four days here. We'll bring it out tomorrow or Thursday. We can go around the resort as well one of the evenings, as there's some great scenery around here."

"Yeah, that's a good idea," she said. "Which slope do you want?"

"How about the one that comes out by our hotel?"

"You haven't had enough already, have you?"

"No, it's just that made the most sense. At least when we've had enough of it then we can just go back into the hotel for lunch."

"Eww, I'm not eating in the hotel any more than I have to."

"Breakfast wasn't that bad."

"Yours wasn't, because it was cooked. But the cereal tasted like cardboard and the croissants were rock-hard. Let's go somewhere else."

"Well, let's do this slope first then, then look for somewhere to eat, then have a few goes on the nearest slope to it."

"Sounds like a plan."

"Unless it's a black run," I added. "I'm not ready for those yet."

"I'll have you on one by the end of the week," she smiled.

The red run that led to the hotel was more complicated than the red runs I'd previously encountered in Austria. It started halfway down the mountain, as the top half was classed as a black slope and had a separate chair lift that ran all the way to the top. There was an almost immediate right-hand kink just after you set off, then the gradient appeared to significantly reduce, before dropping again quite sharply. The trick was to carry enough speed so as not to get caught out on the incline, but slow enough that you didn't take off when the gradient increased. The first time I got it completely wrong, I ended up airborne and landed with my skis not parallel. The back of my skis hit each other, sending my legs separate ways and me sprawling face-first into the snow. I was glad I'd put my balaclava and goggles on, otherwise I'd have had some significant friction burns on my face, but as it happened, I was fine. Michelle was behind me, saw what happened, and almost made the same mistake herself. Fortunately, she landed correctly, managed to bring herself to a stop, and came back up the mountain to check I was ok. My left ski had unlocked, which was a safety feature to prevent serious injury, and it took me a while to spot where it had landed, which was about fifty yards ahead of us on the opposite side of the slope. Michelle skied across to retrieve it, but climbing back up the mountain whilst holding that and her ski poles at the same time was going to be a challenge. So, I unclipped my other ski and gingerly walked across to her, being careful not to get taken out by anyone coming full pelt over the ridge.

"That's why," I said to Michelle when I reached her, still panting for breath slightly, "I wanted to spend some time on the beginner slopes first. I'm glad I didn't do that straightaway this morning."

"I wouldn't have expected that little jump to be there on a red run either," she admitted. "Are you sure you're ok? That looked like a big crash."

"Yeah, I'm fine," I said. "But I'm likely to make that mistake again. Go back around and have a go on your own as you had to abort that run. Once you've worked out how to do it, tell me, and I'll have another go too."

Michelle initially appeared reluctant to leave me, but it didn't take a lot of persuading for her to go. The chair lifts weren't too far from the bottom of the ramp, and I figured that if I walked around with her, I'd be back at the foot of the slope before she'd made it to the top. It took her longer than I expected to reappear, and I started to worry she may have had an accident herself. In hindsight, though, I should have guessed why.

"I went all the way to the top to try the black run," she panted as she re-joined me at the bottom. "I don't know why it's a black run. The jump is the hardest bit. It's just a bit steeper at the top."

"Did you enjoy it?" I asked.

"Yeah, it was great fun. You need to snowplough on the shallow bit," she said, once she'd got her breath back. "Come down as normal, but then kill about half your speed so that you don't take off when it drops again."

"Got it. Are you ready for another go?"

"Yep, come on."

We went back around to make our next attempt. Again, I set off first, heeding Michelle's advice regarding how to handle the ridge. However, this time I slowed down too much, losing so much speed that Michelle had to take evasive action and go around me, making it to the bottom before I did. The next time I didn't slow down enough and fell over again, albeit a little less spectacularly, and it wasn't until my fourth go I properly nailed it. By now, Michelle had given up and had decided to carry on up to the black run, as she was finding this one too easy. I wasn't a natural at this like she was, but I wasn't going to let it beat me. Two runs on a much easier red run later, which I didn't fall over on once, and we made it for lunch to a restaurant that would become our regular spot to eat over the course of the week. The menu choices included all the Italian classics; bolognese, lasagne, carbonara, tagliatelle, along with pretty much every pizza you could wish for. This had convinced Michelle to abandon her diet for the duration of the holiday. We decided we'd work our way through the menu, although we'd save the wine for our evening meal. Skiing was hard enough, for me at least, without attempting it drunk.

The rest of the day passed pretty much without incident or any further accidents on my part. As much as I enjoyed the skiing, my favourite part of the day was afterwards, when Michelle and I proved that you were able to fit two people in the shower cubicle. There wasn't enough room for us to move around without our bodies constantly touching, but I certainly wasn't going to complain about that. This was a new experience for us both, and I enjoyed it so much that I spent much of the next day's skiing preoccupied, thinking about doing the same again that evening. I was so busy daydreaming about it that I fell over twice on the red run I'd easily mastered the day before.

"What the hell is wrong with you?" Michelle asked mockingly.

"Sorry, not concentrating," I called back.

"I bet you still haven't brought that selfie stick out, have you?"

"No, sorry."

"Bloody hopeless, you are."

"You could have reminded me."

To an outsider, it would have sounded like we were arguing, but we weren't. This was just the manner in which we spoke to each other. It was very jocular, and there wasn't a hint of nastiness to it. I concentrated more in the afternoon, and the evening was possibly even more enjoyable than it had been the previous day, to the point it was quite late by the time we made it out to dinner, complete with the selfie stick.

"Are you glad we came?" she asked as we made our way down to the restaurant.

"Do you mean in the room just, or here generally?"

Michelle shot me a look, and her cheeks reddened.

"You know what I mean," she said with a hint of embarrassment.

"Yeah, it's been really good, I'm enjoying it. How about you?"

"The same," she said. "Although I'm sure I've actually been here before as a kid. There's bits of the resort that feel familiar."

"Your mum didn't say when we booked it."

"She wouldn't remember anyway. Dad and Carl would know."

"Drop them a text and ask them, if you want."

"No, Dad can't really do texts and Carl never checks his phone anyway. We'll ask them when we get back."

We got to the restaurant and took what was becoming our regular table. I ordered a traditional spaghetti carbonara, which I was surprised came without any sauce, whilst Michelle had tortellini. She washed hers down with a bottle of White Zinfandel and, as I didn't like Rosé wine, I had a bottle of pinot grigio. Both were much stronger than the wine we drank back in the UK, and one bottle was enough to have us walking back to the hotel tipsy and giggling.

"Let's make snow angels," she said suddenly. "There's some snow over there."

"There's snow everywhere," I reminded her.

"Oh, go away, you know what I mean," she said. "It looks pretty undisturbed, let's go."

We slid across the road we'd been walking in. Not because we were daredevils, but because there was so little traffic that it was safe to do.

"Get your phone out, take some pictures," she said as she took her hat off and then lay back on the ground.

"You're going to get your hair all wet again."

"Oh, it doesn't matter," she said. "I'm having fun. Besides, there's no point taking photos if our faces are covered up."

We spent the next twenty minutes diving about in the snow, taking photos and making memories, and eventually lay back and cuddled up, holding the selfie stick above us for some photos together.

"I love you so much, Michelle," I said to her.

"I know, I love you too," she replied, and we kissed again.

"I'm getting cold, we should get back to our room."

"I know, I'm soaked too."

"Are we going to need another shower?" I asked her cheekily.

"Stop it!" she replied, slapping my arm. "You've had enough of me for one day. Besides, the hotel will be wondering how we're managing to use so much water."

We walked back to the hotel giggling, our arms around each other. It was such a special time, and I don't think I'd ever felt so much in love with her. I was so lucky to have her and be with her here like this, and I was determined that I'd never take it for granted.

Now, this is the thing with men around my age. When they're happy they gain confidence, and when they're confident they get cocky, and when they get cocky, they take risks and do stupid things.

As a result, the next morning we were out on the slopes, complete with phones and selfie sticks, attempting to take some action shots of us actually doing some skiing. To do this, we went back to the nursery and beginner slopes as it was much safer; there were fewer people, they were going slower speeds, and we were able to get some good shots. However, it had felt almost too easy to do, and I was starting to think that, just maybe, I was getting as accomplished at skiing as Michelle was.

It was our last run before lunch, and we were back at the difficult red run which came out by our hotel. Michelle was going to the top to try the full-length black run, and I decided to go with her, which did please her. She was right about it being steep, and I ended up carrying much more speed on to the lower half red run than I would have done had I started at halfway. However, I snowploughed on the flatter bit to kill my speed before the ridge and navigated it safely.

Then I had a moment of madness.

With my selfie stick strapped to my ski pole, I wondered if I could get a picture or a video whilst we were doing this. I held out the ski pole in my right hand and looked at the phone screen to see if there was a way I could start the camera recording. What I hadn't anticipated was how quickly I would deviate off course by not looking where I was going. I was also unaware that Michelle, who was going much faster than I, was about to pass me on the other side. My weight must have shifted ever so slightly onto my left leg as I was trying to get myself into the shot, and I ended up careering straight into something, and someone, at high speed. Something hit me in the back and knocked me clean off my feet, both my skis unlocking and flying off, and I heard a snap as the selfie stick broke in half. It took me quite a few seconds to come to a stop but, despite anticipating a couple of bruises the next day, I was surprisingly unhurt, albeit I was a bit shaken. I got to my feet looking for my skis, Michelle, and whoever I'd run into. An older man in a yellow coat had stopped alongside me, had removed his goggles and balaclava, and was now yelling at me in a foreign language. Presumably, he was telling me what an idiot he thought I was, and I'd have struggled to argue. However, it is disorientating having someone shout in your face and not being able to understand them, especially as I was still shaken from the crash. I held my hands up to the man and said sorry, hoping it wasn't one of his family members I'd careered into. Then I noticed her; about a hundred yards down the slope there was someone lying on the ground in a distinctive pink and purple jacket, and they weren't moving. It was Michelle. There were five or six people around her by this time looking to assist her. I looked at the man, pointed at Michelle, and just yelled, "Help her!".

I ran down to her as fast as I could without paying any attention to where I was going or who else might have been coming over the ridge. I was nearly taken out again by someone who whizzed past me on my left-hand side; I must have run right in front of his path. One of the other skiers had kicked his skis off and was planting them upright in the shape of an X in the snow to warn other skiers that there had been an accident. It felt like it took me forever to reach Michelle but, fortunately, by the time I got there, she was sitting up.

"Are you ok?" I shouted to her as I approached.

"YOU COMPLETE MORON!" she yelled at me. "HOW BLOODY STUPID ARE YOU? YOU COULD HAVE KILLED US BOTH!"

"Michelle, it's me," I said, wrongly assuming she hadn't realised who had hit her and she wouldn't be speaking to me like this if she did.

"I KNOW WHO YOU ARE, YOU IDIOT!" she bellowed. "WHAT THE HELL DID YOU THINK YOU WERE DOING!?"

"I'm sorry," I said. "Are you ok?"

"I'm fine!" she fumed. "Just a bit winded, I think."

For someone who was winded, she was having surprisingly little trouble shouting at me. She tried to get to her feet but winced as she did, and she was holding the lower right-hand side of her chest.

"I can't believe how utterly stupid you are!" she seethed, still bent over as she was struggling to stand up straight. I went over and tried to put my arm around her for support.

"Don't you touch me," she spat. "Go and find all our stuff."

She then let out a cry of pain as she tried to put her weight on her right leg.

"You should sit back down," I said, as calmly as I could, before saying, "Can someone go and get help for her, please?" to the dozen or so people who were gathered around us. I noticed the man in the yellow coat wasn't one of them, and I was hoping he'd already gone to get someone.

"I'm not being carried off this mountain because of you, you daft sod. What on earth did you think you were doing?"

"I was trying to get a picture."

"At that speed?" she said, utterly exasperated. "Are you insane? Do you know how risky and dangerous that is?"

"Well, I do now, yes."

"Is everything ok?" a man asked in English, although I could tell it wasn't his first language. He was wearing the same red puffer jacket as the tutors on the nursery slopes, and I assumed he was some sort of course marshal.

"We crashed into each other. It was my fault," I said.

"Do you know each other?"

"Yes, she's my girlfriend."

The man gave me a look that screamed, "You're in trouble," and he was right. Michelle was still standing bent over. She hadn't yet managed to stand up straight.

"Are you ok, madam?" he asked her.

"It's my ribs, it's hurting me to breathe. My right leg hurts too," she said, much calmer, and I realised it must have really been hurting her to continue screaming at me.

"Are you ok to make your own way down to the bottom or do you need assistance?"

"I'll be fine," she said, then looking at me, scolded, "If I ever get my skis back."

I turned around to look where the skis might have gone, and I heard the man say we needed to move her from the middle of the slope as she was in danger where she was. We were only around 200 yards from the bottom anyway, so if I could find the skis quickly, she wouldn't have far to go. There were four unattended skis to find, not to mention my ski poles; somehow, Michelle had managed to keep hold of hers. Once I'd found the first two, assuming it didn't matter which ones she used, I turned around to return to the scene of the accident, but Michelle and the small crowd had gone. Even the X-shaped skis in the snow had been removed. I looked down the slope and could see them at the bottom. I gathered up everything else as quickly as I could; my phone was smashed, and the selfie stick was indeed broken. I found both bits of it and hoped it had only snapped in two, then I put my own skis back on and returned to the foot of the mountain. Michelle was no longer there, but the man in the red puffer jacket was filling in a form on a clipboard.

"Where did she go?" I asked him.

"Two people are helping her back to her hotel room," he said. "Are you ok?"

"I'm fine, I'm just worried about Michelle."

I assumed he'd let me go, but he then started asking questions about me and Michelle for his accident form. It was only when he asked me to remove my helmet and balaclava that I realised I had injuries too.

"Yeah, she looked a bit like that," he said.

"Like what?" I asked indignantly.

"Blood blisters, facial cuts. You'll probably find others when you get undressed. They'll look worse than they are. They're just friction burns, superficial, but they'll sting for a few days."

"Can I go now?" I asked impatiently. "I want to check she's ok."

"If she's not, tell your hotel reception. They'll get a medical team to come and check her over. Can you sign this, please? I need to give you a copy of it too."

I put our stuff down, took my gloves off, and signed the form. He then gave me a green sheet of paper from underneath the one he was writing on, the customer copy of the accident form.

"Thanks for your help," I said before rushing off to the hotel. I say rushing off, but I was carrying the accident form, two full sets of skis, two snow poles, and the broken pieces of the selfie stick. My left hand was hurting too. I was struggling to grip with it and kept dropping stuff. By the time I made it to the hotel entrance, the people who had helped her were coming back out. I hadn't recognised them, but one blurted out as I passed him:

"She in room. She very angry."

I knew I was in the doghouse already, but I didn't really care. I just wanted to know she was ok. I made my way to the room and let myself in with my key card. Michelle was lying on the bed still fully dressed.

"Baby, I'm so sorry. Are you ok?" I asked her, kicking off my ski boots and climbing on to the bed beside her. She had tears on her face, and I could immediately see what the marshal had meant about the friction burns. She had a big one on her right cheek and another above her left eye. I hadn't looked in the mirror to assess my own damage yet, but I was becoming increasingly aware of pain in both the upper and lower parts of my left arm as well as my left hand.

"I'm so angry with you," she cried. "Why would you do that?"

"Yell at me later," I said. "Where does it hurt?"

"My ribs on the right side and my right leg. That marshal said my face was a mess too."

"You've got a friction burn on your right cheek and another above your left eye."

"I knew about the one on my cheek, it hurts to touch. Are you ok?"

"I'm fine, don't worry."

"Typical, you act like a dickhead and get away scot-free, and I end up hurt." She tried to turn to face me but wasn't able to. "You've got friction burns yourself."

"Yeah, I know. The marshal said we'll probably find others when we get changed. My left arm hurts but I've only just started noticing it."

"I'm getting hot in here. I need to get some of these layers off."

"Do you need any help?"

"Don't even think of trying anything!"

"I'm not going to, I just want to help you. There's no point hurting yourself more if I can help you, is there?"

"I haven't hurt myself, you hurt me."

"Point taken, and I'm sorry, but let me help you."

Slowly I helped her out of her ski gear and back into her casual clothes. She had a huge bruise forming on the right side of her chest and further friction burns down the outside of her right leg and on her right elbow. The left side of her body seemed to have escaped any injury, and I suspected any injury to her ribs might actually have been caused by the impact of us colliding. I went to the hotel reception and got her an ice pack to put on her ribs, whilst she took both paracetamol and ibuprofen that we'd brought with us. For my part, I had a friction burn all around my left eye and onto my cheek. I also had bruising on my upper body, but on the left side, lending support to my view that they were impact injuries. My left arm was most badly hurt, and it felt worse as the day went on. Although I could bend all my fingers and make a fist, I couldn't properly clench it. At least I knew it wasn't broken. My fingers kept tingling though, and the top of my arm was hurting up into my neck. I hoped it would pass after a good night's sleep.

"Do you think we'll ski again whilst we're here?" I asked her once everything had calmed down.

"You can do what you want, but I don't want the rest of the holiday spoilt by your stupidity."

"I didn't mean it. I just wanted to take a good picture."

"Whereas we won't get any pictures now you've smashed your phone to bits."

"The SD card might still be ok. We'll try it in my laptop when we get back."

As it happened, we didn't ski again. We tried to, but the next morning I was struggling with my left hand. It wasn't hurting as such, but I wasn't able to grip my ski pole properly. Our friction burns looked much better too once we'd cleaned them up. Michelle was determined to ski again, but after a single run down a red slope, where she realised she couldn't comfortably put her full weight on her right leg to turn, and that it was too painful in her ribs for her to enjoy it, she gave up. This did not improve her mood.

"You might have cracked ribs," I said to her. "You should probably get assessed by a medic."

"Even if I have, there's nothing I can do about it."

"But at least you would know."

"I'd rather wait until I get home. I work at a hospital. I'll get it checked there."

"Do you really want someone you work with examining your chest?" I asked her.

"We're professionals, Gary," she said, shaking her head. "We see body parts all the time. It's not always sexual, you know."

This meant the holiday came to a less-than-ideal end, but Michelle said her ribs felt easier the next day and was in slightly better spirits, saying she couldn't wait to get home. I was none the worse for wear. I was still struggling to grip with my left hand but not as bad as yesterday. I was hopeful that in a week or so we'd both be fully recovered, and we'd be able to laugh about it, but we were nowhere near that point yet. All in all, I thought we'd had quite a lucky escape, both only receiving minor injuries from such a high-speed impact. I hadn't been brave enough to say this to Michelle yet though.

The journey home was quiet and uneventful. We couldn't really have a play around and a joke as it was hurting Michelle's chest to laugh. It was quite an uncomfortable trip, and we had to swap seats on the plane as Michelle couldn't rest her head on my shoulder with her to my right, both because of her ribs and my arm. We were both feeling tired and bruised by the time we got back to Luton. Luckily, Ed picked us up from the airport, so Michelle, at least, didn't have to drive home.

"I feel awful saying this as she's my best mate, but I do wish we hadn't got Sinead's party tonight," I said to her.

"I was thinking that too, but I bet you'd be pissed off with me if I didn't go, wouldn't you?"

"I'd be disappointed," I said. "But it's my fault you're injured. Are you going to work tomorrow?"

"I'll see how I feel in the morning. I don't know how I'll cover these burns on my face though."

"Can't you just put a load of foundation on?" I asked her. "If it works for you, I might actually have some myself."

"You, wear make-up?" she said, laughing and then grimacing. Ed was approaching my parents' house by this time.

"I'll go in and get ready, then I'll give you a call," I said. "I've got an old handset in the house, so I'll pop my SIM card in there. I should be able to phone you then and we can see what you want to do about tonight."

"Ok, thanks," she said, and we kissed before I got out of the car.

"Thanks for the lift, Ed," I said as I got out.

"No problem," he called back. "Don't forget to take your case out of the boot."

I actually needed the reminder, or I would have gone without it. Ed drove off and I went inside, had something to eat, spoke about the holiday to my parents, was severely scolded by Mum for my stunt that injured Michelle, then went upstairs to shower, wrap up Sinead's present, write her birthday card, and get ready for the party.

The whole process should have taken me less than an hour. However, having had to describe the holiday to my parents and Nicki, and then listen to them lambast me for injuring her, it was nearly two hours later before I was showered, shaved, suited and booted, not to mention also having had to charge my old phone so I could use it until the insurance company sent me a replacement. At least by this time I'd received a text from Michelle:

I will come with you tonight, can you be at mine by 8, and dad will drop us off xxx

Now, I mentioned earlier on that there are times Michelle and I both appreciate a night sleeping separately so, having been together for much of the last week, and given that we had to be up for work at different times in the morning, I'd decided to spend tonight at home rather than at Michelle's. However, I started regretting that decision the instant I saw her in her outfit. She looked breath-taking in a red dress and with her hair curled. I'd seen her wear the same outfit before and found it mesmerising on that occasion too. It almost caused a physical ache thinking that I wouldn't be going home with her at the end of the night. For a moment, I'd forgotten all about her rib injury, until I hugged her.

"Ouch, careful!" she said. "Not too tight."

"Sorry, baby," I replied. "You just look stunning."

"Thank you, you don't scrub up too bad yourself," she said, commenting on my navy suit, pale pink shirt, and dark brown shoes.

The party was at a pub called The Ox and Lamb in Badminton. I hadn't been in this pub before, and my first impression of the place wasn't good. It felt very old and run down. The wooden floors were sticky, most of the tables wobbled, this room had a couple of ceiling tiles missing, and the walls were still painted Artex. However, I was more interested in seeing the birthday girl than assessing the locale.

"Good evening," I said to Sinead, wrapping my arms around her and giving her a big hug. "Happy 21st Birthday! Have you had a good day so far?"

"Yeah, it's been great," she said. "It nearly wasn't though. Mum had another fall yesterday."

"Oh no, she didn't! Is she ok?"

"Yeah, she's fine, she just needs to be more careful. They thought she'd broken her hip, but thankfully it's just badly bruised."

"That's a relief. Here's your card and present."

"Oh, thank you," she said. "Would you mind putting them in that green bag over there by the cake stand, please? Otherwise I'll end up carrying them around for ages. Hello, Michelle, how are you?"

"Pained," she said, breaking off the hug before immediately filling Sinead in on our little accident. Sinead didn't need to say a word. She just shook her head at me in disbelief.

"Mum and Dad are over there if you want to go and say hello," she said. "That's my Uncle Brian and Aunty Siobhan over there. I need to go and say hello. Will you excuse me a minute?"

Sinead went over to greet her relations, whilst me and Michelle made our way over to Eamon and Mary, via the bar of course. As it had been so long since I'd seen her, it was easy to spot the deterioration in Mary's health that the dementia was causing, and it was almost as obvious how much Eamon was struggling to deal with it. In a way, I almost felt glad Sinead had Marcus for support, otherwise she'd most likely end up trying to shoulder the burden for both her mum and dad alone. I also got to meet some of Sinead's extended family. There were a couple of people from school there that I'd not seen in quite some time, and I even bought Marcus a drink. I still didn't like the guy, but he did spend the entire evening on his best behaviour.

I was starving by the time the buffet opened, having not eaten since lunchtime, and the two of us were soon back up for seconds. I was trying to entice Michelle back up a third time, but she insisted on waiting for them to take the covers off the desserts first so that she could have one of those instead. She was also insistent that she needed to be back on her diet tomorrow but I wasn't convinced. Marcus had come over to join us and had a frosty greeting with Michelle. She disliked him as much as I did, but she did follow my lead in being civil with him. The last thing she'd have done was say or do something that would have caused friction between me and Sinead.

"Can't remember the last time I was at someone's family party," Marcus said. "Even as a kid, my family didn't really have them."

"Are you twenty-one already?" I asked him.

"Yeah, last October. Didn't like having to celebrate it inside."

"What did you actually do?" I asked him. I knew he'd been involved in a robbery, but I also knew he'd only been sentenced to ten months and had been released after six, so it must have been a small part.

"I'll tell you about it someday but not here, not tonight," he said. "This is Sinead's night."

"Gateaux!" barked Michelle suddenly. I looked up and they were finally opening the food on the dessert table.

"Come on then," I smiled, rolling my eyes at her. "Are you coming?" I asked Marcus.

"Might as well," he said.

As I stood up, I felt myself go dizzy, and I briefly put my hand on the table for support.

"You ok?" Michelle asked.

"Yeah, just a bit light-headed," I said. "I'm fine now."

We walked over to the dessert table but I still didn't feel right. I didn't feel ill. I just felt a bit weird.

"Do you want me to cut you both a slice?" Marcus asked, having made a beeline for the cheesecake.

"No, it's ok," I said. "We're going to have some of this chocolate gateau here."

"Make it a big piece," Michelle grinned, handing me the knife and then turning to pick up a couple of fairy cakes off the next table.

"You're a greedy bugger," I murmured, as my light-headed feeling returned.

Chapter Six
The Black Line

It was a glorious afternoon in San Francisco; the sun was beating down, but the water was still nice and cool. We weren't the only people swimming here today, but the bay wasn't exactly busy. I swam over to Michelle, who had made her way back over to the canoe we had hired for the afternoon. She was wearing a deep purple halter-neck bikini, and she had her usually curly blonde hair up in a bun in a vain attempt to keep it dry.

"I should have done this when I was here before," I said to her, as we looked across towards the Golden Gate Bridge. "I can't believe I came all the way out here and didn't come down here to see that."

"You didn't really have time, did you?" she responded. "You were only here for one night."

She was right, of course, it had been a very long trip. It was last summer; I'd just finished my first year at university where I was training to be a doctor. I'd flown over there to attend a seminar on virology for undergraduates which was giving guidance on the career path required. I'd departed on the Sunday evening, landed Monday morning Pacific Daylight Time, and headed straight to the four-hour seminar. I then slept the rest of the day before flying back to the UK the next morning. It took over a week for my body clock to realign, but it was the most educational thing I'd ever attended.

"Do you fancy going and grabbing lunch?" she asked me.

"Yeah, come on."

As I clambered back into the canoe, though, I slipped, fell forwards, and landed on my bad arm.

"Ouch!"

I woke with a start.

"Sorry," I muttered, somewhat disorientated. It took me a few seconds to gather my bearings and realise where I was. It certainly wasn't San Francisco, and I wasn't with Michelle either, I was with Sinead. I was lying on my front, my bad arm underneath me; the discomfort this caused in real-life presumably being what woke me up.

"Are you ok?" she asked sleepily.

"Yeah, fine, I was just dreaming, sorry. You go back to sleep".

But she already had.

I got up and went to the bathroom for some water, still thinking about the dream and wishing I really was back in San Francisco.

I gave my head a wobble.

What did I mean 'back' in San Francisco? I'd never been to San Francisco, and I wasn't training to be a doctor. I knew who Michelle was though.

Let me fill you in.

My name is Gary Jackson. I'm twenty-one years old, six foot two inches in height, and slightly underweight at 140lb. I have no job and never have. I'm a long-term mental health patient who has been receiving treatment for depression and post-traumatic stress disorder since I was run over by a lorry just over five years ago. The accident itself was a thoroughly unpleasant experience. I'd been walking to school with a couple of classmates, William and Henry Potts, who were twins. They'd been teasing me about my plans to ask out Michelle when we stopped for lunch at a burger van over the road from the school. Crossing back over, we'd run out in front of a lorry. There was plenty of time to clear it, but unfortunately, my pen fell out of my pocket as I ran. Instinctively I stopped and bent down to pick it up. Wham! The lorry hit me, causing multiple serious injuries, mostly to the right side of my body. A broken leg, broken arm, broken hand, numerous fractured ribs, and a nasty head injury where it bounced off the curb. I'd been told by several doctors and psychologists that I should feel lucky to have survived it, but luck is a relative term. The long term effects are that I still walk with a limp, (I'm supposed to use a stick when walking any great distance, but it feels embarrassing so I tend not to), and I also taught myself to write with my left hand, as the nerve damage in my right means I'm unable to grip with that hand. Other than that, physically at least, I'm reasonably well recovered.

I live with my girlfriend, Sinead O'Brien, and her parents at their house in the town of Badminton, which is situated about halfway between Birmingham and London, and the upper-class neighbourhood of Barchester, which was my hometown. She was about five foot four and quite petite with dark brown hair. I'd known her for nearly ten years now, as we'd been all through secondary school together. She was an only child, born to Mary and Eamon in the second half of their forties after they'd had difficulties conceiving throughout their married life. Sinead was actually an accident as they'd pretty much given up trying by the time Mary finally had a pregnancy she was able to carry to full term. As you can imagine, this means she's doted on by her parents. The two of us had been friends for much of the time we'd known each other, however, after my accident, we became very close; she was one of only a handful of people to really stand by me and support me. We became a couple about six months later and have been together ever since.

Michelle Peyton, on the other hand, had been my crush all through school, although I'm not sure how much she knew about it at the time. She was a couple of inches taller than Sinead and, if I may say so, quite a bit curvier. We'd been friends too, but I think I hid my feelings for her quite well. On the final day of our GCSE exams, I'd planned to finally ask her out. Unfortunately, this ended up being the day of my incident with the lorry and the opportunity passed. I didn't see her all summer but then, on exam results day, I took the bull by the horns and asked her anyway. She turned me down, and I'd resented her for that ever since. I always felt she'd have said yes if I'd asked her when I'd planned, and that the main reason she said no was because of my injuries. As a result, I almost treat her as if she was an ex. I've not seen her for a few years, and it's been a while since I dreamt about her too.

I returned to the bedroom and glanced at the clock. It was 03:42. Saturday morning, the 14th March, and that also meant it was Sinead's 21st birthday today. She was having a family party that evening, and I'd planned to propose to her. I'd been saving up my money and had bought her what was, in truth, quite a cheap ring for an engagement, but it was all I could muster. I'd received a compensation payout from the accident, but I'd blown most of that on gadgets and video games. My regular income came from disability benefits that I claimed as a result of my injuries. It wasn't much, especially after I'd paid board at the O'Brien's', but it was enough to allow me to buy a new game for the PlayStation or the Xbox every month. I'd not done this for the last two months in order to save enough money to buy Sinead a ring. The original plan was to propose at the party later that night, but her mum had suffered a fall at home yesterday and was spending the night in hospital with a fractured hip, so it was unclear currently whether she'd be able to attend at all. If she didn't, then I wasn't going to do it. I'd wait until we were all together.

Mary's fall had been triggered by her vascular dementia, which she'd been suffering from for about three years. She'd had to retire at the age of sixty-four when her diagnosis was confirmed. She had been one of the country's top solicitors but had become a shadow of her former self; you couldn't really hold a full conversation with her now. She can still communicate, and she can still read, as we'd discovered when she read the headline on the front of a newspaper last week, but much of what she says is largely incoherent. She talks about events that haven't happened, seemingly hallucinates, and could quite easily start a sentence on one topic and finish it on another with no idea of what she was doing. She still seemed to recognise us all, although she hadn't referred to any of us by name for several weeks, instead opting for pet names like darling and sweetheart when addressing us. Her condition had been pretty stable for the last couple of months, but then last weekend we noticed her begin to deteriorate again, and this was the second time she'd had a fall this week.

Eamon, Sinead's father, was a retired long-distance lorry driver, having been forced to retire a decade ago as a result of losing his job and his driving licence due to a drink driving charge. He'd have served time in prison too, if not for the fact that Mary had somehow got him off without a custodial sentence. Now in his late sixties, he has his licence back but is quite happy to spend most of his days "enjoying his retirement" as he puts it, which largely involved watching sport and drinking. However, he was now having to take on increasing responsibilities in caring for Mary. Sinead bore the brunt of it, and I helped where I could, as we were all aware her condition was only going to get progressively worse from here.

I lay in bed thinking about all of this, and it made me ponder my relationship with my own family. This is something I don't like doing, and I was annoyed with myself for doing it, as the best word to describe it is "estranged". I have two sisters, Donna who is two years older and Nicki who is three years younger. Donna is a hairdresser and Nicki is a gap year student, having completed her A-levels at the end of the last academic year. Donna and I had a major row after she came out as gay, not because I'm homophobic, but because I thought she was attention-seeking. Rather than telling us all as a family, she made a big announcement about it on social media. Coming out on social media seems to be the approved way of doing it, and it's usually responded to with a plethora of messages saying how brave and how courageous you are. I thought she was craving that level of attention and that being gay was just a phase. However, it really was a serious moment for her, and my reaction upset her so much that my dad punched me. I apologised to Donna the next day, but it didn't resolve anything and just caused more arguments. Dad took Donna's side and told me he was ashamed of who I'd become, which hurt because I couldn't do anything about who I was any more than Donna could. I'd become me as a result of my accident. There was nothing I could do about that now. So, that same day I moved in with the O'Brien's and deleted all of my own social media accounts. I still speak to my mum and Nicki semi-regularly, but I haven't spoken to Dad or Donna since.

I rolled over onto my right and looked at Sinead, who was sleeping with her back to me. It was very rare for us to actually share a bed. Her mum is a Catholic, originally from Kilkyle, in Dublin, and she doesn't really believe in sex before marriage, although she accepts it happens. It does mean, though, we normally have to sleep in separate rooms until we get "the licence" by getting married. However, with Mary being in hospital, and Eamon being far more relaxed about these things, Sinead and I had decided to take advantage of her absence.

The house itself was quite large for a three-bedroom house without being overly elaborate. It was built around the turn of the century, the O'Brien's being the only owners. Each bedroom was large enough to comfortably fit a double bed with room to walk around it, whilst Mary and Eamon's room had a king-size, plus a dressing room, plus an en-suite shower room. Eamon had been contemplating having the garage converted into a downstairs bathroom in the wake of Mary's health problems but had been resisting because of the cost. This week's episodes will probably persuade him that it needs to be done.

I didn't sleep well for the rest of the night and chose to get up at 06:10. I went downstairs and was surprised to find Eamon already drinking his coffee. I hadn't heard him get up, and I wondered if he'd even been to bed at all. However, I have a terrible visual memory and had no idea if he was still wearing the same clothes as yesterday.

"Morning, do you want a coffee?" he asked.

"Please. Couldn't you sleep either?"

"No, I've never been able to when I'm on my own. When I was away with work or Mary was away on a case, I always struggled to sleep. It's not nice seeing her like this."

"You still need to look after yourself," I told him.

"I will," he said. "But I need to be up anyway. Mary's brother and his family are flying into Heathrow this morning for the party. They land at just after eight, so I'll have to leave in a bit to go and pick them up."

"Do you want me to come with you?"

"No, you're ok. There's four of them, so you won't all fit in the car. My two brothers aren't coming until this afternoon, but there'll be six of them in total, so they've hired a car themselves, but Brian wants to come here first to see Mary for a bit before the party."

"Can you visit that early on weekends?"

"Yeah, the ward she's on allows visiting from ten o'clock on the weekend. It'll be about then by the time I get back from the airport. I have an appointment to speak to her consultant at eleven too, although I think Sinead is coming to that with me."

Eamon was right, and Sinead surfaced just after nine o'clock.

"Happy Birthday!" I said, going over to her and giving her a hug and a kiss. Normally, morning breath is horrible, but as neither of us had brushed our teeth yet that morning it was somewhat less noticeable.

"Thanks," she said, with only a half-smile. "Although, I don't really feel like celebrating."

"Worrying about your mum?"

"Mostly. But there was something that happened at university yesterday that was playing on my mind as well. I didn't really settle off until after two."

"Do you want to talk about it?"

"Do you remember that weird stuff I told you we were doing a few weeks ago with Professor Buzzard?"

"The Many Worlds stuff?"

"Yeah. Well, yesterday we were talking about it again, and the subject of death came up. He called it Quantum Immortality. The idea that in a multiverse, if all possible outcomes to any scenario all play out in different Worldlines, and the probability of death at any given point is never one, then we could potentially all live forever from our own perspective."

"An interesting theory," I said.

I had quite a scientific mind myself. Had it not been for the accident, and had I gone to university, I'd have probably found myself enrolling in a similar course.

"It's completely unprovable, of course, as most of these quantum theories are."

"Yeah, I know. I was just trying to relate it to Mum. The idea that she might live forever with this dementia rather than just dying when she's supposed to."

"Then maybe it's a good reason we don't know about this stuff," I suggested.

"Yeah, probably," she paused. "I need to go and get ready. I'm meeting Dad at the hospital at eleven."

I went along also, although I didn't go into the consultation. Sinead, Eamon, and Brian spoke to the doctor. Brian's wife and kids, who I'd never met, had gone to get a tea, and I'd remained on the ward with Mary, who had been asleep ever since we got there.

Hospitals are unpleasant places, and Badminton General was no different. I'd spent long enough in here with my own injuries to be put off the place for life. It was quite old and in need of modernisation, but it was still a popular hospital (if "popular" is the correct word to use), as it had an Accident & Emergency department, the only hospital within an hour's drive that did. It had recently opened two new wings. One was a full maternity unit and the other a cancer treatment centre. Happily, I'd had no reason to visit either of those yet. I'd only been in the main body of the hospital, which was grey on the outside and tired on the inner. It was drab and dreary, and it had that hospital smell that they all have, the one we invariably associate with death.

I sat there playing the new Touch version of Football Manager on my phone, although I was only half paying attention as I was too preoccupied thinking about my dream from last night. I love sleeping and I really enjoy dreaming. I can recall at least one dream most nights. In the last few months,

I've started to try and practise lucid dreaming, which is a state in which you become aware that you are dreaming, and it allows you to take control of the dream. It is a very powerful experience and one I find much more fulfilling and satisfying than most things I regularly experience in the waking world. Unfortunately, I'm not very good at it.

I'd been practising for about six months but had so far only had five lucid dreams. On three of those occasions, the excitement of realising I was lucid dreaming had woken me up, meaning the experience was wasted. As a result, I'd started doing tests in the day, to test that I was awake. Things like checking my right hand for the scars from my accident or reading something before looking away then reading it again to make sure it still said the same thing. Then I sleep, or at least nap, as often as I can to give myself opportunities to experience it. I wasn't having much luck with it though. The dream last night was different. I struggle to remember another quite like it. I hadn't done what usually happens in dreams and gone straight from the canoe to the business trip. I was still in the water, and I was *remembering* that trip, even though from my perspective now neither of those events had ever happened.

"Hello, you!" came a voice, bringing me back to the present. "What are you doing here?"

Mary was awake.

"Hello, Mary. How are you feeling?"

"Oh, you know, like the weather," she said. "Where's the bab?"

"She's with Eamon," I said, assuming she was referring to Sinead. "They're in with the consultant. Brian is here too."

"Brian?"

"Yes, your brother."

"Our Timmy would know all about that," she said.

I had no idea who Timmy was.

"Would he?" I commented, trying to keep the conversation going.

"Yeah, he lost me as a child."

Now I knew. He was her cousin, and I vaguely remember hearing a story about them playing in the woods by their house when they were kids. They'd been playing hide and seek, Mary had gone deep into the woods to hide, and Timmy hadn't been able to find her so had given up looking. Mary had subsequently got lost, and it was about an hour later when her parents found her. However, I also believe Timmy to be dead.

"I remember you saying, yes."

"Remember me saying what?" she asked, seeming genuinely confused.

"About Timmy."

"Timmy? Is he here?"

"No, but Brian is."

"Who's Brian?"

"Your brother, he flew over this morning."

Mary just looked at me; this was getting quite awkward, but it frequently did.

"How's your hip?" I asked, changing the subject before she did.

"Bloody sore," she commented. "I don't know what I've done to it."

"You had a fall yesterday, do you remember? You've damaged your hip."

"I didn't fall over!" she snapped. "I'm not an old woman!"

Happily, at that moment, Sinead, Eamon, and Brian came back around the corner.

"Hello, you!" Mary enthused. "What are you doing here?"

It was the exact greeting and tone she'd used to speak to me, almost as though it was a default setting.

"Hello, Mary," said Brian. "I've come to see my big sister. What have you been doing to yourself?"

"Me? I've already told them," she said.

At that, Brian's wife and kids also appeared on the ward; I confess I didn't know any of their names.

"I've brought Siobhan and the kids to see you," Brian said. "Seamus, Marie, come and say hello to your Auntie Mary."

Now I did.

"Hello," they muttered.

Seamus was about fourteen and I'd have said Marie was around eleven. Seamus was playing on his phone and Marie had got a PlayStation Vita, making her the only person I knew who'd ever owned one. Maybe they were more of a success in Ireland than they were over here. Brian himself looked at least fifteen years younger than Mary. I'd have clocked him as being in his early fifties, although I am awful at guessing these things, I could quite easily have been out by ten years on either side. There did appear a quite decent age gap between the siblings, however. Siobhan looked younger still, maybe mid-forties. She was also sour-faced and looked like she'd rather be anywhere other than here. To be honest, I knew how she felt.

Sinead was now by my side, and I held her hand. Even though the photochromic lenses on her glasses had gone dark due to the light on the ward, I could tell she'd been crying. Her cheeks were red and puffed up.

"Are you ok?" I asked her quietly.

"Of course I'm not, my bloody leg hurts!" piped up Mary, before spotting Sinead next to me. "Hello, darling," she said. "What are you doing here?"

"I've come to see you, Mum. How are you feeling?"

"Oh, you know, like the weather," she said. This was the second time she'd given the same answer to that question, suggesting she had understood it, although I had no idea what the answer meant. I noticed a nurse making her way over to us.

"I'm sorry, we can't have this many visitors around one bed," she said politely as she approached. "Can I ask a few of you to wait outside, please?"

"I'll go, I've been here a while," I said, turning to Sinead. "You stay here with your dad and Brian."

"No, I'll come with you," she said. "You can stay in if you want, Siobhan?"

"No, it's ok. I'm going to take the kids across to the hotel. They said we couldn't check in until two but there's no harm in trying, is there?" With that, she turned and left.

"We'll wait outside," Sinead said to her dad.

"I'll come out in a bit, and you can spend some time with your mum," Brian said. "I've got your cards and present in the boot of your dad's car., Don't let me forget to give them to you."

I considered that unlikely given that the original reason for his visit was for Sinead's party that he'd be attending tonight. If that didn't serve as a reminder, nothing would. However, I declined to make this comment under the circumstances.

We went and sat in the corridor outside the ward.

"What did the consultant say?" I asked.

"They want to keep her in for a few days. She needs to recover from the surgery and have some physio. They're also thinking of doing another CT scan on her brain to see how far her dementia has developed."

"So, she won't be able to come tonight?"

Sinead shook her head.

"They were asking Dad about his ability to continue to care for her, as they were suggesting she might be better off going into a home."

"She won't like that," I grimaced; Mary had always been a strong, independent woman. You couldn't even buy her a drink without her insisting she got you one back.

"No, she won't, and neither did Dad." Sinead removed her glasses and bowed her head so she could rub her eyes to dry them. "She's always said she'd rather die than live to be a burden."

I couldn't think of a helpful remark so stayed silent.

"What's Brian's last name?" I asked her, trying to talk about something lighter.

"O'Connor," she answered, before looking up at me. "Don't worry, he's not Brian O'Brien."

"Well, I'd worked that out," I said. "Your mum is only O'Brien because she married your dad."

"It's funny, had I got Mum's name instead of Dad's, I'd have been Sinead O'Connor."

"Well, nothing does compare to you," I said, quite cornily.

"Very good," she said, rolling her eyes.

She bowed her head again and I could tell her thoughts had returned to her mum.

"We're going to lose her, aren't we?"

"I don't think so," I replied. "The doctor told you when she was diagnosed that she should have about five years, and that was only three years ago. We're going to have her here for a bit longer yet."

"Yet the longer she's here, the longer she's going to suffer for."

She bit down on the knuckle of her index finger, an odd habit she had when she was upset or angry about something.

"It's all rubbish, isn't it?" she said. "I'm twenty-one today, and I'm sitting here at the hospital because Mum is in here. I just want to be able to enjoy myself."

"You will later," I said, realising a moment too late that this wasn't going to be helpful.

"Yeah, without Mum," she retorted. "I'm tempted to call the whole party off."

"Don't do that. Your mum would want to be there, but she also wouldn't want you to cancel it on her behalf. Right now, she's in here and she's safe. That's all you can really ask for at the minute. You could do with going and getting ready yourself. I'm sure it's what your mum would want."

She sat and considered this for a moment.

"Yeah, you're right. We should do exactly what we would have done had she been there. It's what mum would have told me to do."

At that, Brian appeared again.

"Thanks, Sinead, you can go in now if you want."

Sinead entered and Brian walked off. He didn't sit down with me. I wasn't bothered as I didn't really know him, and I'm not good making small talk with strangers.

I pondered for a moment what Sinead had said about behaving as we would if Mary was there and decided, at that point, that I would still pop the question at the party. It would also get me out of a slight hole, as if I didn't offer her the ring, I wouldn't have another present to give her.

Chapter Seven

One thing I hadn't expected at the party was for any of my family to be in attendance. I knew, of course, that Sinead had invited them, but I didn't think any of them would bother to turn up, so I was quite surprised to discover my mum and Nicki there. Whilst I was still on reasonable terms with them both, conversation between us was always exceedingly difficult due to the huge elephant in the room. Mum was about a foot shorter than me, as I got my height from my dad's side, although we probably weighed about the same. She formerly had blonde hair but most of it had turned grey by now. She was in a black top with big bright-coloured flowers all over it. It sounds garish, but she pulled it off quite well. Nicki was of average height and build with long blonde hair. She was in a plain white top with a pale blue jacket over it. I walked over to Mum who embraced me like...I was going to say like a son, but how else would she?

"How are you?" she asked, looking me over; this was the first time I'd seen her in about six weeks.

"Yeah, I'm not too bad," I said. "How are you two?"

"We're ok thanks," Mum nodded and smiled, but the silence that followed was slightly too long not to qualify as awkward.

"So," Mum continued, "How's Mary, I hear she's had an accident?"

I filled them both in on the details of her deteriorating dementia and the injury she had sustained in the fall.

"Oh no," Mum sympathised. "Sinead must be so disappointed that her mum isn't here."

"Yeah, she's pretty cut up about it," I commented. "She considered cancelling the party, but we decided Mary would have probably still wanted her to have it."

"I guess so," she said. "What did you get her for her birthday?"

"Erm…"

"Oh Gary, the girl is twenty-one and she's been so good to you. Don't tell me you haven't got her anything?"

"Yeah, I have," I said awkwardly. "I've just not given it to her yet. Thanks for the vote of confidence though."

"So, what is it?" Nicki asked.

"Oh, now Nicki," Mum said. "If Gary doesn't want to tell us he doesn't have to."

"You've got her an engagement ring, haven't you?" Nicki asked suggestively.

"Why would you think that?"

"Why else wouldn't you have given it to her yet? I reckon you were planning to do it here, but with her mum being in hospital you've not quite decided whether you're still going to or not."

"She hasn't opened any of her presents yet. They're all in that big bag under the buffet table."

"And is yours in there?" Nicki asked.

"No," I answered.

She looked at me as though she was waiting for me to say more; I sat back in my chair and looked up at the ceiling.

"Too bloody clever for your own good, you are," I told her.

"Oh Gary, that will be great if she says yes," Mum added. "We'd be so pleased for you."

"Yeah, well," I continued, "It doesn't feel right without Mary being here. But I've not got her anything else, so I kind of need to or she'll think I haven't got her a present. I'm not sure what to do."

"What does Eamon think?"

"I have no idea. I haven't asked him."

"Oh, Gary! You can't ask his daughter to marry you without telling him first."

"Isn't it a bit old fashioned to ask for permission?"

"Well, maybe. But they're a bit more traditional than we are. I don't think you should do this without asking him first."

"If I see him on his own, I'll ask him," I said. "How's work going anyway?"

"Quiet," she said, which was always her go-to answer. She was a librarian, and she always thought the answer was funny; it never was.

We chatted for about another ten minutes, carefully avoiding the subject of either Dad or Donna. I did learn that Nicki had chosen to study photography at university. I was pleased for her but also a bit underwhelmed by it. Nicki was incredibly clever; she could have been anything she wanted to be. Photography seemed a bit too low for her; I felt she should have been setting her sights higher. However, I didn't really know much about the subject, and it was her decision. Given how my life had gone since I left school, I wasn't in a position to lecture anyone on their choices. I looked up and saw Sinead, who was heading over in our direction. She looked beautiful tonight. She always did, of course, but she's quite low maintenance and doesn't put the most effort into her appearance. I actually quite like this about her, as what you see is what you get, and her attractiveness is natural. But when she does put the effort in, has her hair done and puts some makeup on, her beauty is striking. She was in a black dress with thin white hoops going around it, and she was even wearing heels, which she also rarely does.

"Hi, Alex," she said, referring to my mum. "Hi, Nicki. How are you both?"

"Yes, we're good, thanks darling," my mum replied. "How are you doing?"

"Yeah, so-so, I guess. How are Gregor and Donna?"

That was my cue to leave.

"Excuse me," I said, standing up. "I need to have a word with your dad about something," and I walked off, leaving the three of them to talk about the other half of my family.

Eamon had indeed become free and was walking across to the bar. I had no idea who he'd been talking to. There were between seventy and eighty people here, and I knew no more than about a third of them. The venue itself was the function room of the main pub in Badminton, called The Ox and Lamb. I wasn't that keen on the place. Not because it was rowdy or anything, but because it just felt very run down. The wooden floors were sticky, most of the tables wobbled, this room had a couple of ceiling tiles missing, and the walls were still painted Artex. It felt both old and cold. I always felt people came here for convenience rather than because it was any good, but it was always reasonably busy here. Closing it for a couple of weeks to give it a refurb had never really been on the agenda, even if there was paint peeling off the walls. They did serve Peroni on draught though, which does help make up for it.

"Eamon, do you have a minute?"

"Of course. What's up?" he said, without moving away from the bar. This caused me to hesitate slightly.

"You may have noticed that I haven't given Sinead her birthday present yet."

He turned to face me and rested his elbow on the bar.

"I'd noticed it wasn't in the bag. You have bought her something, I trust?"

"Yes, of course, and I was planning on giving it to her here. But with Mary being in hospital I'm not sure whether I still should."

He eyed me with a hint of suspicion.

"What is it?"

"An engagement ring."

He raised his eyebrows.

"Hmmm. Are you asking for permission?"

"Well, I suppose I am. But, not exactly. I'd intended to do it here at the party as a surprise to everyone, including you. However, with Mary not being here I'm not sure how Sinead would feel about it."

"I see," he said, looking away thoughtfully. "No," he said after a few seconds, "I don't think you should."

"Ask her here or ask her at all?"

"She's your girlfriend. If you want to ask her, I can't stop you. But she'd probably feel embarrassed if you did it here, especially with how emotional she's been feeling today. I think she would prefer it if you did it at the hospital tomorrow when Mary was there."

"At the hospital?"

"Well, she's not going to come out any time soon, is she? Unless you want to wait for a week or two, you'll have to do it there."

"What if she asks where her present is later?"

Eamon put his hand on my shoulder.

"You're a smart boy, make something up."

*****

The rest of the evening passed largely without incident. Sinead, of course, got emotional when making her thank you speech, and she danced with her father to 'Dance With My Father', which was surprisingly clichéd for her. The two of us also had a couple of slow dances which is all I could manage, as twisting and swaying is quite painful for me but, in the main, we were all just happy to get through the evening. I wouldn't go as far to say it had been enjoyable, Mary's absence had certainly been very noticeable, but it had the advantage of taking the limelight largely off Sinead, which she didn't seem to mind.

As we got back home, I was still worrying about her present. I didn't want to bring it up myself, as I didn't know how to tell her without 'telling her', if that makes sense. I also hadn't got an answer ready in case she asked but, fortunately, she didn't. As I lay there that night, though, I wondered what must have been going through her head. I knew she didn't have high expectations of me, but I suddenly found myself worrying that she'd gone to bed and gone to sleep without me acknowledging her birthday. I'd given her a card, of course, and she'd received a lot of presents at the party that she hadn't yet opened. She had made a passing comment about "taking her presents to the hospital tomorrow and opening them with Mum," and I was hoping she'd assume I'd taken the hint, which in a way I had. I took the ring out of my suit jacket that I'd worn to the party and put it back in the inside pocket of my main coat. I was disappointed my plan hadn't come to fruition but, in the circumstances, I did think I'd probably acted for the best.

It didn't take me long to fall asleep that night, but still my dreams were weird. I kept dreaming about the party and about Mary, and I woke up a few times with that familiar disorientated feeling. They didn't keep me awake, though, and I soon dropped back off to sleep.

I was at the party again. This time I was standing at the dessert table cutting a slice off a chocolate gateau. The knife was in my right hand, and my lack of grip in that hand caused me to drop it. I picked it back up with my good hand and looked around the room; Mary was there, and there were a couple of people I recognised from school who also hadn't been at the party. The man to my left, cutting the cheesecake, looked like Marcus Bray, our old school bully. What was he doing here? I turned back to the dessert table, becoming increasingly conscious of the fact that this didn't feel real. I held my right hand up. No scars. I was dreaming; this was a lucid dream.

I was aware of a blonde woman standing to the right of me in a red dress. She had long blonde hair that she'd curled for the occasion; to be honest she looked beautiful. I looked at her, and she turned to look at me.

It was Michelle.

I didn't wake up, and I was instantly quite pleased with myself that I hadn't. I was lucid dreaming, and there was Michelle standing in front of me. I felt the excitement bubble up inside me; I'd felt resentment towards her for a number of years, and I'd fantasised on more than one occasion about punishing her, or hurting her, for the way she'd hurt me. Now she was making appearances in my dreams, twice in two nights, only now I was aware. This was my chance, but what could I do? I looked at the cake knife in my hand then looked at Michelle. She'd turned away again and was focusing on the selection of fairy cakes on the table; with her hair up, the flesh on the side of her neck was fully exposed.

'Look at me', I thought to myself. 'Turn around again and look at me'.

She didn't, and I could feel myself starting to wake up. Without thinking further, I plunged the knife into her neck just under her left ear, behind her jawbone. The shock of doing this immediately woke me up, and I shot up in bed as though I'd been tasered.

"What on earth are you doing?" asked Sinead, who had already woken up.

"What's wrong?" I asked, still shaking.

"You screamed, then shot up in bed. Are you ok?"

I took a few deep breaths to try and slow my heart rate down.

"Yeah, I think so," I said finally. "Just a disturbing dream, that's all."

"Well, lie back down, I was in a lovely sleep then," and she turned over, quite grumpily.

I lay back on my pillow, still trying to get my breathing back to normal. As much as what I'd done had shocked me, it was also a really exhilarating experience. There was no other way to describe it. I'd never have done anything like that in real life, of course, but to punish her like that in the safety of a dream was enthralling. I'd only been awake for a minute or so, and already I was longing to experience it again.

However, I struggled to settle off properly again for the rest of the night and, once more, I was up by just after six o'clock. This was unusual for me, and now I'd done it two days in a row. Once I'd calmed down and the adrenalin burst had subsided, I actually felt slightly guilty, not for my conduct in the dream, but for the fact I was dreaming about Michelle to begin with. There I was, in bed with my girlfriend who was twenty-one that day, engagement ring in my jacket ready to ask her to marry me, and yet I was having fantasy dreams about stabbing another woman to death. Maybe I had a dark heart after all.

Sinead surfaced around eight o'clock, before Eamon was up.

"How are you feeling?" I asked her.

"Yeah, I'm ok," she answered. "I do wish you'd stop waking me up in the night, though. You're a pain in the neck. I'll be sending you back to your own room tonight whether Mum's here or not."

Her tone was light, and I wasn't convinced she really meant it.

"I was having a lucid dream."

"Oh, you managed it. What was it about?"

"I'd rather not say."

Sinead rolled her eyes and walked into the kitchen, probably thinking it had been about sex. She returned a few minutes later with a cup of coffee and a croissant.

"Can I say something to you?" she asked.

"Of course," I replied, although I always get nervous when she asks for permission first. It suggests something serious. "What's up?"

She took a deep breath.

"All of this that's happening with Mum has got me thinking, about how important family is, and how you only get one of each parent. They're special, you know, I think we need to make the most of them."

"Sinead, just spit it out."

She took another deep breath then hesitated again.

"I think it's about time you tried to make peace with your dad and your sister."

Now it was my turn to hesitate. I hated talking about my family problems; by now my dislike for my dad was deep-rooted, and I had no desire or intention of making up with him. I was sad that I didn't speak to Donna, as that was my fault. But I'd tried to apologise to her at the time and it just caused more trouble. From my side, I thought I'd already done everything that I could. I got up from my seat to get my own coffee cup off its coaster on the mantelpiece. Mary didn't like hot mugs on the floor in case they got knocked over, so I'd left it there to cool down. It was my second cup of the morning, and it was still slightly too hot to drink, but I needed a quick excuse to buy myself a few seconds. I took a mouthful and considered my response.

"Why?" I eventually asked her, as calmly as I could.

"It was just chatting to your mum last night whilst my own wasn't there. It made me think about how precious everything is."

"I've called my dad several things over the last couple of years, but 'precious' has never been one of them."

"That's not what I mean. It's just if something happened to him like what's happened to my mum, you may find the fact you're estranged from him more difficult to live with in future than you might think. If it doesn't work, then at least you can have the comfort of knowing you tried."

I didn't like this conversation, but I could tell Sinead was being sincere. She wasn't saying this because she thinks making up is just what people should do. This was being driven by her feelings about her mum, and I couldn't be mad with her.

"I'll think about it," I replied non-committally.

"Ok," she nodded, although I sensed she'd hoped for more. "Thank you."

I sat back down and took another mouthful of coffee.

"Can I ask you something else?" she asked.

"Go on."

"Where the hell's my birthday present?"

"Ah!"

"It's not in any of the bags with the rest of them. You have got me something, haven't you?"

"Of course I have."

"So where is it?"

"You said you were going to open your presents with your mum later. I wanted to give it to you then."

"Oh, ok. Sorry, I thought you'd…"

"Forgotten?" I interjected.

"No, I wasn't sure if you'd managed to get anything."

"It's a good job I did if 'where the hell's my present?' is the response I'm going to get."

"You know I'm only playing," she grinned.

I didn't, and I'm sure she wasn't.

Brian and his family were flying back to Dublin that afternoon, so they'd spent the morning at the hospital with Mary. Eamon had then taken them back to the airport to catch their flight, meaning it was after lunch before we were all together for visiting. As we approached the ward, I stopped.

"I'll be in in a minute," I said. "I'm just going to go and get a bottle of pop from that machine down there."

"Ok, can you pick me one up too, please? Anything will do, I don't mind what."

I headed off down the corridor.

"Hello, darling," I heard Mary cry as they walked on to the ward. "How did your party go?"

That was unexpected. I wouldn't have thought she'd have remembered about the party. As much as it was probably a good sign that she was aware, the fact it had shocked me meant it almost certainly would have an effect on Sinead too. However, as I was walking down the corridor, I didn't hear her reply.

To be honest, I didn't need a drink. I just wanted to make a final check that the ring was ok and that it was sitting straight in the box. It was, and it looked good. It was a silver ring with an emerald gemstone. I wanted something green due to her Irish heritage, and I hoped she didn't find it too corny. I waited a moment to compose myself and then walked on to the ward.

Mary was sitting up in bed, which was an improvement on yesterday already. Sinead was on the far side of the bed holding her hand and talking to her, and neither of them immediately noticed me. Eamon did and, noticing the ring box in my hand, he gave me a wink, acknowledging he knew what I was about to do. I took a step forward and approached the bed.

"Where's the drinks?" Sinead asked.

"Oh, the machine isn't working," I lied. I turned my head towards Mary, whose face had suddenly turned to fury.

"Don't you dare let him in here!" she growled. "Not after what he's done!"

"Mum, what are you on about?" Sinead asked bewilderedly.

"At the party last night. I saw him!"

"Mum, you weren't at the party."

"I saw him, what you did to that poor girl," she scolded.

"Mum there was no girl. He was with me all night."

"The blonde girl in the red dress," she shouted, and she was attracting other patients' attention now. "I saw you. HOW COULD YOU STAB HER IN THE NECK LIKE THAT?"

"MUM! Gary, you should probably go out for a bit," Sinead shrieked, trying to diffuse the situation, but my blood had already run cold.

"WITH THE CAKE KNIFE! IN FRONT OF EVERYONE!" she continued barking. "The poor girl only wanted a piece of gateau."

"Gary, she's delirious," Sinead cried. "Please, just go outside."

I turned around and walked away. Was I still dreaming? I looked at my right hand. My scars were definitely there from my accident. My left hand looked normal. I glanced up at the TV on the wall, which had a rolling news channel on it with subtitles. I read what was on the screen and they formed coherent sentences. I wasn't asleep, I was most certainly awake. What was going on? How could Mary know about something I'd dreamt? I could still hear her shouting from the ward but, in my dazed state, I wasn't picking up what she was saying. She was certainly most agitated; I'd never seen her like that before. I didn't wait in the corridor where me and Sinead had sat yesterday. I kept walking, trying to make sense of what had just happened. I'd had a dream last night, a lucid one. I'd admittedly stabbed Michelle in it, but how could Mary possibly know about that?

I found my way completely outside the hospital and sat myself down on a bench opposite the main car park, my mind still swimming, trying to process what had just happened. It wasn't a quick process, and I must have sat there for a while before eventually Sinead appeared.

"Where have you been? I've been looking all over for you."

"Sorry," I said. "I needed some fresh air and to clear my head."

"Oh, Gary," she said and sat down next to me and hugged me. "I'm so sorry about Mum, she shouldn't have done that. We know she has these hallucinations, but she's never done or said anything like that before."

"I'm not sure what to make of it myself."

"She doesn't mean it. If you went back in there again now, she'd probably be fine with you. Although you'll probably feel quite awkward going back in there, won't you, after what she accused you of."

"I don't want to go back in there yet."

"Please don't be angry with her."

"I'm not angry, I'm just a bit perplexed."

"She just doesn't know what she's saying. Come on, come back inside."

"Sinead, you don't understand."

She looked at me.

"I don't understand what?"

I had no choice. I couldn't hide it from her, it's not my style. I had to tell Sinead what had happened.

"Your mum, what she said. She wasn't hallucinating."

"Of course she was."

"No, she wasn't. Not exactly."

"Well did you stab a girl in a red dress at my party last night?" she said tartly.

"Well, not at your party, no."

She raised her eyebrows.

"So, did you and Mum attend a different party afterwards without any of us knowing?"

"Well, no, not exactly."

"Then Gary, what on earth are you on about?"

This time it was my turn to take a deep breath.

"Do you remember when I shot up in bed last night and woke you up?"

"Yes?"

"Well, I'd had a bad dream. It was a lucid dream."

"Yes, you said, so what?"

"When I told you about it this morning you rolled your eyes at me. Why?"

"I assumed you were fantasising about something."

"Well, in a way I was. You see, I dreamt I was at your party. Michelle was there."

"Michelle Peyton?"

"Yeah. She was standing next to me at the dessert table whilst I was cutting a piece of gateau. She was wearing a red dress and, when the dream became lucid, I..." I paused, as even in a dream state I wasn't sure how she'd take this. "I stabbed her in the neck, just as your mum described."

Sinead looked aghast.

"What!?"

"But how could your mum know that?"

"You actually stabbed her?"

"Sinead, it was a dream."

"I don't care, you don't do that to someone! You don't even fantasise about it!" She seemed genuinely furious.

"Sinead, I was asleep, it wasn't real."

"Mum seems to think it was."

"I know! How can that be? How could she quote my own dream back to me, as if it were real?"

"How the bloody hell should I know?" she snapped.

She turned away and put her head in her hands.

"Even in a dream, in a lucid dream, why would you have stabbed her? You knew what you were doing." She was speaking slightly calmer now, although she was biting down on her knuckle again.

"I don't know. You know I've always been bitter about her turning me down."

"Well, maybe you'd have preferred she hadn't, and then you wouldn't have to be with me."

"You're being ridiculous."

"No, I'm not. You hate the girl so much you have to fantasise about killing her at my birthday party."

"Sinead, it was a dream, it's not important."

"I think it is."

"Well, it isn't. What's important is how on earth your mum knows about it."

"And how do you expect us to find that out?"

I sat back on the bench and looked out across the car park.

"I have no idea."

We sat there for a moment, both processing what had just happened. It was Sinead who spoke next.

"What's that in your hand?" she asked.

I looked down; I was still holding the box with the engagement ring in it.

"Oh shit!" I accidentally said out loud.

"What is it?"

"It's your birthday present."

"Can I have it?"

"No," I said, slightly sharper than I meant to.

"Why not?"

"I hadn't intended to do this here. I wanted your mum and dad to be there."

"Be there for what?"

The cat was out of the bag, and there was nothing I could do about it. It was now or never. I opened the ring box and slid down off the bench on to one knee.

"Sinead O'Brien," I blurted out. "Will you marry me?"

Chapter Eight
The Blue Line

There was a loud high-pitched noise and a sharp pain as something crashed into the back of my head, knocking me clean off my feet and face-first onto the sticky floor. Maybe the initial dizziness was more serious than I first thought, as I suddenly felt like a bomb had exploded inside my brain. I was pinned to the floor and felt like there was a heavy weight holding me down. Out of the corner of my eye, I could have sworn I saw Michelle fall down the same time I did. Had a bomb gone off? Had someone fired a gun? And what was that weight on my back? My arm was also at a funny angle and I could feel pain from my skiing injury. Maybe the accident had caused a head injury, and this was a delayed reaction.

As I started to regain my sense of where I was, I was suddenly aware of people screaming and shouting. A man in an Irish accent was calling for an ambulance, and I noticed my jacket felt wet. What on earth was going on? I tried to move but the weight was holding me down. It felt like another person. Had Michelle landed on me? No, this person was heavier. Even if she had been on me, I'd have still been able to move. It was someone's knee, I was sure of it, and it was in the base of my back. It was also a person gripping my arm, although I wish they'd let go.

"What's going on?" I gasped, barely able to breathe.

"Stay down," Marcus growled at me.

"Get off me," I said with increasing difficulty.

"Trust me, I'm doing you a favour," he snarled. "Now shut up and stay there."

"Where's Michelle?" I asked.

He twisted my arm tighter still.

"Don't you dare!" he said in the most menacing voice I could remember hearing. "Your best chance is to stay there until the police get here. One more word or one more movement, and I swear I'll kill you."

It must be another robbery, and he must have planned this. I could hear a woman who sounded like she was performing first aid on someone close to me, suggesting something must have gone wrong. But where was Michelle? And where was Sinead? If Marcus had ruined her party, it would be me doing the killing, if I could ever get the fat lump off me, of course.

I could hear sirens approaching the building. That hadn't taken long, or it didn't seem to have. I lay there, motionless, praying it was the police and that they'd soon have the situation under control. There was still a commotion within the room, and I became aware that the disco music had stopped and that the lights had come up. It was also apparent that the pain in my head wasn't just from a blow. Marcus was also pressing my head into the floor with his other hand. It was at least at a slight angle allowing me to just about breathe, but I couldn't exactly inhale with his bulk on top of me. I was, however, aware what the wet liquid was that was soaking into my shirt and jacket. I knew it wasn't someone's drink as it was too warm, but now I came to realise that it was blood.

I could hear a man yelling to keep applying pressure; was he talking to Marcus? Why was it so important he held me down? The lady who was performing first aid was now counting.

"One, two, three, four, five, six, seven…" She went all the way up to thirty then stopped. Then started again from one. She was performing CPR. Was someone dying next to me? I might be joining them in a minute if Marcus didn't shift. I tried again to get up, but he punched me hard in the back of my head and my face smashed into the floor.

I must have lost consciousness for a minute or two as, when I came around, I was lying on my left-hand side in the recovery position being treated by a female medic. My entire upper body hurt, my head and my face especially from where Marcus had hit me, and both my back and my arms ached. I couldn't see the buffet table, but there was blood all around me, and the room had been emptied of party guests.

"What's happened? What's going on?" I croaked at her.

"Try not to move, sir," she said assertively, before looking past me. "Inspector, he's regained consciousness."

"He hit me," I said. "Marcus Bray, he hit me."

"Marcus Bray is the least of your worries," the medic said; she was using quite a vicious and sinister tone of voice.

"Do you need to keep him?" I heard another woman ask. It was the medic who answered.

"He's got a nasty facial wound and most probably a concussion. We need to take him in."

"Can he speak?"

"Apparently so."

A lady in flat black shoes appeared next to the medic. She seemed incredibly tall, although from my vantage point of the floor most people would. She was black, slim to medium build, probably around the fifty mark. I'd never seen her before.

"Do you know who you are?" she asked sternly.

"Gary Jackson," I confirmed, although I was still dazed and struggling for breath.

"Do you know where you are?"

Actually, I didn't. I knew we were in Badminton but, in that moment, I'd forgotten the name of the pub we were in.

"Sinead's party," I said.

"And are you here alone?"

"No, I'm with my girlfriend, Michelle Peyton. Is she ok? She's in a red dress, blonde hair, have you seen her?"

The lady looked confused that I was asking such questions, and I was hoping that meant Michelle had managed to get away before the police arrived. If she had, and she knew I hadn't, she'd probably be worried sick now. I was hoping she was with Sinead and they were both safe.

"Do you think you can stand?" the medic asked me again. In another time and place, I'd have thought she was pretty. She looked slightly older than me, with dark hair in a short ponytail. She looked quite stocky, although that was probably the uniform and the medical gear she was wearing.

"I think so," I said.

At that, a uniformed police officer appeared on each side of me and helped me quite forcefully to my feet.

"Take him to an ambulance," the medic instructed.

I turned my head to see what was happening behind me, but one of the officers pushed it back forward.

"This way, please," the man said authoritatively.

Because of this, I only caught a glance, but I knew what I'd seen. There was a blanket on the floor covering a person up. Not even their face was visible. Someone had died here.

"One moment, please," came the black woman's voice again, and we stopped walking whilst she reappeared in front of me.

"You're going to the hospital now," she said. "But two of my officers will be staying with you at all times."

"Thank you," I said. "What's happened here?"

"After you've been discharged from the hospital, you'll be released directly into our custody," she continued.

"Custody? Wait, what's going on?" I protested.

"Gary Jackson, you are under arrest for the murder of Michelle Peyton. You do not have to say anything, but it may harm your defence if you fail to mention, when questioned, something you may later rely on in court. Anything you do say may be given in evidence. Do you understand?"

My legs went from under me, and I must have lost consciousness again.

*****

I was destined to spend the entire night in hospital, to everyone's apparent annoyance, not least my own. I was lying on a bed in a cubicle in Barchester General A&E, on my own, while two officers stood outside. I'd been ordered to hand over my clothes and so was wearing nothing but a hospital gown. I tried asking questions around what was happening, but everyone was giving me the silent treatment. I suddenly felt very scared as, from what I'd been told...well, what I'd been told couldn't be true; there must be some mistake. I could see the police officer who had apparently arrested me speaking to the doctor who'd been treating me, just outside the cubicle. I strained my hearing to eavesdrop on what they were saying.

"I'm sorry, Detective Inspector," I could hear the doctor say. He was smaller than the detective, with short black hair all the way around the huge bald patch that sat on the top of his head. "He's lost consciousness twice this evening. He'll be kept in for observations and most likely released in the morning."

"He's our prime suspect in a murder investigation, doctor. We need to speak to him as soon as possible," the detective replied.

"He is awake. I can give you a few minutes now if you wish."

"I can't, he's under arrest and entitled to legal counsel whilst being interviewed. I can't question him here, not officially. Her family are going to want answers though, and soon."

"I'm aware of the situation, but he's still my patient. He'll be released into your custody in the morning, assuming there's no cause for alarm overnight."

"Detective," I called, and she looked past the doctor and straight at me. "Can I talk to you, please?"

She passed the doctor and entered my cubicle.

"What is it, Mr Jackson?" she asked calmly.

"I appreciate this may sound odd from your perspective, but what the hell has happened? Why am I here? Why am I under arrest? And where's Michelle?"

"All in good time, Mr Jackson, I'll be happy to fill you in at the station in the morning. You should follow the doctor's advice and get some rest because, believe me, you're going to need it."

"Detective, do my mum and dad know I'm here?"

"If they don't yet, then they will soon enough," she replied and hastily left.

That, frustratingly, was the sum of the information I could gather that night. As a result, I spent the evening in the cubicle, seemingly under guard, but otherwise alone, pained, and utterly scared to death. I didn't believe Michelle was dead. She couldn't be. It wasn't possible. As for me being responsible, I'd just have to wait tonight out and clear everything up at the police station the next morning. It was only at that point I realised why the two uniformed police officers were there; at first, I thought it was to protect me, like I might be in danger from Marcus or his ilk. It took me longer than it should to work out they were actually there to ensure I didn't go anywhere. Not that I would. I wanted to know what was going on more than anyone.

My parents must have been informed, as the next morning, I was passed clothes; boxer shorts, jeans, a jumper, socks, and shoes, all of which were my own and could have only been got from home. What had they told

Mum and Dad, and what must they be thinking? I was hoping Michelle would go over to them and prove it was all a massive misunderstanding. Of course, I didn't know for certain either her or Sinead were ok, but they were decent enough friends in their own right, and I was confident they would look after each other.

When I was finally discharged from the hospital the next morning I was, as I'd come to expect, escorted straight to the police station. I'd never been in trouble with the law before. I'd never even stolen sweets from a Pick N' Mix as a child. I'd always place a glass over a spider and a piece of paper underneath to move them outside rather than kill them as, even though squashing them wasn't yet a crime, I still felt squeamish doing so.

I was shown into a room where I was met by a short, plump man who I'd have clocked to be in his late forties.

"Warren Dawlish, duty solicitor," he said, shaking my hand. "Detective Braithwaite will be in to interview you in a few minutes. My job is to brief you before she does. What do you remember about what happened last night?"

"Everything, and I haven't killed anyone," I said assertively. He gave a slight frown.

"If you're unclear on the events…" he began, but I cut him off.

"I'm perfectly clear on the events. I haven't done anything."

"Then my advice would be to say nothing."

"Why?"

"So as not to make things worse by incriminating yourself."

"How can I incriminate myself when I haven't done anything?" I fumed.

At that, the door opened. The detective from last night returned, and I noticed she was wearing different clothes. She must have been off duty and then come back on again. She was followed in by a young blonde lady in police uniform. Under different circumstances, she might have given me the horn.

"Gary Jackson, please be seated," she ordered as she came in.

She started the tape recorder.

"Interview with Gary Jackson, Sunday, March 15th, 2015 at 09:53," she began. "Present in the room are the suspect, his duty solicitor Mr Warren Dawlish, myself, Detective Inspector Yasmin Braithwaite, and Police Constable Whitney Clarke. Tell me, Mr Jackson, do you know why you're here?"

"Not really," I confessed. She eyed me with suspicion and, I felt, a hint of loathing.

"What happened last night?" she asked.

"Me and my girlfriend, Michelle, went to The Ox and Lamb in Badminton for my best friend's 21st birthday party," I said calmly.

"And?" Braithwaite prompted. Assuming she wanted me to explain the incident with Marcus, I continued.

"We were at the dessert table. There was a loud screech, I was knocked to the floor, Marcus Bray pinned me down, punched me in the back of the head, knocked me out, and when I woke up you arrested me for murder."

"Anything else?" she asked mockingly.

"Look, before we go any further. Where's Michelle? Is she ok?"

Braithwaite sat back in her chair and folded her arms, as though she was weighing me up.

"Is that a serious question, Mr Jackson?"

"Of course it is. Since Marcus knocked me down, I haven't seen her, heard from her, been allowed to speak to anyone. Nobody has given me any information. Forgive my tone, but what the hell is going on?"

"You are in here," she said, in a slow patronising tone, "Because you have been arrested for the murder of Michelle Peyton."

"Michelle isn't dead," I corrected, in as strong a voice as I dared.

"She's dead, you killed her, and I want you to explain why," Braithwaite ordered.

"I did no such thing," I said forcefully, unable to fathom why she was continuing with this bizarre line of questioning.

"I don't have time for this. DI Braithwaite leaving the room at 09:55," she said. At the time, I hadn't registered that she'd left the recording running.

"Are you ok?" PC Clarke asked.

"I don't know," I admitted. "I don't know what's happening."

"Start from the beginning," she said. "Tell me everything that happened at the party."

"I'm not saying anything until I know what's happened to Michelle," I said.

"Mr Jackson, Gary. Can I call you Gary?"

I nodded.

"Gary, it is in both yours and Michelle's best interests for you to tell me what happened last night," PC Clarke said.

"So, she is alive?"

"No. Michelle Peyton was murdered last night. I need you to tell me what happened at the party."

"But, how?" I asked, tears forming uncontrollably in my eyes and rolling down my face. "How can she be dead? She was right next to me."

"Gary, please start at the beginning," Clarke repeated. "What happened when you first got to the party?"

"We greeted Sinead," I said. "We gave her card and present to her. Then we headed to the bar, then we had a chat with her mum and dad."

"Miss Peyton's parents were at the party?"

"No, I mean Sinead's mum and dad, Mary and Eamon. Mary is ill, she has dementia We were talking to her."

"What happened after?"

"We went back to the bar and got a second round of drinks, then went and sat at a table with a few old school friends."

"Did anything out of the ordinary happen?"

"Michelle wouldn't let any of them hug her. She'd hurt her chest when we were skiing in Italy last week, and we injured each other colliding on one of the slopes. It was my fault."

"Did you eat at the party?"

"Yeah, we did. We went up to the buffet twice. They didn't open the food until half past nine and we hadn't eaten since lunch. We were both starving."

"Then what happened?"

"I wanted a third course, she wanted to wait for dessert."

"Did you argue about it?"

"No, of course not. Marcus came over and started talking to us."

"This would be Marcus Bray who you mentioned earlier?"

"Yes, he's an ex-con and the one who assaulted me. He should be in here, not me."

"We are getting a statement from Mr Bray. Please, do continue. Did you go to the buffet again?"

"No, we waited for the dessert table to open. Michelle noticed them taking the cover off the gateaux and nudged me to go up with her."

"And did you?"

"Yeah, the three of us went up. Marcus went for the cheesecake, and I cut me and Michelle a slice of chocolate gateau."

"Do you remember cutting the gateau?" she asked curiously.

"Actually, no I don't," I said.

"What do you remember?"

"Michelle handed me the knife to cut the gateau. She asked me to make hers a big piece. The next thing I knew there was a loud squeal and Marcus Bray was on top of me, pinning me to the ground. I thought him and his cronies were robbing the place."

"There was no robbery," PC Clarke confirmed. "What happened between those two incidents?"

"What two incidents?"

"Between you being handed the knife by Miss Peyton, and you finding yourself restrained by Mr Bray."

"Nothing," I confirmed.

"Think carefully. You don't recall anything of note occurring between you picking up the knife and you being restrained?"

"I didn't pick up the knife, Michelle gave it to me. And no, nothing happened in between. They both happened at pretty much the same time."

At that, DI Braithwaite entered the room and announced herself, doing so for the benefit of the tape. She was holding a couple of papers she hadn't had before.

"Mr Jackson," she began. "You say you remember Miss Peyton giving you the knife?"

"Yeah," I confirmed.

"Can you describe it?"

"No," I admitted. "It was dark, there were disco lights on. I didn't pay any attention."

"Was it plastic, metal, long, short?"

"It had what felt like a wooden handle, but the knife was metal It was a kitchen knife, I think."

"Anything else?"

I shook my head, unsure what more information I could give.

"Colour of the handle, shape of the blade?" she prompted.

"No idea," I confessed.

She showed me a photograph on a piece of paper.

"Showing the suspect Exhibit 1A," which was a picture of a blood-stained knife. Black handle, serrated blade. It was a bread knife.

"Was it this knife?" she asked.

"No, there was no blood on it," I said stupidly. "I'd have remembered."

"This is a waste of time," Braithwaite said again, once again standing up to leave. She was furious. "We don't need a confession from you, Mr Jackson, we already have more than enough to charge you. We have the murder weapon containing her blood on the blade and your DNA on the handle. We also have her blood on your clothing, at least twenty witnesses, some of whom are traumatised from having watched you do it, and CCTV footage from inside the venue clearly showing you stabbing Miss Peyton in the neck. Now I ask you again, is there anything else you wish to tell me?"

"You have CCTV footage?" I asked.

"Yes."

"I want to see it."

She glanced at Warren Dawlish next to me.

"He has that right, to see the evidence against him," he confirmed.

"Why would you wish to watch it back?" Braithwaite asked me.

"Because somewhere there has been a terrible mistake," I said. "Michelle isn't dead, she can't be, and even if she was, I most certainly wouldn't have killed her. That tape will clear me, and I want to be present when you watch it."

"Very well," she sneered. "Interview suspended, 10:09."

She stopped the recording.

"PC Clarke, with me please," she said, and they both left the room.

"You're telling the truth, aren't you?" Dawlish asked. "About not remembering, I mean."

"I'm telling the truth about all of it," I stated.

"The evidence against you does appear very strong."

"But if this video shows the incident, it will prove I didn't do it."

"What if it doesn't?" he asked.

"Of course it will, what else would it show?"

"I should point out, Mr Jackson, that I have already seen this tape."

I turned to face him and looked intently at him.

"Then you know I'm innocent," I said.

"I think it probably is best that you see this tape for yourself," he commented. "Although I warn you, the content is pretty graphic."

"That's ok, I'm prepared," I said.

"Actually, I don't think you are," he said.

When the two officers returned, the sense of conflicting emotions was like something I'd never experienced. I still felt disorientated, and my head felt like I'd been swimming underwater. I didn't feel grief for Michelle yet as I didn't for a second believe she was dead, and my adrenaline was pumping somewhat at the fact I was about to prove it. Despite the solicitor's warning, I couldn't compute the idea that there was anything on the tape other than proof of my innocence. If it did indeed show someone attacking Michelle, and at this point I didn't entirely believe this either, then I was as eager as anyone to find out who it was. The two officers sat down, and PC Clarke started playing the tape. The camera was directly overlooking the dessert table, and I spotted Michelle and I at a table not far away. She was standing and nudging me to join her for gateaux.

"Pause the tape," Braithwaite ordered, and Clarke did as she was asked.

"What's happening here?" Braithwaite asked me.

"We're about to go up for dessert."

"For the record, can you point out both yourself and Miss Peyton on the recording?"

"Yeah, Michelle is the blonde woman in the red dress standing up," I confirmed. "I'm the man next to her. At the minute, she has her arm on my shoulder. Marcus Bray is the man sitting to my left."

"Play the tape," Braithwaite ordered again.

"Before I do," Clarke interjected. "Gary, will you say 'pause please' at the first sign of something you don't remember?"

"Yes, of course," I nodded, and I'm sure Braithwaite scowled at her for asking the question.

PC Clarke pressed play, and I felt my heartbeat speed up. I was about to prove my innocence and I'd be free to go and find Michelle. I watched as we walked over to the dessert table. I saw Michelle pick up the knife and hand it to me. I looked across at Marcus standing at the cheesecake. Then I dropped the knife.

"Pause," I said, and Clarke did so. "That didn't happen."

"What didn't happen, Mr Jackson?" Braithwaite asked.

"I didn't drop the knife. That's not me."

"Is it the same man you confirmed was you just a moment ago?" she sneered.

"Yes, but I didn't do that. I didn't drop the knife."

"Then what did you do?" she asked.

"I don't remember," I said blankly. "But not that."

"The video would suggest otherwise," she said, in a rather sarcastic tone. "Play the tape, PC Clarke."

The constable did so. I watched myself as I picked the knife up; I had no memory of the events that were currently happening. I was looking at Michelle who I noticed turned back to face me. I didn't remember that either. She looked away again and was picking at the fairy cakes. I was just staring at her. What was going on? Then, without warning, I watched myself plunge the knife directly into the left-hand side of her neck. My hands shot up to my face instinctively and I burst into tears, but I continued watching myself as I pulled out the knife, just as Marcus threw his plate down and punched me full force in the back of the head, knocking me to the ground. A number of people came running over to assist Michelle as Marcus restrained me. I couldn't actually see myself now. I looked away from the TV screen, removed my hands from in front of my mouth, and vomited all over the floor.

Chapter Nine
The Black Line

Sinead sat forward, put her head in her hands, and burst into tears.

"That's not quite the reaction I was hoping for," I said hesitantly.

"It's just all too much," she sobbed. "So many things going on, so many conflicting emotions, I just can't take it all in."

"Sinead, I'm sorry, I shouldn't have done this now. I wanted to surprise you with it at the party last night, but it didn't seem right with your mum not being there."

She looked up and shook her head.

"I'm glad you didn't."

"Once you saw the box, I had to ask you. I couldn't get out of it then without tipping my hand. I'm sorry."

I closed the lid on the box and went to put it back in my pocket.

"No, don't," she said, grabbing my wrist.

"If you don't want to, then you don't have to."

"No, I do want to. I'm sorry, it's all just a bit overwhelming."

"So, is that a yes?"

Sinead smiled through the tears and gave me a hug and a rather wet kiss. It was nothing like what I'd planned or wanted to do, but the result was the same. I'd done it; we were engaged.

"Does Dad know about this?" she asked.

"Yeah, he does, although I only told him about it yesterday. It was him who convinced me not to do it last night and that I should do it here today. That's why I had no drinks when I came on to the ward. I hadn't gone for pop, I wanted to check the ring was ok. It was in my hand because that's what I'd come in to do when your mum kicked off at me."

"Let me see it," she said, reaching for the box. I opened it and showed her the emerald. "Oh Gary, it's beautiful."

"Do you want to put it on now or wait until we're back on the ward with your mum and dad?"

She took the ring from the box and placed it on her finger.

"What, and pretend you haven't already done it?" she smiled, although she still had tears streaming down her face. I was glad she wasn't still wearing her eyeliner from last night.

"I'm sorry it wasn't more romantic."

"It was typically you," she said.

I'm still not entirely sure what she meant by that.

We walked back inside the hospital holding hands and made our way back up to the ward. My heart was beating nineteen to the dozen, and I knew what Sinead meant when she spoke about conflicting emotions and everything being overwhelming. I genuinely had no idea what was going to happen next. Would Mary turn on me again? If she did so, how was I ever going to be able to visit her, or live with them going forward, if that was how she reacted? And how could I possibly marry her daughter? On the same note, how would Eamon react now? He was expecting to see this proposal, and now we were going to walk back in and tell him it had already been done, on a little wooden bench outside the hospital. I imagine he had higher expectations than that for his only child.

We reached the entrance to the ward, and I automatically stopped at the door.

"Are you ok?" Sinead asked.

"My anxiety is kicking in."

"Yeah, I'm quite nervous too."

"Do you want to go in first? Just see how she is, if she's still agitated. I don't want to upset her further."

"I'll tell her you're here and ask her if she wants to see you, see what she says."

I sat down in the corridor, on the same chair I'd sat on yesterday, and did what I always do in these situations; automatically reached for my phone. However, playing a game or browsing the internet wasn't going to be enough to distract me this afternoon. I'd recently started a new Football Manager game, starting at the bottom in the Conference South, but as I hadn't been concentrating when playing it the last couple of days, I'd not won any of my opening four games and, as a result, was already losing interest in it; I didn't like losing. It was difficult to focus on anything, currently. The panic about Mary's reaction and the delight at Sinead accepting my proposal were causing odd sensations in my stomach.

Sinead and Eamon exited the ward together.

"She's still distressed. I don't think you should go back in there today," Eamon said.

"Ok," I nodded. "I'll wait in the café for you to finish."

"We won't be long," Sinead said. "We're trying to see if we can calm her down and get her off to sleep. Once she settles, we'll go."

"You wanted to open your presents with her."

"It doesn't matter," she said sadly. "She's not in the right frame of mind today."

"I see she's opened one already," Eamon commented.

"Oh," I said. "You noticed then?"

Eamon nodded his head.

"Sorry. I didn't want it to happen like that."

Worldlines

"It's ok, you didn't really have another choice. This isn't an ideal situation for any of us."

He reached out and shook my hand.

"Well done," he said, "And congratulations."

*****

The events of the afternoon weighed heavily on my mind as we went into the evening, but it was bedtime before Sinead and I were alone again to be able to talk about things. Both her and her dad had been quiet since leaving the hospital, and I knew she wouldn't want to go up to her room and leave her dad on his own, so I stayed with them both. Barely a word was uttered between the three of us all evening, bar the usual pleasantries when offering around drinks. Eamon had even more whiskey than he normally does, I had a couple of beers, and Sinead polished off two bottles of Rosé wine. I think we all needed the alcohol to calm our nerves after the weekend we'd all had. When we finally retired for the evening, I remembered what Sinead had said that morning.

"Am I allowed in, or am I banished to my own room?" I asked her cautiously.

"You can come in but keep still and don't wake me up."

We got changed and got ready for bed; Sinead went and got changed in the bathroom as she normally did. I must admit this frustrated me immensely as I loved seeing her undressed; I was hoping it was a habit she'd get out of now we were formally engaged.

"How do you feel now about what happened with your mum this afternoon?" I asked her when we finally got into bed.

"I don't know what to make of it. Maybe it was just a coincidence, what she said."

I shook my head (in the dark).

"No, it can't have been. She was too precise. She described it perfectly."

"What do you think of it, then?" she asked.

"I have no idea. But I do hope it isn't going to stop me from seeing your mum going forward."

"True. If she reacts that way again it's going to make you living here very difficult when she comes home."

"Yeah, I'd thought that myself."

We lay there for a while, and I thought she'd gone to sleep.

"I wonder if any of this has anything to do with Professor Buzzard's theories that he's been talking about lately," she said eventually.

"What theories?"

"The Many Worlds stuff I was telling you about. Parallel universes and alternate Worldlines and all that."

"I don't see how."

"No, neither do I. But he might," she rolled over to face me. "Are you doing anything tomorrow?"

"Not really. There's a World of Warcraft event from six until ten tomorrow night, but I'm not doing anything before that."

"Come to the university with me in the morning. My lecture doesn't start until ten, but if we get there about nine, we can try and talk to Professor Buzzard about it before classes start."

"Will he be there that early?"

"I don't know, but I guess it's worth a try."

So that's what we did. The next morning, I was again up by six; I genuinely couldn't remember the last time I did that three mornings in a row. We had to have left by seven o'clock as it was a good hour and a half to the university campus; a fifteen-minute car journey, forty minutes on the train, and then an additional half an hour on the tube. It's not a pleasant journey.

First, we had the joy of listening to Matt and Helen, the local breakfast show hosts on mid counties radio. My attention was drawn back to the radio by the over-enthusiasm of the DJs. Nobody should sound that happy that early on a Monday morning, and today they were talking even more nonsense than usual.

"The A35 heading south has one lane blocked because of a lorry having its tyre changed just after the Badminton turn off. It's taking you about half an hour to get through there," Helen said.

I looked over at Sinead who was driving. She had a grey Vauxhall Corsa that was about fifteen years old and on its last legs, but as long as it continued to pass its MOT, Sinead would persevere with it.

"Have we not just come down that stretch of road," I asked, "And wasn't it clear?"

"It seemed it," she said. "Maybe it happened earlier, and it's cleared up now, and they just don't know yet."

"Now for the weather," Helen continued after she finished the travel bulletin. "It's going to be mostly dry across the region with the slight chance of an odd shower this afternoon, highs of twelve Celsius which is fifty-four Fahrenheit."

Sinead had her windscreen wipers on because of the drizzle.

"They're just making this stuff up, aren't they?" I said.

Sinead smirked but kept driving. I hoped they were wrong about the shower; the rubber seal around the rear left door was worn and, if it rained too heavily, there'd be a puddle behind my seat by the time we got back.

We made it to the train station where we were free of the DJ's ramblings and, happily, we even managed to find two seats together on the train. We were travelling backwards but that didn't matter. I put my earphones in and turned on my Sherlock Holmes audiobook. The chapter I was listening to was thirty-eight minutes long, which was the perfect length for this train journey.

When we eventually got into London, we followed the signs for the Northern Line and joined the queue for the escalators, a task made more difficult in recent weeks by the fact they'd closed one of them to refurbish it. There were signs all around the station telling us that, over the next two and a half years, they were going to refurbish each escalator in turn, and that each one was going to take five months as they were tailor-made and had to be refurbished on-site, before apologising for the inconvenience caused. I was fascinated by, and loathed, the London Underground in equal measures. I hated it because it just seemed to be busy all the time, or at least whenever I was using it. Trains are several hundred feet long and run pretty much on the minute every minute, and still you were sardined in; signs in the carriages warned you to mind your hair and clothing in the doors, as there was usually no guarantee that just because your legs had made it onto the train that there would also be enough room for your head and your arms. Drivers announcing "Please move right down inside the cars and use all available space" was a station by station occurrence, although where they expected you to go, I'd never quite worked out. It amazed me that in this Health & Safety-driven world of 2015 the damned thing was still allowed to exist in the manner it does; although if it takes them five months to refurbish one escalator at one station, the chances of them doing anything about its more fundamental issues seem unlikely. It makes you wonder how, one hundred and fifty years ago, they ever managed to build it to begin with. The chaos when they eventually shut it down will be unimaginable.

We eventually arrived on the university campus. I'd been here twice before; once when Sinead came to look around when she was deciding which university to attend, and once during her Freshers Week, but it had been about eighteen months since my last visit. The place kind of reminded me of a holiday park site you'd find by the seaside. There were buildings with halls of residence within them, there was a big reception office at the top of the site, a student union bar, an entertainment complex, an onsite mini market, a laundrette amongst a host of other things. There was even an old red phone box there, although I had no idea if it still functioned. The only thing it really felt like it was lacking was a path to the beach.

Once we were inside the main building, I quickly lost my bearings. All of the corridors looked the same, and I had no idea where we were or which direction we were facing in relation to where we came in, so I just followed Sinead until we came to the correct room; she knocked on the door.

"Come in, come in," said a voice from the other side that I took to be Professor Buzzard. Sinead opened the door and we both stepped inside.

I'd heard a lot about Professor Leyton Buzzard from Sinead, and I had an image in my mind of what I thought he would be like. He was exactly how I expected him to be. He was tall, thin, about sixty, long grey hair, a small beard, thick-rimmed glasses, and he was wearing a white technician's coat. He was everything your stereotypical mad science professor should be. If you saw him in the street out of context, you'd just know he was a scientist.

"Good morning, Professor," said Sinead.

"Miss O'Brien," said Buzzard with a hint of surprise. "You're an hour early. You do know the clocks don't adjust until the end of the month?"

"Of course, Professor," she said. "I wanted to speak to you before class about something that happened over the weekend, if I may?"

Professor Buzzard returned to his desk and sat back in his chair.

"By all means," he said.

"This is my fiancé, Gary."

"Fiancé, you say. My, my, you have had a busy weekend. A coming of age birthday and a proposal. Congratulations to you both."

"Thank you, Professor," she continued. "But an incident has occurred that neither of us can explain. We're hoping you may be able to shed some light on it?"

"I can't promise that," Buzzard said. "I'm always here as a counsel to my students, though. Tell me what happened."

I'd only known the man two minutes, but already I could see why Sinead held him in such high regard. His mannerisms were infectious, and his posh accent just added to his charm. I already felt completely relaxed in his company.

"Maybe you should explain the first bit," she said, turning to me.

"Probably," I said, and I gave Professor Buzzard a rundown of the dream I'd had, the lucidity of it, and the actions I took. His eyebrows raised and his mouth opened slightly when I mentioned the stabbing, but he didn't interrupt or pass comment until I'd finished.

"Interesting," he commented, turning back to Sinead. "But, I'm curious as to why you think I'd be able to interpret dream meanings for you. You'd need a psychoanalyst to help you do that. Whilst I have a more than passing interest in the subject, I wouldn't say I was an expert in it."

"It wasn't the meaning we were interested in, Professor," she added. "It's what happened next. You are aware my mum is ill with dementia?"

"I am, yes. I worked with her on a professional basis about fifteen years ago. One of her business partners, Betsy Cohen, is also an old friend. She was a formidable woman back then. I trust she still is?"

"Maybe less formidable now than she was," Sinead replied. "She had a fall on Friday and is currently in Badminton General recovering from a fractured hip."

"I'm sorry to hear that. Tell her Leyton sends his regards when you next see her."

"I will do, Professor. However, when we went to see her yesterday, she was calm at first. But then she saw Gary and boiled over with anger, saying she couldn't believe what he'd done to that girl at the party. I didn't know about Gary's dream at the time and just assumed she was hallucinating or delusional. But Professor, she was describing his dream back to him."

Professor Buzzard sat right forward in his chair, resting his arms on the desk.

"Really!" he said enthusiastically. "Tell me more."

"There isn't really more to tell. It freaked us both out, to be honest, and neither of us can explain it. However, we've been doing Many Worlds stuff for the last few weeks, and I wondered if it fit in with any of those theories, somehow, and if there was a way to try and understand what happened?"

Buzzard sat and thought for a moment.

"Do you know what happens to our consciousness when we go to sleep?" he asked.

"No," we both said.

"Nobody does," he continued. "Not really. There are theories and suggestions but no concrete proof. Does it just switch off? Does it go somewhere else? Nobody really knows. But dreams have always fascinated me. I wake up in a morning, and I can recall a dream. This means I have made conscious memories, in my sleep, whilst I was unconscious. How do you explain that?"

Sinead and I both just looked at him blankly.

"Now imagine for a moment that the Many Worlds Theory is, in fact, true. We live in a multiverse rather than a universe, and that's how life is set up. One of the main hypotheses around Many Worlds is it supports the assumption that consciousness can't really be terminated. There will always be a 'path of least resistance' where the conscious state survives. But unconsciousness, and sleep by definition, would seem to disprove that theory. And yet we dream and make conscious memories in our sleep. The two facts don't tally. There must be a missing link."

I glanced across at Sinead, who appeared to be taking this all in far more successfully than I was.

"That missing link would be the answer to the question, 'What happens to our consciousness when we go to sleep?' and that's something we can't answer. However, if you analyse a normal dream, what do we notice about it?"

"That they're really messed up," I commented.

"Exactly! They don't make any sense in the waking world. If you dream that you're in a pet shop buying a rabbit, and yet moments later you come out of that pet shop with a fish tank, you don't look at that and go 'where's my rabbit?' In the moment, the fish tank makes complete sense., You don't recall asking for the rabbit and, therefore, you don't realise that it's all 'messed up' as you put it."

"Now if you believe the Many Worlds theory to be true, and I personally do, could there not be a rational explanation in there? Is it not possible that whilst we sleep, our consciousness drifts into neighbouring Worldlines, passing through different eventualities, each one making perfect sense in that moment? Yet you wake up, you remember the journey through those Worldlines, and it's only then you think about the lack of continuity. At this point, you just shrug it off as a weird dream, but what if it's not? What if, Gary, in your act of lucid dreaming, you'd actually found a way to control yourself in one of those other Worldlines?"

"Are you suggesting I may have really stabbed someone, just in another Worldline?"

"I'm saying that it's not impossible, that you can't prove that you didn't. Think about some crimes here. Only last month a man in Croydon was sent to prison for killing his six-year-old daughter. The case struck me as odd, as the family were not known to social services, there were selfies of the man with his daughter posted to his social media account just forty minutes before the tragedy, they were happy, the family had no concerns about the child's wellbeing. Then for no reason at all, he just strangles her with his bare hands. There was no motive, he claims to have no memory of it, and he's always denied the charge. Yet nobody believes him and, as a result, he was sent to prison for life. Something about the whole thing just didn't sit right with me."

"Are you suggesting he was taken over by another him from a different Worldline and that he killed his daughter without knowing about it?" Sinead asked.

"What we don't know about life, death, and all of these things is far greater than what we do know. There is nothing to disprove it so, theoretically at least, it is possible."

"But I don't care who you are," Sinead said. "You're not going to go and murder a child, even in a dream, are you?"

"Miss O'Brien, fifteen minutes ago I'd have said you wouldn't voluntarily stab someone in the neck with a cake knife in a dream either. Yet your partner here would seem to disprove that theory."

"Forgive me, Professor," I interrupted. "But this all sounds like nonsense to me."

"Maybe it does, and maybe it even is," said the Professor. "But if you don't mind, Mr…?"

"Jackson," I responded.

"Mr Jackson, may we explore your dream further and see if we can draw any further clarity from it?"

"Go ahead," I said.

"What's the first thing you remember about the dream?"

"Realising I was back at the party."

"And did you realise immediately that you were dreaming?"

"Not straightaway, no."

"What triggered that?"

"It was when I dropped the knife."

"You dropped the knife? When was this? Before the stabbing?"

"Yes, I was cutting the gateau."

"What caused you to drop the knife?"

"It was in my right hand, it hurt."

"You are left-handed?"

"I am now."

"What do you mean by 'now'?"

"I had an accident a few years ago. I can't grip properly with my right hand anymore."

"Ahh yes, the incident with the lorry, I assume? Miss O'Brien did tell us that little tale in one of our lectures a few weeks ago when we were discussing near-death experiences," he turned to Sinead. "It was around the same time you told us about your daredevil driving manoeuvres, I believe."

Sinead's face reddened, and I knew the incident he was referring to. She was driving down the M1 when she passed a van that was lane hogging. In her irritation, she made an elaborate move across the lanes to pass him, only to suffer a tyre blow out on the way back across the road and coming dangerously close to killing us both. Happily, she drives a lot calmer now.

"Let us continue," he said. "So, you've dropped the knife. Then what did you do? Pick it back up again?"

"Yes."

"With, in your perspective, your correct hand."

"Yes."

"And are you aware you're dreaming at this point?"

"I'm becoming aware."

"Tell me, as I'm unfamiliar with the concept, how does one become aware that they are dreaming?"

"I use visual clues to tell me whether I'm awake or asleep."

"Such as?"

"I look at my right hand for my scars."

"From your injury?"

"Yes."

"And there were none?"

"No."

"Do you use any other clues?"

"Only if the scars are there. Sometimes they are."

"And what would those clues be?"

"Reading text. Looking away, reading it again to see if it still said the same thing, or if it was a coherent sentence."

"Did you do that this time?"

"No."

"Because your scars were missing, so you'd already established you were dreaming?"

"Yes."

"Hmmm, ok. And then what, was it at this point you stabbed the girl?"

"No, not straightaway, I wasn't immediately aware of her. I looked around the room to see who else was there. I noticed Mary, actually. That was another clue I was dreaming, as I could remember she wasn't at the party."

"This is all getting very interesting isn't it," he commented, looking back and forth between us. "So, when did you become aware of the girl?"

"When I turned back around. Her red dress caught my eye. I thought it looked like Michelle, she turned to face me and smiled, and it was her. She turned back and I remember willing her to turn and face me again."

"Out loud?"

"No, I don't think so."

"And did she?"

"No."

"And then you stabbed her?"

"I felt myself starting to wake up. I thought I was losing control of the dream, so I lashed out quickly before I woke up."

"And when you did lash out, what happened then?"

"I did wake up."

"I see. Tell me, where exactly did you stab the girl?"

"Just under her left ear, behind her jawbone."

"And straight through the carotid artery, no doubt. It probably killed her almost instantly."

He said it with such flippancy that I couldn't believe he was proposing it as something that might have really happened.

"Sorry, Professor," Sinead interjected. "But how does my mum's hallucination fit into all of this?"

"If what you're saying is true, then it's not really an hallucination. But it is an interesting point, isn't it, and one I've not really thought about in relation to Many Worlds. Can we conclude on the dream first though, if I may? Gary, I want you to imagine for a moment that you never had your accident that day. What would you have done that day?"

"Sat my English Literature exam, and then I was planning to ask Michelle out after it."

I could feel Sinead scowl as I said it, even though at the time it had actually been her idea.

"Michelle being the girl you stabbed in the dream?"

"Yes."

"Ok, so in a Many Worlds scenario, do you think it's plausible that had you avoided the accident, you'd have gone to the exam, asked Michelle out, been successful in that, and had a relationship with her as happy as the one you now have with Miss O'Brien here?"

"It's plausible, I suppose."

"Did you two know each other at the time of the accident?"

"Yes," Sinead said. "I witnessed it."

"And the two of you were friends already?"

"Yeah, I was reasonably friendly with Michelle too, but I lost touch with her after she and Gary fell out."

"Excellent! Most excellent. So, it is highly likely that, in the scenario described, Gary and Michelle may still have attended your party?"

"I wouldn't say highly likely, but not impossible."

"And in that Worldline, Gary would still be right-handed."

"Yes," I said.

"Cutting a cake, when this Gary in this Worldline grabs control of his consciousness in the form of a lucid dream and stabs his girlfriend to death."

"I don't know that it killed her, or that she was my girlfriend. As I said, I woke up."

"If you stabbed her there with a knife that wide you would most likely have killed her. She'd have died of blood loss if she'd not immediately perished from the injuries. It's a fatal wound you inflicted on her."

"Assuming any of this is real," I corrected.

"Assuming that, yes."

"If it is real," I asked. "What can I do about it now?"

Buzzard considered the question.

"I don't think there's anything you can do The event has already happened."

"But if I had that dream again, could I not simply correct the error by not stabbing her?"

"In theory, you'd be able to avoid making the same mistake in two separate Worldlines, but as for the one you witnessed on Saturday night, that crime has already been committed."

"And the version of me you spoke about, the one who avoided the accident, what about him? Is he just sitting in a prison cell now unaware of why he's there?"

"Again, it's not impossible."

I looked at Sinead.

"I need to do it again," I said. "I need to find out."

"Sorry, Professor," Sinead began. "I still don't understand where my mum fits into all of this. How do we convince her that Gary hasn't really committed a crime?"

"I'm not sure you can. Your mother suffers from vascular dementia and experiences what we identify as hallucinations as a result of this, correct?"

"Yes, that's right."

"And if we are hypothesising that in dreams, the consciousness is escaping into additional Worldlines, is it not also possible that hallucinations could work on a similar premise?"

"Well, when she hallucinates, she does often claim to see things that aren't there or refers to events that haven't happened."

"But somewhere inside, what she's seeing must be real to her. It must have some basis in fact from her perspective. If we assume her consciousness is drifting through other Worldlines the same way Gary did, how do you convince her what she's seeing isn't real? Even if you do convince her, you can't rely on her remembering the conversation. Your best bet is probably to hope she forgets about the party."

"What are you saying, that the decaying of her brain is actually just the releasing of her consciousness into multiple different Worldlines simultaneously, and she just happened to occupy the same one at the same time as Gary when he was murdering Michelle?"

"We don't know she's dead!" I shouted, but they both ignored me.

"Sounds preposterous, doesn't it?" Buzzard said. "And yet, can you think of another explanation?"

"No," she said. "Although the absence of another explanation doesn't mean there isn't one."

"Quite true, but you came here for clarity and for some sort of explanation on how it might be explained using Many Worlds. Based on nothing but assumptions, conjecture, and hypotheses, that's my best guess. Now, if you would both excuse me, I have to prepare for your lecture, Miss O'Brien. Frankly, it should all be child's play to you now given what we've all been discussing."

"Sorry, Professor," I said. "One more thing. If everything you've said is true, there must therefore be a way to communicate with that Worldline again, get a message to them and explain what's happened."

"Gary, imagine the three of us hadn't had this conversation. Then someone comes up to you and explains a crime in the manner we've just described. What are you going to think?"

"That they're a bit mental," I admitted.

"Precisely. You wouldn't just have to communicate with that Worldline, you'd have to communicate with the right person in that Worldline too."

"Such as Sinead?"

"This didn't make any sense to her before this conversation either. Really, you'd need to talk to me, and this version of me, in the Worldline in which you committed the crime. That's asking a lot, particularly if you're in prison now."

"Professor," Sinead interrupted. "If Many Worlds is really about all scenarios playing out in infinite Worldlines simultaneously, the scenario Gary requires, the one you just described, must exist in at least one Worldline."

"In theory, it will exist in infinite Worldlines, although less infinite than all the possible alternatives of course."

"Then we have to try," I added. "We're assuming we can connect with other Worldlines through dreams or hallucinations. Is there any other way?"

"Even if there were, and even if you managed it, how would you control which Worldline you visited?"

"Well, the party was on my mind on Saturday night, that's why I dreamt about it."

"How did Michelle get there?" Sinead scoffed.

I hesitated again.

"I dreamt about her on Friday night also."

"Oh, did you?" she retorted.

"Yes, but it wasn't a bad dream. It was weird though, that's why it was playing on my mind."

"So, the combination of the party, and Michelle occupying your mind anyway, led you to dream about Michelle being at Sinead's party. You then performed your visual check to establish you were dreaming, and then in a lucid state enacted your fantasy to kill her," Buzzard asked.

"I didn't want to kill her, just, just hurt her."

"Hurt her, then? The premise is the same."

"Basically, yes."

"And now you want to atone for that mistake?"

"If possible, yes. I would never want to hurt her really, or anyone for that matter," I said.

Buzzard thought for a moment.

"Let me discuss this with the other science professors here. I want a second opinion before I suggest anything further. Professor Charnock, who you will know, Miss O'Brien, from your chemistry sessions, and Dr Cross from biology will also have an interest in this. Can you come back and see me on Thursday evening once we've had time to discuss it?"

"Certainly," I said.

"Splendid. Now, if I may Miss O'Brien, Mr Jackson, I really do need to prepare for my lecture."

We crossed back over the room and Sinead opened the door.

"One other thing," Buzzard asked. "The murdered girl, Michelle. What was her last name?"

"Peyton," I said.

"Thank you," he said. "See you on Thursday. And you, Miss O'Brien, I'll see you in a few minutes."

Chapter Ten
The Blue Line

In light of the evidence against me, I was immediately charged with Michelle's murder and remanded in police custody to await my first court appearance. In truth I didn't care, not with Michelle gone. It was Sunday afternoon, and right now I should have been sitting with her having dinner with my family. I attempted to compartmentalise my thoughts; first I had to deal with the fact Michelle had died, suddenly and unexpectedly. How she'd died, I'd have to deal with later.

The initial hearing at the Magistrates' Court was scheduled for Tuesday morning, where I was told by Mr Dawlish that I would most likely be sent to HMP Badminton to await trial. Although I wasn't obligated to give a plea at that hearing, he advised that if I intended to plead guilty that I should do so at the first available opportunity. Apparently, this would be my best course of action, but he made the mistake of thinking I was analysing this with a rational mind. I'd seen the evidence myself and it was damning, but I knew in my head that I wouldn't, and didn't, kill Michelle.

At least I was in a cell on my own, which I was relieved about as I wanted some time by myself. It seemed impossible that this was happening to me, and I needed to try and understand it. The idea that this might be my life for the next twenty years made me wish I'd turned the knife on myself during my apparent blackout, and I wondered if I might have done had Marcus not intervened. I cried for Michelle all night. She was the love of my life and my soulmate. We were looking forward to moving in together, having a home, starting a family at some point in the future. Now she was gone, with no explanation, and I wasn't even going to be allowed to grieve for her. Had she been snatched away by someone else, or in an accident, I don't know how I'd have ever come to terms with it. Now, apparently, I was responsible, although I had no memory of the event. In a way, I was glad I couldn't recall it, as I wouldn't want to live with those memories. Maybe that was the point and the reason I couldn't. I wish I could erase the memory of the video also, but that would remain etched in the front of my mind until the day I died.

I also cried for Ed and Denise, who had been so good to me over the last five years. How could I ever explain to them what had happened when I couldn't explain it to myself? I wanted to see them, to tell them what I knew and what I didn't know; that this was all a horrible mistake that I couldn't rationalise, but that I would never have knowingly done this. I'd like to think they'd know this anyway, but if they'd seen the evidence I had then they probably hated me by now. Carl would be furious too. He'd lost his little sister, and I wept for him also.

What of my own family? Mum and Dad had treated Michelle like a daughter for the duration of our relationship. Donna hadn't been overly close to her, but Nicki had always looked up to her as if she was her own big sister. And how about Sinead? She'd been my best friend for years, and now her 21st birthday had been ruined. I didn't see her on the video, and I was hoping she hadn't witnessed it or else she'd be traumatised by it forever. Although no doubt Marcus would have filled her in on his heroic performance by now. The grief I'd given him for being in prison, and now here I was myself. I hoped he was looking after Sinead.

She'd also be the one tasked with initially explaining what had happened to Professor Buzzard at the university. How would he react? Maybe between the two of them, they could fashion a scientific explanation from all of the Many Worlds theories, but I couldn't see how. I have always been brought up believing that all problems had a solution or an explanation, but I couldn't find one for this situation. There had to be one though because this was wrong. It shouldn't be happening.

Apart from the desk sergeant bringing me food at mealtimes, which I didn't eat anyway, I didn't see a soul until the following afternoon. As I was on remand, I was allowed up to a ninety-minute visit each afternoon, which is something I didn't realise at the time. I was collected from my cell by PC Clarke because I was told I had a visitor. It seemed odd given that she was the officer who had conducted my interview, but I did quite like her. Of course, it was entirely possible that her and DI Braithwaite were deliberately doing a good cop/bad cop double act, but she seemed genuinely nice. I could only imagine, however, what she must have thought of me.

Unsurprisingly, the visitor was Mum. She looked like she hadn't slept in days either, and her eyes looked sore from all the crying she'd clearly been doing. She gave me a stern, almost cold, look as I entered the interview room. I wanted to hug her, but PC Clarke had already warned us that there was to be no physical contact.

"How are you?" Mum opened with.

"I don't know," I replied honestly. "I'm in shock, I think. None of this makes any sense."

"Join the club," said Mum. "Forgive me, but I have to ask you outright before we go any further. Did you do it?"

"No, of course not. They've got video evidence though, Mum, I've seen it, it's conclusive. But it wasn't me. I don't know what's happening."

Mum frowned.

"I have no memory of doing it," I went on. "Michelle and I were standing at the dessert table at Sinead's party, I was about to cut her a piece of gateau, and the next thing I knew Marcus had pounced on me and was pinning me to the ground. I assumed him and his gangmates were turning the place over, but apparently, he was reacting to me. But it can't have been me, Mum, I love her so much, I wouldn't do that to her. I wouldn't do it to anyone, but certainly not to Michelle," I was crying again.

Mum just sat quietly without passing comment, and I sensed she was unsatisfied with my explanation. To be honest, I wasn't happy with it myself either, but what else could I add?

"How is everyone else?" I asked.

"Dad is furious, Donna is confused, Nicki is devastated. She really loved Michelle. We all did. We're not allowed to see any of Michelle's family for obvious reasons, although we've already been informed that Ed has cancelled the work contract with your dad. Sinead is coming to see you shortly. We were told we had an hour and a half of visiting, but we could only

Worldlines

come in one at a time, so she'll be here in about half an hour. Have you been assigned a solicitor?"

"Yeah, but he's a bit useless."

"Why would you say that?"

"He's told me to plead guilty. Basically, he thinks I should just admit it and take my punishment."

"Why?" she asked, seemingly taken aback.

"Because the video shows me stabbing her, and I can't explain it. I can't defend it. I can't even confirm it. But there it is, me killing her. How could I have, Mum? Something has gone wrong somewhere. This isn't right. This isn't how things are supposed to be."

"That doesn't sound like that's the solicitor's fault. Has he mentioned any possibility of getting bail?"

"I'm not going to get bail if I plead guilty to murder, Mum."

"Go back to the start," she said. "Tell me everything from the beginning. What happened after you left the house on Saturday night?"

I recounted the whole tale to her, meaning I must have spoken non-stop for about twenty minutes. Everything from how beautiful Michelle looked when I picked her up, to the most minute detail such as when we had to swap sides in the car because the seat belt was hurting her ribs. How hungry we both were after the flight and not eating since lunch. How Michelle's face lit up when she saw the desserts being opened up. Marcus going for the cheesecake whilst we went for the gateaux, the subsequent scuffle when he had me pinned to the floor, realising there was blood soaking into my suit and not knowing whose it was, and Marcus then knocking me out with a punch to the back of the head. The cuteness of the medic who was treating me, Detective Braithwaite placing me under arrest before the ambulance took me away, having to give up my clothes for examination, and not being given any information at the hospital. The interview with Braithwaite and Clarke where I denied everything and demanded to see the CCTV evidence that they said they'd got. Then the indescribable horror of watching it, seeing myself plunge a knife into Michelle's neck, and subsequently spewing up all over the floor. Mum listened earnestly throughout without interrupting, which I appreciated. She could save her questions until the end.

"So, you really remember nothing about the incident itself, until you watched it back on the video?" she asked when I'd finished.

"Mum, I still don't remember it. I remember the video clearly, the sheer awfulness of it will be etched into my memory until the day I die. But the incident itself, I don't remember anything about it at all. I have a gap from when she handed me the knife to when Marcus knocked me to the ground."

"Could Marcus's punch have caused the damage?"

"I hadn't thought of that. It's very specific if it did. It's not like I've forgotten the entire party There's about twelve seconds that I don't remember. Has Ed really broken off the contract with Dad?"

"It wasn't really a contract. Ed always insisted on keeping the agreement informal. There's no documentation around it. Your dad always felt he kept it that way in case anything did go wrong between the two of you. Admittedly, we never expected it to be anything like this."

"It wasn't exactly high on my list of expectations either."

"Don't you get that attitude with me!" Mum snapped, letting her guard slip. "This isn't just tough on you, you know. Have you seen the news?"

"No, I've not seen anyone or anything since I got here."

"It's been on local and national news, and we're dreading The Gazette coming out tonight. You know how hot the media have been on knife crimes with all the gang stabbings in London, and now we're part of that statistic too."

"Mum, even if I wanted to kill her, why would I have done it there? There were literally a hundred people in the room. I'd have done it in Italy, when we were alone in a room by ourselves for the week."

"You might have even arranged an accident to take her out as she was skiing down a mountain."

"Mum! That was an accident!"

"I know, and I'm sorry, but we've been questioned about her other injuries and I imagine you will be too."

"What other injuries? It was only bruising she had from the holiday."

"They said she'd got three broken ribs."

"From the skiing accident?"

"That's what they were asking us."

"Well, at least I can prove everything about the holiday," I said. "Will you be coming to the hearing at the Magistrates' Court tomorrow?"

"I will," Mum confirmed. "Dad's been adamant he won't ever since it happened, but I assume he'll come around in time. Nicki wants to come, as does Will. Donna is trying to get the morning off work but isn't sure she'll be able to."

"Why doesn't Dad want to come?"

"I don't know, I think he's too angry."

"Oh, poor Dad."

"Sarcasm won't do here!" Mum snapped again. "If you act like that in court, it's not going to go down well with a jury, is it?"

"Neither will the video. I know in my own heart, and my own mind, that there's no way I could have done something like that, not to anyone. Yet the evidence is conclusive. I know I didn't do it, but I'm intelligent enough to know that, if I were anyone else, not even I'd believe me."

"If you plead guilty, though, then it really is all over. You'll never clear your name."

"I'm not sure I can anyway."

"Maybe Sinead can help you make sense of it."

"I'm amazed she still wants to speak to me."

"She's an amazing woman. So was Michelle."

"Please don't speak about her in the past tense."

"How else should I?" Mum said. "She's gone, to pretend otherwise insults her memory. I think Sinead wants an explanation more than anything."

"Then she's going to have to help me find one, because I can't tell her anything that I haven't already told you."

There was a knock at the door. PC Clarke opened it and I heard a man, who wasn't visible to me, inform her that there was another visitor waiting in reception.

"That's my cue to leave," said Mum. "I'll let Sinead come in and see you."

"Mum, one more thing. My suit, I wore it to the party. It's covered in blood and being used as evidence. It means I won't have one to wear in court tomorrow. Is there any way you could sort me one out please and bring it in?"

"I'll see what I can do."

"Thank you for coming," I said.

Mum smiled, but only with her mouth. The pain in her eyes never vanished for a second.

"We'll see you tomorrow," she said.

PC Clarke opened the door and escorted Mum back to reception, which meant that for the moment at least I was in an unlocked room, by myself, with no handcuffs on. I assumed this was a breach in procedure somewhere, as if I was ever going to abscond it would probably need to be now. Unfortunately, I hadn't come up with an escape plan so, even if I tried it, I didn't know where I'd go or what I'd do. I was also extremely cynical and wondered if the police were just testing me to see if I would try and leave the room. For all I knew an officer was standing guard outside the door. I decided to put my sensible head on and stay seated until PC Clarke returned with whom I presumed would be Sinead.

I didn't know how far reception was from the interview room I sat in, but it took PC Clarke a couple of minutes longer to return than I expected, but I was pleased to see that she did indeed have Sinead with her. My best friend entered the room and took the seat opposite me. Her eyes were swollen behind her glasses and I knew she'd been crying a lot. Normally I would hug her, but we were still under the no contact rules I'd been under with mum. Sinead just sat there, trying to remain expressionless and seemingly avoiding my eyes. It was as though she was waiting for me to do or say something. This was, of course, the first time I'd seen her since Saturday night.

"How are you?" I asked her.

"Pretty messed up, to be perfectly honest," she said. "My party was an absolute blast though," she added cattily.

"Yeah, about that," I began, but she was in first and, for the first time, turned to properly face me, the anger and upset in her eyes now immediately apparent.

"What on earth did you think you were doing?"

"I didn't think I'd done anything," I admitted. "Not until I saw the video footage."

"You don't remember any of it?" she scolded.

"Not a thing. Nothing from cutting the cake to Marcus flooring me. I was convinced when they showed me the video it would prove my innocence. It felt like watching someone else though. I ended up vomiting all over the floor."

"At least you didn't bleed to death on it," she said scathingly.

"Sinead! I'm at least as shocked by all of this as you are."

She just stared at me.

"Sinead, you know me better than anyone, except perhaps Michelle. You know more than anybody how much I loved her and how happy I was with her."

"Then how do you explain what's happened?"

"I can't explain what's happened! My solicitor wants me to plead guilty, but I can't in good faith plead guilty to something that I know, 1,000 per cent, I wouldn't have done."

"Marcus saw you stick the knife in. He's traumatised by it. He said when he closes his eyes, he can still see the handle protruding from her neck."

"Sinead, please don't."

"I don't know what else to say to you. But given we're supposed to be best friends, I wanted to give you a chance to explain what had gone wrong."

"Sinead, we are best friends, and right now I need you more than ever. But I can't explain it to you. One moment everything was fine, the next it wasn't. When I came around, I kept asking where Michelle was because I had no idea."

Sinead's eyes narrowed.

"You are telling me the truth, aren't you?" she asked, and it was phrased as a question more than an observation on her part.

"Of course I am. I've never lied to you, ever. If I could explain this I would, and if I could remember doing it, I'd admit it. Denying it would be an insult to Michelle, but I can't confess to something that I know I wouldn't do. But I can't explain the memory gap."

"How much don't you remember?"

"It was about twelve seconds. Mum thinks it could be damage from when Marcus punched me, but I doubt it would be that specific."

"Yeah, he said he'd hit you, said he'd done it twice actually. He was worried he'd get sent back to prison as he's still on parole. It did mean we had to tell Mum and Dad about his past, though, when the police questioned us on Sunday morning."

"What did they say?"

"Dad wasn't happy, but Mum was largely oblivious. She was furious as she heard it, but five minutes later it was as though she'd never been told."

"Are the two of you ok?"

"We're helping each other through it," she said.

"How about Michelle's family, do you know how they are?"

"How do you think they are? The car lot was closed yesterday and still is today, nobody has seen Denise, but Carl has said he'll kill you if he ever sees you again."

"Good thing I won't be out on bail then, isn't it, although I'd be the same if Will ever hurt my little sister," I admitted.

"So, what do you think happened? Why do you think you can't remember?"

"I have no idea. I was wondering if Buzzard might have any ideas."

"Why would Professor Buzzard know?"

"Just with what we've been talking about regarding the Many Worlds stuff, and with him saying about the idea of your consciousness drifting through different Worldlines, whether he might have a theory about this."

"You think you might have been possessed by someone from another Worldline, just at the moment we're discussing the possibilities at university?" she asked. I couldn't decide whether she was being serious, or if she was mocking me.

"I don't know," I said. "But something has gone wrong. What I do know is that this me, inside this head, would not have done what this body apparently did. There has to be an explanation. What did Buzzard say when you told him about it all this morning?"

"I didn't go," she said.

"How come?"

"Gary, on Saturday night at my 21st birthday party, my friend was murdered in front of me by her boyfriend, and my best mate. You don't just get up the next day and carry on your life as if nothing has happened."

"Did you see what happened?"

"No, I was talking to a relative. But I did see Marcus holding you down, and I could see someone on the floor behind you. I couldn't get closer, though, as someone pulled me away, but I could tell it was Michelle as I recognised her dress. I can't imagine what she must have felt."

"No, me neither. I hope it was nothing. That she was just there one minute and gone the next without feeling any pain."

"She was pronounced dead at the scene according to the reports, and her face was covered by a blanket when they carried her out."

"I can't process all of this," I said. "It's like there's been a glitch in the matrix."

"That would be no more far-fetched a theory than you having been possessed by someone from another Worldline," she commented.

155

"Yeah, I know, but right now I can't think of anything else that fits."

"You're not seriously considering it as a defence?"

"It might be the only defence I have, providing I need one. If I plead guilty it won't matter anyway. Will you speak to Buzzard about it, please? I can't spend the rest of my life in here not knowing why. I'd have rather died myself."

"If you've seen video evidence of you actually committing the crime then it's going to be difficult for Professor Buzzard to come up with anything that's going to get you off," she said.

"Yeah, I know," I admitted. "But, even if there was just some way of trying to explain all this, it might make it easier for everyone to compute and to deal with, and for me to grieve for Michelle. Do you know when her funeral is?"

"No, the police haven't released her body yet. They're not going to let you out to go, are they?"

"I haven't asked yet."

"Gary, you can't, think of Michelle's family if her killer shows up at her funeral."

"I'm not a killer," I said strongly.

"I'm sorry to break it to you, Gary, but unless something comes up to explain all this in a way other than how it looks, then I'm afraid you are."

At that, she stood up to leave.

"I'll speak to Professor Buzzard on Thursday morning, but don't hold your breath. Good luck in court tomorrow."

"Will you be there?" I asked her suddenly, as she turned away.

"Do you want me to be?" she asked, somewhat reluctantly.

I thought for a second then nodded my head.

"Then I will be," she said, and off she went.

Chapter Eleven
The Black Line

"What did you make of all that?" I asked Sinead as we walked back down the corridor, oblivious to the dark turn her mood had taken.

"I find the fact you keep dreaming about Michelle quite insulting," she snapped.

"Why?" I asked; Sinead stopped walking and turned to face me.

"Gary, what are we?"

"A couple?" I offered as an answer.

"Yes, but more than that, we're engaged to be married, and you're a part of my family. You proposed yesterday because you didn't get the chance on Saturday, which was my 21st birthday, because my mum is lying in a hospital bed. And yet, on Saturday night, you went to bed and had a fantasy dream about murdering the girl you fancied at school. Do you understand why I'd have a problem with that?"

"Yes, in a way," I admitted. "Once the adrenaline wore off, I felt quite guilty about it myself. But Sinead, I didn't go to bed wanting to dream about Michelle. I was dreaming about the party. That's how I started realising I was dreaming. I was thinking about your mum not being at the party, and I dreamt about the party and your mum was there. It's just in the Worldline I went to, Michelle was there too."

"Oh, get stuffed Gary!" she spat furiously. "You don't buy any of that stuff he just said in there, and don't pretend that you do. Not even I believe most of it, and I'm studying the damned subject! I can't believe you can stand here, look me in the face, and try and use it as an excuse for what happened."

"Well, what do you dream about?" I asked her.

"I don't know," she snapped. "I never remember any of my dreams."

"Ever?"

"Not very often, and I've never lucid dreamed. You knew what you were doing!"

I thought about answering her but figured anything I said on the subject would just rile her further, so I tried to change topic.

"Where shall I meet you after your lecture?" I asked, turning to start walking again.

"Just go home. I want some time on my own."

I was upset by her reaction, but I did as she wished.

On a Monday, she was usually home by around four o'clock, but this evening neither Sinead nor Eamon appeared until after seven. I was hungry; not that I demand that someone else cooks my dinner for me, but we usually all eat together. Mary is the only person in the house who can cook and, given we'd been eating leftover party food all day yesterday, I wasn't entirely sure what 'dinner' was going to entail tonight. I needn't have worried, as when they did appear, they were carrying takeaway pizzas they'd picked up on the way home.

"Is everything ok?" I asked, sensing it wasn't.

"No, Mum's really ill."

"What's happened?"

"She's got an infection from the surgery she had on her hip on Friday," Eamon said. "She's been put on intravenous antibiotics meaning she's going to be in there for at least another five days, possibly seven."

"That's not good. How is she feeling?"

"We couldn't really tell, she slept most of the time we were there. I think she's in a lot of pain, though."

I turned around to speak to Sinead, but she'd already gone upstairs to her room.

159

"Is she ok?" I asked Eamon, gesturing towards the door.

"She tells me you've had a row."

"It wasn't a row exactly. We argued briefly this morning, but it was nothing serious."

"Well, Sinead thinks it is," Eamon added coldly, giving me no further clues.

I was unsure what to do next; I went up the stairs myself, but it was only when I got onto the landing that I decided to try Sinead's room first before going into my own. If she'd wanted to talk to me, she presumably wouldn't have walked off, but it's not wise to let these things fester. With a hint of trepidation, I knocked on the door.

"Sinead, it's me," I said softly. "Can I come in?"

"Do what you want," came the reply.

I opened the door and went in, trying to tread carefully both physically and metaphorically.

"Sinead, what's wrong?" I asked her. She dried her eyes before responding.

"Do you know why I took you with me to university this morning?"

"Yes, to speak to Professor Buzzard."

"Why?"

"To ask him about the dream, to see if it fit into the Many Worlds Theory."

"To what end?"

"To see if there was anything we could do about it."

"No."

"No what?"

"No, that isn't why I took you."

"Then why did we go?" I asked, confused.

"Well, my objective was to try and help Mum," she snapped. "She's hallucinating, she's seeing things we can't see or comprehend. Your dream and her reaction gave us a possible insight into what she might be going through. But what did you spend the entire meeting talking about? You, you and Michelle. How you could save her, and how you could ease your own conscience. Twice I tried to bring the conversation back to Mum, and both times you both ignored me."

"I hope you gave him a hard time over it in lecture," I retorted.

"No, Gary, I didn't. Because he's a science professor, interested in all the science bits, and you're my partner who is supposed to care about how I feel and what this family is going through. When you were injured, when you fell out with your family, you had my full, unequivocal support, and you still do. But to you, Mum's condition is secondary, going on in the background of your own little dream world, where you're fantasising about someone else. I'm hurt, I'm upset, I'm struggling, and for once I need you here, in this Worldline. I need your support."

This was rare for Sinead; she's always been an emotional girl, but she's also a strong, independent woman who I admire a lot. She'd never reached out to me for support like this before, and I wasn't sure what signs I was meant to be picking up on. I walked over to the bed and wrapped my arms around her.

"Baby, I'm sorry," I said. "I didn't realise you were struggling so much."

"Gary, I've barely stopped crying all weekend. How could you not notice?"

"I guess I have been overly preoccupied with all of this, I'm sorry. I think we should probably cancel the meeting with Buzzard on Thursday We won't bother going back."

"And leave me to explain why to him when I have him for lecture?"

"Can't you tell him on Wednesday?"

"I've got Charnock this Wednesday. That's not what I want anyway. I'm a scientist too remember, and this interests me as well. But it doesn't take precedent over my mum and her health. It's not the most important thing going on in this house and in our lives at the minute."

"Ok, I understand," I said, kissing her on the forehead.

"You understand, but do you care enough?"

"Of course I do, I love you, you know that."

She wiped her eyes again.

"What have you done this afternoon?"

"Not a lot," I admitted. "I played a FIFA tournament on Xbox Live, but I couldn't concentrate. I got knocked out in the second round."

"Have you spoken to your mum yet?"

"No, why?"

"Do you not remember our conversation from yesterday morning? I asked you to think about how you might make up with your family. Have you?"

"No, not yet."

Sinead freed herself from my arms.

"Would you mind sleeping in your own room tonight, please?" she asked. "I want some time on my own."

I didn't sleep well again after that. I think part of me was worried about going to sleep and the possibility of dreaming and impacting other Worldlines again after the other night. I was bothered that I'd upset Sinead and that she was hurting, but I confess I was sleeping slightly easier knowing that Mary was remaining in hospital for the week. I wasn't looking forward to seeing her again, call it a guilty conscience, and I was secretly quite pleased that such a reunion had been postponed for an extra few days.

I didn't see Sinead at all the next day, and the fact that it was St Patrick's Day almost completely passed me by. I eventually dropped off to sleep sometime around four o'clock and then slept until nearly eleven. It was the first time in ages that I was unable to recall any of my dreams either, but under the circumstances this was probably a good thing. Sinead was out, her dad was at work, and I didn't see anyone until Eamon got back around 5:30 pm.

"How's Mary?" I asked him.

"She's more stable now," he said. "Sinead has been up there most of the day. I'm going up there to her now, and then we're going to The Ox and Lamb for a drink and some dinner. Are you joining us?"

"It's probably best that I don't," I replied. "Sinead is still annoyed with me over yesterday, and if Mary is ill, I don't want to risk upsetting her again."

"You'll have to see her at some point. You can't live here if the two of you can't get on."

"Yeah, I know," I said, unsure if he was referring to Sinead or Mary.

Eamon got changed and went out, and the two of them didn't get back until just after closing time. I'd already turned in, as I didn't want a confrontation with Sinead. I had my bedroom door ajar and the light on so she could see I was awake; it was then her choice if she wanted to speak to me or not. I heard her and Eamon laughing downstairs and was pleased that they'd had a good time, but when Sinead came upstairs, she went straight into her room. I lay there for hours, wondering how I could fix this.

By the next morning, I'd decided. Sinead left early for university and would be gone for most of the day. No doubt she would stop by the hospital on her way home anyway. Eamon also had a few errands to run, so I waited for him to leave, then I got up and dressed, had my coffee and my cornflakes.

I was about to leave the house when I decided that, on a journey this long, I'd be better off taking my walking stick. So, with a considerable amount of trepidation and a fair amount of embarrassment, I made my way into town to catch the bus into Barchester.

It had been over a year since I'd last set foot in my hometown, and to be honest, I hadn't really missed it; compared to Badminton, it was a bit of a dump. There were two main estates; Birchtree, which is where I grew up, and Sycamore Village, which was where Michelle used to live, or possibly still did. Between the two estates was the main road where I'd had my accident, and off that road was the White Willow industrial estate, which meant the smell of factories was noticeable in the air. It hadn't been when I lived here, but now I'd been away for a while the scent stood out more than I'd previously noticed. The main road also contained a bakery warehouse, a double-glazing store, and a second-hand car dealership. The latter of these, Peyton's Automotives Ltd, was actually owned by Michelle's dad. Opposite the entrance to the industrial estate was my old school, now called The Barchester Academy, which sounded much better than Blackthorn Comprehensive, which is what it had been called in my day.

I got off the bus outside the school and made the short walk into Sycamore Village, towards the Central Library where Mum worked. I should have probably called ahead and told her I was visiting, but that would have involved a bit of forward-thinking which is why it hadn't occurred to me. I wasn't even sure if she was working today; it would be a bit of a wasted trip if she wasn't.

Happily, my luck was in, and I spotted Mum almost immediately. As you enter the building, there is a prayer room to the left and an open staircase in front of you which I'd never been up. The entrance to the main section of the library was to the right and through a set of automatic sliding doors that you get on the front of supermarkets. All very posh, and all very different to the last time I was here. Mum was sitting at the desk, which was about halfway down and to my left. She hadn't yet noticed me. I stood there in the doorway for a moment waiting to see if she would, but the longer I did that the more likely I was to turn around and head back home, so I took the bull by the horns and walked in.

"Gary!" she enthused, as I approached the desk. "What are you doing here?"

"Hello, Mum," I said, as she walked around the counter to hug me.

"Twice in less than a week I've seen you," she said. "To what do I owe this pleasure?"

"Sinead, mostly," I said.

"Have you proposed to her yet?"

"Yeah. I did it at the hospital on Sunday."

"And, what did she say?"

"She said yes."

"Oh, Gary, congratulations," she said, hugging me again. "I'm so pleased for you. I wish we could celebrate it."

"Actually, that's part of the reason I'm here," I said.

"Just a minute," she said, and called over to another staff member who was stacking books back on a shelf. "Jana, do you mind if I take my break a bit early? My son is here to see me."

Jana nodded; she looked familiar, but I couldn't place her.

"Shall we go to La Zona Rosa? We can talk there."

La Zona Rosa was an American themed café two buildings down from the central library. The building had been vacant the last time I was here but was now under new owners; a Texan couple called Amy and Austin, Mum informed me. The café wasn't large, about the size of your average terraced house, although its decor made it feel much bigger than it was. It had a diagonal black and white tiled floor, and a dado rail around the middle of the walls, which had plain bricks below, and full mirrors running the length of both sides of the café. Added to the big glass front, it was surprisingly bright in here. The back wall was plain brick and, oddly, had a red electric guitar on the wall above the "Staff Only" door. The booth nearest the far end was free, and Mum and I took it. It allowed me to rest my stick against the wall without the risk of it falling over and tripping someone else up.

"Why would you come all the way from Texas to open a café in Barchester?" I asked.

"Why wouldn't you?" was mum's somewhat vague reply. "I'll get these. What do you want?"

She ordered an American Latte and a cheese and tomato toastie, whilst I had a regular coffee with a tuna and sweetcorn baguette, even though it was still only 11:30 in the morning.

"So, what brings you here?" Mum asked.

"Sinead thinks it's time we all buried the hatchet," I said.

"Ok," Mum replied, nodding curtly. I got the impression that Sinead may have mentioned this to her at the party, and therefore my visit was perhaps slightly less surprising than she was making out. "What do you think?"

"To be honest, Mum, I'm quite happy with how things are. I speak to you and Nicki. I'm sorry I upset Donna, but she's made her position clear, but Dad's a moron, he's always been a moron, and I can't imagine ever thinking anything else. It was only a matter of time before we came to blows. I'm only surprised it took as long as it did. But circumstances change, don't they? It's probably in everyone's interest to try and move on"

"He does miss you, you know."

"I'm sure he does," I said, but Mum picked up on the sarcasm.

"He does. We were speaking about it last week. You've already moved out, Donna is moving in with her girlfriend in the next few weeks, and

Nicki wants to go away for university. All our babies have grown up but, unfortunately, not everything has gone to plan."

"You mean I've not lived up to his expectations."

"No, it's not that. Nobody is happy about what occurred between you and Donna, but time heals Gary, and you've not spoken to either of them in so long."

"I'm not coming back to the house with you," I said sharply.

"I know," she said, "And I wasn't about to suggest it. Not today, and not on your own. But we are family, and Sinead is now part of that family too. If you're interested in trying to move on, why don't you and Sinead come over on Sunday for dinner. Not to the house, we'll go to The Red Chestnut if you like."

The Red Chestnut was the local pub on the Birchtree Estate; it had a terrible reputation and had been shut down twice during my childhood. It was probably only a matter of time before they closed it again.

"No, that place is horrible."

"Your dad likes it in there."

"I thought he might."

"It's not as bad as it used to be."

"Mum, you've been saying that for the last ten years."

"Well, how about The Loch & Quay around the corner then? You used to like the food in there. It's neutral ground too, you can see everyone there without the added pressure of going to the house."

"I'll run it by Sinead when she gets home, if she's talking to me."

I gave Mum a heavily edited version of what had happened since the party; Mary flipping out at me because she's hallucinating, the fact me and Sinead had fallen out, and the potential difficulties in continuing to live with the O'Brien's if both situations didn't get resolved. I left out the parts about the dream and the conversations with Buzzard.

"So, you do have a personal interest in making up, in case you need to move back home?" she said.

"No, I wouldn't move back home. I couldn't live under the same roof as Dad and Donna."

"You'll always have a home here, Gary."

"I didn't have one two years ago when Dad kicked me out."

"And he shouldn't have done that. It's a mistake he wouldn't make again."

I took a bite from my baguette without replying.

The two of us chatted for another twenty minutes until Mum had to go back to work; actually, it was really nice to have some alone time with Mum, as it hadn't happened in quite some time. Despite the dread of going back, I found that I'd quite enjoyed it.

When I left her, I walked back out of the village to the bus stop. The bus back obviously left from the other side of the road, the one I was run down on, and I always had a shiver go down my spine whenever I had to do this. Today was no different. I found myself walking slower than normal to ensure I didn't trip, despite trying to get out of the road as quickly as possible. Despite the unlikelihood that, should I ever get run over again, it would only happen here, I also waited for a huge gap before I crossed, so much so that I almost missed the bus.

As there was no direct bus from Barchester to Badminton General, I had to go into Badminton town centre and then back out again. I'd decided I was going to go and see Mary, and that I'd rather do it on my own initially, just in case it went badly. I was trying to spare Eamon and Sinead the awkwardness and myself the embarrassment. Visiting didn't commence until 2 pm, and I was at the hospital before 1:30, meaning I spent half an hour sitting on my favourite seat in the corridor outside the ward.

It amazes me how much people are creatures of habit. This corridor contained six chairs, and I'd now sat here a few times. Even though none of them were my seat, I always sat on the same one, the second one in. Had someone else already been sat here, it would have irritated me far more than it rationally should have done. I knew it wasn't just me though. People who catch the bus or the train at the same time every morning tend to make a beeline for the same seat where possible. Sinead always likes the same parking space when she goes into town. These things don't matter, but we are happiest when we're dealing with the familiar.

When I went on to the ward, I could see that Mary was awake, but wasn't looking in my direction. The knot in my stomach tightened further. How should I play this? I decided I'd speak to the nurse first.

"Excuse me," I said to the first one that passed, a young slim Asian lady who made up for in hair what she lacked in natural height. "I'm Gary, I'm Mary O'Brien's son-in-law," I wasn't being presumptuous; she did call me that.

"Yes, you were here on Saturday, weren't you? I asked you to leave as there were too many visitors around the bed."

I could have sworn it wasn't the same woman that did that, but apparently it was.

"Yes, that's right," I said. "Well, when I was here on Sunday, she reacted badly to me. She was hallucinating and she got aggressive towards me. I've not seen her since and I'm a bit nervous about walking in there in case I upset her again. Would you mind coming in with me initially please, just until she spots me? If she reacts badly again and needs calming down, I won't be able to do it as I'll need to leave."

"Ok," she said, but she sounded unsure.

Ever so slightly scared, I walked on to the ward.

"Hello, Mary," I said, trying to sound as normal as possible. "How are you feeling?"

She turned to face me; this was the moment of truth. It felt like it took her an age to respond but, in truth, it was only a couple of seconds.

"Hello, you," she said. "What are you doing here?"

"I've come to see you, haven't I?" I answered, breathing a huge sigh of relief. "How are you feeling?"

"I'm alright," she said. "Have you come to take me home?"

"Is everything ok now?" the nurse asked.

"Yes, I think so," I said. "Thank you."

I turned back to Mary.

"I can't take you home, can I? You need to finish your antibiotics first."

"Oh, you've come to give me some more, have you?" she scoffed.

"No, I've just come to visit you, to check you're ok."

"Well, obviously not, I've already had one lot of you coming around this morning prodding me. You all need to leave me alone."

"Do you want to see Sinead? She'll be here in a bit."

"Where's Sinead?" she asked.

"She's at university, she's on her way back. She'll be here soon."

"How do you know where she is, are you stalking her?"

"Mary, she's my girlfriend."

This revelation seemed completely incomprehensible to her. Not only had she forgotten about the dream, she'd forgotten who I was completely.

"How's your hip?" I asked.

"You lot should know," she snorted. Clearly, she thought I was one of the hospital staff.

"Only you know how it feels, Mary. You need to be able to tell us."

"Tell you what?" she asked.

"How your hip is?"

"My hip? It really hurts, I don't know what I've done to it."

"I'm sure it will get better soon," I said, trying to sound reassuring.

"How was the party?" she asked, and my anxiety levels shot straight back up.

"Yeah, it was good," I answered, before I gave her a rundown of the night's events. I was almost certain she wasn't following what I was saying, but she didn't talk over me or change the topic; if anything, she appeared to be studying me. When I finished, we sat quietly for a while; I was clock watching. I was expecting Sinead at any time now. Even though I'd not spoken to her since Monday evening, I'd still feel better when she was here. Being on my own with Mary, I never really knew what to talk about.

Sinead arrived just before three o'clock when her mum had just dropped off to sleep. She looked great. She wasn't dolled up, she just looked really pretty. She was in a pale pink pleated blouse, a knee-length skirt and a grey overcoat. I felt quite scruffy in t-shirt, jeans, and a bomber jacket next to her.

"What are you doing here?" she asked when she saw me.

"I came to see your mum."

"On your own?"

"Yeah. I wanted to see how she'd react to me, but I didn't want you and your dad to get upset if it went badly, so I came by myself. I did get one of the nurses to come in with me though, just in case she needed calming down."

"How long have you been here?"

"About an hour and a half. I sat outside the ward until visiting hours started."

"Has she been asleep all the time?"

"No, she's only just dropped off."

"So how was she with you?"

"Fine, although I don't think she knows who I am."

"She doesn't know who any of us are."

"You come and sit here," I said to her, standing up. "I need to find the gents. Do you want me to get you a drink?"

"Not from in there," she said, and for the first time I thought I heard her tone lighten.

"I can get you a tea or a coffee if you'd prefer?"

"No, you're ok, thanks," she said, taking my seat.

We stayed at the hospital until afternoon visiting ended at four o'clock and, as Sinead was in the car, I was able to get a lift home. Conversation between us was civil, but there was still something bothering her.

"How was your lecture?" I asked.

"Yeah, it was ok," she said. "I struggled to concentrate, but the bits I did catch sounded interesting."

"What was it about?"

"Chemical releases in the brain."

"In a physics lecture?"

"It wasn't physics today. We had Charnock, the chemistry professor."

"The one Buzzard wants to talk to?"

"Yes, and before you ask, no he didn't say anything about it."

The mention of this seemed to irk her again, but the conversation continued.

"How about you, what have you done today?"

"I went to Sycamore to see Mum."

Sinead took her eyes off the road for a split second to look at me.

"Really, how come?"

"I was thinking yesterday about what you said, so I thought I'd start by going back and chatting to Mum for a bit."

"How did it go?"

"She's invited us out for dinner on Sunday to The Loch & Quay."

"With your dad and Donna?"

"Yeah, I think so."

"Is your mum booking the table? What time is she booking it for?"

"I don't know, to either question. I didn't ask."

Sinead smiled and shook her head.

"Never change, Gary," she said.

Her mood seemed to improve quite markedly after that, and she told me about the night out they'd had at The Ox and Lamb. They'd had an Irish folk band on, as well as an Irish dance group. She doesn't often miss living in Dublin, but she does wish she was there for St Patrick's Day as she misses the big celebrations on O'Connell Street. I made a mental note that next year, I would take her.

I stayed at home that evening whilst Sinead went back to the hospital with her dad. Mary had slept through Sinead's visit earlier, and I was hoping she'd get to see her awake this time. It was a weight off my mind that we appeared to be on decent terms again, and I assumed she appreciated the effort I'd tried to put in today. I also hadn't fancied going to tomorrow's meeting at the university with the two of us still on bad terms either, but happily, that looked unlikely now. I sent Mum a text asking about the meal on Sunday, and she'd replied saying she'd booked it for two o'clock for eight people. Mum, Dad, me, Sinead, Donna, her partner (who I hadn't met), and Nicki. Who was the 8th person? I didn't ask, I'd find out on Sunday.

"How was your mum?" I asked, when they came home, with two big bags from the Chinese takeaway. I felt Eamon was just putting off having to prepare his own food, but he'd have to at some point. Even when Mary returned, she wasn't going to be in the right state physically or mentally to continue cooking for us.

"She was ok. Nothing more than ok, but she was ok."

"Was she awake?"

"Yeah, and she was talking. But she seemed to be making less sense than ever."

"Yeah, I felt that earlier."

"Thanks for going up to see her this afternoon," Eamon added. "I'm glad she was ok with you."

We polished off the Chinese in double quick time, given how much food there was. Sinead was off the wine tonight after how much she'd drunk the last few days, but I had a single can of beer whilst Eamon continued to drink more straight whiskey than he should. It had been quite an emotional day, and the heavy meal combined with my poor sleep the last few nights had made me very tired.

"I'm going up to my room," I announced. "I need an early night."

"Yeah, I might do the same," said Sinead, getting up off the sofa at the same time. "Goodnight Dad."

"Goodnight both," he said.

We climbed the stairs, and at the top, I went left towards my room whilst Sinead went right.

"Gary," she called, and I looked across at her. I noticed she'd opened the buttons on her blouse to halfway down. "You don't have to sleep in there if you don't want to. You can always come in here."

Chapter Twelve
The Blue Line

I slept awfully that night. Every time I closed my eyes, I was back in the interview room with DI Braithwaite and PC Clarke, watching the video footage of myself stabbing Michelle. I wondered if it was significant that my visions were of being shown the incident, rather than the incident itself. Surely if the memory was stored somewhere in my sub-conscious, it would come racing to the surface when I went to sleep? It was Monday night and I'd normally be with Michelle now; I went to her parents' house on Mondays after lecture and didn't go home again until Wednesday night. I was missing her so much; I had no idea how I was going to get through the rest of my life without her.

The next morning, I was again escorted from my cell to an interview room, but this time it was for a meeting with Warren Dawlish, who was to brief me on what was to happen on my first court appearance. Mum had pulled out all of the stops and had managed to get me a suit. It was black, and she'd also sent me in a crisp white shirt with a black and grey striped tie. She'd also sent in a bag containing three changes of clothes, a small address book with hers, Dad's, Donna's, Nicki's, and Sinead's mobile numbers, and £20 in cash consisting of £15 in notes and then five £1 coins. She'd also added an A4 writing pad, a pack of envelopes, and a book of first-class stamps. For someone who had no experience in preparing anyone for a trial, she appeared to have covered all the bases quite well.

I was shown into the interview room by a police officer I hadn't seen before, and this time he didn't stay in the room, meaning Dawlish and I could speak in private.

"I'm here to advise you on the events of today," he began. "Do you know what to expect?"

"No, not really. I know I'm going to prison though."

"We're not making an application for bail, so, yes, you will be."

"Could we make one?"

"It's very rare for someone charged with murder to get bail. I would advise against it."

"I'm not pleading guilty."

"You don't actually need to enter a plea today unless you specifically want to plead guilty. However, these cases aren't heard by the Magistrates' Court. It will have to go to the Crown Court anyway, even if it's only for sentencing. Did you want to enter a plea?"

"No, I need to try and process all of this first."

"Then all you'll need to do today is to confirm your name, address, and date of birth. The case will then be immediately adjourned and passed to the Crown Court. Do you have anyone attending court today?"

"My family, hopefully, and Sinead, my best friend."

"Are you aware that the family of the victim will most likely also be present?"

This should have been obvious, but I hadn't anticipated that at all, and I found the thought of seeing them quite chilling, although not as chilling as hearing him describe Michelle as 'the victim'.

"I hadn't realised."

"Well, they will be, unless they choose not to be, but you should expect it. It will get emotional, and it goes without saying that they will not be pleased to see you. It may get uncomfortable."

"How long will it last?"

"The discomfort or the hearing?"

"Both."

"The former depends on you and how thick your skin is. The latter, about fifteen to twenty minutes. Just make sure you respect the court, answer any questions that are put to you honestly, and don't say anything else unless you're asked to, or instructed to by me."

The journey to court, via prison van, was not a pleasant experience. However, unbeknownst to me, it was to be the easiest and most stress-free part of the day. It was hot and cramped, but at least it was quiet. The transfer to the prison began at 10 am as our case was due to be heard at noon. The only thing I'd ever arrived two hours early for before was an airport flight, and the court process was a bit like that given that both I and Mr Dawlish had to go through the full-body airport scanners, as well as having our bags put through a similar device, presumably scanning for weapons, corrosive liquids or signs of explosives. Once we'd cleared the security checks, the court usher transferred us into a room on our own so that we wouldn't be intercepted by any of Michelle's family when they arrived. I assumed at the time this was for my benefit but, in hindsight, it was more likely for theirs. I think I should have appreciated the calm before the storm, as the worst was clearly still to come. When we were finally called in, I felt myself break into a cold sweat, as the magnitude of where I was and what was happening was about to sink in.

Inside the courtroom, which felt very imposing, were three magistrates. As I looked across the room, I saw Mum, Nicki, Sinead, and Marcus sitting together. Dad wasn't there, and this really pissed me off, although I was in the wrong place to be showing annoyance. Sat slightly apart from them were Ed, Denise, and Carl. Denise looked very ill, although I could understand why. I wanted to shout and tell them how truly sorry I was for everything that had happened, but I knew better than to do so. Carl glared at me and didn't stop doing so throughout the entire hearing. As for Ed and Denise, neither of them looked at me once.

I was ushered into the dock and the hearing then went pretty much as Mr Dawlish had described that morning. I spoke to confirm my name and address, and a summary of the case was read out to the magistrates by DI Braithwaite. The court adjourned the case without me needing to make a plea. The lead magistrate confirmed that no application for bail had been received and that, therefore, I would be remanded to HMP Badminton pending my trial date at the High Court being set. It felt like it was over very quickly, but I also felt like I hadn't taken much in. After the hearing, I was escorted, still cuffed, back to the prison van which was to transfer me to my new home.

The process was excruciatingly slow. There were four of us inside the swelteringly hot prison van, and I was regretting wearing a blazer with my long-sleeved shirt. I felt sweaty, and because I was still cuffed, I couldn't remove the jacket either. Two of the other three prisoners were clearly acquainted, as they were telling each other how easy it would be to complete their respective ten-month and eight-month sentences. I did my best to tune out.

We'd been driving about fifteen minutes when I felt the van stop. Then there was a high pitch screech of scraping metal which I took to be the prison gates opening. We were stopped again, the driver got out, and then a few moments later we were escorted, one by one, to a holding cell. I was in there well over an hour as the other three prisoners were all processed first; I was the last to be collected by the prison officer. I was taken to a small room, where I was subjected to a deeply degrading and intrusive strip search by one male prison officer whilst another observed. To be fair to the officer, he did inform me that he hated this part almost as much as I did.

Once that part was over, I was asked a number of questions about myself. Previous criminal convictions, whether I used recreational drugs, drinking and smoking habits, questions about my health and medical history, whether I was suicidal or was suffering from violent feelings towards myself or others. Finally, having given them my life story, I had my picture taken and was issued with an identity card containing my name, picture, date of birth, and prison number. I was told to keep it with me at all times as I'd need it for pretty much everything in the prison. Then, having once again confirmed I was not a smoker, I was provided with a non-smokers pack containing some biscuits and a bottle of orange squash.

Once the checking in process was over, I was escorted to another small room, where I was to meet my first fellow prisoner. I was told he was an 'insider', which was basically a long-serving, but relatively trusted prisoner who could relate to my position, understand what I was going through, and answer any immediate questions.

"If you're quick, you can make it to your cell and be introduced to your roommate before dinner," was the first thing he said when he walked in.

He looked in his late fifties, with grey hair that was slightly too long to be described as short, without actually being long. He had tattoos on his arms and looked surprisingly tanned. "My name's Tyler Brooks, I've been here forever, and I know everyone. I'll probably still be here when you leave. On remand for murder, I was told?"

"Yeah, that's right," I confirmed quietly.

"What's your name?" he asked.

"Gary Jackson."

"Have you been in prison before?"

"No."

"Why did you do it?"

"I don't know, I don't remember doing it."

"Oh yeah, one of them, are you?"

"I genuinely don't remember."

"Makes no difference to me," he shrugged. "I'm just here to give you the info. It's half four now, dinner will be served at five, you'll be locked up at six and you won't be unlocked until eight the next morning when you'll go for breakfast. After that, you'll begin your induction process."

"What does that involve?"

"The same as all inductions involve anywhere. Learning the rules, guidelines on how to survive in here. You'll have to enrol in a job or an educational course They'll tell you what's on offer. They'll also tell you about visiting rules, how to get money or clothes sent in, and stuff like that."

"I am a physics student."

"And?"

"It's just you mentioned educational courses."

"You'll have to talk to the officers about it. You'll also be given the option to speak to the drugs team, make sure you take it. They'll also assess you medically, again. Any other questions?"

To be honest, my head was spinning, but as no specific questions came to mind, I just shook my head.

Afterwards, I wished I'd asked him who my cellmate was, as the prisoner I met upon being shown to my cell proved to be far from forthcoming with any information. There were two beds in the cell, if you could call them beds, one on either side of the cell. As I walked in, he was lying on the one on the right but was facing the wall. He was in the standard prison uniform of grey jumper and soft grey trousers and had a bald head which made me suspect he was quite a bit older than I was.

"Si, cellmate," the prison officer called as he took me inside. Si, which I assumed (wrongly, as it turned out) was short for Simon, didn't say a word. I put my bag down and sat on the other bunk as the door banged. I suddenly felt very nervous; I had no idea who this man was or what he was in prison for, or how he'd react when he woke up to find a new stranger in his cell. I decided to sit there and stay alert until he did, in case he attacked me. After about ten minutes, though, he spoke.

"Jackson, isn't it?" he asked in an American accent, without rolling over to face me.

"Gary, actually," I answered. This time he did roll over.

"Gary what?" he scowled.

"Jackson," I admitted. Surprisingly, he laughed, but not pleasantly.

"I hoped so," he said, before rolling back over.

"What's your name?" I asked.

"You'll find out," was all he answered.

That was literally all he said to me between when I arrived and when we were called down for dinner. His introduction had made me feel worse, and I was unnerved that he appeared to already know who I was. I didn't appreciate at the time that he was attempting to show he was above me on the food chain, that I'd moved into his cell and he was top dog. I had no problem with that, as long as he left me alone.

However, it didn't appear he was going to. He ordered me out of the cell first when the warden came to collect us for dinner and followed me a little too closely for comfort as we made our way down to the kitchen area. He appeared to be doing everything possible to make this as awkward and unpleasant an experience as possible. He stood next to me in the queue and was almost brushing against me as I made my way along the line of prisoners. He was about three inches smaller than me but a slightly bigger build. He wasn't fat, though. He looked strong and muscular.

I had very low expectations of prison food, but we were apparently getting gammon and chips, which was more than I expected. The tall, thin, gaunt-looking man who put the gammon on my plate didn't say a word to anyone, but the shorter, plumper, man serving the chips.

"One of the newbies?" he asked loudly and cheerfully. It was the first cheerful voice I'd heard in days, but it did have the unfortunate consequence of drawing everyone else's attention to the fact I was there.

"And Mr Cyrus," he said to my cellmate next to me. "You have a new friend to play with."

"Just serve the food and shut up," he ordered. I hoped I never got to the stage where I spoke to the staff with that attitude.

"Anything you say," the chef replied in the same cheery tone, before turning to me. He spoke good English but had a foreign accent, although I couldn't tell where he was from. "You've got a good one here. Requested you personally, he did."

Cyrus punched the counter, startling the chef slightly.

"Maybe I should have had you moved in there," he growled, and this wiped the grin from the chef's face.

"Welcome to the prison," he said to me, more formally this time, as I realised he was also a prisoner.

After I'd collected my food, I started making my way to a table at the far wall.

"Where do you think you're going?" Cyrus said sternly.

"Just over there," I said, more meekly than I intended.

"That one!" he said, pointing to a table near the centre that was already occupied.

"I'm alright over there, thank you," I naively answered.

"A word of advice," he said, "And it's the last one you'll get for free. Don't piss me off! You're on that one."

I looked around for Tyler, but he hadn't come in yet. I thought about just ignoring him then, realising I'd probably have to spend pretty much every moment with this man going forward, I did as he said. I expected him to follow me but was surprised to find he went to the table I originally made a beeline for, and he was immediately joined by other prisoners. I took the seat he'd pointed me to, which meant I had my back to him. The people already at the table looked as dissatisfied as I was that I'd come to join them.

"You're not welcome here," said one of the men already at the table. He was tanned, in his forties, and had short scruffy dark hair with a moustache and beard. He also had a tattoo of a snake on the back of his hand.

"This is where I was told to sit," I said, growing increasingly irritated with myself that my voice sounded so weak in response to anyone, yet I didn't appear to be able to do anything about it.

"I know," he said, momentarily smiling, before immediately turning serious again. "But I've just told you, you're not welcome here."

I got up and was about to move when a voice from behind yelled out.

"Oi," it went, and I turned around to find my cellmate standing up. "I said that one!"

He was talking to me and again referencing where I should sit. I looked back at the bearded prisoner, who was still seated and smirking. He picked up his drink.

"And I've said you're not welcome here. The choice is yours."

"Is there a problem?" came a woman's voice, and I turned to the side to find a female prison warden standing next to our table. She was short, blonde hair in a short ponytail, of medium build, and her appearance caused a chorus of wolf whistles to go up from the other prisoners.

"Only that you're overdressed, again," sneered the bearded man.

"That's funny, I always thought Governor Waylon was more your type," she retorted tartly, causing raucous laughter from some of the other prisoners. She then turned to me.

"You can sit where you want," she said. "Don't let them intimidate you."

I sat back down in the same seat, and the lady went back to her post.

"She wouldn't be saying that if she knew why you were in here, would she?" the man derided. "Now, eat up quickly before I really lose patience with you."

He then proceeded to stare at me for the entire duration of dinner. I was so uncomfortable and anxious that I hardly ate a thing, so I got up and went to scrape my plate into the bin.

"Don't you dare waste that," the chip chef called as he watched me. "I've stood in here cooking that this afternoon. Now, sit back down and eat."

I glanced over to the lady warden who had intervened moments ago, but she remained expressionless this time around. She clearly wasn't coming to my aid this time. I sat back down in the same seat and hoped, if I didn't look up, I could pretend Beardy wasn't staring at me for the entire time. It didn't work, but I forced myself to eat the food, even though I was feeling more and more nauseous with every bite. I'm glad it was only a child-sized meal. I'd have never stomached an adult one.

After dinner, we were shown back to our cells. I muttered a thank you to the female warden as I exited the kitchens, but she either didn't hear or chose to ignore me.

"Goodnight," called a different warden as he slammed our cell door shut. That bang as the door closed was the most horrible noise; not the sound itself, but the meaning of it. I sat on the bed in my cell and looked across at my cellmate, who was laying on the bed and had picked up a magazine that he must have already owned. It had a picture of a Ferrari on the front of it. I decided to try and make conversation.

"So, your name is Mr Cyrus?" I said.

"Nope," he answered. "And, I don't remember telling you that you could talk."

"Do I need permission?" I asked.

"In this cell, you need my permission to fart, now be quiet."

"I just wanted to talk for a bit."

"Well, I don't. Now shut up and go to sleep."

Given that it was only just after six o'clock, sleep felt unlikely, but I did do as instructed. I lay on my right with my back to him, trying the same trick I'd attempted in the kitchens; if I don't look at the other person, I can pretend they're not there. It must have worked as, surprisingly, I was soon fast asleep.

Chapter Thirteen
The Black Line

Suffice it to say, I slept a lot better that night, and I was in a much better mood the next morning. Sinead didn't go to university on Thursdays, so we got to spend the day together, which was nice. It was the first time since the previous Thursday we'd gotten any time to just relax and really do nothing. We did go into town for some lunch and to watch the new Kingsman movie at the cinema. At two o'clock, we left town and started making our way to the university. Unbeknown to me at the time, the following conversation had taken place between Professor Buzzard, Professor Charnock, and Doctor Cross since our initial meeting with Buzzard on Monday morning.

"Does anyone have any other business?" Doctor Cross asked, at the end of their weekly staff meeting on Wednesday evening.

"I have something interesting I'd like to bring up," Buzzard began. "You're both familiar with the Irish lady in the second year, Sinead O'Brien?"

"I am," said Charnock but Cross shook his head.

"She came to see me on Monday morning with her boyfriend. Well, fiancé, as they got engaged last Sunday. Anyway, they came to see me because of an incident that had happened to them over the weekend. Her fiancé, Gary Jackson, has been experimenting with lucid dreaming. Last Saturday night he experienced a lucid dream where, in it, he committed quite a serious offence. However, on Sunday afternoon, Miss O'Brien's mother, who is currently hospitalised with a form of dementia, claimed to have witnessed that crime."

"That's not possible," Cross commented dismissively.

"Well, that's what I'd have thought too," agreed Buzzard. "But the incident is quite compelling."

Professor Buzzard then detailed out the dream, the incident with Michelle, and the subsequent delirium suffered by Mary at the hospital on Sunday.

"It sounds like quite the coincidence," Cross dismissed again.

"Not really, not if you apply multiverse logic to it."

"Oh, come on," scoffed Charnock. "You're not seriously suggesting he may have really committed this crime, are you?"

"The event would seem to tick several boxes around many current assumptions and hypotheses that support the multiverse theory."

"So, you're suggesting that dreams allow you to commit crimes in other Worldlines and ultimately get away with it?"

"I'm suggesting that may be one possible consequence, yes."

Doctor Cross shifted uncomfortably in his seat.

"Would the person who occupied the Worldline at that time be aware of what was happening?" he asked.

"Ultimately, that's what we'd like to find out."

"And how do you propose we do that?"

"If we work on the assumption that anything we experience outside of our normal level of consciousness is actually an unconscious interaction with another Worldline."

"Forgive me, Professor," Charnock interrupted, "But that is quite an assumption."

"Granted, but let's assume for a moment it's true."

Both Charnock and Cross gave the look of treating this idea with a huge amount of scepticism, but they kept quiet and allowed Buzzard to continue.

"If you accept that to be true, then anything that triggers any form of hallucination, such as a dream or a mental illness, would allow you to interact with different Worldlines. What we want to try and do is get back to the Worldline in question and assess the damage."

"Assess the damage?" asked Charnock. "In what way?"

"I believe he'd have killed her given where he stabbed her. He is concerned that, in that Worldline, he is now rotting in a prison cell for a crime this Worldline's version of him committed. Mr Jackson wants to try and help his 'other self' if you will."

"Professor, you are aware of my cynicism around Many Worlds," Cross began. "I think it places a lesser value on each of our lives and our actions within it. However, say this is true. At the point Gary stabbed Michelle, wouldn't infinite Worldlines have formed? Worldlines where she died, where he missed the artery altogether, where someone saw him and stopped him. Likewise, even in the Worldlines where she did die, wouldn't there be an infinite number of them by now? Some where he's in prison, some where he's on the run. Unless he's going to go back to them all, he's never going to undo all the damage. Besides, Many Worlds supports the notion of all eventualities all of the time. Surely if that's true, then the girl being stabbed in the neck is just one possible outcome of her going to fetch cake at that party It would have happened whether he was dreaming or not. What I'm saying is, if Many Worlds is false this is a waste of time, and even if it's true, I fail to see the point."

"The point is about advancing our knowledge, Doctor Cross. I know he'll never undo what happened in the dream, but it will ease his conscience in this Worldline and the other infinite Worldlines that form off it after this point. What it will allow us to do is test a few theories. For Mr Jackson, it's about saving the girl or saving himself. For me, it's an opportunity to test some hypotheses that have always appeared untestable."

"So, this is just a good excuse to run a few experiments?" asked Cross.

"Crude, but reasonably accurate," confirmed Buzzard. "I know there'll be Worldlines where that girl survived. Her chances of death, even given she

was stabbed, is never a probability of 1. However, it would be in the 0.9s and, therefore, finding a Worldline where she did perish seems the most likely outcome, should we be successful at all, you understand. Now if Gary stumbles across one where she survives and he's not in prison, that will close the case for him. But if he discovers one where she's dead, then he needs to be prepared for encountering that, so I've told him that's what's happened."

Cross and Charnock sat without passing comment.

"Now, getting back to how we may achieve this. The most obvious way to do it would be the way he did it before, through his dreams. But this happens very irregularly and could take quite a long time. I was wondering if there was any way to induce that type of deep dreaming medically?"

"You mean any legal way?" Cross asked.

"Of course," Buzzard clarified.

"This is all hypothetical, I assume?" asked Charnock. "Or are you actually going to suggest we run with this after we've discussed it?"

"It's hypothetical for the moment. But if there's a safe and easy way to run an experiment like this, I'd be very interested to know how it would work and, potentially, to try it. Just to complete the picture, they know I'm talking to you about this. I'm meeting them both after lectures tomorrow to discuss this further."

"What are they expecting from that meeting?" Cross asked.

"Mr Jackson asked me if there was a way he could get back to that Worldline. I said I wanted a second opinion first and would discuss it with the two of you."

"I'm curious," commented Charnock. "What's your first opinion?"

"That if everything I've proposed really is true, that it should be possible. What I'm not sure of is whether there's any licenced drugs that would allow it to happen. That's your area, Richard," he said, addressing

Charnock. "I wanted you in here, Andy," he said turning to Cross, "Because we may need your hospital to do it."

"You're not doing it at the UCH," Cross said.

"Why not?"

"The girl you mentioned, the one who was murdered, Michelle Peyton. She's one of my student nurses. She works there."

"Oh, really?" said Buzzard with a hint of surprise. "Are you sure it's the same girl?"

"Absolutely. And if, as you suggest, the fiancé has fantasies about murdering her, then I have a duty of care to my staff. I don't want any risk of him knowing she's there, or of him coming to our hospital and encountering her."

"You might not need to," said Charnock. "Are you aware of a drug called Phencyclidine?"

"Angel Dust?" asked Cross.

"Yes," Charnock confirmed. "It's a psychoactive drug, very dangerous when used recreationally. We're doing some research alongside our neurology and psychoanalytical departments where we're running some clinical trials using Phencyclidine, ironically, for dream analysis."

"In what way?" asked Buzzard.

"We're monitoring brain wave activity in subjects whilst they sleep. Normally, this is done at one of our clinics, not at an actual hospital. It monitors the brain wave pattern on a normal night's sleep for three nights, then we administer a dose of a diluted form of Phencyclidine before bed, with the intention of triggering a more vivid dream experience, and the impact it has on the brain waves whilst the subjects sleep. It's a two-week trial, three days off the Phencyclidine, one day on, for a period of fifteen days. They only actually take the Phencyclidine three times, as it's still much too potent to use more frequently or for a longer period. We only monitor five subjects at a *time, well, ten if you include the ones who are taking the placebo, and we're running the experiments monthly for a year. We're currently halfway through month ten. If Gary enrolled in the programme, and he passed our preliminary tests to prove he's not psychotic, we could potentially extend next month's programme to six subjects. It would also allow us to monitor dreams that may be occurring in a lucid state, which is something that was originally deemed out of scope for these experiments."*

"How have the first nine months of experiments gone?" Cross asked.

"We noticed some odd behaviour after the first dose, that's why we leave it three days before administering the next. After the first dose, it takes about twenty-four hours for brain activity to return to normal. However, after the third dose, that recovery time has increased to between thirty-six and forty-eight hours, depending on the mental stability of the patient. Hence the reason we can't run this experiment more than three times on the same subject."

"Any long term effects?"

"Four patients now suffer migraines when they didn't before, which is about ten per cent. One of the subjects from month three has also suffered from meningococcal meningitis since, but it happened four months after the experiment finished, so we're not currently sure if it's related."

"But there's an open question around the long-term health effects of this experiment?" asked Buzzard.

"A slight one," Charnock reluctantly admitted.

"I don't like it," said Cross. "You'd be exposing a random person to an unknown risk."

"That's effectively why they're called medical trials, Doctor, you should know this," Charnock retorted.

"And what is the end goal? What are you trying to achieve with these trials?"

"This is the second phase. Last year we ran an experiment analysing people who dream, and it seemed to suggest that people who can remember their dreams feel more refreshed than those who fall asleep and then appear to wake up an instant later with it being morning. People who regularly recall dreams tend to feel like they've slept longer on the nights they can recall dreams as opposed to the nights they don't, so if we can get people dreaming and remembering dreams, it may help as a cure to so-called 'tired all the time' syndrome. We're a long way from a solution. This is the first round of trials. We know already that the drug is far too potent to be taken on a regular basis, but we think it's safe enough to allow us to complete our study and collect our full sample of data."

Charnock turned to Buzzard.

"If Sinead's fiancé wants to try it, I'm prepared to let him sign up to next month's programme, but he must pass our preliminary tests first. If he fails them, it's a non-starter."

"Understood," said Buzzard. "I'll have the meeting and let you know what they say."

"We'll have the meeting," Cross corrected. "I think we all need to be in there. We'll come along tomorrow."

This meant that, naturally, when I arrived at the university, we ended up meeting all three science professors.

"Miss O'Brien, Mr Jackson," Buzzard began. "Please meet Doctor Andy Cross, our Head of Biology, and Professor Richard Charnock, our chemistry expert. Now, since our initial conversation on Monday morning, the three of us have had a chat, and we have an idea that may give you the opportunity you're looking for. Professor, would you care to explain."

Professor Charnock then gave us an overview of his dream experiments, and the desire to monitor brainwave patterns whilst people slept. I was fascinated by the idea of them being drug-induced, although I'd never heard of Phencyclidine.

"You'll have to undergo a psychiatric evaluation before you enrol in the programme," Professor Charnock informed me.

"Why?" I asked.

"To evaluate your psychiatric state and to make sure there aren't any underlying mental health problems."

"But there are," I said.

"What do you mean?"

"I was injured in a road traffic accident five years ago. I've been treated for depression, anxiety, and post-traumatic stress disorder ever since. I still take Venlafaxine nightly to help treat it."

"Not to mention the reason he wants to enrol is because he thinks he might have murdered someone. Not an obvious candidate for your programme, Professor," said Doctor Cross coldly. To this point, these were the first words he'd spoken.

"I'm not interested in the programme, though. I just want access to the drug."

"Trust me, Mr Jackson," said Buzzard. "That sort of comment is not going to help your cause."

I thought back to the conversation I'd had with Sinead on Monday night and the idea of using this primarily to help Mary. If I went for that angle, I figured I may have more luck.

"But this isn't just about Many Worlds or brainwaves when dreaming, is it?" I began. "This is about something much bigger. We're here not because of the dream I had, but because Mary, Sinead's mum, witnessed it in a hallucination triggered by her dementia. If we can start to understand this, it might help you understand the effects of other degenerative illnesses or anything else that triggers hallucinations. If I have to take a risk in order for us to understand that, then so be it. I'm a twenty-one-year-old with serious long-term health issues, both physical and mental. I don't work, I have no career prospects. This could be my chance to do something really useful with my life, to contribute to the world. So what if there's a risk to my mental health? Everything I do is a risk to my mental health these days. And, if I may be candid Professor, it's my health to risk."

Sinead's eyes had narrowed, and she looked furiously at me.

"We'll consider your request," said Charnock officially. "But I would suggest you don't get your hopes up."

We exchanged pleasantries, then Sinead and I left. We'd barely closed the classroom door, though, before she turned on me.

"I don't believe you!" she snapped. "Do you not listen to a word I say?"

"What have I done now?"

"When I said I wanted you to think about Mum more, I didn't mean as a last resort, and you shouldn't use her condition to try and get your own way."

"Sinead I…"

"Don't. Just don't."

The rest of the journey home was spent largely in silence, with Sinead seeming so angry I was surprised there wasn't any steam coming out of her ears. She didn't even sit next to me on the train and kept biting down on her knuckle, which was always a sign of how upset she was.

"I'll walk back," I said when we got to the station at the other end. It was my intention to get her to say something positive in response.

"Fine," she said instead, before exiting the station, crossing the car park, getting in her car, and driving off. To be honest, I was starting to wonder if I'd woken from that dream in a different Worldline to the one I went to bed in. Me and Sinead rarely argued, and now we'd done it twice in a few days. This wasn't like us, and it wasn't like her. I knew she was upset about her mum, but I felt like I was missing something.

So, yet again, I was back in my own room that night and, yet again, I didn't see Sinead the next morning as she'd already left for university by the time I got up. I was aching too. I'd done a lot of walking yesterday, and as the walk back from the train station last night had been unexpected, I'd done it without having my walking stick. I knew I'd need to rest it tomorrow, but I was feeling lonely in the house. Usually, I was more than happy being on my own all day, but this time I was starting to feel a little bit lost. Aside from the issues with my family, I don't really have any friends either. The ones I did have back in my school days had largely deserted me after my accident; they didn't understand how badly I'd taken it. I'd become reclusive in the intervening years, and as a result, I didn't really have much of a life outside of Sinead and her family. I played online games a lot, usually with the same group of people, but I wouldn't go as far as to say any of them were friends. I'd never met any of them, several of them claimed to live in other countries, and even when we did converse it was in written form via the chat window in the game. There was very little verbal communication between me and anyone I knew online. For the first time since I'd moved in here, the life I had was beginning to feel under threat. Maybe this meal with my family on Sunday was a good idea after all, as if this did suddenly fall apart, I was going to need a contingency plan.

I stayed in my room all day the next day, apart from the occasional ventures downstairs to get food and drink. I'd had a Broken Sword game for my laptop for quite some time that I'd never played, but I was in need of mental stimulation, so I loaded it up and spent much of the day trying to work my way through the various levels and puzzles within it. I made sure I'd grabbed a couple of beer cans from the fridge and that I was out of the way and back in my room by the time Sinead and Eamon got back from the hospital that evening. However, I'd already drunk them both by the time they got home. I was considering whether to go down for some more when, to my surprise, Sinead came to my room.

"Hello, are you ok?" I said pleasantly as she entered.

"Yeah, I'm fine," she said quite coldly. "I'm sorry for making you walk home last night, especially without your stick. Are you ok?"

"Yeah, I'm alright. I've ached a bit today, but I did a lot of walking the other day too when I went to see Mum."

"Did you take your stick then?"

"You know I did. I had it when you came to the hospital."

"Oh, yeah. Anyway, I came to give you these and tell you that Charnock said yes. He doesn't want you at the clinic, so he said this is completely unofficial, but he's given me the three tablets to give you. You're supposed to take them three days apart, to give yourself time to recover from each dose."

"He's given you unlicensed trial medication to just take away with you? Is he mad?"

"If he is, then he's not the only one," she said, turning to leave.

"Sinead, wait a minute, please."

She turned back to face me.

"Can we just talk for a bit?" I asked her.

"About what?"

"About us. Things haven't been right this week, and I don't fully understand what all the problems are. I can't do anything about it if I don't."

"It's nothing, I'm just struggling a bit."

"But I want to help you. What can I do?"

"The best thing you can do is to take those tablets, have your dream, do what you need to do, and for us to then move on and never speak of this again."

"I don't understand why it's bothering you so much."

"Gary, you stabbed someone!"

"In a dream!"

"That doesn't matter. A woman wronged you, then in your mind you fantasised about stabbing her before acting it out. As the woman who's engaged to be married to you, do you not understand why I'd have a massive issue with that?"

"Sinead, I'm not going to stab you, am I?"

"Aren't you?"

"Of course not."

"And what if we split up?"

"We're not going to split up...are we?"

"I don't know, nobody knows what's going to happen in the future. Think back to last Friday before Mum had her fall. Did you really expect this week to play out like this?"

"Well, no, of course not."

"Exactly, so who can say where we'll be in six months, or a year, or five years' time. Last Friday morning I woke up looking forward to my party. Since then, I feel like the world is falling apart. Mum's been in hospital for a week, we're doing nothing but living off takeaways, I've got engaged, you've been so obsessed with this dream thing that you haven't been able to think about anything else. I've taken you to my university twice to see my professors about it, I've brought you the medication home you need, and you've spent all this time thinking about another woman and fantasising about hurting her whilst I've got all this going on. It's like I've seen a different side to you, and I'm not sure I like it."

"Then I'll not take the pills, I'll throw them in the bin, and I'll try and forget about all of this."

"But you won't be able to, will you? You'll be like a dog with a bone. You won't be able to let it drop."

"What else can I do?"

"Just do what you need to do as quickly as possible. But please then come back to me, because right now I need you."

With that, she turned and left.

I lay back on the bed and thought about what she'd said. Naturally, I thought she was overreacting, but I knew better than to suggest it to her. I hadn't done anything overly wrong this week in my eyes; I didn't really think you could be accountable for things that you do in a dream. Punishing someone in the real world for something they'd done in a dream seemed weird to me. I could just about understand her concern regarding whether I'd fantasise about hurting her in the event we split up, but even if I did, it still shouldn't really matter to her. Without meaning to sound kinky, there were several things I fantasised about doing to Sinead, although I certainly wasn't going to tell her about them now. I had a vivid imagination and occasionally I had dark thoughts, but it didn't make me a bad person and I wasn't a danger to her, yet she was implying I was. I wouldn't even act that way in a dream again, let alone in the real world.

Still troubled, I went downstairs to get a beer out of the fridge.

"How was Mary?" I asked Eamon, who was pouring himself a whiskey as I entered the kitchen.

"She seems a bit better. The markers in her blood have gone back to normal so the doctors are hoping she'll be able to come out on Monday."

"Oh brilliant, that'll be good."

"Yeah, it will," said Eamon, somewhat less enthusiastically than I expected.

"Is everything ok?" I asked.

"I'm just not looking forward to the future," he said glumly. "Her memory is going, her mobility is going, and we're going to have to start planning for life without her, unfortunately. It doesn't really bear thinking about."

"What can I do to help?"

"Just support Sinead. I don't know what's gone on between you two this week, but whatever it is, coupled with her mum and the party, she's taken it all very badly and I'm worried about her. She needs you to help her."

"I am trying, but she keeps pushing me away."

"Well, keep trying," he ordered.

I went back upstairs and drank my beer, my head swimming. Once I'd finished the drink, I decided to take the first pill and turn in. Sinead had requested this was all over as quickly as possible and, even though it wasn't quite 10 pm yet, I figured there was no point in waiting. I had no idea what effect they'd have or what I expected to happen, but I went to sleep straightaway.

Or I must have done, as the next thing I knew it was 01:45. I was still in the same position, I'd had no dreams, and aside from a headache that I'd had for most of the day anyway, I felt perfectly normal. I was about to drop back off to sleep when I decided. I was going to put all my eggs in one basket. I was going to take all the pills together, it would either work or it wouldn't, and if it didn't after all that then nothing would, and I could try and move on with Sinead. If I suffered adverse effects, well, Sinead was doubting me anyway so what difference did it make? Without even a hint of trepidation, I took the other two pills and was soon back asleep.

Took 3 tablets.

Chapter Fourteen
The Blue Line

It was light when I opened my eyes, so I knew I must have slept straight through. Given that I was in an unfamiliar place, in a less than comfortable bed, in the same room as a, presumably, dangerous man, this surprised me. When I rolled over, I wasn't exactly shocked to see Mr Cyrus, or whatever his name was, sitting facing me. He looked amused.

"Sleep well?" he asked.

"Better than I expected," I said.

"At least you don't snore."

"I do when I have a cold, apparently."

"The murdered girl told you that, did she, or was it someone else?"

That caused me to take a backwards step, metaphorically at least. This guy knew who I was and why I was in here. Then I remembered what Mum had said about the incident being on the news, and I began to suspect he'd probably heard about it from there.

"Yeah, that was her," I said sadly.

"Did you do it?" he asked. "Kill her, I mean."

I shook my head and shrugged.

"Apparently," I said. "Although I don't remember it."

"Of course you don't," he laughed.

"I don't. One minute I'm cutting us both some cake, and the next minute I'm pinned to the floor covered in blood. There's nothing in between."

"That much is apparent," he said, and it took me a few seconds to realise he was referring to 'between my ears'.

"See what I mean?" he chuckled again.

"Why are you here?" I asked him.

"Because I was a naughty boy," he said mockingly. "This your first time inside?"

"Yeah, it is. I've never been in trouble before."

"And you've gone straight to murder," he commented. "Interesting, isn't it?"

"It's not the word I'd use," I said.

"What word would you use?" he asked, still speaking in a mocking, patronising tone.

"Messed up," I said.

"That's two words. But we're all in here for the same reason."

"You're all convicted murderers?" I shuddered.

"Are you a convicted murderer?"

"No, I'm on remand."

"Well, then. No, we're all in here because we all messed up. That's the thing with places like this, it's one of the few places in the world where everyone here is here on merit."

"On merit?" I asked.

"Yeah. You go to hospital, you have people with illnesses that they didn't expect to contract. Go to a school and there's kids there who will never amount to anything, just wasting their time. Church, even then some have been coerced into going. But here, everyone in here is here because they deserve to be. Because they messed up, as you put it."

"How did you mess up?" I asked.

"I allowed myself to get caught," he said, still not giving anything away. "But this is the thing you need to realise. There are people in here who have committed all sorts of supposed crimes. People who have killed or hurt people. Drug lords, people traffickers, armed robbers, and, yes, even one or two murderers. Then there are the others, the ones who are really depraved. The paedophiles, the rapists, the abusers. Those men who commit crimes specifically against women and children. They are the lowest of the low even in places like this. You murdered your girlfriend, in cold blood, and that makes you a marked man in here, my friend."

"We're not friends," I remarked.

"Oh, you'd better hope we are," he said, standing up and leaning over in my face. "Because if you're going to survive in here, it's people like me who are going to get you through it."

We sat there for a moment in silence whilst I absorbed what he said.

"Did you really request that I was put in your cell?" I asked.

He considered the question before answering, as though he was worried about showing me his cards prematurely.

"Yes," he said finally.

"Why?"

"I owe a debt to an old friend, and they've called it in. Asked me to look after you in here."

"Who?" I said.

"They said you were naïve," he chuckled. "Now I know what they meant."

"What should I call you? I asked.

"Sir," he replied. "Until I tell you otherwise."

"Thank you for agreeing to look out for me," I said.

"Trust me, it wasn't my choice." He scowled.

That was pretty much all I could get from him, and I was learning quickly not to push him for information. At breakfast, I sat in the same seat I was in the previous day, but the bearded man didn't sit opposite me. This morning he sat talking to Tyler, who had served as my insider yesterday. Tyler nodded his head to me as a form of acknowledgement, but the bearded man never looked up.

"Maybe they're planning your execution," my cellmate murmured in my ear.

"They're welcome to it," I thought to myself.

After I'd finished my porridge, I was taken by a prison officer to the first of my induction sessions. There was one session before lunch and one session after lunch for three days, covering the chaplaincy, the drug team, the medical team, education, probation, and the gym. I was also told I was entitled to a single, two-minute phone call. Naturally, I tried to call my mum, but she must have been at work as it rang through to voicemail. I didn't leave a message as I assumed I'd be allowed to try again later. It was only when I hung the receiver up that I was told that the attempt counted as my call, and that was it.

The chaplaincy felt like it was going to be a waste of time; I wasn't religious and never had been. I was of the view that my mind was too scientific to be taken in by religion. However, the other five prisoners on the induction, including the three from yesterday's transfer from the court, all seemed deeply interested in it. I also remembered what Marcus had said about finding religion in prison, and I wondered if it might just be a source of comfort. I didn't believe in heaven or hell, but if there was any way at all that I could feel spiritually closer to Michelle then I was prepared to take it at this point. So what if it wasn't real? None of this felt real anyway.

It was ironic when meeting the drug team to discuss any history of substance abuse that this was the first time in my life I'd have actually considered using them. Some drugs apparently give the user an incredible high, and given the despair I was feeling right now, that sort of pick-me-up would have been more than welcome. I knew better than to admit to it here, though.

I did, however, admit to the medical team the next day the feelings of utter despair I was experiencing and how I didn't feel able to grieve for the loss of Michelle. The fact that everyone believed that I was responsible meant I didn't really feel I had the right to grieve for her in the normal manner, and I was missing her desperately. I told them that I don't have any memory of the crime, and that the only flashbacks I get are of being shown the video at the police station. The gentleman on the team I was speaking to appeared sympathetic to what I was saying, but when I asked about the possibility of attending Michelle's funeral, he told me in no uncertain terms that it was never going to happen.

The education department was the most interesting, although the series of initial tests they made us do to assess our English and maths levels were very basic, and I couldn't believe a grown adult would seriously be incapable of answering them correctly. However, answering questions and having to solve problems on the maths test was the first time all week I'd focused on anything other than Michelle. There were a variety of science courses on offer and, even though I was more interested in physics than I was in either chemistry or biology, I decided I'd try and work through them all. If I was locked up as long as I expected to be there would certainly be time.

For that reason, Friday morning's session with the probation team felt like a waste of everyone's time. If, by some miracle, I got cleared of this then I'd be free to go anyway, and if I wasn't then I suspected it would be at least ten years before I had to worry about probation. Finally, there was the gym, which wasn't really my thing, but I signed up for it anyway. If I was in danger in here because of the crime I was locked up for, then bulking up and being able to defend myself was going to be a useful skill to have.

Upon completion of the induction course, I was introduced to my Personal Officer. This was a prison officer who was to be my main point of contact during the stay, and I was pleased to discover it was the lady officer who had intervened in the dinner room on my first evening when the bearded man, who I'd since learned was named Blaine, was trying to intimidate me. Her name was Kirsty, and she filled me in on details such as how to get phone credit, so I could try my mum again, as well as how to book visitors. She also informed me that a Miss O'Brien had made a request to visit the prison to see me, and she'd be there at four o'clock. It was after three now, and I was pleased that I didn't have long to wait to see Sinead.

I spent the short period in between back in my cell. Happily, my cellmate was absent, and it was the first time I'd been alone in here since I was brought in. I'd learned from Tyler that my cellmate was called Cyrus Ramsey and that he was a bit of a nut job. Apparently, he'd been in and out of prison for nearly thirty years for a range of crimes including burglary, armed robbery, and carjacking. He raised an eyebrow when I told him that Ramsey had requested me as his cellmate in order to repay a debt to an old friend. We discussed the idea of it being Marcus but Tyler dismissed the idea. He did say he would look into it but how he would, or indeed whether he would, remained to be seen.

Kirsty, the prison officer, reappeared at the door at exactly four o'clock. Say what you like about prisons, but they did know a thing or two about punctuality.

"Jackson, visitor, room two," she said. "Ramsey, you have one also, room one."

My cellmate chuckled to himself.

"I thought I might get one today," he said, looking at me.

I suspected his visitor might be our apparent mutual friend that he, and I, were indebted to, and I wondered if it was Marcus. We weren't friends, but I didn't know anyone else who had been in prison. Also, given that I was meeting Sinead today, it wasn't impossible that Marcus had come too, to see someone else. However, the fact we were in different rooms meant I wouldn't be finding out of my own accord. It was the first time since I'd met him that we'd been separated, and also the first time I wished he was actually there.

Sinead sat at a table and gave me a half-smile when she saw me, but remained seated as I approached.

"Hello," I said. "I would hug you, but we're not allowed physical contact with visitors."

"I know, we were warned on the way in too."

"We? Who else is here?"

"I meant all the other visitors."

"Is Marcus here?"

"Why would Marcus be here?"

"My new cellmate, Cyrus Ramsey, claims we have a mutual friend who wants him to look after me. I wondered if it was Marcus."

"It's not, he doesn't speak to anyone in here. How are you anyway?"

"Struggling a bit, to be honest. This all feels so surreal, and it's all so degrading and humiliating."

"Why?"

"Do you know, after I was transferred from the court, I was subject to a strip search on the way in? It was invasive, too. They were making sure I hadn't smuggled drugs in any orifice, if you get my drift."

"I had quite a personal search too. Do you know, some lady officer put her hand up my top to check I hadn't got any drugs in my bra. It was so embarrassing. They'd even got sniffer dogs there, so there really wasn't any need."

"I hope they don't do that to Mum or either of my sisters when they come to visit."

"They probably will. You look quite rough. Have you not been sleeping well?"

"Actually, I slept really well the first night I was here, but I think I was just so exhausted from everything that had happened that I just shut down. It's a shame I ever had to wake back up, really."

"Don't say things like that. I wanted to apologise to you anyway."

"Apologise to me? Why?"

"I was furious with you when I saw you on Monday, but having spoken to Professor Buzzard I think it may have been unfair."

"Why, what did he say?"

"Nothing conclusive, but he said he did 'acknowledge the theoretical possibilities of what you were suggesting', about being possessed by another Worldline. He said he's heard of cases like this before. Last year a man killed his daughter, apparently, and argued the same thing you have, that he'd never do it and can't have done it."

"What happened to that man?"

"Nobody believed him, and he was sent to prison for life."

"Oh, great."

"The two main things I took from it was that at the minute, scientifically, there's nothing he or anyone else can do to prove you weren't in control of your own actions at the time of Michelle's death. However, from what he knows both of the case and of you as a person, he said he does believe you."

"Does that mean you believe me too?"

"Yeah, I do, which actually makes me feel worse than when I thought you were guilty."

"I can't believe you ever thought I was guilty. Me, kill Michelle. You know I'm not capable of that."

"And yet Marcus and about twenty other people saw you do it. Even considering how well I know you, and how long for, I couldn't see another

207

explanation. I believed you couldn't remember it, as I think you'd admit to it if you did, but I couldn't see how it couldn't have been you."

"So now you feel guilty for doubting me?"

"No, I think what I thought was rational. But at least if you had done it then you being in here was justified. Now it isn't, and I don't know what to do about it."

"Me neither."

"Even if, for the sake of argument, you did get away with it. It's not going to bring Michelle back, and it's not going to ease the pain you and her family feel."

"At least I'd be able to go to her funeral and say goodbye. I miss her so much, Sinead. The year after we got together, she went to Cape Verde for two weeks with her mum and dad, and that's the only time since we got together that I've gone this long without seeing her. I just want her back. I'd do anything for it."

Sinead put her hand on top of mine, but Kirsty saw it immediately.

"No physical contact," she barked.

"Sorry," Sinead replied.

"So, what do we do now?" I asked her.

"I don't know. It feels wrong to just accept this, but I honestly don't know what else we can do."

"Your mum was a solicitor. Surely, she must have a contact or someone we can talk to, get a better legal team than the duty solicitor I've been dealing with since I was arrested. He just wants me to plead guilty."

"You can't do that," she said. "Once you say you did it then you'll never be able to clear your name. Science may be able to find an answer one day."

"And I'm just meant to rot in here until it does?"

"It's not right, is it?" Sinead acknowledged. "But I don't know what else to do for you. Don't give up though, and neither will I. Between us we will think of something."

Chapter Fifteen
The Red Line
The day of Sinead's party

I confess, I was disappointed to be going to the party without Michelle. She was still struggling with her skiing injuries, and the accident was entirely my fault, but it still bothered me that she hadn't come, especially as she was still planning to go to work the next morning. However, having mentioned this to the family when I got home, Nicki had offered to step in as my 'plus one', no doubt swayed by the potential of more free drinks at her big brother's expense.

The party was at a pub called The Ox and Lamb, in Badminton. However, as there was no direct route there from our estate, we had to take a bus into Barchester town centre first, and then another one back out. Nicki thought this was the main reason I was annoyed about Michelle not coming, because she hadn't been able to drive us there. She may have had a point.

I hadn't been in this pub before, and my first impression of the place wasn't good. It felt very old and run down. The wooden floors were sticky, most of the tables wobbled, this room had a couple of ceiling tiles missing, the walls were still painted Artex. However, I was more interested in seeing the birthday girl than assessing the locale.

"Good evening," I said to Sinead, wrapping my arms around her and giving her a big hug. "Happy 21st Birthday! Have you had a good day so far?"

"Yeah it's been great," she said. "It nearly wasn't though. Mum had another fall yesterday."

"Oh no, she didn't! Is she ok?"

"Yeah, she's fine, she just needs to be more careful. They thought she'd broken her hip, but thankfully it's just badly bruised."

"That's a relief. Here's your card and present."

"Oh, thank you," she said. "Would you mind putting them in that green bag over there by the cake stand, please? Otherwise I'll end up carrying it around for ages. Hello, Nicki, how are you?" Sinead said, spotting my sister next to me and giving her a hug. "Where's Michelle?"

"She's not come."

"Oh no, why? Is everything ok?"

"Yeah, it's fine, she just had a bit of an accident on holiday. She's struggling with pain in her ribs and she's got work in the morning. She'd rather just rest."

"That's a shame, I haven't seen her for a while, it would have been good to catch up with her."

"Actually, are you doing anything tomorrow evening?"

"Nothing, as far as I know, I'll probably see Marcus, but we don't have any set plans. Why?"

"Michelle has asked me to invite you for dinner tomorrow evening at The Loch & Quay, if you're interested. She wants to make up for not coming tonight."

"What time?"

"She said about four, as she's working until two."

"That'll be great, yeah. Is Marcus invited?"

"Yeah, of course," I said. Michelle and I hadn't actually discussed that scenario, but if he was to be Sinead's boyfriend, and the two of us were to remain best friends, I'd have to get used to him being around.

"Thanks," she said, hugging me again before spotting a relative who had just arrived. "That's my Uncle Brian and Aunty Siobhan over there. Will you excuse me a minute?"

"Yeah, of course," I said, and off she went.

The rest of the party passed largely without incident. I got to have a chat with Mary and Eamon, Sinead's parents, as I hadn't seen either of them for several months. As it had been so long, it was easy to spot the deterioration in Mary's health that the dementia was causing, and it was almost as obvious how much Eamon was struggling to deal with it. In a way, I almost felt glad Sinead had Marcus for support, otherwise she'd most likely end up trying to shoulder the burden for both her mum and dad alone. I also enjoyed spending some time with Nicki, I got to meet some of Sinead's extended family, there were a couple of people from school there that I'd not seen in quite some time, and I even bought Marcus a drink. I still didn't like the guy, but he did spend the entire evening on his best behaviour.

Michelle wasn't the only one working the next day. Freya and Will were also both at work, meaning Sunday lunch with my family really was just a family affair; me, Mum, Dad, and my sisters.

"This is nice, isn't it," Mum began. "We don't often get just the five of us on our own anymore."

She was right too. Whilst we all technically still lived under the same roof, it was very rare for all five of us to be there together. I spent a couple of nights a week at Michelle's, Donna was pretty much living with Freya even though they weren't meant to move in together for another fortnight, and Nicki was so besotted with Will that she wanted to spend every waking moment with him. This must have been the first time the five of us had had a meal together on our own in the last six months.

"Not quite the same, is it?" Nicki said with a hint of disappointment.

"It makes dinner cheaper," laughed Dad.

"How are Michelle's ribs?" Mum asked.

"Ribs? What has she done?" Donna asked, unaware of our little holiday mishap.

I filled her in on the details, although I was getting tired of telling the story and being told what an idiot I was for it. I'd told the story to Mum,

Nicki, and now Donna, and got the same reaction in all three instances. I knew in hindsight it had been a daft thing to do, but I consoled myself with the thought that the outcome of my stupidity was still relatively minor.

"Have you managed to save the rest of your photos?" Nicki asked.

"I haven't tried yet. This phone doesn't have a camera on it so I can't check."

"After dinner let's go upstairs and try on my laptop, see if we can pull them off the SD card."

"You have your own laptop? When did you become a tech whizz?"

"It's an old laptop of Will's that he doesn't use anymore. He gave it to me when I told him what Shell said last week about possibly studying photography at university. He'd suggested the same thing to me, so he's given it to me, and I've been loading it up with software I've been able to find and download online."

"They're going to be more for editing photographs. If the SD card is damaged, you'll need something that'll be able to recover data."

"Henry should be able to do that. He's studying IT or something around that."

Henry was Will's twin, the other witness to my lorry encounter.

"We'll have a look then after dinner. If it doesn't work, would you mind giving it to him to have a look at when you see him?"

"Yeah, of course," Nicki said. "There's no embarrassing or naughty photos on there, are there?"

"Not on that one," I winked.

"Moving on," said Mum quickly, turning to Donna. "Have you got your moving in date yet?"

"Friday the 27th. Actually, I wanted to ask you, Dad, would you be able to take the day off to help us move?"

"I'll see what I can do," he said. "It shouldn't need all day, should it? It's only the stuff in your room."

"Freya has a load of stuff too though, but no, it should only take a few hours. Gaz, would you be able to help too?"

"Yeah, if you want," I said. I hated manual work, but I had no pre-planned excuse to avoid it. I made a mental note to talk to Michelle and see if she could help me come up with one.

The rest of the conversation played out with a lot of idle chatting, without anyone really saying much. At the end of the meal I went up to Nicki's room but, unfortunately, her laptop didn't have a slot for an SD card. I gave her the card and asked her if Henry could have a look at it for us.

"Did you say you were going to The Loch & Quay later?" she asked me.

"Yeah, we're meeting Sinead and Marcus for dinner at four."

"Are you staying for the pub quiz at seven?"

"I don't know, we haven't discussed it."

"I was wondering if me and Will could join you when he finishes work. He gets off at six o'clock."

"You could, but it might not be a good idea."

"Why not?"

"Marcus was in our year at school, and he wasn't very popular with us. I couldn't stand him, and Will hated him even more than I did. I doubt he'd want to socialise with him now."

"Do you mind if I at least ask him?"

"Of course, go ahead."

So, anticipating Nicki and Will joining us later regardless, I made my way over to Michelle's at half past three ready to go for dinner.

"How are you feeling?" I asked.

"In pain. I'm going back tomorrow to have a chest X-ray as the doctor I was with today thinks I might have a couple of cracked ribs. She said she'll get Doctor Cross to assess me during lunch tomorrow. How's your hand?"

"It's getting there. Glad it's my left hand and not my right one, though, otherwise I might not have been able to cut my meat up."

Even though we were ten minutes early ourselves, Sinead and Marcus were already there by the time we got to the pub.

"We thought we'd come in for a pre-meal drink," Sinead said cheerfully.

We hadn't booked a table. However, our regular one was free, whereas they had sat at a different one. Michelle sensed what I was thinking.

"Let's go over to the booth over there," she said.

"What's wrong with here?" Marcus asked.

"Nothing, it's just that's our booth," I said and headed over. Sinead followed, but Marcus looked bemused.

"Did you have a good birthday?" Michelle asked Sinead, whilst Sinead then filled her in about the events of the day.

"How about you?" she asked. "Gary said you'd had an accident on holiday and had hurt yourself. Are you feeling better?"

"Doctor at work thinks I've fractured a couple of ribs. I've got to go in tomorrow for an X-ray."

"Oh my God. What did you do?"

"Has he not told you?" Michelle said, eyeing me.

So, for the fourth time, I recited the story of the accident. I would have edited the story this time around to make myself look less foolish, but I doubted Michelle would have let me.

"And you thought that would be a good idea?" Sinead laughed when I got to the part about taking a picture mid-run.

"I didn't anticipate the accident happening," I said.

"You berk!" Marcus added, as if he just wanted to be sure I knew I'd done something rather silly.

"Thanks," I muttered.

"Did you get hurt?" Sinead asked me.

"Only my hand and my arm, but it's my left one so it doesn't really matter. It's getting easier though."

"What happened to the selfie stick?" Marcus asked.

"Snapped, and the SD card with all our other photos on it may be damaged too. Henry works in IT so Nicki is going to ask him to have a look at it for us, see if he can retrieve the data off there."

"There's nothing naughty on there is there?" Marcus asked.

"Why does everyone assume that?" I countered, but Marcus just grinned his stupid grin.

At that, Mill Lane appeared at our table.

"Hello, strangers," she said. "I wondered where you were the other night when you didn't come in for your regular meal."

"We've been on holiday," Michelle responded.

"Oh right, did you have a good time?"

"I think it's fair to say it was a holiday of two halves," I said.

"What do you mean?"

I was about to answer but Michelle got in there first.

"The first half was great," she said. "But then this dope thought it would be a good idea trying to take selfies whilst coming down a big ski slope. he lost control and took me out. Think he's fractured a couple of my ribs."

This was a much more edited version of the story than I'd been telling, but it was succinct and to the point. Mill just shook her head at me.

"Can I get you a drink to make it feel better?" she asked.

"Can I have a large Sauvignon Blanc, please?" Michelle said.

"I'll have White Zinfandel please, just a regular size," Sinead added.

"Just water for me," added Marcus, taking me by surprise.

"And I'll have a Moretti," I finished.

I was sat next to Sinead and opposite Michelle, with Marcus to her left.

"So how about you two," Michelle began. "I was surprised when Gary told me you were together. How did that come about?"

"This will sound clichéd, but I found God in prison," Marcus said.

"What was he in for?" I asked sarcastically.

"You know what I mean. But it's changed me a bit, that's all. I don't know many people who follow the Bible, but Sin always has." I made a mental note that he'd just called her Sin. "So, when I came out, I reached out to her. We've got closer, and we've decided to give a relationship a try."

"If you'd reached out to me, I'd have told you to sod off," I said. Michelle kicked me under the table.

"That's why I didn't," he said. "And besides, I never really fancied you."

Sinead giggled, but he was getting my hackles up.

"I always thought you'd end up with her myself, to be honest," he said, in front of Michelle.

"It was Sinead who got him to ask me out," Michelle admitted. "I must admit I was in two minds at first."

"Were you?" I interrupted.

"Of course. I'd never had a proper boyfriend before. But I wouldn't change a thing," she said. "Well, maybe his antics on the ski slope last week, but not other than that."

"He said he was attracted by my eyes," Sinead grinned.

"He's lying to you then," I said.

"What, why?" and "What's wrong with my eyes?" both Marcus and Sinead said together.

"Nothing. It's just no man has ever been attracted to a woman purely because of her eyes before."

"Yes, they have," Sinead protested.

"Sinead, men our age fall into three categories. We're either attracted to your boobs, your bum, or your legs. There is no fourth group. No man has ever gone out with a woman based on her having a nice round juicy pair of eyes," I said.

The other three all sniggered.

"Which one attracted you to Peyton?" Marcus asked. He'd now called Michelle by her surname. However, the mood did unexpectedly seem lighter, so I went with it.

"I liked her boobs and her bum," I admitted.

"What's wrong with my legs?" Michelle exclaimed, albeit light-heartedly. She knew how attracted to all of her I was.

"Nothing, it just wasn't one of the first things I noticed about you."

"You won't see them anymore, then," Michelle grinned.

"None of mine are any good," Sinead commented.

"I've only ever seen your legs," I said. "So I couldn't comment."

"I could," Marcus smirked, and my desire to punch him came instantly flooding back. Sinead went crimson with embarrassment and put her hand to her face whilst giggling to herself. Happily, at that point, Mill returned with our drinks.

"Are you ready to order food?" she asked.

"I've not even looked at the menu yet," Sinead admitted.

"You've been here ages," I exclaimed.

"I know, but we didn't decide what we were eating."

"Can you give us another five minutes, Mill, please?" Michelle asked.

"Of course," she replied and off she went again.

At that, a cheer went up around the lounge. I noticed the big screen in the other room was showing live coverage of the Manchester United versus Tottenham game, and it looked like United had taken an early lead. I suddenly remembered that Marcus was a Spurs fan.

"Didn't fancy watching the match today?" I asked him.

"Not really, I knew we'd lose. They'll probably get another one in a minute."

The conversation continued in this manner until our food arrived, and whilst I did continue to make mental notes of all the little things Marcus did that wound me up, he was being less of an irritant than I'd found him at school. Sinead continued to seem taken with him, but it was going to take him a significant amount of time to fully earn my trust.

I was still relatively full from Mum's dinner, so I opted for the smaller of the two mixed grills, whilst the other three all ordered starters as well as mains. Michelle normally wouldn't, but as her diet had gone out of the window with our holiday and, as Sinead and Marcus had ordered, she decided to indulge herself. I didn't mind though. It meant mine would take an extra half an hour or so to come out, so I had more time to make room for it.

"I'm just going to pop to the ladies' before this comes out," Sinead said after we'd ordered. "I'll be back in a minute."

"Yeah, I'm going to pop out and have a puff on this," Marcus said, pulling out one of those e-cigarettes. It was the first sign I'd seen that he was a smoker, and I wondered if really it was just an excuse as he didn't fancy sitting on his own with me and Michelle.

"I bet he waits for Sinead to come back before he does," I said to her.

"Probably. He does seem different though, doesn't he?"

"You mean less psycho and more normal?"

"Well, yeah."

"I'm still worried about Sinead being with him. I don't like it."

I didn't actually hear Michelle's response, as Mill had returned with the starters, and the thought of Marcus hurting Sinead made me drift off into my own little world as I automatically reached for my drink.

Chapter Sixteen
The Black Line

"Thanks, Mill," I said to the waitress as she brought the starters out to the table. I picked my beer up to have another mouthful before I started eating, but I found I couldn't grip it and immediately dropped it. The glass didn't break, but there was nearly half a pint in there, and the wetness as it ran off the table and on to the leg of my jeans caused me to jump up. Why would I have put the glass that side?

"Are you ok?" she asked with a hint of alarm. I looked across the table. It was Michelle.

I looked at my hand. No scars. I looked around the pub we were in; the place was familiar, but it took me a second to realise where it was. It was The Loch & Quay in Barchester. There was a TV showing a football match. Manchester United were playing Tottenham; they were currently leading 1-0.

"Oh, Michelle," I said uncontrollably. I was so pleased to see her.

"Gaz, are you ok?" she asked again.

"I'm dreaming," I said to myself out loud.

"You seem awake to me."

"No, you don't understand," I said, sitting back down. The chair was wet from the beer, but I didn't really care. I looked across at Michelle, who looked thoroughly confused.

"Do you know who I am?" I asked her.

"What sort of a question is that?"

I was starting to panic, and if I did that I'd wake up. Michelle was presumed dead in the Worldline I'd committed the murder, yet here I was sitting in a pub apparently having a meal with her. I couldn't be in the correct Worldline, but it may well be the best chance I got. I was already lucid dreaming so, if the theory was correct, she was going to get spooked anyway

Worldlines

when I woke up and she got this Worldline version of me back. I decided to run with it; providing I didn't get an uncontrolled urge to stab her again with my steak knife, what was the worst that could happen?

"Michelle," I said, before pausing and just looking at her for a moment. She was truly gorgeous. I'd wanted to date her for years, and yet in this Worldline, I apparently was. I didn't feel pain, I had no scars, and I was with the most beautiful woman. If this was a real Worldline, then this guy's life was considerably better than my own.

"Michelle, can I ask you something? I warn you, this is going to sound very strange from your perspective."

A cheer went up around the pub; United had scored a second goal.

"You say lots of strange things so go ahead."

"What do I do here?"

"You eat your meal and drink your beer," she said sarcastically.

"That's not what I mean. In this life, what am I?"

"An idiot," she laughed, the sassy cow. "Stop it, just eat your dinner."

"Michelle, I'm being serious."

The jovial look disappeared from her face.

"Ok, I'll bite. You're a physics student."

"Physics, at university, with Professor Buzzard."

"Yeeesss," said Michelle in a long, slow tone. She acted like I was being thick.

"Is Sinead there?"

I saw her eyes narrow.

"You know she is. What is this about?"

"Michelle, please, stick with me. Did you go to Sinead's party?"

"No, you know I didn't." She was getting irate. "Gary, what is going on?"

"This isn't the right Worldline," I said to myself.

"Worldline? Are you still on about those?"

I looked at her.

"We've spoken about this before?"

"Yes, in this very pub, before our holiday."

"Holiday?"

She looked at me with utter bewilderment. I was running out of time. Quick as a flash, I made a decision. This Gary knew Sinead and he knew Buzzard. If I could get Michelle to record what had happened and explain it back to her Gary when I woke up, he may have more luck with this than I was having.

"It doesn't matter," I said. "Do you have your phone with you?"

"Yeah, of course."

"Then can you put the camera on and record this."

"Our conversation?"

"Yes."

"Ok," she said, but I figured she was saying ok out of curiosity rather than obedience.

She reached down under the table to grab her handbag, and I found myself studying her. She looked exactly as I remembered from school; beautiful blue eyes, curly blonde hair, a curvy figure. She was wearing very subtle makeup, the pale blue eye shadow bringing the colour out in her eyes. I wondered if I could get away with kissing her, but the excitement of doing that would probably wake me up. I had to stay focused.

"Let me know when you've started recording, then please don't cut me off or stop recording until I say, no matter how strange what I'm saying may seem."

"Gaz, you're starting to scare me."

"I don't mean to, but this is important."

She pressed a couple of buttons on her phone.

"Ok, I'm recording."

"Gary," I began. "This is going to sound very strange to you as you'll most likely have no memory of this. The work you're doing at university currently with Buzzard and Sinead, the stuff around Many Worlds, it's all true. But it goes deeper than you think. When you dream, your consciousness is drifting through those Worldlines. In my Worldline, I'm able to lucid dream which allows me to effectively take control of you. Now, I've only recently discovered this because last week I had a lucid dream where I stabbed Michelle at Sinead's party. Sinead's mum, Mary, has dementia in my Worldline and suffers hallucinations. This is part of it too. She hallucinated and saw me stab Michelle. But neither Michelle nor Mary had been at the party in my Worldline, only in the dream. That led me to believe all this is real. I'm trying to reach that Worldline, as that Gary is most likely now in prison for my crime and I want to help him. The key to clearing him is the science and proving he wasn't in control of his own body. You'll do that because of my injury. Five years ago, on my way to a school exam, I was run over by a lorry. I suffered a lot of injuries, including long term nerve damage in my right arm. I can't grip with that hand anymore, and it means I'm left-handed. I stabbed Michelle with my left hand. Explain this to Professor Buzzard and Professor Charnock at the university. Between them they'll be able to understand."

I was beginning to lose control of the dream. I looked at Michelle, but she hadn't got her phone anymore; it wasn't even Michelle. I was starting to wake up.

"I need your help to find him. Please help me."

I sat up in bed, my heart racing. I'd done it, sort of. I couldn't wait until the morning. I opened my door, crossed the landing, and went into Sinead's room.

"Sinead," I whispered as I sat on the bed. I put my hand on her shoulder hoping to wake her gently and not startle her. "Sinead, I did it. It worked."

"What worked?" she asked sleepily.

"The tablets. I had a lucid dream, I saw Michelle, I explained everything. It's all over now."

"And you've woken me in the middle of the night to tell me this because?" she groaned at me.

"I thought you'd want to know. It's been upsetting you, and now it's dealt with."

"Good, now go back to bed," she said.

She was less enthusiastic than I'd hoped, but maybe it should have been what I expected, given how she felt and the fact I'd woken her in the middle of the night. I hoped she'd be more interested in the morning. As it turned out, when we were both downstairs having breakfast the next morning, it was Sinead who approached the subject first.

"So, what happened last night then?" she asked.

"I took that tablet before I went to bed but nothing happened. I woke up at half one having not had any dreams at all. So..." I hesitated, she wasn't going to like the next bit, "...so I took the other two as well."

"You took all three together?"

"Yeah, but I feel fine, don't worry about it."

"I knew you'd do that."

"Do what?"

"Take them all in one go."

"I hadn't realised I was so easy to read."

"Gary, you've been obsessed. Luckily, those weren't the right tablets."

"What do you mean?"

"Gary, you took a placebo."

"A placebo?"

"Yes. Professor Charnock turned you down for the dream programme because of your mental health. I went to see him after Buzzard's lecture yesterday and asked him to reconsider as I didn't think you'd let the matter drop until you'd done something about it. He said the only way around it would be if you got the trial drug by an unofficial route and asked me if I wanted him to make that happen, but the catch would be that you'd be on your own. You'd have to follow the instructions they gave you, but you wouldn't be monitored to check that you did. I told him I didn't think you would follow them, that you'd either take them three nights in a row or all three together. That's when he suggested the placebo drug. They monitor patients who both do and don't take the drug, although they all think they're taking the real one. Some of those on the placebo have also shown an increase in dream activity. Therefore, he suggested even if you had the placebo, if you thought you were taking the real drug and you took it inappropriately, you may still have had some success. It turns out he was right."

I sat there open-mouthed.

"So basically, you think I'm an idiot, you protected me from myself, then lied to me about having done so to see if I'd do the stupid thing you thought I'd do?"

"In essence, yes."

If it's possible to feel equal levels of annoyance and gratitude at the same time, then this is it. I was irritated that she'd lied about the drug and fed me a placebo. But she'd done the wrong thing for the right reasons, as she clearly knows me better than I know myself. She thought I'd do something stupid and I did. What does that say about me?

"I don't know what to say," I said.

"'Thank you' would be a good start," she retorted.

"Thank you," I said. "I don't like the fact you lied to me about it, but I understand why you did."

"Believe it or not, I don't like the fact I had to lie to you about it either. I felt so guilty last night when I went to bed, and I even toyed with the idea of coming back and telling you. I've never lied to you about anything before, but you've been so obsessed by this that I didn't know what else to do. If I'd got you the proper drug, you'd have clearly overdosed on it, and I couldn't deal with that. If I'd have come back with nothing, you'd have had a bee in your bonnet about it and you wouldn't have been able to stop thinking about it. And, if I'd told you that it was a placebo, well then, it wouldn't have worked so what was the point in that? This felt like the least bad way."

"I can understand your logic, yes," I admitted, although I confess that I really didn't like it.

"So, what happened in the dream itself?" she asked.

I gave her a rundown of what had happened, being in The Loch & Quay with Michelle, spilling my drink, the weird conversation I had with her initially, and the video message I recorded for myself on the phone explaining all of this. When I finished Sinead was sniggering.

"So, if this is all real," she said, "When you woke up, that Worldlines version of Gary is going to find himself sitting there with soaking wet jeans and no recollection of how he did it?"

"Basically, yes," I smiled back.

"I wonder what he'll make of the video," she commented.

"I guess we'll never know. But I do think I've done all I can now. Even if I dream about Michelle again, and I hope I don't," I added quickly. "I can't keep reliving this in every dream I ever have. You're right, I have to move on from it."

After that, we actually had quite a pleasant day. Nothing overly exciting happened, but to feel like there was no animosity between us was a welcome break from much of the rest of the week. I also felt like I had a bit of closure from the dream saga. We went to the hospital at lunchtime to see Mary. As it was Saturday, the visiting was on from 10 am and it meant we could go earlier. She looked a lot better, although she still wasn't making much sense when she was talking. I wasn't sure if it was my imagination or what, but she seemed to be eyeing me with more than a hint of suspicion.

"We won't be up tomorrow," said Sinead as we were leaving. "Dad will come up, but me and Gary are going for dinner in Barchester with his family."

"Oh, that's nice," Mary said. "Where are you taking me?"

"No Mum, you're not coming with us. It's with Alex and Gregor, Gary's mum and dad. Do you remember them?"

"Oh yes," she said. "It was lovely, wasn't it?"

"It was, yeah," we both agreed automatically. It was odd. If I was in a conversation with Sinead and she made a random comment in the middle of a conversation that was completely out of context, it would throw me and take me a second or two to gather my thoughts again. With Mary, however, it was as though we were slowly training ourselves to respond automatically to whatever she happened to say next, as there was no logical way to predict it. Life would be interesting when she came home on Monday, and I suspected it wouldn't be in a good way.

Two o'clock the next afternoon came around much too quickly, although at least with Sinead coming to the meal also, it meant I had a lift there and we didn't have to mess around going into town to catch a bus.

"How are you feeling about this?" she asked in the car on the way there.

"Terrified, to be honest," I replied. "This isn't a good idea. It's all going to go wrong."

"Well, it will if you go in with that attitude."

"It's difficult not to. It feels like every conversation I've had with Dad since my accident has been confrontational."

"There's been a lot of time since the last one though, today might be different. I'm here to support you too, so you're not facing it alone."

"I know, thank you," I said.

We got to the pub and parked in the car park. We were a few minutes early but when we got into the pub Mum and Dad were both already there, as was Nicki. Sitting next to her, bizarrely, was William Potts, my old school friend, the one who'd witnessed my accident. What was he doing here? Mum stood up to greet us.

"How are you feeling, son?" she said as she hugged me.

"Yeah, I'm ok, a bit nervous," I said.

"That's understandable. Hi, Sinead," she continued, hugging her also. "It's great to see you."

Dad stood up and offered me a handshake. I looked him in the eye for a second or two before deciding it was probably best to take it.

"Hello again," Nicki said, and I gave her a kiss on the cheek. "I wasn't expecting to see you so soon."

"Sorry to disappoint," I said, turning my attention to William. "What are you doing here?"

"Will is my boyfriend," said Nicki cautiously. I looked at him.

"You're shagging my kid sister?" I said; I loved Nicki and I always felt drawn to protect her.

"It's ok," said Dad. "They've been together for a while."

"And you didn't tell me because?"

"Because I knew you'd most likely be a jackass about it," Nicki said.

William stood up and, like Dad, offered me a handshake.

"Hello mate, how are you doing?" he said.

Again, I hesitated, glancing across at Sinead, who nodded her head. I met his handshake.

"Yeah, I'm good thanks," I said, taking a seat the other side of Nicki. Sinead sat next to me, with Mum and Dad on the other side of the table with the spare seats for Donna and her girlfriend. The silence felt immediately awkward.

"Where's Donna?" Sinead asked, breaking the silence.

"She'll be a few minutes late," Mum answered. "She's working until two o'clock herself. Freya's picking her up and then they're coming here."

"Is Freya her girlfriend?" I asked.

"Yes, have you not met her?"

"How long have they been together, Mum?"

"Nearly two years."

"Then clearly not."

"Who wants a drink?" Dad asked, rising from his seat. "Gary, Sinead?"

"I'll have a Moretti," I replied.

"Just a lemonade please," said Sinead. "I'm driving."

Dad went to order our drinks and the tension subsided temporarily.

"Thank you both for coming," Mum said quietly. "It can't have been easy for you walking in here like this."

"I had Sinead with me, I was alright."

"Gary Jackson," came a voice from the past. "Long time no see!"

I turned around and a waitress was trotting over to me. It was Milly Lane, a girl who had been the year below me at school.

"Hello, Mill, I didn't know you worked in here," and I gave her a quick hug before remembering that I should have known. Mill had been the waitress who served me and Michelle in here in the dream I had last night.

"Been here since last summer," she said. "How have you been?"

"Yeah, I'm ok, just catching up with family," I said.

"I'll leave you to carry on," she said. "But if you want anything give me a shout."

Dad returned from the bar and the conversation continued in a surprisingly civil manner. Nicki and Will had been together since just before Christmas. I didn't like the idea of one of my school friends with my sister, but they did seem genuinely taken with each other. The photography course she'd enrolled in at university was actually his idea; Nicki had been unsure what she wanted to do in life, and Will had commented on her talent for taking quality photographs. It wasn't much, but it was enough to give Nicki a steer on where to go next. If he treated her well and didn't hurt her, I guessed I should be happy for her.

Donna arrived a few minutes later. She'd changed since I last saw her. She'd put on weight, her hair was cut short, she'd had two nose piercings, and there was a big tattoo running down her right arm. She still looked quite pretty though, dressed all in black. Freya wasn't my cup of tea at all She was a big woman with multi-coloured hair styled with a side parting. She was in an oversized black t-shirt with some rock band emblazoned on the front, and a choker chain around her neck. It was easy to see the influence she'd had on Donna. Donna gave a generic, "Hi everyone," and sat down at the table without directly speaking to or addressing me.

"How are you?" I asked her.

"Fine," she responded, completely avoiding my eyes.

"And this is Freya," Mum said cheerfully.

I looked at her, and she gave a slight nod of acknowledgement, although I could see she was scowling on the inside. I could only imagine what Donna had said to her about me these last couple of years.

Everyone except me and Nicki ordered starters. My stomach was too knotted to eat currently, and Nicki was watching her weight, which was ridiculous given she was on a par with Sinead as the slimmest person at the table.

"Your dad's business has picked up lately, hasn't it, Gregor?" Mum said, trying to steer the conversation. Dad was a mechanic and owned a garage on the edge of the Birchtree estate where they lived.

"Sure has," he said. "I've got an agreement with Peyton's on the main road. You remember Ed Peyton, don't you, Michelle's dad?"

Sinead, who had been eating her prawn cocktail next to me, dropped her spoon.

"Sorry," she muttered.

"Yeah, I remember," I said.

"Well, I repair and MOT all the cars before he sells them. Even without the passing trade, there's comfortably enough work for us. I think I'm going to take on another mechanic."

"I assume you still need a job, don't you?" Donna said, although her tone was confrontational.

"I don't work yet, no," I said.

"I didn't think so," she smiled sarcastically.

"It wouldn't have to be a manual job. I know you still struggle with your arm and your leg," Dad said. "I think Ed is recruiting for someone himself, maybe you could ask him?"

"Yeah, I'll think about it," I said non-committally.

"That's a no," retorted Donna.

Sinead squeezed my hand under the table. She knew Donna was trying to provoke me. If she carried on, she'd probably succeed. However, Mum must have picked up on it too.

"I need to go to the ladies'," she announced. "Donna, can you come too, please? I need your help with something."

"In the ladies'?" she asked.

"Now!" Mum replied firmly.

Whatever she said away from the table it must have worked, as when they returned Donna's snarky comments ceased, and the rest of the meal was relatively pleasant. I still didn't eat all my dinner, although I did manage a dessert. By just after four o'clock the meal had concluded, and we were all preparing to leave. Conversation had been placid; Mum had taken more interest than seemed natural in Sinead's engagement ring, whilst Dad had been on his best behaviour, presumably under Mum's orders to do so. Nicki had been her normal self, whilst Donna and Freya had hardly spoken since they arrived, giving the impression they were even more uncomfortable about being there than I was.

"Let's do this again," Mum said. "How about once a month, just all meet up as a family. I've really enjoyed having you all together today."

"Can do," said Dad, who'd been far too nice for his own good throughout the afternoon.

"I'd like that too," Nicki added.

"Can if you want," Donna shrugged.

"Gary, what do you think?" Mum asked.

"Yeah, I'll think about it," I nodded.

"Got lots of thinking to do, haven't you?" Donna piped up.

"Don't spoil it," snapped Mum.

We said our goodbyes and made our way out of the pub back to the car.

"That went ok, didn't it?" said Sinead on the way home.

"Yeah, as well as could be expected, I suppose."

"You did well not to bite at Donna. She had a few digs at you."

"Yeah, I noticed. Thank you for coming with me."

"I wasn't going to leave you to deal with that on your own, was I?"

"I guess not."

We were nearly home by the time either of us spoke again.

"With Mum coming out of hospital," Sinead began, "We've decided it might do her good to take her back to Ireland for a while."

"Are you sure that's wise? She's very confused and her mobility isn't great."

"I know, but dementia patients sometimes give the impression they've gone back in time, and we think that's started to happen to Mum. We're going to take her back to the area where she grew up, see if it can lift her spirits a bit. We're not flying, we booked a ferry last night for Tuesday afternoon, but we'll be back on Sunday. Me and dad will share the driving to and from Anglesey."

"You've already booked it?"

"Yeah."

"And am I invited?" I asked indignantly.

"Honestly?" began Sinead. "You weren't going to be. After how things have been lately, I thought a few days apart might do us good. But if you want to come then you can."

"Not if I'm not invited," I said, slightly offended at this turn of events.

"That's why I've just mentioned it to you. It may be nice for all four of us to go together."

"And it may not," I replied. "If I go and we continue arguing, you'll regret taking me, and that'll do us more harm than good. No, I'll stay here."

"If you're sure," she said. "It might do us good to miss each other a bit."

"Yeah, I suppose," I said, not at all convinced.

Chapter Seventeen
The Red Line

My lack of concentration had clearly caused me to drop my glass, as the next thing I knew there was beer on the table and my jeans were soaking wet.

"For goodness sake," I said, jumping up. "Mill, can I have a cloth, please?" but she'd already left the table.

"Is everything ok?" Sinead asked as she returned to the table.

"Yeah, I've just spilt my drink," I said. "That was quick, I hope you remembered to wash your hands."

"What took you so long?" Marcus asked, also reappearing, in direct conflict with what I'd said. I swear, the man could annoy the life out of me without even trying.

"Michelle, what's wrong?" Sinead asked.

I turned to face her. She was a white as a sheet and was shaking like a leaf.

"Baby, are you ok?" I said, going around the table and putting my arm around her.

"What just happened?" she quivered.

"Oh, bloody hell," said Marcus, who had turned to face the TV. "I told you they'd concede another. Was it a good goal?"

"I don't know, I didn't see," I said, irritated that this is what he thought was important. "Michelle, what's wrong?"

"I don't know," she said; she was trembling quite violently.

"Are you feeling ok? Do you feel ill?"

"No," she said, looking at me, tears starting to roll down her face. "It was you."

"Me?" I said, confused. "What have I done?"

"Michelle, what's happened?" Sinead asked, coming around the table and joining me the other side of Michelle. Mill had also reappeared.

"Is everything alright?" she asked.

"Yeah, fine," I said. "Just give us a minute. Michelle, do you want to come outside and get some fresh air, calm down a little bit?"

"No, I'm fine," she lied. "What just happened?"

"I don't know what you mean," I said. "Sinead went to the toilet, Marcus went out for a smoke, Mill brought the starters over, I dropped my drink, Sinead came back. That's it."

"No, that's not it. What happened between dropping your drink and Sinead coming back?"

"Nothing," I said, perplexed.

Michelle's shaking had eased, and she was now giving me a stern and serious look.

"You don't remember talking to me about all that Worldlines stuff you've been doing at uni?"

"No," I said, my bewilderment growing by the second.

"Gaz, if this is you messing about trying to scare me then stop it, please, because it's really working."

"Michelle, I haven't done anything, I swear. What do you think I've done?"

"You were talking to me about something called lucid dreaming. You said you'd dreamt you'd stabbed me, and you needed Sinead and Professor Buzzard's help to get you off."

"What?" I exclaimed, and looked at Sinead who was wearing the same puzzled expression as I. Marcus was still facing the other way watching the game.

"You asked me to record you saying it," she said. "Here, it's on my phone."

She handed me her phone, and I went to her media gallery. Sinead had come around to stand next to me so that she could see also. There was, indeed, a video clip with the current date and time on it showing me, which was weird as I didn't remember her doing it. I hit play and turned the volume up. The video clip played as follows.

"Gary, this is going to sound very strange to you as you'll have no memory of this. The work you're doing at university currently with Buzzard and Sinead, the stuff around Many Worlds, it's all true. But it goes deeper than you think. When you dream, your consciousness is drifting through those Worldlines. In my Worldline, I'm able to lucid dream, which allows me to effectively take control of you. Now, I've only recently discovered this because last week I had a lucid dream where I stabbed Michelle at Sinead's party. Sinead's mum, Mary, has dementia in my Worldline and suffers hallucinations. This is part of it too. She hallucinated and saw me stab Michelle. But neither Michelle nor Mary had been at the party in my Worldline, only in the dream. That led me to believe all this is real. I'm trying to reach that Worldline, as that Gary is most likely now in prison for my crime and I want to help him. The key to clearing him is the science, and proving he wasn't in control of his own body. You'll do that because of my injury. Five years ago, on my way to a school exam, I was run over by a lorry. I suffered a lot of injuries, including long term nerve damage in my right arm. I can't grip with that hand anymore, and it means I'm left-handed. I stabbed Michelle with my left hand. Explain this to Professor Buzzard and Professor Charnock at the university. Between them they'll be able to understand."

This time it was my turn to go white. I literally felt the colour drain from my face as I was watching it.

"Michelle, I swear to you, I honestly don't remember doing that. And I've certainly never had a dream where I've hurt you. I feel bad enough for cracking your ribs."

"I know, I believe you," she said. "That's what's scared me so much."

Marcus had turned to face us again and was now humming the tune from The Twilight Zone.

"Oh, shut up," Sinead snapped at him before turning to me. "Gary, what does this mean?"

"I have no idea," I said. "But we probably should take it to Professor Buzzard tomorrow."

"Good idea," Sinead replied. "Michelle, can you send this video to me, please?"

"Yeah, sure," Michelle replied, taking her phone back. Her hands were still shaking.

"Are you sure everything is ok. Can I get anyone anything?" Mill said, having returned to our table.

"We're fine, thanks, Mill," I said. "I'll call you across if we need something."

"I don't think I can eat that now," Michelle said, looking at her prawn cocktail. "I'm too shaken up."

"Let's go outside, get some fresh air," I said to her. "Sinead, are you coming?"

"I'd better stay here with Marcus," she said.

Michelle and I went out to the car park The breeze felt nice and helped bring me back into the moment.

"Do you think it's possible?" Michelle asked. "What's just happened, I mean. That we can be possessed like that?"

"Ten minutes ago I'd have said no, but this is really freaky. You do believe me when I say I'm not messing about, don't you?"

"I didn't at first, but I do now. I don't think you'd let it go this far if you were winding me up and besides, you're not that good an actor."

"So, what do you think?"

"You're the scientist, you tell me," she said. "I know one thing, if someone came into the hospital and said they'd experienced what we just have, we'd be carting them off to the mental home."

"Makes you think, doesn't it?"

"I want to go home," she said. "Can you ring Dad and tell him I'm not feeling well? Ask him to come and pick us up, and to bring Carl with him to drive my car back."

"Yeah, of course," I said, taking her phone back from her. "Can I watch that video again?"

"Can you ring Dad first, please?" she insisted.

I did as she asked and then went back inside to tell Sinead and Marcus what was happening.

"I'm not surprised," Sinead said when I told her Michelle was heading home. "It's probably scared her to death, the poor girl. Do you honestly not know anything about it?"

"Of course I don't, I swear."

"Let's go into uni early in the morning. Our lecture is at ten, but if we get there by nine, we can speak to Professor Buzzard about it for a bit before we start."

"Sounds like a plan. Would you mind picking me up, please? I don't want to wake Michelle on her day off to drop me at the station."

"Yeah, of course, I have to pretty much pass yours on the way to the station anyway. Will you be at home or at Michelle's?"

"Probably Michelle's, but I will text you later to let you know."

As it happened, I ended up at home. When Ed and Carl turned up, Michelle asked Carl to drop me off at home whilst she went back with her dad. It was an awkward car journey, Carl desperately quizzing me on what I'd done and why we'd fallen out. He didn't accept "Nothing," and "We haven't," as acceptable answers, and I was grateful to get out of the car.

"If you have hurt her," Carl said as I got out of the car, "There'll be hell to pay."

I could understand the sentiment; Michelle was his younger sister just as Nicki was mine. If I thought Will had hurt her, I'd have reacted in a similar manner.

Because Michelle had sent the video to Sinead and not to me, it meant I hadn't actually got a copy of it to watch myself. I decided it was best to let Michelle calm down in her own time, and text Sinead to tell her I was at home and ask her to forward it to me. Unfortunately, she was having some trouble with her mobile network, meaning I didn't actually watch it again until I was in her car the next morning. I hadn't slept well and neither, by the looks of it, had she.

"How's Michelle?" she asked as I got in the car.

"I don't know, I've not spoken to her. I texted her last night but she's not replied yet."

"I hope she's ok," she said with genuine concern.

"Yeah, me too."

"Here's my phone," she said, handing it to me. "The video clip is on there."

I watched it through three times back to back, trying to make sense of what I'd apparently said. I was so focused on it that I hadn't realised we were sitting in stationary traffic.

"The A35 heading south has one lane blocked because of a lorry having its tyre changed just after the Badminton turn off," said Helen, the lady presenter on the radio. "It's taking you about half an hour to get through there."

"Wish they'd reported this before we joined the back of the queue," I said.

"Maybe they did," Sinead said. "I'm barely paying attention to it."

"Now for the weather," the lady continued after she finished the travel bulletin. "It's going to be mostly dry across the region with the slight chance of an odd shower this afternoon, highs of twelve Celsius, which is fifty-four Fahrenheit."

The temperature displayed on Sinead's dashboard already said eleven Celsius, although at least they were right about it being dry. It didn't take us long to get moving and, as luck would have it, our train was slightly delayed anyway, meaning we still ended up on the same one as if we'd had a clear run.

"What do you think Buzzard will say?" Sinead asked me after we'd boarded.

"I have no idea. I imagine he'll think we're winding him up."

"Why? If he believes these theories himself, you'd think he'd believe us."

"I know, but think about it. Freaky event happens to us, right in the middle of us studying this very topic. The timing's a bit suspect, don't you think? That's what I'd be thinking if I were him."

The rest of the journey was quite quiet for one involving me and Sinead, both lost in our own thoughts on this topic, and both thinking any other topic not really worthy of discussion by comparison. I was pleased when we finally reached the university and found Professor Buzzard already in his lecture hall.

"Come in, come in," he said as Sinead knocked on the door, and we both stepped inside.

"Good morning, Professor," I said.

"Mr Jackson, Miss O'Brien," said Buzzard with a hint of surprise. "You're an hour early. You do know the clocks don't adjust until the end of the month?"

"Of course, Professor," Sinead said. "I wanted to speak to you before class about an incident that occurred yesterday that neither of us can explain. We're hoping you may be able to shed some light on it."

"I can't promise that," Buzzard said. "I'm always here as a counsel to my students, though. Tell me what happened."

"Maybe you should explain the first bit," she said turning to me.

"Probably," I said, and gave Professor Buzzard a run-down of what happened in the pub yesterday. From the normal events at the start of the meal, to Sinead leaving to use the ladies' room, to Marcus going outside for a smoke, to my apparent memory loss for a few moments until Sinead's return, Michelle's reaction, and finally the revelation of the video that was on Sinead's phone.

"Interesting," he commented, turning back to Sinead. "May I see the video?"

"Yes, of course," she said, passing him her phone so that he could watch it. At the end, he handed Sinead her phone back and sat, his elbows on his desk and his fingers intertwined, his thumbs resting on the bridge of his nose, apparently lost in thought.

"Before we go any further," he began, "Can I make absolutely sure that this isn't being staged in any way?"

"It isn't, Professor," I confirmed.

"Because if you are attempting to make either myself or someone else look stupid as a result of this, then both I and the university in general will be most displeased."

"Everything you've seen and everything we've told you is entirely genuine," I said, in my most assertive voice.

"Very well," he said. "We will begin with the assumption that events have occurred as you've described them. Before I offer you my opinion I must ask, what do you think is going on?"

"Not a clue," I admitted.

"Come now," he said. "I've taught you better than to react like that. Miss O'Brien, do you have an opinion?"

"I have a couple," she said. "But each one seems increasingly more absurd the more I think about it."

"Let's discuss what you consider to be the least absurd one."

"Well, the most logical explanation is that Gary is winding us up."

"I'm not!" I exclaimed.

"Yes, I know," Sinead said, "and I believe you. But you have to admit, you must understand why someone might think it."

"Indeed," said Professor Buzzard, and I reluctantly agreed. "However, if we are working on the assumption that everything you've both told me is true, and everything on the video is genuine, what is your least absurd hypothesis that fits that assumption?"

"Then the least absurd theory," Sinead began, "Which is still completely weird, is that Gary was momentarily possessed by another instance of himself from a different Worldline."

"Meaning what?"

"Meaning, at that moment, I wasn't in control of my own body and mind," I said.

"Why?"

"Because my consciousness had been replaced, I guess, by someone else's."

"Not really someone else's," said Sinead. "Just another Worldlines instance of you."

"To me, that's pretty much the same thing."

"To me also," acknowledged Buzzard. "How do you think this has happened?"

"If the Gary in the video is telling the truth, he's managed it via lucid dreaming," Sinead said.

"What is lucid dreaming?" I asked.

"It's when one becomes aware that they are dreaming and can then effectively take control of the dream. It's meant to be a very exhilarating experience, although it's something I've never been able to do myself," Buzzard explained.

"But how would that person dreaming allow them to take possession of me?" I asked.

Buzzard sat and thought for a moment.

"Do you know what happens to our consciousness when we go to sleep?" he asked.

"No," we both said.

"Nobody does," he continued. "Not really. There are theories and suggestions but no concrete proof. Does it just switch off? Does it go somewhere else? Nobody really knows. But dreams have always fascinated me. I wake up of a morning, and I can recall a dream. This means I have made conscious memories, in my sleep, whilst I was unconscious. How do you explain that?"

Sinead and I both just looked at him blankly.

"Now imagine for a moment that the Many Worlds Theory is, in fact, true. We live in a multiverse rather than a universe, and that's how life is set up. One of the main hypotheses around Many Worlds is it supports the assumption that consciousness can't really be terminated. There will always be a 'path of least resistance' where the conscious state survives. But unconsciousness, and sleep by definition, would seem to disprove that theory. And yet we dream and make conscious memories in our sleep. The two facts don't tally. There must be a missing link."

I glanced across at Sinead, who appeared to be taking this all in far more successfully than I was.

"That missing link would be the answer to the question, 'What happens to our consciousness when we go to sleep?' and that's something we can't answer. However, if you analyse normal dreams, what do we notice about them?"

"That they're really messed up," I commented.

"Exactly! They don't make any sense in the waking world. If you dream that you're in a pet shop buying a rabbit, and yet moments later you come out of that pet shop with a fish tank, you don't look at that and go 'where's my rabbit?' In the moment, the fish tank makes complete sense. You don't recall asking for the rabbit and, therefore, you don't realise that it's all 'messed up' as you put it."

"Now if you believe the Many Worlds Theory to be true, and I personally do, could there not be a rational explanation in there? Is it not possible that whilst we sleep, our consciousness drifts into neighbouring Worldlines, passing through different eventualities, each one making perfect sense in that moment? Yet you wake up, you remember the journey through those Worldlines, and it's only then you think about the lack of continuity. At this point, you just shrug it off as a weird dream, but what if it's not? What if your doppelganger, through the form of a lucid dream, had found a way to control himself and, by definition, control you, Gary, in a Worldline separate from his own?"

"That's a frightening idea," I shivered.

"Why?" Buzzard asked.

"It means someone could potentially take control of me and do anything without my knowledge, commit a crime or something. How would I ever prove I wasn't in control of my actions at the time?"

"I believe that's already happened."

"Because of what the me in the video says?"

"Precisely."

"So, what do we do about it now?" Sinead asked.

"May I see the video again?" Buzzard asked.

"Yes, of course," she said, handing him the phone back.

Buzzard watched the video through very intently and kept pausing it every few seconds to make notes. Then he watched it through a second time, ticking off the notes to confirm he'd got everything.

"I suggest we talk through the events described in the video one at a time," Buzzard said, handing Sinead her phone back. "However, that is going to take longer than we currently have before lecture. Are you both free afterwards?"

"Yes, Professor," we both confirmed.

"Then before we do park this for the morning, there is one thing that I wish to know. It is mentioned by the Gary in the video that during one of his lucid dreams, he stabs a lady called Michelle. This is your partner, Gary, I understand, and the lady who recorded the video?"

"That's correct."

"How is she? How has she taken this?"

"Badly," I confirmed. "She hasn't spoken to me since."

"I suggest you give her a call before lecture starts. Whatever she witnessed and experienced yesterday, it's important that she recognise that it wasn't you. Is she of a scientific mind?"

"A bit. She's a student nurse at the University College Hospital."

"Is she working today?"

"No, but she is going there for a chest X-ray. She got injured on our holiday last week. We think she's cracked a rib."

"Then go away for a few moments and check how she is, but make sure you're back in here for when lecture starts at ten o'clock. We'll pick this up again at twelve when we've finished."

I did as Buzzard suggested, whilst Sinead went to get us both a coffee from The Oasis before lecture started. Unfortunately, Michelle wasn't answering my calls. Her mobile went to voicemail, and the house phone rang through to the answering machine. I tried her mobile again, deciding I'd actually leave her a message if she didn't pick up this time, which she didn't.

"Hi, Michelle, it's me," I said after the beep. "I'm worried about you, and I want to know you're ok. Can you call or text me when you get this, please? Thanks. I love you."

"Any joy?" Sinead asked when she returned with our drinks.

"None whatsoever, she's still not talking to me," I said.

However, at that my phone beeped; it was a text from Michelle.

"I'm fine, just leaving to go to the hospital. X-rays will be at 12. Will text you this afternoon when I'm done. Love you too xx"

"It's a start," said Sinead. "At least she doesn't hate you over it and still loves you."

"Then why won't she speak to me?"

"She's probably pretty freaked-out. I think I would be in her place," she said.

"But I'd never hurt Michelle. She knows that."

"Perhaps, but yesterday she learnt that you might."

"But I wouldn't."

"I know but think what she heard. You sat opposite her having a nice meal, and then suddenly you're asking her to record you saying you've stabbed her in a lucid dream. I know it wasn't you but, in that moment, to her it was. She's not training to be a physicist like you and me. She won't be able to separate the you and the not-you bits quite so easily as we might. She just needs time."

We made our way back into the lecture theatre. Some other students were already there, so Sinead and I took our regular seats.

"Can I ask you something personal?" she whispered.

"Of course."

"Do you ever have fantasies about hurting her?"

"No, of course not."

"Neither of you are into BDSM or anything? You're not into violent love-making? There was no master and slave role-playing whilst you were in Italy?" She'd grinned as she'd asked the last one.

"No, none of it," I confirmed. "We're all a bit too passionate for that."

"Just wondering," she asked, but I sensed there was more to it than that.

"Why, is that what Marcus wants to do to you?"

Sinead opened her mouth to answer then hesitated, then opened it again.

"Well..." she began but, at that, Buzzard interjected.

"Good morning, class," he began. "You'll be delighted to know we'll be moving off Many Worlds for today's lecture."

Great, I thought and tuned out. I could suddenly feel my adrenaline pumping, partly because of Michelle and what happened yesterday, but mainly over the idea Marcus might be forcing Sinead to let him hurt her. She was wearing a long-sleeved top with a high neck, and proper jeans without holes in them, so there was no way to check her for bruises or anything. However, she must have sensed my angst, because she whispered to me.

"I'll tell you about it later."

*****

I must admit I have no idea what the lecture was about. I saw Sinead scribbling down notes, at various points, that I'd ask her if I could read over at some later date, but for now I was too preoccupied. I wished I'd been at the hospital with Michelle to support her whilst she had her X-rays, I wished I'd been able to beat the shit out of Marcus at school and wondered what he was trying to get Sinead into, but most importantly, I was wishing that yesterday afternoon had never happened. Such was my daydreaming, I was barely aware that the two hours were up and Buzzard had ended the lecture until I felt Sinead get up next to me.

"Are we going to go and speak to Buzzard?" she asked.

"In a minute," I said. "Wait here first."

I waited until the rest of our row was clear.

"What has Marcus done to you?"

"He hasn't done anything."

"Ok, what does he want to do to you?" I asked. I was aware the conversation might get a bit explicit, but it wasn't unusual for Sinead and me to talk on these terms. It wasn't an everyday occurrence, but if there was anything deep and personal that we needed to talk about, then the other was where we went for support.

"He's just a bit more adventurous than I am," she said quietly. "Privately, I mean."

"I think I can work it out. Is he pushing you into stuff you're not ready for?" I said, lowering my tone to hers.

"You know me," she said. "I've never really been in a long-term relationship like you and Michelle. I'm not as experienced in these things as most people our age. I don't really understand what's normal and what's not. We didn't even sleep together until Saturday night, but now he's talking about wanting to..."

She stopped and looked away.

"Wanting to what?" I pushed.

"He wants to choke me," she whispered.

"Choke you?"

"Yeah, he said it's more intense that way. Said his previous girlfriends all let him do it early on."

"All those previous girlfriends he's no longer with?"

"His last one left him when he got sent to prison, and she's in a new relationship now."

"That's not your problem."

"I know, it's just, on Saturday night he lay down right on top of me and put both his hands around my throat. I didn't feel like I could breathe, he's a lot bigger and stronger than me. I tried to throw him off."

"And did you manage to?"

"He got off himself when he saw I was distressed."

"And what did he say?"

"He apologised and said it was just him doing what he normally does."

"What happened then?"

"We finished what we were doing after he promised not to do it again, but it kind of spoilt it. I wasn't feeling it after that."

"I'm not surprised. Has he said anything about it since?"

"Yeah, when we got back from The Loch & Quay, he asked if it would still be a problem next time if I knew to expect it beforehand?"

"What did you say?"

"I told him I'd think about it."

"And what do you want?"

"I don't know," she shrugged. "I don't really know what's normal and what's not."

"I'm ready when you both are," called Buzzard from the front of the hall.

"Coming, Professor," I said back, before turning to Sinead. "We can carry on talking about this later if you want."

She nodded, but she looked troubled. I felt a bit guilty now too. She was having her own troubles and yet she was still prioritising helping me with this.

"Right, where were we?" said Buzzard, to himself as much as us. "I think it's best that we run through the events described in the video as they're mentioned. It begins with your other consciousness stating that when you dream, your own consciousness is drifting into various Worldlines. So far, from what we know, I think that much is believable."

"Does that mean dreaming, as we know it, isn't really dreaming at all? It's just us witnessing other events outside of our own Worldline?" I asked.

"It's an interesting idea, isn't it?" he said, "That we only see snapshots of other Worldlines when we're asleep, rather than dreams being something contrived from our own thoughts and memories."

"But to communicate with Michelle, and us, through his own lucid dreams, that Gary must have found a way to control where his consciousness goes when he's asleep," Sinead suggested.

"Let's take it one step at a time," Buzzard replied. "The next comment is that those dreams allow him to take control of your body and mind. Again, we seem to be seeing evidence that this is true. Next, we have the description where he says he stabbed Michelle at Miss O'Brien's party. Was Michelle at the party?"

"No," I said, "her skiing injury kept her away."

"That's how we ended up in the pub yesterday," Sinead interjected. "She wanted to buy me dinner to apologise for missing my party."

"Understood. Next, he says that your mother is suffering hallucinations as a result of her dementia. Is that true?" Buzzard continued.

"Yes, she does. She comments about things and people who aren't there, talks as if she's seen relatives who are dead, that sort of thing."

"Yes, I have some experience dealing with family members who suffer dementia," Buzzard admitted. "Although, I'd never considered that the hallucinations may be anything more than that. However, the next comment about your mother hallucinating and witnessing the crime Gary committed in his lucid dream is quite remarkable, don't you think?"

"It's a little bit freaky," I confessed.

"Freaky, perhaps. But it would rationalise the hallucinations, would it not?"

"So, Mum's consciousness is drifting between Worldlines in the same way as if she were asleep?" Sinead asked. "And that's why she makes no sense whilst she's talking, because she's effectively in more than one place at a time?"

"Let's assume that's what the other Gary thinks, and that's what he's trying to communicate to us," Buzzard went on. "Because now he's saying that if this is true, he may have really stabbed the girl in one Worldline and that an innocent man may now be in prison for his crime, something you said you were fearful of this morning, Mr Jackson."

"That's right," I said.

"Then he attempts to offer evidence of this by citing an accident where he was run over by a lorry five years ago. This sounds like it may well be the accident you yourself avoided, Mr Jackson, when you were telling us your story last week."

"I was thinking that too," I said.

"Those injuries have caused him to lose some of the abilities in his right arm and he is now predominantly left-handed. However, the Gary who committed the crime isn't and, therefore, couldn't be in control of his own actions as he'd have used his right arm to commit the crime, rather than his left."

"He'd have had a job using my left arm to commit it," I said. "I also had minor injuries skiing. I'd have struggled to grip a knife with that hand on Saturday night, although it's feeling better now."

"Interesting," Buzzard continued. "And now he's asking for help to release who we will refer to as Gary number three."

"How on earth do we do that?" Sinead asked.

"Your mother used to have a work colleague, a very formidable lady called Betsy Cohen," Buzzard said to Sinead. "I've maintained a loose friendship with her over the years. She's a practised lucid dreamer, takes it all very seriously. She's also got a very scientific mind. I had more than one in-depth debate with her on various subjects, so she should take you seriously."

"Are you suggesting we should speak to her?" I asked. "If she's a lucid dreamer, and a lawyer, she may be able to help us."

"There would be worse places to start," Buzzard admitted.

"She may also think we're insane," Sinead suggested.

"Quite possibly," Buzzard smiled. "But if you tell her you've discussed this with me it may help her. I'd also like to speak to Michelle at some point."

"Why?" I asked.

"We're missing some big information here. We have the video, but how did Michelle end up filming it? I'd like to know what happened between you being possessed, as we will call it, and the moment she started recording. What other information did she gather?"

"I'll talk to her," I said cautiously.

"What about the other professor Gary mentioned?" Sinead asked. "Professor Charnock, do you know who he, or she, is?"

"I have no idea," Buzzard said, shaking his head. "It's not a name I've come across."

"They don't teach at the university?" I asked.

"Not that I know of."

"We need to find them," I said.

"I will ask the other science professors whether anyone with that name is a part of their network anywhere. Your doppelganger seemed to take it for granted that if you knew me, you'd also know Professor Charnock. Therefore, there must be a link somewhere. Let me enquire and see if I can track them down. In the meantime, it may be worth speaking to your mother about Betsy Cohen. If she were able to introduce you, it would allow you to speak to her regarding this."

"That might be a problem," said Sinead. "I don't think she'd even remember who Betsy was at this stage."

"If you have trouble then let me know and I'll try and dig her details out. Although it might be after Easter by the time I've done that."

"I don't really want to wait that long," I said.

"No, me neither," Sinead agreed.

"Then I think that determines our next step," Buzzard said. "I'll try and locate a Professor Charnock. Miss O'Brien, you will speak to your mother, and Mr Jackson, you will attempt to get Michelle to join us here on Thursday evening after lecture to discuss this further. Not to mention the other homework I've asked you to do for then, of course."

"Of course, Professor," said Sinead, turning to leave.

"Thank you, Professor," I said and followed her.

"Have a good afternoon," he called.

We closed the classroom door and walked away down the corridor.

"What homework?" I asked Sinead, with a touch of panic. Sinead just laughed and rolled her eyes.

"I'll tell you on the train," she said.

Chapter Eighteen

The task Sinead said Buzzard had given us was to find out about something called The Dirac Equation, so we could discuss it prior to Easter. I had no idea who or what that was at this point, and at this precise moment, I didn't care. We got to the tube station and I checked my phone. Still nothing from Michelle, but she must surely be in with the doctor by now. I'd try and ring her when we got to Euston.

"So, what are you going to say to Marcus?" I asked her.

"Oh, I don't know," she groaned. "I'm not used to having misunderstandings with a partner. Maybe I'm stressing about it more than I need to."

"Well, how do you feel about what happened, or the idea of it happening again?"

"I guess I'd just like him to be normal with me for a while, whatever normal is. I want to get used to being with him, and take smaller steps, before we jump in at the deep end with both feet."

"Then tell him that."

"But if he's never known any different, he may not know how to handle it either. I don't want to upset him."

"Why not?"

"Because he's my boyfriend."

"Well, let me upset him then."

"Gary!"

"Sorry."

We boarded the tube; it was quiet for the time of day. All the seats were taken, but we could stand and chat in relative privacy without anyone's armpit in either of our faces or anyone breathing down our necks.

"I know you're only trying to protect me and look out for me," she said, looking away from me. "But, if you are right and I am making a mistake here, then, respectfully, it is my mistake to make."

"Are you trying to make a mistake?"

"No, of course not."

"And if I could prevent you from making one, wouldn't you want me to?"

"I don't know," she sighed.

"Sinead, what is it? I feel like there's something I'm missing."

"Oh, it doesn't matter."

"Sinead," I said, putting my hand on her cheek. "You're my best friend and I love you. If you get hurt, I'll hurt for you too. I want you to be safe, and I want you to be happy. I don't want you putting yourself at risk for scum like Marcus Bray."

"He's not scum."

"Either way, something about this just isn't right. This isn't how I'd expect you to handle someone like him."

"Maybe that's the point," she said, moving away from me.

"What do you mean?"

"How would you describe me, in three words?" she asked.

"Warm, genuine, loyal."

"Ok, now describe Michelle in three words."

"Sexy, charming, funny."

"Do you see the difference?"

"No," I admitted.

"You said I was warm, genuine, and loyal. Do any of those things apply to Michelle?"

"Yeah, all of them, I guess."

"Now take Michelle's qualities, sexy, charming, and funny. How many of them am I?"

I hesitated for a fraction of a second but it's all it took.

"See what I mean?" she said.

"Sinead, why are you comparing yourself to Michelle?"

"Because you're right, Michelle is sexy, she always has been, even I can see it. But Marcus tells me he thinks I'm beautiful, and I've never had anyone say that to me before. It's empowering, it makes me feel confident and good about myself. I've never had anyone make me feel like that before."

"Unless he's playing on your insecurities to get what he wants from you."

"Well, I had thought that. But if he doesn't get what he wants, he might leave me."

"If he's that sort of person, he'll take what he wants from you and then leave you anyway."

"I'd thought that, too. But, at least that way, I can be sure that I've done everything that I can. It's not going to be me letting him down that causes the relationship to fail."

"But how are you going to feel afterwards?"

"That's where I might need your help," she said mournfully, as the train pulled into Euston station.

"Sinead, if you're taking risks because you're generally unhappy about things in life, I'd rather help you resolve those issues than stand by and watch you get hurt by someone like him."

"I know you would," she said, "And I appreciate it. Thank you. Are you heading back with me or are you going to wait here for Michelle?"

"I hadn't thought of that," I said, checking my phone. "She's not called or texted, so I assume she's still in there. I don't want to wait, though, in case she's gone back without telling me, and I end up standing here for hours like a lemon. Can I come back with you?"

"Of course," she said.

The conversation weighed heavily on my mind, along with everything else, although neither of us mentioned Marcus again all the way home. There are five women in the world that I truly love: my mum, Donna, Nicki, Michelle, and Sinead. I'd take a bullet for any of them, and I'd dish a couple of my own out if I thought it would protect them.

Although Badminton was the posher area, it was Barchester which sat on the mainline and was, therefore, the quickest route into London. We were almost back in Barchester by the time I heard from Michelle.

"Three broken ribs, they want to operate and have booked me in for next Friday, the 27th. Signed off work too, gutted."

I showed Sinead the text.

"Poor thing," she said. "She must be in so much pain with it. And she went to the trouble to come out with us yesterday too, feeling like that."

"Yeah, for all the good it did," I said. "I'll go and see her later."

Sinead dropped me at home, by which point Michelle and I had exchanged another few texts. I wasn't going to see her that night, but she said I could go over the next morning. As a result, I didn't sleep well as I had so much going through my head. Would yesterday fundamentally change something between me and Michelle? What could have possibly happened had I been hit by the lorry to make me want to hurt her? Is that dark side really within me? If so, can I use it to stop Marcus hurting Sinead? Is Sinead going to be able to find Betsy Cohen? How are we going to stop her thinking we're insane? Even if we do, how could any of this possibly help my counterpart in the other Worldline who could even be up on a murder charge as a result of all this? It was enough to make my brain start dribbling out of my ears.

I felt very nervous making my way to Michelle's the next morning. It's only a twenty-minute walk, but it did take me past the spot where the lorry had nearly hit me. I hadn't thought about the incident pretty much since the day it happened until recently, when I recounted it in class. I hadn't really considered it a key moment in my life. I'd nearly died on two other occasions too, once before that incident, and once last year, but it was the lorry moment that jumped out at me at the time. I wondered if any of this would be happening had I picked one of the others.

As I expected, Michelle's car was the only one in the drive when I got to her house. I knocked on the door and she answered quite quickly; she looked like she hadn't slept for days. I mean, she was still beautiful, but she looked rough. She wasn't wearing any makeup, meaning the friction burns to her face from the skiing accident were still clearly visible, as were mine which I'd largely forgotten about.

"Oh, baby," I said, wrapping my arms around her and giving her a hug. "Are you ok?"

"Ouch, not too tight," she replied.

"Sorry," I said, giving her a kiss. She hadn't brushed her teeth either, but I wasn't going to tell her I'd noticed. "How are you?"

"I'm a bit all over the place, to be honest."

"I thought you were. I'm so sorry about what happened the other day."

"It's not your fault. It wasn't you, was it?"

"No."

"And that has really freaked me out," she admitted. "How can someone else possess you like that?"

I explained to her the conversation Sinead and I had had with Professor Buzzard, about the theory of the other Worldlines, and the idea that when we dream or hallucinate it may be because our consciousness is drifting into those other Worldlines.

"It's deeply unsettling, isn't it?" she said.

"It is, but it doesn't really change anything, does it?"

"What do you mean?"

"Well, if the world is set up that way, then it's always been set up that way. It's not just started happening now. It's our knowledge of how things work that's been increased."

"Then I think I'd rather not know."

"Ignorance is bliss sometimes, isn't it?" I said.

We sat and hugged for a while without saying a word, although we were both still thinking about it.

"It's strange that it doesn't happen more often really, isn't it?" she commented.

"Why would you think that?"

"Well, even though there are, apparently, an infinite number of these so-called Worldlines, when you consider that we sleep for eight hours a day, we must be asleep in around a third of them at any one time."

"I guess so."

"So that's only two awake Worldlines for each sleeping one. This must be happening all the time, all day long, but without any of us picking up on it."

"You think every time we daydream or stop concentrating, that it leaves us vulnerable to other Worldlines?"

"It's no more far-fetched than anything else I've heard about this so far, although I do wish this consciousness of mine had chosen a Worldline where I haven't got three broken ribs."

"You could be in one where you had four broken ribs," I joked.

"Yeah, or one where I died."

"Don't say things like that."

"Or one where you weren't stupid enough to do it in the first place," she continued.

"Or one where we never went on holiday."

"Or even one where we're not even together."

"Don't say things like that either," I said.

"I'm only joking," she smiled. "But I guess if everything else is true then that could be too."

"I guess so," I said again.

"I'm a bit annoyed I'm going to be off work for so long. We're supposed to be saving to move."

"I haven't been back to work yet. I'll ask for extra shifts when I go in this evening, see if I can pick some up whilst the uni is closed over Easter."

"At least you get out of helping Donna to move."

"Oh yeah, your operation's the same day. Well done, did you pick that date on purpose?"

"No," she laughed before wincing again. "It's just the first date they could get me in. They need to put a plate in to hold the ribs in place whilst they heal."

"I didn't think they operated on broken ribs."

"Normally they don't if it's one or two, as they heal in about six weeks anyway, but the more there are the longer it takes and the less likely they'll heal naturally. I have three broken all next to each other, so they think I'll need some help."

"I'll come to the hospital with you on the day."

"I know you will," she said.

I suddenly remembered what Buzzard had said about finding out what had happened before the video.

"How did you end up filming in the pub?" I asked.

"You asked me to."

"But, why? What happened before then? When did you know something was wrong?"

"It took me a while. Mill brought the starters over."

"I remember that."

"Then you dropped your beer."

"I don't recall that. I remember noticing my jeans were wet."

"That was several minutes later."

"What happened in between?" I asked.

"I thought you were winding me up at first, as you said you were dreaming and asked if I knew who you were. You told me you were going to say something strange, and I made a comment about the fact you often do. You asked what you were in this Worldline, and I said you were an idiot."

"Thanks," I said.

"You told me you were being serious, so I said you were a physics student. You asked about Sinead and Professor Buzzard, and I started losing my patience with you as I still thought you were messing about. You seemed genuinely confused when I mentioned our holiday, then you asked me to get my phone out and start recording. I didn't understand, but I did what you asked. I recorded the message and, as I stopped recording, you jumped up when you noticed you'd spilt your beer. That's when you were back, and that's when I freaked out."

"It must have been scary for you."

"It was. I just wish it had happened whilst we were all there, or whilst you were with Sinead as that's who you seemed to want to speak to."

"Did I give any indication who Professor Charnock was?"

"No, who's Professor Charnock?"

"My counterpart mentioned him in the video but nobody knows who he is."

"Why would you need to know?"

"Because the other me was asking for help. I was going to try and see if I could give it."

"You can't be serious?"

"Of course, I am."

"Why?"

"We think that version of me, via a lucid dream, committed a serious crime against you. However, because that me was dreaming, it'll be another different version of me who's potentially in prison for that crime, which they'll have no memory of committing."

"So, you're going to go off and try and communicate with all these different Worldlines in the hope of what, finding him and releasing him?"

"I don't know yet. We're trying to reach out to one of Sinead's mum's business partners. She's also an old friend of Professor Buzzard, and he said she's a practised lucid dreamer. We're hoping she'll be able to help us."

At that, my phone beeped in my pocket. It was a text from Sinead, saying she'd contacted Betsy Cohen and arranged an appointment with her at three o'clock tomorrow.. I told Michelle about it.

"You're going to want me to come with you, aren't you?" Michelle asked.

"You don't have to but you can if you want."

"I don't want to. As I said, I'd rather not know about these things. But now I do, and it was me who had the experience with the other you. I guess I should come with you."

The next afternoon really couldn't come around quickly enough. Work was boring as it usually was, and then university on Wednesday morning (with a different professor) did little to stimulate my brain or steer it away from the Worldlines stuff. I was delighted to get to lunchtime so Sinead and I could get the train home and then head for our appointment with Betsy. We went around to Sycamore Village to pick up Michelle, then the three of us set off. I hadn't seen Professor Buzzard that day, but I really wished he was with us. However, if Betsy Cohen was as open-minded as Buzzard had suggested, we should hopefully be ok.

*****

"Let me get this straight," said Betsy Cohen, as the three of us sat in her office having muddled through attempting to explain this situation to her. "You're presumed dead," she said, eyeing Michelle, before turning her attention to me. "You killed her. Except it wasn't you, and it wasn't even Presumed Dead Michelle's boyfriend. It was yet another instance of you, committing the crime in a lucid dream."

"That's about the size of it," I confirmed.

"Except none of this happened, only in someone else's dream. And there's no murder to solve because the three of you are all still here."

"I appreciate how this sounds," I said.

"No, Mr Jackson, I don't think you do."

Buzzard had been correct about Betsy Cohen's appearance; she really was a formidable-looking woman. Close to six foot, mid fifties, well built, broad shoulders, shoulder-length hair dyed a dark red, and a deep, gruff voice that sounded like it had been caused by years of smoking, although there was no smell of tobacco in the office.

"Professor Buzzard told us that you practise lucid dreaming," Sinead said.

"Yes, what of it?"

"We were hoping we could use that in some way to help the Gary in prison in the other Worldline."

"I am, if I may say so," Betsy began, "Quite a good solicitor. I get innocent people off all the time and maybe, on occasion, I've even helped the guilty walk free. But even I am going to struggle to free someone who's committed a crime as someone else in a different dimension."

"Is there any way you think you might be able to help us?" I asked.

"To do what?" she protested, sounding flabbergasted. "I'm a solicitor, Mr Jackson, and you and your friends are scientists. You deal in theory, whereas I deal in evidence and proof. You can't prove any of what you're saying."

"But the video," I protested.

"The video shows you, sitting in a pub telling a story, that from my perspective, and from the perspective of everyone in this room, including you, hasn't happened. It proves nothing."

"How often do you manage to lucid dream?" I asked her.

"On average, about once a week," she said.

"For how long?"

"Since I was around your age, so about thirty years."

"So, let's call that fifty dreams a year, that's 1500 lucid dreams you'll have had."

"Ok," she shrugged.

"So that's 1500 Worldlines you've impacted over the years, 1500 versions of you who have had their lives affected by your actions."

"Be very careful, Mr Jackson," she warned.

"Mrs Cohen," said Sinead, "You've known my mum a long time."

"Indeed, I can't believe she's sent you here to argue this case, even in her current condition."

"She doesn't know I'm here. Even if I'd told her she wouldn't remember now. Her condition has deteriorated an awful lot lately. If you came to our house now, she wouldn't remember who you were."

"I'm sorry to hear that," said Betsy, her tone softening.

"If this were my mum arguing the case rather than me, what would you say to her?"

"I'd tell her she was bloody puddled."

"But if she insisted, would you send her away or would you try and help her?"

Betsy leaned back in her chair, causing it to make an awful creaking sound as she did.

"What exactly do you want me to do?" she asked.

"At the minute, nothing. But we're meeting Professor Buzzard tomorrow evening at the university to try and discuss the next steps. It's at six o'clock. Is it possible you could join us?"

"Most likely, we might ask you to teach one or all of us the method to lucid dream," I added.

"Who else will be there?" Betsy asked.

"The three of us, Professor Buzzard, and possibly someone called Professor Charnock, if Professor Buzzard can track him down."

"Richard Charnock?" she asked suddenly. "How is he involved in this?"

"I have no idea. Nobody knows who he is except my doppelganger on the video. Do you know him?"

"Yes, he's the Head of Pharmaceuticals at the University College Hospital. He applied for a job as the professor of chemistry at your university the summer before last but was overlooked for it."

"Do you know how we can contact him?" I asked.

"I could probably do it," said Michelle. "I do work there, after all."

"Yes, and you're signed off for a month," I countered. "I'll do it."

"No, I'll do it," said Betsy. "I'll contact Leyton at the university then I'll give Richard a ring. If he agrees to go to your meeting tomorrow, I will come also, out of pure curiosity if nothing else."

"That's all we can ask for now," I said. "Thank you, Mrs Cohen."

I spent that night at Michelle's. As tomorrow was Thursday, our lecture wasn't until after lunch, and our meeting with Professor Buzzard was for after the lecture, so we had nothing to get up for. Michelle would normally drop me off at the station, but as her ribs were preventing her from driving, Sinead had agreed to pick me up.

"Can you believe," said Michelle as we lay in bed hugging, "That this time last week we were getting drunk and making snow angels in Italy?"

"Has it really only been a week?" I said.

"Yeah, it was last Wednesday night. Thursday morning was when we crashed on the mountain. Things feel so different now, don't they?"

"It's certainly been a bit surreal since we came back, hasn't it?"

"When we were over there, I felt like we hadn't a care in the world," she continued. "Now I don't feel like I even know what the world is anymore."

"It's the same as it's always been. It's just we've been exposed to some of life's more weird quirks the last few days."

"I'd call them more than quirks."

"But life is the way it is," I explained. "There's nothing we can do about it, except learn and try and get along with it."

"I'm not sure I'm going to find it that easy," she said.

"You have no choice, really," I said more bluntly than I intended. "But you won't have to deal with this on your own. We'll work through it together."

"Every time I drift off or go a bit absentminded, I worry that someone else, or another me, will take over me. I'm trying so hard to remain focused and concentrate all of the time, but it's exhausting. I feel so tired."

"We don't know what causes it though. We still don't even know if it's real, I guess. We've just been exposed to things that make us think it is. Let's get this meeting with Professor Buzzard out of the way tomorrow, and then hopefully we can find a way to start putting all of this behind us and move on with our lives a bit."

"Yeah, I hope so," she said. She tried to lean over to kiss me, but it was too uncomfortable for her, so I went to her.

Sinead and I met Michelle in The Oasis at 5:30 the next day, once our lecture had finished. Sinead had told me that Marcus had wanted to join us, but she'd managed to convince him otherwise. Apparently, he'd gone off in a huff about it, but I rejected the urge to try and convince her to end it with him. I was her best friend, and I needed to support her, not be against her in this. If I fought with her about Marcus, I might end up losing her to him.

By the time the three of us made it back into Professor Buzzard's office, Betsy Cohen was already there, along with a small, thin, dark-haired man who I took to be Professor Charnock.

"Come in, come in," Buzzard called in his usual manner. I pulled the door open and let the two ladies through ahead of me.

"Miss O'Brien, Mr Jackson," Buzzard said, before turning to Michelle and shaking her hand. "You must be Michelle. I've heard quite a bit about you recently, take a seat. How are the ribs?"

"Sore, but thank you for asking," she said.

"Mrs Cohen here has just been introducing me to Richard Charnock," Buzzard said. "I think I now understand how your comrade knew of him."

"Yeah, I applied for a job here a couple of years ago but I didn't get it. I guess in another Worldline I must have been more successful," he said.

"Mrs Cohen was telling us yesterday. She'd said you'd applied for the Head of Chemistry," I said. "Although I don't really see how this would fall into the area of chemistry."

"We have just been discussing that," he said. "But can we start from the beginning? What's happened, and why are we all here?"

Sinead, Michelle, and I all retold our stories of the events of the last few days for what felt like the umpteenth time, and the video was again passed around. We all watched it through even though Charnock was the only one of the group who hadn't seen it before.

"A very interesting sequence of events," Charnock commented. "I'm glad you summoned me for this. Thank you, Professor, Betsy."

"What do we do now?" I asked. "Do we just forget it and pretend it never happened, or is there a way to help my counterparts in the other Worldlines?"

"From what I can gather, there's only one of you that needs help," Buzzard said. "There's another one of you who's requested help on their behalf, that would be the Gary in the video. Then there's you, who has been tasked with providing it."

"I'm going to need to learn to lucid dream, aren't I?" I said.

"That's what I thought," Sinead said.

"I disagree," said Buzzard. "I don't think it can be you."

"But you just said..." I began but Buzzard cut me off.

"I know, but think about it. Imagine for a moment Michelle had attended Sinead's party, and you had indeed been possessed at that point, meaning you stabbed her without your knowledge. Where would you be now?"

"In prison, most likely," I said.

"Exactly! And if you lucid dream and find yourself in a prison cell, to start talking about different Worldlines and being possessed, it's unlikely to be heard by the correct audience. You'd most likely find you'd get your counterpart out of prison but straight into a mental institute, and again with no idea what he did to get there. No, it can't be you."

"Me, then," said Michelle.

"You may well be dead," said Buzzard, in a far more casual tone of voice than I'd expected. "Therefore, there is no chance of you reaching the correct Worldline."

"Surely she is dead?" said Charnock, "And alive, and every other result that comes from a stabbing."

"Quite possibly, so we need to contact the Worldline with the most severe outcome, as that is the Worldline with the most extreme punishments for our innocent party. That would mean you will be dead, and therefore it can't be you either, Michelle. I'm sorry."

"Could I do it?" asked Sinead.

"Of the three of you, you would certainly be the best candidate. But I don't think you're the right choice either."

"You're not suggesting you do it yourself, are you, Professor?" I asked him.

"No, I don't have the first idea how to lucid dream," he replied, turning to Betsy. "But you do."

"I know about lucid dreaming, but I don't understand any of the science stuff. What would I do?"

"You'd need to defend Gary, of course, and you would need to explain this to your counterpart in the other Worldline."

"How would I do that? I can lucid dream, but I can't control where I lucid dream, and I can't do it for a long time. What would I even say? It's not like I can take the video clip in there with me."

"I believe that's where Mr Charnock may be able to help us," said Buzzard, turning his head to our resident chemist. "Do you have any drugs or medications that would help to induce lucid dreaming?"

"Pfft," said Charnock. "We've got nothing licenced that would do it."

"Anything unlicensed? Anything in the trial stage? Anything hypothetical?"

"We are trying to get approval to trial a drug that contains Phencyclidine, what you might know as Angel Dust. It's a dissociative hallucinogenic drug that we want to use to monitor brainwave patterns in people as they sleep."

"To what end?" asked Betsy.

"We believe people who recall dreams actually sleep better than those that don't. People who never recall dreams are more likely to suffer from so-called Tired All The Time syndrome. If the trials ever get off the ground and we can prove it, we may be able to prescribe it to help induce dreaming in patients and help them stop feeling so fatigued. How you could have got wind of that though," he said, turning to me, "Is beyond me."

"I knew nothing about it until just then," I said. "I still don't understand it now."

"I think this could potentially be more evidence of the other Worldlines," Buzzard commented. "One thing we don't understand is how time affects these things. It could be that in that other Worldline your medical trials are approved, or maybe they've even been successful."

"I guess so," said Charnock, who looked like he had a hard time believing this.

"Forgive me for saying so, Leyton," said Betsy. "But this is proper freaky, with no real basis in fact."

"I fully understand you saying so," Buzzard replied. "But surely there's enough here to pique all of our scientific interests? If there's a chance to learn and evolve our theories, then I'd like us to explore it."

"You mean you'd like me to explore it," she said tartly.

"You are the logical choice, but you're not forced into anything. If you decide not to help us, we'll find another option, possibly involving Miss O'Brien here."

Betsy Cohen rolled her eyes.

"How will this work?" she asked.

We sat there for about another half an hour thrashing out the details. Betsy Cohen explained how she would normally induce a lucid dream. Richard Charnock described the expected effects of the drug and how it might help give Betsy more control over the dream. Professor Buzzard talked her through the details of the video again and the information she would need to pass to the other Worldline. The three of us mainly just sat there, adding the occasional comment or clarifying facts. However, by the end of the meeting, we appeared to have a plan. Betsy was going to take a tablet to induce a lucid dream. Charnock suggested she do it as soon as possible whilst these events were fresh in her mind and she was more likely to naturally dream about this topic. She'd then need to investigate whether Michelle's apparent murder had been committed by me at Sinead's party, then leave a written account of the event for her own counterpart in that Worldline to pick up to enable her to try and defend him. It sounded very complicated and very convoluted but eventually Betsy agreed.

"There's one other thing you'll need to do whilst you're there," said Buzzard.

"Oh, just one more thing?" Betsy replied sarcastically.

"We'll need to know whether you've been successful. That instance of you will need to find a way back here to give us the result of the case, assuming you all wish to know it?" he said, asking the group. We all nodded.

"How do we know that version of me can lucid dream?"

"Because you've been doing it for years and the murder only took place at the weekend, it stands to reason you are more likely to be able to than not. However, you may need Mr Charnock's drug to do it. You must include that in your note."

"It's going to be more like an essay," she sighed. "And I still think the whole thing is insane."

"Quite possibly," Buzzard acknowledged.

Betsy Cohen got up and reached for her coat and bag.

"Will you do it?" I asked.

"How hard can it be?" she said in that same sarcastic tone.

Chapter Nineteen
The Blue Line

My trial was scheduled for the first week in June which, given that Michelle had died on the 14th of March, meant I'd have been in prison for nearly three months by the time the trial came around. I wish I could say that life was getting easier during that period but it wasn't. Granted, I'd settled into the routine of prison life. We were awoken at eight o'clock and went straight down for breakfast. Morning was for either work or education, and I'd chosen the latter. Lunch was at twelve o'clock, then there was outdoor time followed by time in the gym or religious time. This time I'd chosen the former. Then it was back to the cells until dinner at five unless you had a visitor, and that was usually around 4 pm. Back in your cell after dinner and lock-up was at 6 pm until the next day. I hated being there, and my mental health was deteriorating, but there was a structure, organisation, and discipline to the setup and the activities that I begrudgingly admired.

Visiting itself had also become routine; my mum came on a Monday, my sisters on a Wednesday alternating between Donna and Nicki from one week to the next, and Sinead visited on a Friday. Dad hadn't been once, and I was beginning to wonder if I'd see him at all over the next twenty years. Nicki and I had always been closer to Mum, whereas Donna had been dad's favourite; if she'd been in here, then I'm sure he'd have come up every day. However, he clearly couldn't give a toss about me.

It was during my fourth week inside when my mental state took its first major blip, which was the week of Michelle's funeral. Even up to the day of the service, I kept thinking some miracle would occur that would mean I'd be able to go and pay my respects to her. That there hadn't been, and the fact there'd never been any likelihood of it, despite me knowing I'd not done anything wrong, left me with feelings of anger and resentment. Not towards anyone in particular but to life itself. She was my girl, my one and only. Nobody at that funeral would have loved her like I did. Her parents and her brother would have loved her as deeply, but the deep, spiritual and emotional connection I had with her couldn't be surpassed by anyone. We knew each other intimately, and I missed everything about her. The way she looked, the way she smiled, the way she laughed, how she'd take the mickey out of me when I said stupid things. Her enthusiasm for life and for our relationship, her tendency to make decisions on a whim, the meals we had in the pub, the train rides we took in silence after work. The nights in the summer when the sun would wake me up shining through the curtains at five in the morning, and it was light enough in the room for me to watch her sleeping. Every single part of it hurt like nothing I'd ever experienced before. And yet I couldn't talk about it in here. Yes, there were medical staff, and the chaplain, and even Kirsty, but they all had something in common. They all believed I was guilty, and that my feelings stemmed from guilt around what I'd done. None of them truly accepted that I hadn't done anything wrong. I could understand fully why that was the case, but it certainly didn't make it any easier to deal with.

The only person I could talk to was Sinead, but even that was difficult. I only saw her for about half an hour a week, which was nowhere near enough time. Her mum had been hospitalised after another fall, and this time had broken her hip. They thought it might have been fractured from the previous fall the day before her party, but somehow, they hadn't spotted it. She was also having trouble with Marcus, who himself was struggling to come to terms with the events of the party. She'd also said he had some weird kinks that she wasn't entirely comfortable with, but up to now, she'd not elaborated on what she meant. I'd gathered she'd meant sexual, but asking her about her sex life when she'd come to visit me in prison didn't feel right somehow. I could have bought phone credit and called her, but I suspected those calls were monitored, and I wasn't going to talk about personal stuff on that line.

She'd also not been able to get anywhere with Buzzard in trying to find a scientific explanation for what had gone on that night, and I was facing the prospect of a long prison stretch for a crime I hadn't committed. My mum and my sisters believed me but, apparently, Dad didn't and that, according to Mum, was his main reason for not visiting.

My solicitor wasn't helping, and I'd ended up telling him I'd plead guilty just to stop him badgering me about it. The downside to this was that he wasn't actually preparing a defence, but I couldn't see what he'd be able to do anyway. I didn't like the man, and I didn't trust him to act in my best interests. If the situation were less serious, I might have pleaded not guilty just to piss him off. In truth, though, I hadn't really decided what I was going to do.

My relationship with my cellmate had at least softened somewhat. He still had a superiority complex and liked to be referred to as Mr Ramsey. Apparently, I wasn't important enough to call him by his first name yet. However, he had stepped in twice to assist me when other prisoners had taken exception to me being there and the reasons behind my incarceration. He made it quite clear on both occasions that he begrudged having to do it, and I felt indebted myself to whoever it was he was repaying his debt to.

It was Wednesday of the last week in April. I'd just returned to my cell after an hour in the gym lifting weights. I had at least been able to shower, and I'd earned the right to do it unsupervised now. Despite my mental health worries, drowning in the shower wasn't the way I wanted to go. My muscles were aching though, in my arms, legs, and across the centre of my chest. I was looking forward to seeing Donna, as it was her week to visit. However, I was surprised when Kirsty came to the door and announced an unexpected change.

"Jackson, visitor, there's a man waiting for you in room two."

"A man?" I said.

"Yes. You do know what one is, I assume?"

"I think I've encountered them before," I responded sarcastically, as even though she was the prison officer, I felt I got on quite well with her. "Who is it?"

"No idea," she said. "I'll take you to the room, though."

I knew it wouldn't be Warren Dawlish. He didn't have to wait until visiting time. As my solicitor, he could just turn up whenever he wanted, as long as it was between the hours of eight and six. Kirsty, who was a tiny woman at least a whole foot shorter than me, noticed the shift in my attitude.

"Are you really so surprised that you may have a male visitor?" she asked.

"Yes. I've been in here six weeks and not had any male visitors. It'll be either Marcus, my best friend's partner, or Will, who's my sister's boyfriend. He and his twin brother, Henry, were best mates with me at school."

"I find it odd that someone who is in here for the crime you are in for would have so many female visitors," she said. There was no accusation or cynicism in her tone, she was merely just commenting. "Were you quite the ladies' man on the outside?"

"Oh, God no!" I said. "It's only four visitors, my mum, my two sisters, and my best mate."

"Yeah, I get on better with men, to be fair. It's why I work in a male prison rather than a female one. I might get lewd comments occasionally, but I can be reasonably sure none of the inmates are going to beat me up. I wouldn't feel so safe surrounded by women."

"I don't feel safe in here," I said. "If it wasn't for Cyrus standing up for me, I'd have been beaten up at least twice already. They think Michelle was just another victim of domestic violence but she wasn't. She was my first love and only love. I knew how lucky I was to be punching so far above my weight, as she was way out of my league really."

She didn't pass comment, and I was glad she didn't. I expected her to ask why I'd killed her, but I'd told her before that I didn't remember, meaning she either believed and respected that, or didn't see the point in pushing me on it again. She opened the door and led me into room two where, sitting waiting for me at a table against the far wall, was my dad.

For weeks I'd been furious with him for not being bothered about me rotting in here, and I'd sworn I'd give him a piece of my mind when I did next see him. However, his visit had taken me so much by surprise, and I was feeling so low in myself, that it all just faded away in that moment and I found myself genuinely just pleased to see him. I think I was even smiling when I got to the table.

"How are you, son?" he asked in that gruff voice of his.

"I've been better," I admitted. "I didn't think I was going to see you until I was released."

"Neither did I," he said.

"So, why are you here?"

"I wanted to make sure you were ok."

"Surely Mum has been giving you updates?"

"Yes, she has, and she's getting more and more worried about you. I wanted to come and tell you that you're not alone in here."

"I think you'll find I am."

"Believe it or not, I do know what it's like," he said calmly, and he looked around the room like someone surveying a house they were planning to buy. "I swore I'd never set foot in this place again."

"What? You've been here before?" I said, genuinely confused.

"A long time ago," he said. "Before you were born."

"You've done time in here?" I said, bewildered.

"1988 to 1991," he said. "I was a getaway driver in a series of armed robberies."

"Of course you were," I said dismissively.

"Who do you think asked Cyrus to look out for you?"

"It was you!" I said, unable to believe what I was hearing. "You know Cyrus Ramsey?"

"Yep. I used to work for him back in the late 1980s. Me and your mum always swore we'd never tell any of you about this, but I think you need to know. I'd only been going out with your mum for about a year, but she stood by me and waited for me to come out so we could get married. That's how she knew what to include in your prison bag, as she'd done it nearly thirty years ago for me. Cyrus was a TV and video engineer, which in the mid-80s was quite a good profession. He lived in Milton Keynes. I was an apprentice mechanic at the time. I was only about nineteen, and I'd just moved down from Scotland to be with your mum. I'd recently passed my driving test and was a bit of a boy racer. I'd taken out a loan to buy a ten-year-old Chevrolet Chevelle Laguna. It was the model of car that was used in NASCAR racing in the late 1970s. However, I'd bitten off more than I could chew and was struggling with the repayments. Cyrus was impressed by my speed and manoeuvrability when driving the vans around and asked me if I wanted to earn some extra money at evenings and weekends doing some driving for him. He was only two years older than me, but he was clearly quite affluent for his age and stature. Naturally, I said yes. Anyway, to cut a long story short, they started robbing nightclubs on weekends. Northampton, Milton Keynes, Luton, we did about seven all in all. I knew they were turning places over, but I wasn't involved in any of the robberies directly and I never hurt anyone. I was just the group's getaway driver. Anyway, the police got wise to what Cyrus and his crew were doing, and one week when we were in Luton, they knew we were going to be there and surrounded us the second I started pulling away. The thing is, the night we got pulled, Cyrus wasn't with us. His wife was heavily pregnant at the time, and she'd gone to the hospital with stomach pains. He'd gone with her and left one of his lieutenants in charge. However, the police knew Cyrus was the ringleader and he was who they wanted. They arrested him but were struggling to prove his involvement, so they offered me a deal. Rat on the group, tell them everything I knew about Cyrus, and I'd walk away scot-free. Cyrus would have been off the street the same day, but it also meant he'd miss the birth of his son. For all his wrongdoings, he'd helped me out a lot, so I refused to break ranks and got sent down with the rest of them. I got six years and three months defending that son of a bitch, of which I served three years, two months, and eleven days. Cyrus was eventually convicted too of course,

Worldlines

but not before he'd got to see his son be born and spend time with his new baby. He's always said that was due to me, and described it as a debt that could never be repaid. I hadn't seen him in nearly twenty-five years, but when you got caught up in this business with Michelle, I immediately looked him up. I booked a visitor's slot and came here to see him the day your mum came to see you at the police station. I told him that if he truly felt indebted to me that he would look after you, and we could finally wipe the slate clean. He said he'd see to it. So, now you know."

"What the hell!" was all I could think to say, such was the scale of what Dad had just told me. He'd had this entire secret life before he'd had kids, and now he'd suddenly blurted it all out. Uncontrollably, I found myself suddenly laughing out loud.

"This is nonsense!" I said hysterically. "How have you even managed to hide this all these years?"

"It's why I was so angry with you, as you were suddenly making the same mistakes I had. It's also why I don't believe this scientific rubbish Sinead keeps pedalling, as I know it's in our genes to do bad things. I've done them."

"You think it's genetic?"

"You're the middle child and the only son. If anyone was going to seriously mess their life up, it was going to be you."

"Oh, thanks."

"Have you ever wondered why I've always been harsher on you than I have on the girls? They take after your mum, especially Donna. You're cut from the same cloth as me though, and I was worried you'd end up making similar mistakes to what I did. Didn't think you'd go this far wrong, though."

"Dad, I didn't kill Michelle," I said, my serious face returning immediately. "Whatever happened, whatever possessed my body to do that to her, it wasn't driven from this brain. I absolutely mean that one million per cent."

282

"I don't really care," said Dad. "I came to make sure you did the right thing at your trial."

"And what would that be?"

"Plead guilty."

"Dad, are you insane?"

"No, but you must."

"Why?"

"Do you love her?"

"Of course, I do."

"And her family?"

"Dad, they are my family as much as you and Mum are."

"Then spare them. Don't make them sit through all the gory details of how their little girl was butchered to death by you in the hope you can get off on some Mickey Mouse theory. Whether you like it or not, you are responsible for her death, just as I was as responsible for those robberies as anyone else. Whether you're consciously aware of it or not, your body was the vehicle that delivered that fatal blow to her, and if she means anything to you, you won't make her family go through it."

"You'd rather I spent the next twenty years in here for something I didn't do?"

"You're going to spend the next twenty years in here either way," he said. "Because, believe me, we've seen the evidence ourselves and you're not getting away with this. If you truly love her, don't put them through that ordeal. Do the right thing, plead guilty."

I could see the logic to his argument but couldn't help thinking he was massively missing the point. I was also quite offended by the idea that he'd always expected I'd end up throwing my life away; I mean, it's not like I'd been in trouble before. I was a fully-grown man with a completely clean record who was in prison for a crime I didn't remember committing. It was hardly the same as him consciously agreeing to drive getaway cars for Cyrus half a dozen times whilst he went robbing nightclubs. Five minutes after I'd left the room, the feelings of anger I felt towards him before our meeting returned and intensified.

I wasn't in a good mood when I got back to my cell, and I wasn't exactly thrilled to see Cyrus either. My relationship with my dad had always been slightly fractious, and I always felt I'd disappointed him as a son even though I'd never really done anything wrong. Now I understood it was because he was looking for his own deficiencies within me, deficiencies that Cyrus had helped to find within him. Any problems with the relationship I had with Dad, they were all this man's fault.

"So, it was my dad," I said, sitting down on the bed. Cyrus burst out laughing.

"Oh my God, he actually told you about it?"

"Just now."

"Bad blood runs in your family it would seem."

"Then how come he never came back here after his release?"

"Because of me," he said, "and your mum, of course. He saw what being inside away from my son was doing to me, and how it was affecting his development also, growing up without a father. When he got out of here, he still had money left over from the work we'd done together, but it wasn't enough. He intended to finish the apprenticeship he started as a mechanic, and then marry your mum, get a place together and start a family. I offered to let him pick up where he left off and to introduce him to a few friends of mine. Unfortunately, three months after he got out, your mum got pregnant with Donna, and he decided at that point to keep his nose clean. He could have avoided prison time altogether if he'd grassed me up. He didn't though, and I got to see Nicholas born and spend the first four months of his life with him before the police finally had the evidence to charge me. Of course, I then went the other way. My girlfriend left me, and I rarely saw Nicholas until he was an adult. I'd try and make the effort when I was out to make amends, but I always got lured back into crime and ultimately back here. I've spent more time in here than out in the last twenty-five years."

"When are you due to be released this time?"

"I'll be eligible for parole in November. Until then, I've got your back."

Those conversations had given me a lot to process, and as a result, I didn't sleep well that night. What the hell had gone wrong with the world lately? My girlfriend had been killed, I was a murderer, my dad was an ex-con, and his old boss was now my cellmate. How had all of this happened? I also didn't understand how they'd managed to keep it secret for all these years. Of course, now I had to keep it too, but I couldn't keep something like that from Donna and Nicki indefinitely. It would be a week until I saw either of them again anyway, so it did at least give me time to decide what to do. I couldn't wait to tell Michelle about it all.

My head dropped and the tears began again. This wasn't the first time this had happened, where I'd got so excited about seeing Michelle that, for a brief moment, I'd forgotten she was gone. It seemed an odd thing to happen given where I was and what I was going through, but there were occasional moments when I thought about her and got the butterflies feeling I always got when I was going to see her. The pain of it being pulled away time and again when the realisation kicked in was indescribable.

It did allow me to have my first proper dream about Michelle, though, since she'd died. Of course, it was even more horrible when I woke up to the real world, but at least, in a weird way, I got to see her face again.

I dreamt we were in San Francisco, swimming in the bay by the Golden Gate Bridge. Michelle looked beautiful, wearing a deep purple halter-neck bikini, and she had her usually curly blonde hair up in a bun in a vain attempt to keep it dry. I was talking to her about a previous visit to San Francisco, which was odd given that I knew I'd never been. She asked me if I wanted lunch, but as I climbed back into the canoe, I slipped and fell forward.

The shock of falling caused me to kick out in real life, and I ended up booting the cell wall with my foot.

The pain subsided after a few minutes, but I didn't sleep well again for the rest of the night and, as a result, I was really tired at breakfast the next morning. I was also due to start a new module on the biology course I'd enrolled in, but didn't really feel I had the mental strength to concentrate on anything difficult for a long period of time. However, as I was waiting to be collected, Kirsty appeared.

"Jackson, your solicitor is here to see you. She's waiting in room one."

"She? My solicitor's a man."

"She said she's taken over your case. Were you not aware?"

"No," I said with a hint of annoyance. "Any idea who she is?"

"I have seen her before, but no, not really. I'll take you down to her."

In a way, I was pleased to be rid of Warren Dawlish. In terms of useful advice, he'd given me exactly none up to now. However, I wasn't entirely sure what a new solicitor would do to change that.

Kirsty showed me into the interview room where I was introduced to a really formidable-looking woman, she intimidated me just standing up. She was about six-foot-tall, in her mid-fifties, well built with broad shoulders, and shoulder-length hair dyed a dark red.

"Mr Jackson," she said in a deep gruff voice that sounded like it had been caused by years of smoking. "My name is Betsy Cohen. I'm a partner in a legal firm that was previously co-owned by Mary O'Brien, and I'm also an old friend of Professor Leyton Buzzard. I'm here to take over your case."

"Sorry, what?" I said, unable to compute what she'd just said.

"It's probably better if we sit down."

I did as she requested.

"Can we start at the beginning," she asked. "What do you remember about the murder?"

"Nothing, and I've already been through this so many times."

"I understand, but this is important. Your case file says you have a small memory gap?"

"Yes, about twelve seconds long," I said with a hint of irritation at having to re-live this again. "It starts from the moment Michelle handed me the knife to cut the gateaux to the moment Marcus Bray hit me in the back of the head and knocked me to the ground. I can remember nothing between those two events."

"This will sound like a strange question, but have you ever been run over by a lorry?"

"What? No, of course not."

"Any near misses?"

I thought for a moment. There was the time when I was going for the school exam, the story I'd told Professor Buzzard about in lecture, but how could this woman possibly know about that and what relevance could it have now?

"Once," I said. "I was on my way to school to sit my English Literature GCSE. I ran across the road when there was a lorry coming, and I dropped my pen. Instinctively, I bent down to pick it up, but the two lads I was with swore that I was inches from the thing flattening me. Why do you ask?"

"I was just fact-checking," she said with a hint of a smile. "I must admit I had no idea who you were, and I'd never heard anything of your case until two weeks ago when this note arrived at my desk."

She took a folded A4 piece of paper from her bag and handed it to me.

"I'd just finished a long and tiring case. I went back to the office to do some paperwork before heading off, but I must have dozed off at my desk. When I woke up, that note was there, written in my own handwriting."

I opened up the note. It read as follows:

Betsy,

You will have no memory of writing this, although I hope you recognise it as your own handwriting. I am writing this through a lucid dream that I'm having in a different Worldline, and I'm hoping you're also a practised lucid dreamer and can relate to what I'm saying.

In my Worldline, we've learned that dreams are a form of reality. When we remember dreams, we're seeing our consciousness drift through those different Worldlines. A lucid dream appears to allow our consciousness to briefly possess our own bodies in those Worldlines. Your old friend, Leyton at the UCSE, will be able to explain it to you better than I can.

On your computer screen, you'll see a news article for a murder that was committed on March 14th. The man in prison for the crime, Gary Jackson, is innocent, although it won't appear that way when you look at the case. He stabbed his girlfriend in the neck at a friend's party, and there's evidence of him doing so. However, he was being possessed by another consciousness from a different Worldline, and as a result, he'll have no memory of the crime. The version of Gary in the offending Worldline carries lifelong injuries from an accident where he was hit by a lorry in his teens and is unable to use his right hand. If you can prove that the Gary native to your Worldline committed the crime with his left hand, you may be able to prove his innocence. Leyton can help you, and so can Mary's daughter, Sinead. She's Gary's best friend. You should also talk to Richard Charnock. He's experimenting with a drug called phencyclidine. It should allow you to get back to my Worldline and tell me what happened.

I'm going to wake up in a minute and so are you. Please don't dismiss this. Please act on it. An innocent man's freedom depends on it.

Kindest regards,

Betsy

"What do you make of that?" she asked.

I read the note again to make sure I'd read it correctly, as the content seemed to explain my situation, but also seemed completely and utterly absurd.

"Did you write this?" I asked her.

"Apparently so," she said. "It is my handwriting, but I have no recollection of writing it. The CCTV in my office shows me doing so, though."

"The CCTV footage from the party shows me stabbing Michelle too, but I don't remember doing it."

"I believe you. Our job now is to convince a jury of that."

"How on earth are we going to do that?"

"Leave that with me for now. I've already spoken to Professor Buzzard and I'm discussing it further with him this afternoon. I'll probably call him as a witness to your trial. I've also spoken to your friend Sinead. I attempted to talk to Mary also, but I believe you are aware of the state of her health. However, I think that video is proof of your innocence as much as it proves your guilt."

"How?"

"You did commit the crime with your left hand."

"Did I?" I said. "I hadn't noticed."

"You did. What I need to do is find a body language expert to effectively read that video and prove that the person at the table isn't the person that walked up to it. Not mentally, anyway. If they can detect the change in body language, and the subsequent change back, we may still be able to corroborate your story. I'm not going to lie to you, I'm kind of staking my reputation on this, and it's a hell of a long shot."

"Then why are you doing it?" I asked, feeling dazed by what I was hearing.

"I believe in justice, Mr Jackson, and you deserve justice for yourself as much as Michelle does."

"Yes, but you could have ripped that note up and thrown it in the bin, as even to me it sounds a bit absurd, even though it does explain things. Why have you picked my case up?"

"The note you've just read refers to lucid dreaming. Do you know what that is?"

"Isn't it when you become aware that you're dreaming?"

"More or less," she said. "It allows you to take control of your own dreams. It's a very powerful, very enriching experience. I've been practising it for years and years, have done it hundreds of times. What I didn't understand until now is that I was experiencing other realities, or Worldlines, as you term them. I've impacted all of those Worldlines with my own actions, and I understand how something like this might have happened to you, even if I don't understand the 'sciencey' bits. That's what I need Professor Buzzard's help with."

"So, another version of me, in another Worldline, had a lucid dream, where their consciousness drifted into this Worldline, which then took possession of my body before stabbing Michelle and then leaving again."

"As ludicrous as it sounds, that's what we think, yes. That Gary would have probably woken up at the instant he stuck the knife in, which would have been when Marcus Bray knocked you to the ground."

"So why did that person want to stab her?"

"I have no idea."

"And what will happen to him now?"

"Nothing, most likely. In his Worldline, Michelle is still alive so from that perspective he hasn't actually committed a crime."

"He hasn't committed a crime? He's murdered my girlfriend!" I said furiously.

"Mr Jackson, please calm down. As you are no doubt aware, things you do in your dreams are not considered crimes. Now, I have no idea what's happened in other Worldlines that has resulted in me ending up with this note. However, the only explanation I can come up with is the Gary who has committed the crime in his Worldline has learned that, somehow, he's impacted others, and is now trying to rectify it."

"He's not going to be able to bring Michelle back, is he?"

"No, he isn't. But he may be able to help prove that you weren't responsible. He'll have made an innocent mistake in a dream that you are paying the price for, and having realised that, he's managed to get a message to me, via myself, to try and clear your name."

"It's Michelle who paid the price. She's dead now because of him."

"There's no way he could have known that."

"Why would he have wanted to stab her in the first place?"

"I can't answer that either."

"Then how on earth is this going to fly in court?" I was raging now and had stood up. Kirsty had also come over to intervene.

"Jackson, calm down or I'll take you back to your cell," she ordered.

"I'm here to try and assist you, Mr Jackson," Betsy stated. "But if you'd rather I didn't, then I won't. Enjoy your sentence."

"No, wait," I said, sitting back down. "I'm sorry, I know none of this is your fault. It's just I always knew there had to be another explanation for what had happened. Now you've given me one and it makes sense, but to know that it really was someone else who did this, and that I may end up being convicted for it because they're out of reach in another Worldline makes me so angry. I didn't mean to take it out on you."

"I understand the anger, and I don't mean to be the bearer of bad news, but proving this is your only chance of clearing your name. Do you want me to pick this up and run with it on your behalf?"

"Yes, please," I said. "Do whatever you can. Speak to my family too. It will be good for Dad to realise I'm innocent too."

Chapter Twenty

I should have been pleased, and in a way, I was, but I also knew now that even if Betsy Cohen's defence worked, we were never going to get justice for Michelle. In a way, it would be easier for her family if I was convicted, as at least they may get some peace from it. However, it had given me a fair hope that I may not spend the next few decades locked up in here, even if I did feel guilty, under the circumstances, of being happy about it.

Betsy was as good as her word, and for the next six weeks, she worked tirelessly trying to amass evidence and testament from scientists across the world to try and back up the claims that I wasn't in control of my own actions at the instant Michelle was fatally wounded. She went through the video meticulously and, although I found the stabbing itself too harrowing to continue watching, I was able to clarify some points for her. She was correct about the crime being committed with my left hand, something I should have been unable to do as I had injured my hand on the skiing holiday, and shouldn't have been able to grip the knife as I did in that hand. To support this, there was CCTV footage from earlier in the night, where we went over to speak to Sinead's parents. We'd just been to the bar and I was carrying my drink. Instinctively, I tried to put my drink in my left hand to shake Eamon's hand with my right, but I hadn't been able to grip it and had had to put it down on the table before being able to properly greet him. Betsy indicated that this may be significant, however, she also stressed that the verdict would eventually come down to whether the individual members of the jury bought into the science. If we were fortunate enough to get twelve physicists then we might be ok, but she warned of the need for unanimity in these cases, and that any closed-minded jury members could jeopardise our bid for freedom.

I was also expecting that Michelle's family's legal team would call all sorts of witnesses to put the boot into me, but Betsy advised this wasn't the case. Witnesses would only be called to testify if we disagreed with the evidence in their witness statements, which by and large we didn't. We weren't disputing that Michelle was dead, and we weren't disputing that my body was the vehicle responsible for her death, merely that I wasn't in control of my actions at the time. Therefore, the two dozen statements that said I picked the knife up and stabbed Michelle with it weren't really in dispute. I queried why several of the statements failed to mention that it was Michelle who had handed me the knife, or that I had dropped it and picked it back up, but Betsy said this was largely irrelevant. Even if only five of them had actually seen the knife go in, the video was the key piece of evidence and, once we'd confirmed the authenticity of that video, whether there was one statement or twenty backing that up was inconsequential. Betsy was more interested in the fact that none of the witnesses had suggested that the incident was a culmination of anything that had gone before. Nobody had suggested we regularly argued, or that our relationship was anything other than it was, which to me was perfect. She explained she would use this in our defence when attempting to prove that I was a different character during the incident. She did also point out that the prosecution would also want to use the interview I originally gave to DI Braithwaite and PC Clarke when I was arrested, and I had no issue with this, although I did want the sections where I was asking where Michelle was, and also to see the video to be included. Betsy said she would arrange this with the prosecution team, which was being led by a lady called Elsie Lamb, a lady who Betsy described as being around even longer than she had been; of being small, slight, but vicious in the courtroom.

Then we came to my own evidence, and she advised that whilst I wasn't obligated to give evidence to the court, it wouldn't look good if I didn't, and therefore she would recommend that I did. This did mean, though, that I'd be opening myself up to cross-examination by Mrs Lamb. Betsy was more concerned about this than I was, as I felt that given that I'd done nothing but tell the truth all the way through this, she had nothing to catch me out on.

By the time we got to the night before the trial, I was a wreck. My mental health had actually improved in recent weeks as I'd been focusing on building the defence with Betsy, and I now had representation from someone who truly believed I was innocent. I also had hope, which is something I'd been lacking entirely whilst Warren Dawlish was responsible for my case.

However, I also felt guilty actively working against Michelle's family. They weren't science people, and there's no way they'd understand if I got acquitted. Carl might, as he's a clever bloke, but he was also emotional and would probably lose his objectivity. I thought long and hard about abandoning the whole plan and just taking Dad's advice, pleading guilty and sparing them all the heartache. But, as Sinead had pointed out to me at Friday's visiting, there's no way Michelle would have wanted that to happen. So, through slightly gritted teeth, I tried to mentally prepare for the next day. My cellmate, whose attitude towards me had mellowed somewhat since Dad's revelation (I still hadn't really started coming to terms with that, and I'd decided against telling my sisters, for now), and he had some unusually helpful advice.

"Expect to get sent down," he said.

"Why?" I asked.

"Because it's easier emotionally when you do. I know you want to believe in your solicitor and her defence, but prosecution lawyers are nasty pieces of work. They'll torment you, try and provoke you into showing aggression. They'll pull apart your relationship, your character, your life history, and will do everything they can to portray you as someone you're not. Most jurors aren't clever enough to see through it, so you'll probably end up back here."

"Geez, thanks," I said mockingly.

"I'm speaking from experience. You know what they say, think about how stupid the average person is, and then realise that half the people are even more stupid than that. Do you believe the average person would believe your scientific explanation of why you're innocent?"

"No, probably not," I admitted.

"Exactly, so at least half the jury aren't going to comprehend what your solicitor is saying. They'll see the prosecution's evidence, they'll see you stabbing her, and they'll decide you're guilty there and then. They won't really pay attention to the rest."

"But this is slightly different from any of your trials," I said. "When you've been in the dock you've always been guilty."

"I've always been found guilty, four trials and four guilty verdicts. But I was only really guilty on three occasions."

"If you were guilty, why did you bother going to trial?"

"Just in case I got away with it," he shrugged. "But after I was wrongly sent down, I realised that juries don't really care. This is their opportunity to have the power to send someone to prison, and they take it. Whether you are guilty or not doesn't really matter."

"So why did you still plead not guilty at your next trial?"

"To pee everyone off," he laughed. "I was in for a long sentence anyway, so I decided to try and have some fun, waste everyone's time and money. Now go to sleep, you'll need to be rested in the morning."

I arrived at court the next morning after another horrible trip in one of those swelteringly hot prison vans. At least this time I'd had the good sense to take my jacket off before going down to the van to make the journey slightly less uncomfortable. I immediately met with Betsy for our final pre-trial briefing.

"We've got Justice Christopher Hope as our judge," she said. "He's very good. I've known him a long time, as has Elsie. But he'll also know I wouldn't have taken this case on unless I seriously believed I could win it."

"Justice Hope," I commented. "Maybe it's a sign."

"Everyone says that," she smiled. "Both prosecution and defence. His name means nothing, though. Now, are you fully prepared?"

"I think so," I confirmed. "As ready as I'll ever be."

After we finished our briefing, I was taken into the court for the trial to begin. I'd never attended a trial before and, under different circumstances, I'd have found the experience hugely interesting. The courtroom itself was very daunting and intimidating, and there were far more people in there than

I expected. There was the judge, the twelve jurors, Elsie Lamb as the lead prosecution barrister, Betsy representing me, and they also had an assistant each. There were also two ushers, the Clerk of the Court, both mine and Michelle's families, along with a packed public gallery and, surprisingly, members of the press. I noticed Sinead and Marcus sitting with Will. Nicki, of course, sat with Donna on either side of Mum and Dad. I appreciated the togetherness they were all showing, although I wondered if the girls would feel the same way if they knew what I did about Dad's colourful past.

I was ordered to stand up in the dock while the Clerk of the Court read out the charge against me, the first-degree murder of Michelle Peyton on Saturday, 14th March 2015, and asked me how I pleaded.

"Not guilty," I answered, as clearly as I could.

Elsie Lamb's opening speech informed the jury of why I was on trial, that I had (allegedly) murdered my girlfriend in cold blood at a mutual friend's birthday party, and that the evidence should support this. Betsy then advised that the defence wasn't around whether the murder had been committed by me, but whether I was responsible for my actions at the time.

Naturally, the prosecution started with the CCTV footage from the night of the party. The jurors were warned that the content got very graphic very suddenly but were urged to watch it closely. I'd seen this several times by now but, apart from the first time in the police station, I'd always avoided paying a great deal of attention to it. It was too brutal and too horrific to watch. However, this time I did try and observe it as if I were a juror. I watched again as we walked up to the table. Marcus is to my left cutting some cheesecake. I'm grinning as I turn around to see Michelle holding the knife out to me. She handed it to me in a way that meant the knife was already pointing towards her, as she was passing me the handle. After I took it, I turned to face the gateaux, and then inexplicably dropped it. It was as though I suffered a spasm in my hand, as I wasn't nudged and nothing had happened, I just lost my grip on it. Betsy was right, I did pick it back up with my left hand, even though the position of the knife made it easier to pick up with my right, but I never attempted it. I looked back at Michelle who had turned to face me again, and she was smiling. As she turned away, I began looking around the room, and I'd turned full circle before turning back to face Michelle. I found myself looking at her for two or three seconds, although you couldn't see my facial expression due to having my back to the camera. Then, for no apparent reason, she was attacked. I looked away as the knife went in, I couldn't help it. There were gasps around the courtroom, and I resisted the urge to look over to either of our families or the jury. I just sat with my head bowed, and I realised once again just how damning this evidence was. Even I had to admit the unlikeliness that unproven scientific theories were getting me off this.

The rest of the prosecution's case was made up of the witness statements, which were plentiful and consistent. It didn't seem necessary for there to be so many, but each one was read out in full. They were also delivered in a surprisingly fair manner. They weren't spun to imply things that hadn't happened, nobody was suggesting there was previous animosity. Betsy informed me that this was actually a good thing, especially the statements from the ambulance crew, the medical report from the hospital, and the statements from DI Braithwaite and PC Clarke. All referenced my apparent confusion after the event, and they all confirmed I was asking where Michelle was and if she was safe. Whilst Braithwaite said she didn't believe my explanation, PC Clarke surprisingly said she was confident I was telling the truth when I said I didn't remember. She also commented on me vomiting when I saw the video, and believed my shock was genuine. Betsy said a lot of the content in these statements, even though they were officially prosecution statements, would in itself form part of our defence.

Once the prosecution had presented all of its evidence and rested its case, it was our turn. Betsy was encouraged, claiming that all they really had was the video. However, given the video showed what appeared to be me committing the crime I was accused of, I personally still thought we were up against it. As the case resumed, I took the stand, and the oath. Betsy questioned me first.

"Mr Jackson, can you please explain in your own words what happened that night?" she asked.

I gave the full account, which was something I'd said so often in the weeks between Michelle's death and her trial that I felt like I was repeating it on autopilot, and I was hoping it didn't sound too monotone to the jury.

"Can you also please describe your relationship in the weeks leading up to the tragedy?"

"We were great," I said. "We'd been planning on moving in together before the end of the year. We had a date a week or so beforehand, and Michelle suggested we went away to celebrate her work placement finishing. On a whim, we booked a skiing holiday to Italy, and I took a couple of days off work and university so I could go. The university wasn't happy, but Carl, Michelle's brother, agreed to cover my work shifts as we work together, so I was able to go."

"How was the holiday?"

"Fine, for the most part. The journey wasn't nice but, after that, the first half of the holiday was great. Very romantic, we really enjoyed it. But on the third day, we had an accident and crashed into each other on one of the slopes. It was my fault, I was being stupid, but she hurt her chest and I hurt my hand, and we both had friction burns on our bodies from the snow. We didn't ski again after that."

"How did Miss Peyton react?"

"She was angry with me, but with good reason I guess."

"Did it damage your relationship in any way?"

"Not really, she still went to sleep on my shoulder on the plane home, although we did have to swap sides because it was hurting her chest to lean the other way."

"What happened when you got home?"

"We went back to our respective homes and got ready for the party."

"Was Miss Peyton really fit to attend?"

"Possibly not, and she had toyed with not going. She had work the next morning and she thought that was more important. But Sinead is my best friend, and she was responsible for us getting together in the first place. Michelle didn't want to let me or Sinead down."

"How would you have felt if she hadn't gone?"

"I do wish she hadn't gone," I said.

"Hypothetically, Mr Jackson. Had you gone to the party without her, would you have been annoyed with her?"

"Slightly," I admitted. "But we wouldn't have argued over it. She'd have most likely met up with Sinead separately a day or two after to try and make up for it."

"No further questions, Your Honour," Betsy confirmed.

Elsie Lamb got to her feet.

"Mr Jackson," she began. "Are you well mentally?"

I expected Betsy to object to the question, but she didn't.

"I've felt better," I admitted.

"Do you take mental health medication currently?"

"No, I never have."

"You have no medical history of amnesia, or anything similar?"

"No, I don't."

"So how do you explain the apparent twelve second gap in your memory?"

This was the moment; I was almost dreading saying it, as I could anticipate the reaction.

"I think I was possessed," I confirmed.

"Possessed?" Elsie said incredulously. "By a ghost? By a ghoul?"

"Objection," Betsy said. "The prosecution is mocking my client."

"Not at all," Elsie said. "But the defendant has just claimed that, apparently, a supernatural event is responsible for his actions on the night in question. I am keen to hear his explanation."

"I'll allow the question," Justice Hope announced. "But tread carefully."

"Mr Jackson," Elsie continued. "Do please explain why you believe this?"

"Because I just wouldn't have done that," I said. "I wouldn't have hurt Michelle, ever. I wouldn't have done that to anyone, let alone my soulmate."

"But you did, we all saw you do it on the video clip."

"That wasn't me, it can't have been."

"Because you were possessed?"

"Correct," I said.

"I ask again, by what? What is your explanation?"

"I believe, and we have witnesses later who will attempt to back this up scientifically, that I was possessed by another version of me, that exists in a different Worldline."

"A different Worldline? So, another dimension?" she said mockingly.

"Basically, yes."

"Ok, and how would they have managed that?"

"We think they were probably in the middle of a lucid dream."

"Forgive me, Your Honour," said Elsie Lamb, turning to the judge, "But this is nonsensical. This is a court of law that deals in fact and hard evidence. What we have here is pure fantasy."

"Yes," said Hope. "I do hope Mrs Cohen that you have evidence to back up these 'theories'?"

"We believe we do, Your Honour," Betsy confirmed.

"Then, in that case, Your Honour, I have no further questions," Elsie confirmed.

"I have one further question," Betsy stated. "Mr Jackson, if we are successful in this defence, what do you intend to do with your freedom?"

"I'm not entirely sure," I said. "I don't have Michelle anymore, so I don't really know what I'll live for. I'll probably try and teach myself to lucid dream myself, see if there's a way I can reach this other Gary, and somehow get justice for Michelle."

"Because you want justice for her as much as anyone else?"

"Of course I do."

"No further questions," Betsy said.

I stepped down from the stand, thinking I'd got off quite lightly. Elsie Lamb had ridiculed the basis of our defence, but we expected that. However, I hadn't been grilled on it for hours, and I was now sitting back in the dock. My part was done. It was now down to everyone else.

Next up was Professor Buzzard, who gave a very detailed and very in-depth view of how the "phenomenon" we were describing, as he put it, may have occurred. Under questioning from Betsy, he detailed the Many Worlds Theory, the idea that everything that we experience is real, and the possibility that when we dream our consciousness is drifting through these Worldlines. He theorised that a lucid dream may well show that consciousness taking control of one of those Worldlines, and acting in that

Worldline as if we were native to it. It all sounded very convincing to my scientific mind, but then he was cross-examined by Elsie.

"Professor Buzzard," she began. "Can you please demonstrate a lucid dream to us?"

"That's not possible," he replied. "I can tell you how a person can enable themselves to lucid dream, but it can't be demonstrated."

"Why not?"

"Because, in this scenario, the outcome of the lucid dream would be played out in the receiving Worldline."

"You mean the Worldline which the dreamer ended up possessing?"

"That's correct."

"Ok, let's try the other way. If someone in this courtroom was suddenly possessed in the manner you describe, by someone lucid dreaming in a different Worldline, how would we know?"

"They would start acting out of character, they would start showing the behavioural characteristics of themselves from that Worldline."

"Ok, and how would we prove that?"

"There would be a memory loss similar to the one witnessed by the defendant."

At that, Elsie Lamb picked up all of her court papers and folders and hurled them across the courtroom, taking literally everyone in the room by surprise and leading to audible gasps; she then marched over to the exit doors from the court, causing quite the commotion. Justice Hope was on his feet.

"Mrs Lamb, you are out of line," he barked. "If you do anything like that again I will rule against you in this case."

Elsie Lamb stopped, turned around, and then looked at Justice Hope with a confused expression on her face.

"I apologise, Your Honour, I'm not sure what happened there. One moment I was questioning the witness, the next I'm standing over here. What just happened?"

"Mrs Lamb, return to your position at once."

"Certainly, Your Honour."

She returned to her bench.

"May I please retrieve my papers from the courtroom floor?" she requested.

"At your convenience," snarled a clearly furious Justice Hope.

"My apologies, Professor," she said as she finished picking her things up. "I believe I may have just suffered one of the incidents you were describing. I think I was possessed by someone lucid dreaming in another Worldline."

A snigger went around the public gallery. The audience was clearly enjoying her performance.

"Perhaps," said Buzzard, who was the calmest man in the room.

"I honestly don't recall what just happened," Elsie claimed sceptically. "Professor Buzzard, do you believe I was just possessed by another Worldline?"

"Theoretically possible," Buzzard acknowledged.

"I didn't ask you about theories, Professor, I asked if you believed me?"

"Objection, Your Honour. Professor Buzzard is not on trial here," Betsy added assertively.

"Agreed, Mrs Lamb please rephrase your question and get to the point. My patience is wearing thin."

"Forgive me, Your Honour," she said, before turning back to Buzzard. "Professor, you say that during my apparent memory loss just now that it was theoretically possible that I was possessed by another Worldline. Is it the only possible explanation?"

"No, of course not," Buzzard confirmed.

"What other scientific explanations could there be?"

"Any number of them." He was trying desperately hard to keep his powder dry.

"Of all those possible explanations, which one is most likely?"

"Given the suspect timing of your episode," he began, "The most likely scenario is that you do remember, and you put on that show to prove a point. However, in a Many..."

"That will do, Professor," Elsie interrupted. "You've answered the question to my satisfaction. No further questions, Your Honour."

"Just one more question, Your Honour," Betsy said. "Professor, given what has just happened in the courtroom, you were about to give an explanation on how that might manifest itself if we are indeed living in a Many Worlds scenario. Could you please elaborate on that?"

"Of course," he said. "What I was about to say is that Many Worlds supports the idea of all possible outcomes to all possible scenarios playing out simultaneously in an infinite number of Worldlines. Mrs Lamb being possessed in the manner she alleges is one potential outcome, and therefore in one Worldline or another that would have happened. However, whether it happened here or whether Mrs Lamb was merely putting on an elaborate show for the benefit of the court, I am unable to confirm."

"Thank you, Professor. No further questions."

Buzzard had clearly done his best, but if Elsie Lamb was attempting to prove how ridiculous my defence sounded, then she'd done an excellent job of it. I didn't buy for a second that she'd been possessed, which I thought spoke volumes about the likelihood of a jury believing I had. We had one more witness to call, the body language expert, a lady I'd never met called Ella Mellow.

"Miss Mellow, I'd like you to watch the following video clip and describe your impressions of the man highlighted."

She played the CCTV footage, but it cut off at the point Michelle handed me the knife. The man highlighted in the video was me and, whilst I wasn't a body language expert and most of what she said was over my head, I grasped that she was describing me as calm, confident, affectionate to my partner, very warm, and seemingly happy.

Then we watched a second video, a very short clip just a few seconds long, of the stabbing itself.

"Miss Mellow, is it conceivable, in your professional opinion, that the person highlighted in video one, is the same person as the one highlighted in video two? Or would you suggest they are different people?"

"If I were watching these videos for the first time, with no context, I would have said they were different people," she confirmed.

"As you did the first time that I showed you these, without the context?"

"That's correct, yes."

"Why do you believe they're different people?"

"The person in the first clip is right-handed, the person in the second is left-handed. In the first clip, the person stands naturally well balanced, in the second clip there is a definite leaning to putting the majority of their body weight on their left leg, that wasn't present in the previous clip. When, in the second clip, the person turns around their eyes look different. Much narrower and more menacing than they were before."

"For the benefit of the court, can you please confirm that you have also seen the full unedited video clip from the night in question?"

"I have."

"Then how do you explain the sudden difference between the two?"

"In a real scenario, there is no rational explanation for the sudden changes."

"Could a person put it on, so to speak, to try and give themselves an excuse?"

"It's possible. If this was a shoot from a movie set, I might assume the director had just said action, and that the defendant had instantly got into character."

"But all the same, the actor would then still be playing a different person."

"Correct."

"In your experience, do people have the ability to make the changes to their posture and body language so suddenly, in the manner you described?"

"Not ordinarily, no."

"So, do you believe we're watching two different people, occupying the same body, at different points in time?"

"If it were possible, it would seem a feasible explanation."

"Thank you, no further questions," Betsy confirmed.

Elsie didn't cross-examine either, meaning she must have been happy with the explanations given. This also concluded our defence, and, after a brief recess, both solicitors gave their closing statements to the jury. As was apparently normal, the prosecution went first.

"What you have heard in this court over the last few days is a very imaginative defence, for a very serious and very tragic crime. I have no doubt that the defendant feels regret and remorse over his actions on the night in question, but they were his actions," Elsie said authoritatively. "Nothing I have heard over the course of the defence persuades me in the slightest that the defendant is anything other than guilty. They have offered scientific theories, but none of it is provable. There is no evidence for what they are proposing, and a not guilty verdict would open the floodgates for every criminal all over the world to use the same defence for any crime they'll ever commit ever again. It is your job to ensure that does not happen, and I implore you to find the defendant guilty as charged."

Betsy Cohen was equally authoritative in her own summing up.

"We have seen proof," she said, "That the man who committed the crime is so unlikely to be the man who approached the dessert table that a body language expert initially believed they were different people. We have heard from twenty different witnesses, none of whom make any suggestion of violent tendencies in the defendant, none of whom have made any suggestion that the couple were anything but happy, none of whom suggested they have ever felt the victim was in danger, none of whom believe there was even the slightest warning of what was about to occur. We have police and medical statements confirming the defendant's confusion when being treated, and his frantic requests to find out where his girlfriend was, and his extreme reaction to seeing the video which, up to that point, he believed completely would prove his innocence. He doesn't have the personality, the characteristics or the profile to commit the crime he's accused of. And yet, we do concede that the video shows it. It doesn't add up, and it's not right. We believe it's explainable and believe we have done that. Therefore, I urge you to find the defendant not guilty."

There was an obvious recess whilst the jury deliberated, and I was returned to a holding cell. As I sat there, I tried to imagine how I might rule on this case if I was a juror. I was scientifically curious by nature, and I'd have certainly found the explanations provocative and interesting, but would they have been enough to persuade me of a defendant's innocence? In truth, probably not, and I was taking Cyrus's advice in expecting a guilty verdict.

It took less than two hours for the jury to deliberate and for us to be called back into the courtroom, and I was led to believe this wasn't a good sign. Everyone gathered in the courtroom, and I was ordered to stand in the dock. I was shaking, and my palms were sweating, even though I felt freezing cold. My entire life was going to be decided in the next few moments.

"Will the foreperson of the jury please stand?" said the court usher, and a man in his sixties sitting at the far end of the jury bench got to his feet.

"Have you reached a verdict in which you are all agreed?"

"We have, yes," he confirmed.

"Then, on the charge of first-degree murder, do you find the defendant guilty, or not guilty?"

Chapter Twenty-One

"Guilty," he said.

"Yes!" Carl shouted out, getting to his feet, punching the air. His mum and dad remained seated and largely expressionless, however. Generally, there was a bit of commotion. I looked over to my family to see Mum sobbing on Dad's shoulder. That's it, it was all over, I was now a convicted murderer. How on earth was I going to live with this?

"Order! Order!" called Justice Hope, and waited for the room to settle, before addressing the jury. "Members of the jury, this court dismisses you and thanks you for a job well done."

The members of the jury stood and filed out of the courtroom. The Judge then turned to me.

"Gary Jackson, you have been found guilty of first-degree murder. Whilst during the trial I have established that you have a strong sense of emotional loss regarding the victim's death, it is also noted that you have accepted no responsibility for what you have done. The crime you have been convicted of carries a mandatory life sentence in prison, and I rule that you must serve a minimum of fifteen years before being eligible for parole. This court is adjourned."

I was re-cuffed and taken back out of the court by the two prison officers. I just caught sight once again of my parents, both in tears, before I was removed from the courtroom. I was expecting to be taken straight back to the prison van, but I was instead shown into an interview room.

"Your solicitor wants a quick chat with you before we take you back," one of the prison officers said.

I sat and waited, feeling numb. I could hear activity outside the door, which I took to be the members of the public gallery making their way back outside, then it all went quiet again. In a way, I just wanted to get back to the prison, get back in my cell and go to sleep, at least to get this day over with. It felt like it took an age before Betsy Cohen appeared.

"Gary, I'm sorry," she said, as she closed the door. "We knew it was a long shot, but I didn't expect our defence to be dismissed out of hand quite so quickly or so brutally."

"It was Elsie's histrionics that really showed how ridiculous we were being."

"I did warn you she was good. We weren't being ridiculous, though. Everything we said was true, and you know it was."

"I know, but convincing a jury was always going to be a bit whimsical. I should have just pleaded guilty."

"You'd have still got life in prison."

"But I'd have spared Michelle's family from having to go through all of that," I said.

"You say that, but I've just spoken to them. They're not quite as closed- minded as some of the jurors. One of the things they've been longing for since the tragedy is an explanation of how things could have gone so wrong, so quickly and so dramatically. They've never understood how you could have turned on Michelle in that manner, and they've never believed you wanted her dead. Had you pleaded guilty you'd have gone straight to sentencing and they'd have never got to hear your version of events. They have now, and they take comfort from it. I'm also not entirely convinced that they think you're guilty, although they didn't go as far as to say that."

"Carl certainly believes it."

"Some people will, the jury proved that. But the people who know you, and I mean really know you, will be less quick to dismiss our explanation as you might think."

"I'd love to see them and talk to them, to be able to remember Michelle properly. To tell them how much I love her and miss her."

"That's unlikely," she conceded. "We do have to consider an appeal. Would you like me to request one?"

"No," I said. "Not yet, anyway. If I appeal there needs to be something new, a way to guarantee winning. That evidence just doesn't exist yet."

"So, what are you going to do with your time now?"

"I don't really know. Educate myself, most likely, continue studying the sciences in prison. You asked me on the stand what I'd do if I got out, and I said I'd try and teach myself to lucid dream so I could find the offending Gary Jackson in his native Worldline and see that he's brought to justice. I think I'm going to attempt it anyway."

"How will you do that?"

"I have no idea, but I have the rest of my life to do it."

"Take care in there," Betsy said, shaking my hand. "When you're ready for an appeal, do please let me know. I'll be happy to represent you again."

"Thanks for all your help," I said, and with that, she left the room.

Straightaway, I was escorted from the room and back into the prison van. I was still feeling numb, and I remembered nothing of the journey whatsoever. I was pleased to be the only prisoner in the van, though. There were officers present, but they didn't speak to me.

The prisoners were all at dinner, and everyone watched me as I came in, wanting an update on how the trial was going. However, I couldn't face any further scrutiny tonight. The officers started escorting me towards the kitchens.

"Don't," I said. "I want to just go back to my cell."

"Without any dinner?" the officer asked.

"I can't walk in there with all of them sitting there and tell them all I was found guilty."

"They're going to find out sooner or later. We all knew you were coming back here after the trial."

"Just take me to my cell, please," I requested, and they did as I asked.

In truth, I just wanted half an hour of quiet time before Cyrus came back. He had helped to defend me in the prison up to now, but that was as a prisoner on remand. What would they all think now I was a convicted murderer? The only thing certain now was that I was going to find out. Not today, I'd managed to put it off until tomorrow, but this was my life now.

Kirsty, the prison officer, appeared at the cell door.

"I hear it didn't go well," she said. "Are you ok? Do you want to talk about it?"

"Not really," I said. "Although if you could make me an appointment with the prison doctor tomorrow please, that would be good."

"For what reason?"

"I'm worried about my mental health. All I can think about at the minute is wanting to be with Michelle, and the only way I can do that is if I'm dead. So, I need some help, or I'm going to end up wanting, or trying, to jump off the roof."

"I will speak to the medical team to get you assessed," she said. "How do you feel about the verdict?"

"In a weird way, I am glad it's all over."

"You're not the first prisoner I've heard say that."

"I just want to be able to grieve for Michelle, and I don't feel I can. It doesn't feel like I'm allowed to, it doesn't feel right."

"A lot of killers do feel the need to grieve for their victims."

"You speak as though as I'm an ordinary murderer."

She looked at me as though she was weighing me up.

"Whether you believe you're innocent or not, in the eyes of the law you are now a convicted killer. You are going to have to get used to being treated as such, even if you don't think you deserve it."

"All the more reason I need that mental health appointment," I said.

I could hear chattering in the corridor, and it meant the prisoners were all coming back to the cells from dinner.

"I'll get it booked in and get one of the medical team to assess your needs," she said, getting up to leave. She was barely out of the cell before Cyrus Ramsey appeared.

"Good news," he said.

"Oh yeah, brilliant," I replied sarcastically.

"What's up with you? Are the jury out yet?"

"Out, returned, and convicted me all in about two hours."

Ramsey burst out laughing.

"I told you they'd be too stupid to understand your defence, didn't I?"

"Yep."

"Well, may I be the first to officially welcome you to the prison?" he said, rather too jovially for my liking.

"Thanks," I said.

"Oh, come on, it's not like you didn't expect it."

"I know, it's still difficult to swallow. So, what is the good news?"

"Oh, that the parole board has decided I can apply for parole early. My work with you has gone some way towards that, apparently. My solicitor is going to submit an application, and I could be out within about six weeks."

"Great news," I agreed.

"You are going to have to look out for yourself at that point, though," he said.

"I'll do it from now," I said. "I don't really care anymore. Someone wants to stab me and kill me, I'll let them. It's no worse than Michelle got, and no doubt I deserve it."

"You're a miserable sod tonight, aren't you?" he said.

"What did you expect?"

"Look on the bright side," he said. "Once I'm out of here, this will be your cell, until some other lowlife ends up in here. Then you can induct him into prison life the same way I did you."

"I wouldn't do that," I admitted.

"Why not?" he asked.

"They might be innocent."

"Of course they will!" Cyrus laughed.

Chapter Twenty-Two
The Red Line

On the journey home, Michelle, Sinead, and I all agreed that, at this point, we'd all done pretty much all we could to assist my counterpart, and that now we were just waiting to see if Betsy Cohen was successful in her lucid dreaming attempts. It didn't seem a particularly satisfactory ending, but we didn't seem to have any other choice. Betsy was the lucid dreamer, and the most likely to make an impact in the appropriate Worldline, so it was best for my other counterpart that we left it in Betsy's hands now. The fact that university had finished for the Easter holidays meant we wouldn't even see Professor Buzzard in the next few weeks for an update and, whilst we had a contact number for Betsy, it felt wrong to keep bugging her for an update. In the meantime, our main job seemed to be getting our lives back in order.

In addition to the full Saturday and Tuesday evening I already did at work, I'd agreed to extend that to all day Tuesday and Thursday for the duration of the three-week Easter holidays. As the store was open from eight to eight during the week, this meant I'd be doing thirty-two hours for each of those weeks, whilst remaining free to attend the family lunch on Sunday, Michelle's pre-op appointment on the Wednesday, and her actual operation on the Friday. It also meant I'd finally get to know what it was like to work one of Michelle's twelve-hour shifts, something she assured me I would not find pleasant. It was when I left work on that Saturday evening that I got my first update on the Worldlines problem from Sinead. She told me she'd just received the following text from Betsy.

Had lucid dream and found evidence of Michelle's murder. Left a note for my equivalent, no idea if it will work. Will let you know when I hear anything. BC.

"At least it's something," Michelle said when I got home and told her. "Do you think she'll get a response?"

"I hope so, but you know what it's like with murder trials, it could take months."

"I still find it really unnerving that a version of you could actually wish to kill a version of me," she said.

"I've got a ready-made defence now if I ever decide to," I joked.

"They'd never believe you," she responded.

"Then what chance has the other Gary got?"

Michelle was getting very nervous about her operation, to the point she was considering cancelling it. She vomited on both the Sunday and the Monday before because of stress, although her mood was improved by the fact Henry had been able to both retrieve and print our holiday photos from the damaged SD card. However, I still felt bad leaving her on the Tuesday to go to work. For a soon-to-be qualified nurse, I was surprised how terrified of hospitals and medical procedures she was. I was hoping, once she'd had the pre-op, she might calm down a bit and even if she didn't, then at least by the weekend it would all be over for her.

It was very much a relief to get up on Wednesday morning and make our way to the hospital. Michelle had been sick again before she left, which actually made her more scared, as if they thought if she was ill they'd cancel the operation. As much as she was dreading it, she was also struggling to deal with the pain so knew it was for the best.

We came out of the train station and took the short walk down Euston Road to the hospital. My phone buzzed in my pocket, and when I checked it was another text from Sinead.

Can I meet you later, need to talk to you? Doesn't matter what time, I'm free all day. Happy to come to The Loch & Quay if it's easier for you.

"Do you mind if I do?" I asked Michelle.

"No, go ahead," she answered. "I'll want to go to bed when I get back from here, so won't be great company tonight anyway."

"Well, I'll meet Sinead for a bit, then come back to yours. I don't like you being left on your own when you're feeling down, it's not good for you."

"That's fine, then."

As Michelle and I went inside the hospital, I texted Sinead back saying I'd meet her in The Loch & Quay at six o'clock. I wondered whether, being staff, Michelle would get preferential treatment, and this was confirmed when we were shown into a consulting room by a Doctor Andy Cross, who introduced himself as the hospital's most senior consultant. This also made him one of Michelle's top bosses. She'd met him a few times before, but I had no idea who he was.

"I don't run a clinic for everyday patients," he explained. "But I do take care of our own staff and any patients who have any sort of public profile. You're here today for a pre-operation assessment to repair a few broken ribs, so we can insert a plate to hold them in place, and also check for possible pneumothorax."

"Pneumo-what?" I said.

"Pneumothorax. In plain English, it's to make sure that there are no jagged edges to any of the fractures that may be in danger of causing a lung puncture. It seems unlikely with your kind of fracture, but if we are operating, we should check this too."

I nodded to confirm I was happy with the explanation, but Michelle hadn't said a word.

"How is the injury?" he asked her.

"Still painful," she said.

"Are you having any trouble breathing?"

"It hurts too much to breathe in fully."

"How about movement?"

"I can't drive at the minute as the seat belt hurts as I move. It also hurts when I laugh or sneeze or cough."

"I understand. Today we'll just ask you some questions about your current health and wellbeing, do a urine test and a few blood tests, just to check you're otherwise healthy before the operation on Friday. Does that sound ok?"

"Yeah, that's fine."

"How are you feeling generally?"

"Terrified," she admitted. "I don't like doctors, or hospitals."

"Not many nurses do," he smiled. "Are you happy for it to be myself that carries out the tests today?"

"Yeah, it's fine," she confirmed again.

He said this to her but then didn't actually perform any of the tests himself. He sent Michelle to the ladies' to do a urine test, and a phlebotomist came in to take the blood tests.

The medical questionnaire was pretty standard stuff too. Did she drink – yes. Did she smoke – no. Did she do drugs – no. Was she pregnant – no. Did she have any underlying health conditions – no. Did she have any allergies – no. Did she take any other medication – Not currently but occasionally for hay fever. Afterwards, we were shown back to the waiting room whilst the blood tests were analysed.

"That was all rather quick and painless," I commented. "I thought we'd be here for hours."

"We have been here over an hour," she said.

"Well, yes, but I expected us to still be sitting in reception waiting to go in, and you're nearly all done. How are you feeling now?"

"Not too bad, stomach feels a bit knotted but other than that I'm ok."

"I haven't seen you eat anything today, actually."

"I had some toast for breakfast. To be honest, I've been struggling to eat since what happened in the pub the other week, although at least it's helping me lose the weight I gained on holiday."

"Do you want to go for a meal later? Have some food and some wine?"

"You're meeting Sinead."

"Yeah, but it won't be all night. If I see her at six, we can meet about half seven if you want."

"No, I don't fancy it," she said, shaking her head.

"Michelle, would you like to come back through, please?" called Dr Cross from the doorway. Michelle went in, and I went with her. I noticed the look of mild concern on Cross's face.

"Is everything ok?" I asked.

"There's an unexpected anomaly in one of your blood test results," he said to her. "But it may have just returned an erroneous result. Do you mind if we take another, just to double-check?"

"Yeah, of course," said Michelle, and the phlebotomist returned to take another sample. "Which one is abnormal?" she asked.

"Let us double-check first, I'll be back in a few minutes."

"I wonder which one it is," she asked as he left the room.

"What were they checking for to begin with?"

"I don't really know. I assume it's just things like hormone levels and iron levels."

"Your iron might be low if you haven't been eating well. You'll need a big juicy steak to boost it back up."

"I couldn't eat anything like that at the minute," she said.

It didn't take long for Cross to return again. He was wearing an expression I'd best describe as bemused. He sat down at his desk and looked at Michelle.

"Your second sample has returned the same result as your first, and as a result, we have to take it seriously," he said.

"What's wrong?" Michelle asked, even before I did.

"I'm not sure anything is actually wrong," he said. "But we're not going to be able to perform surgery. The levels of the Human Chorionic Gonadotropin hormone in your blood indicate that it would be unsafe to give you an anaesthetic."

"Human what?" I asked, but Michelle was ahead of me.

"My HCG levels? But that would mean..."

"It would indicate that you are in the early stages of pregnancy," Dr Cross explained. "As a result, any anaesthetic we give you could be potentially damaging to the embryo."

I'd stopped listening after 'pregnancy'.

"She's pregnant?" I asked.

"Between four and five weeks according to the blood test results. I assume this is unexpected."

"Just a bit," said Michelle. "Although I have been being sick the last few mornings, and I am late on my period, so I did wonder."

"You thought you might be pregnant, and you didn't tell me?" I said, turning to her.

"I thought it was just as likely to be stress since we came back off holiday. I didn't want to worry you unnecessarily."

"Is this unwelcome news?" Dr Cross inquired tentatively.

"No, no it's not," Michelle replied cautiously. "Just unexpected."

"That's one way of describing it," I said.

"I know this is a lot to take in for you both," Cross continued. "I suggest, Michelle, you book an appointment with your own GP and also book in to see the midwife as soon as possible."

"Midwife?" I said dumbly.

"You know what a midwife is," Michelle scoffed.

"My immediate concern now is how we manage your rib fracture. You have quite a nasty break which we'd prefer to operate on, but it should be manageable without surgery, it will just take longer. You'll also need to be careful around pain medication whilst you're pregnant."

He rambled on for another few minutes, and I hoped Michelle was listening because I wasn't. Pregnant. How could she be pregnant? I mean, I knew *how* she could be pregnant, but we were always so careful. How would this affect her recovery, our ability to get our own place, our jobs, our whole lives? It was all about to change.

They finished the assessment, and Cross handed Michelle some leaflets on pain management and potential exercises she could do, as well as the best way to sit and lie to prevent aggravating the injury to her ribs. By the end, I was just glad to be out of there and back in the street.

"Michelle, are you ok?" I asked her, as soon as she stepped outside.

"Yeah, I'm fine," she said, far calmer than I'd expect from someone who had just found out she was unexpectedly pregnant.

"Did you know about this?" I asked.

"No, of course not. But I had symptoms, so I did suspect."

"You should have told me."

"I know, I'm sorry. Are you happy?"

"I don't know," I said. "I'm too in shock to think how I feel at the minute. I'm still trying to process the news. Are you happy?"

"Yeah, I think so," she said. "Granted, I'd rather not be pregnant, I don't think the timing is right. I'd rather we got our own place and got some money behind us first, but I'm not disappointed that this has happened. I always wanted children, and I did expect to have them with you, just not yet."

"So, what do we do now?" I asked.

"Well, I'm going to catch the train, then I'm going home to bed like I'd planned. You're going to see Sinead."

"You know what I mean."

"I know I do, and to be honest I don't know. You're not supposed to tell anyone until you've had all the checks at the twelve-week scan."

"Maybe this is why you were dreaming about your friend Jana, and her partner, having a pregnancy scan the other week?"

"Actually, I dreamt he was having an affair, and it was his other woman we were scanning."

"But if you're five weeks pregnant, you'd have been pregnant then also."

"That's true, maybe it was an early sign," she said.

"We can't keep this quiet, we have to tell our parents at least. And I can't go and see Sinead tonight and not tell her. She'll know something is wrong the second she sees me."

"It's not wrong," Michelle said bluntly.

"I know, but she'll know there's something heavy weighing on my mind. This is a shock and I need to talk about it, and I'd rather talk to Sinead."

"Fine, you can tell her, but only if Marcus isn't there. I want us to tell our parents first though, but then nobody else until we've had a scan."

"If that's what you want," I said.

Telling your parents that you're expecting your first child is an oddly terrifying experience, especially when that child is unexpected and unplanned. My mum, who was only a year older than Michelle is now when she fell pregnant with Donna, shrieked with joy and hugged us both. Dad called us a pair of stupid bastards for doing this before we had our own roof over our heads, but Mum reminded him they were in the same boat twenty-five years ago. Dad explained that their circumstances were substantially different, and that he remained concerned that it was a different world now. Nicki, who was also there, burst into tears and hugged Michelle before me. Michelle's parents' reaction was more in tune, but less blunt, than Dad's had been. They asked how long we'd been planning it and actually seemed to take reassurance from the fact we hadn't planned it at all. Denise had been nearly thirty when she first got pregnant with Carl, and their primary concern was how young we were. Carl himself just said, "Nice," and walked off to his room.

During the commotion of the afternoon, Sinead had text again.

Bring Michelle too if you can, had news from Betsy.

"It's probably best I came anyway given what's happened today. I think I'd rather be with you when you told her."

We made it to the pub at bang on six. Sinead was already there, sitting at mine and Michelle's favourite table, but on her own.

"I'll get the drinks," Michelle said. "And I'll take my time. Give you a few minutes to talk about what Sinead wanted. Is it Rosé wine she normally drinks?"

I could see the wine glass on the table. It was still a third full.

"I'll get her one anyway," Michelle said.

"Ok, thanks. And don't forget, no alcohol for you."

"Oh, damn, I hadn't thought of that," she said.

I went over to Sinead. Had I had less on my mind, I may have been able to tell before she spoke that she was troubled, but I genuinely hadn't noticed.

"How are you?" I said. "Michelle has gone to the bar so we can speak on our own first. Is everything ok?"

"Not really, I've ended it with Marcus."

"How come?"

"I thought about what you said on the train last week, and you were right. The things he was saying to me seemed too choreographed to be entirely genuine."

"You know what they say about women's instincts," I said.

"These weren't my instincts, though, they were yours."

"You said you'd thought it yourself too."

"I guess I just didn't want to believe it. I let him try the choking thing too, it wasn't pleasant, and he was going to keep wanting to do it. I wouldn't have been able to get used to it."

"How did he react?"

"He just shrugged."

"And how do you feel?"

"Vindicated, after that's all he did. Had he got upset or protested I'd have felt really bad, but he didn't. He just left."

"How's your mum?" I asked.

"She's out of hospital. We're going to take her back to Ireland tomorrow for a few days whilst I'm off university. They say people with dementia sometimes go back in time, so we're going to get a ferry and take her back to where she grew up. It might help her a bit. It might also be the last time the three of us get to go away together as a family. That's one of the things that persuaded me to end it with Marcus. He isn't part of our family, and I don't think I want him to be."

Michelle had just returned to our table with the drinks.

"Do you mind if I tell her?" I asked Sinead.

"Yeah, go ahead," they both said in unison, and Sinead looked at Michelle with some confusion.

"Sinead's news first," I said to Michelle. "She's ended it with Marcus."

"Oh, congratulations," Michelle said. "Are you ok?"

"Yeah, I am. I'm a bit disappointed it didn't work, but I think the leopard had changed less spots than I thought. Do you have something to say too?"

"Let's do the update from Betsy first," I said, but I should have known Sinead wasn't going to buy that.

"No," she said. "Something's not right. What's happened?"

"Nothing's wrong, it's just…"

"I'm pregnant," Michelle jumped in.

Sinead momentarily sat there open-mouthed.

"Oh, wow," she finally said. "That's a massive shock."

"To both of us too," Michelle said.

"Are you both ok?" she asked, with more concern in her voice than either of our families had shown.

"I am," said Michelle. "I'm not sure Gary is yet."

"It hasn't quite sunk in yet," I said. "Michelle has had signs for the last week so has had time to prepare herself a tiny bit for the news, but it caught me fully on the hop this afternoon."

"So, what are you going to do now?" Sinead asked. "Where are you going to live?"

"That's all still to be decided," I said. "Now can we do the update from Betsy, please, before we talk anymore about this, otherwise it'll be a distraction."

"It didn't work," Sinead said.

"I thought she said it had?" I replied.

"No, she did, and the message got through. But the Betsy in the other Worldline didn't win the case. That Gary got sentenced to life in prison for murder."

"Oh no," I sighed, leaning back on the bench. "That's awful."

"There's nothing more we could have done," Sinead said. "We were fortunate to be able to do as much as we did."

"Try telling that to him," I said.

"Since I got the message, though, I've been thinking about something Professor Buzzard said in one of the lectures. I think it was the one you missed when you were in Italy. It's that if every possible outcome to every possible scenario played out in separate Worldlines, he was always going to."

"What do you mean?"

"It was one possible outcome, so it would have happened somewhere. Likewise, there must be a version where he got off too. That Worldline just hasn't interacted with ours yet."

"Doesn't that mean they would have both happened with or without our help?"

"There'd have still been infinite numbers of Worldlines for both, but the balance between guilty and not guilty may have changed with our input. I guess we'll never know the scale of the full impact, but I suspect the three of us are sitting in this very pub at this very moment, in several other Worldlines, celebrating his freedom. We just don't know about it in this one."

"There's a sobering thought," I said.

"I'm only going to be having sober thoughts for the next nine months," Michelle joked.

"Longer than that if you breastfeed," Sinead winked.

"Oh stop it, don't say that," Michelle giggled, before wincing, again.

"I know it's come as a shock, but are you both happy?"

"I am," Michelle said.

"Yeah, I think so, I will be when the shock wears off."

"Then allow me to congratulate you," Sinead said. "And raise a toast, to the three of you.

Chapter Twenty-Three
The Green Line

"Not guilty," he said.

"No way!" Carl shouted, and got to his feet, gesticulating at the jury. His mum and dad remained seated and largely expressionless, however. Generally, there was a bit of a commotion, and I looked over to my family to see Mum sobbing on Dad's shoulder. I felt like I'd had a weight lifted off mine. That's it, it was all over, I was a free man, and now I could grieve for Michelle properly.

"Order! Order!" called Justice Hope, but Carl was still remonstrating.

"You murdering scum, Jackson! You killed my sister! You killed my sister!"

"Can we have that man removed from the courtroom please?" Hope ordered.

"Watch your back, Jackson," he called, as he was led away. "I'll have revenge on you. Watch your back!"

His reaction had shaken me. It was the last thing I'd expected to happen. The Judge was speaking again though.

"Members of the jury," he began. "This court dismisses you and thanks you for a job well done."

The members of the jury stood and filed out of the courtroom. The Judge then turned to me.

"Gary Jackson, you have been found not guilty of first-degree murder. While some people in this courtroom may have doubts around that decision, this is a Court that abides by the rule of law. You are therefore a free man. This court is adjourned."

I was released from the dock by the two prison officers and was finally free to go where I wanted. I made a beeline for my family, and Mum ran across the court and hugged me. Due to the no contact rule for visitors in the prison, this was the first time I'd hugged her, or anyone, since the night of the party.

"I'm so pleased for you," Mum said. "I didn't think they were going to believe you."

"Neither did I," I admitted, releasing mum and hugging Nicki.

"What are you going to do now?" Nicki asked.

"Grieve," was all I answered. Donna was next in line for a hug.

"I'm so glad it's all over, this has been horrible for all of us."

"I know, and I'm so sorry."

"It wasn't your fault," she acknowledged. Even Dad gave me a hug.

"Thanks for looking out for me," I said quietly. "Cyrus did a good job."

As our family embrace ended, I looked across the Courtroom. Ed and Denise had left, and I imagined they'd gone looking for Carl. I wondered how long it would be until I could speak to them. I'd lost Michelle, and I didn't really want to lose her entire family if it was avoidable. It was still my hope that we could help each other.

"Congratulations, Mr Jackson," said Betsy Cohen, as she approached me and shook my hand.

"Thank you so much," I replied. "You were amazing!"

"It always helps when the defence is telling the truth. I also don't think Elsie's histrionics particularly helped their cause. It was always going to either convince a jury or turn them against her. Today we got a bit lucky."

"It could have easily gone the other way," I acknowledged.

"Very easily," she admitted.

"Please don't take this the wrong way," I said to her. "I do hope I never have to deal with you again."

"I understand," she smiled. "Take care of yourself."

"Where's Sinead?" I asked.

"She was in the public gallery," mum said. "She's probably waiting outside."

Mum was right. I made my way out of the courtroom and Sinead was standing waiting for me. I embraced her even more warmly than I had my sisters.

"Thank you so much for believing in me," I said. "Where's Marcus?"

"He left with Carl when the verdict was read out."

"He doesn't believe me?"

Sinead shook her head.

"He never has," she said. "He always says that he knows what he saw. It's caused a lot of friction between us, the fact I've stood by you."

"Sinead, I'm sorry, I didn't realise this had caused you trouble like that too."

"It's ok, he has to accept it now."

"I hope it doesn't affect our friendship."

"Trust me, if he doesn't it will be him rather than you that loses me."

She smiled and I hugged her tightly again.

"Do you know where Michelle is buried?" I asked.

"Yeah, she's in Barchester cemetery. The headstone was put on a couple of days ago."

"I want to see her, will you come with me please?"

"You may want to wait a while, as that's probably where Carl and Marcus have gone. Go home now, and we'll go in the morning."

"I want to go today," I insisted.

"Then at least give them an hour or so. Go back home and calm yourself down. The cemetery is open until eight o'clock. I'll pick you up at six."

I did as she suggested and went home with my family. It felt very surreal, sitting in the back of the car, Donna and Nicki either side of me with Mum and Dad in the front. There was a togetherness about us that I hadn't felt for a long time. I was also pleased that Will and Freya weren't here. Nothing against either of them, as they clearly made Nicki and Donna happy, but I didn't want their partners around when I was having to deal with losing mine.

"How does it feel to be out?" Donna asked.

"Weird, to be honest," I said.

"At least you'll be able to sleep in your own bed tonight," she said.

"Do you know what you're going to do now?" Nicki asked.

"No idea," I admitted. "I just want to see Michelle. Sinead is picking me up at 6 to take me to the cemetery."

I was ready half an hour early, but Sinead was right on time. I got in the car and could see she'd been crying.

"Are you ok?" I asked.

"Me and Marcus have split up," she said. "He's told me he doesn't want to be with someone who associates with a murderer."

"Sinead, I'm sorry."

"It's his problem," she retorted. "It's not like he's never done anything bad himself. He's been preaching religion all this time, but where's his forgiveness for you?"

"I don't need his forgiveness. I just want you to be happy."

"I will be," she said. "Everything happens for the best."

"Maybe not everything," I said.

She drove to the cemetery, and we got out of the car. I didn't know where Michelle was, but I could see Ed and Denise a hundred or so yards away with their backs to us.

"Let's wait here," I said. "They're probably not going to want to see me yet."

"You might be surprised," she replied.

After about five minutes the two of them left the grave and started walking back towards us. Ed noticed me as they reached the end of the row of graves and said something to Denise. However, they didn't break their stride and continued slowly walking back my way.

"Should I speak to them?" I asked Sinead quietly.

"Leave it up to them," she said. "Let them speak first."

It was good advice, and Ed did speak as they approached.

"I wondered if you'd come straight here," he said.

"I wanted to, but I thought Carl might, and I figured it was best to avoid him for now."

Ed had stopped walking, but Denise had carried on without speaking.

"I'm so sorry for everything that's happened," I said. "I hope you know I'd have never knowingly hurt Michelle in any way."

"I think I do," he said. "Denise can't process it yet, and Carl can't see past the end of his nose. But neither me nor Denise have ever understood why you'd have wanted to hurt Michelle, despite what the evidence said. I don't fully understand the explanation you gave in defence, but it has to make more sense than what the video suggested."

"How are you all?" I asked.

"Wounded, and empty. Carl wants justice, as we all do. But if what you say is true, we're never going to get it, are we? My little girl is gone, and nobody is going to pay for it. We all need a little bit of time to get used to that."

"I appreciate you still talking to me. Had it been anyone else who had done this we'd have all been helping each other to grieve. I hope we still can, because I love her and miss her enormously."

"I think Michelle would want us to still be a family," Ed said. "Give us some time, though, we'll reach out to you when we're ready."

"Thank you, and take care of yourselves," I said as he walked away. Denise stood by their car watching us.

"That probably went as well as you could expect," Sinead said.

"I guess so," I acknowledged.

"Michelle's grave is just up here," she said, leading me up to the row of graves where Michelle lay. "It's down there on the left-hand side."

"Are you not coming with me?"

"I will, but I assume you'll want a few minutes alone first."

She was right, and I walked along the row until I came to her headstone. As I read it, I immediately broke into tears.

Here lies:
Michelle Elizabeth Peyton
20th October 1993 – 14th March 2015
A beautiful and perfect daughter and sister
Love and miss you always
Mum, Dad, and brother Carl xxx

"Oh, Michelle," I sobbed. "I'm so, so sorry for everything. I didn't know what was happening, I couldn't fight it. They all thought I'd killed you. But I'd never do that, I love you so much. I don't know what I'm going to do without you."

I'd been wanting to see her for so long, and now I was here I couldn't think of anything else to say. I just knelt there and wept.

"Are you ok?" said Sinead, who had now made her way down to me.

"I just don't know how I'm going to deal with this," I cried. "What do I do now? I just want to be with her again."

"Michelle wouldn't want you to waste your life," Sinead said. "She'd want you to carry on, live your life as you were meant to. Honour her memory and make her proud. She'll always be watching over you."

I turned to look at her.

"Do you really believe that?" I asked mournfully. "Given everything we've been through in this case, could she possibly be? Or do you think she's continuing to live on in some other Worldline without me, oblivious that any of this has happened?"

"What do you take more comfort from?"

"The second one."

"Then believe that," she said. "And if she is living on, it won't be without you. She'll live the life you were meant to have, and you'll continue to make her happy."

"I hope you're right," I said.

"My worry is this Worldline, and the infinite number that will branch off from it going forward. I want to try and make sure you're ok, in all of them."

"I don't know what I'd do without either of you."

"I'll look after you," she said, crying herself by now. "That's a promise. A promise to both of you," she said, looking at Michelle's headstone. "You can always come back here every day if you want to, she's not going anywhere. She'll always be here. Come on, let's get you home."

And with that, she took my hand and led me back to her car.

Chapter Twenty-Four
The Black Line

That night I slept back in Sinead's room on the basis that, with Mary coming out tomorrow, it might be the last time we got to for a while. She had warned me not to expect anything, though, as she'd started her 'lady time', as she put it. She even apologised for it, which I found cute and unnecessary in equal measures. It wasn't like there was anything she could have done about it. I was still irritated the next morning, though, that they'd planned their break to Ireland without me, and I think Sinead sensed it. I wasn't going to argue with her about it, though. If they were going away for a few days, I didn't want us to part on bad terms. However, something Dad said in the pub yesterday had struck a chord with me and, added with my disgruntlement with Sinead for planning to go away with her family without me, I decided, perhaps unwisely, to act. I waited for them to get the call that Mary was to be discharged, which came mid-morning, and once her and Eamon were both out of the house, I grabbed my stick and caught the bus back to Barchester.

Peyton's Automotives had been there at least ten years. I remembered it opening in the summer before we started secondary school. I'd been inside the place about three times, but I did know Michelle's dad, as I had been reasonably good friends with her when we were at school. I still had a fair amount of anxiety, though, as I walked in and approached the lady at the reception desk.

"Hello, is Mr Peyton in?" I asked her.

"I'll just check," she said. "Do you have an appointment?"

"No, my dad said he was recruiting for someone. I wanted to ask him about it."

"I can help you with that," she said pleasantly.

"No, it's ok," I said quickly. "I'm actually an old friend of his daughter's, so I was hoping to be able to see him."

"I'll check if he's in if you'd like to take a seat. What's your name?"

"Gary," I replied, before sitting myself down in the waiting area. The place was quite big, with a light tiled floor and a big glass frontage; this presumably made it easier for them to get the cars in and out of the showroom. There were four cars in here currently; a silver Ford Focus, a sky blue Peugeot 206, a hideous looking canary yellow Ford Ka that Sinead would have probably liked, and a deep red Jaguar X-type on the far side, the one I assumed Dad had mentioned servicing the day before. I wasn't much into cars, especially since my accident, but they always seemed to look better inside a showroom than outside on the forecourt.

Ed Peyton appeared a couple of minutes later.

"Gary Jackson," he said. "Your dad told me I might be seeing you today."

"Did he?" I said, with a tone of surprise.

"Yes, I don't know what surprised me most. The fact he said it or the fact you're here."

"Yeah, well, I've decided it's time to try and rebuild my life. He said you had a job going, so I thought I'd come in and see if it was still available."

"It's not, unfortunately, I've already decided to give it to our Carl. He's also looking to rebuild, so I've given him a chance to join the family business. However, his old job at Cables will be coming available once he's worked his notice. I can ask him to put a word in for you if you're interested."

"It would need to be a sitting down job, as a cashier or something."

"Carl works on the shop floor, but I can get him to ask and see what they say."

"Yeah, that might be good," I said. "What does Michelle do these days?"

"She's a student nurse. She works at the UCH just outside Euston station. She'll qualify and graduate this year."

"Oh, wow, she's doing well for herself."

"Yeah, she is, we're all very proud of her."

"Actually, Mr Peyton, if you don't mind me asking. If I'm going to rebuild my life then I'm going to need to make new friends, and that may be easier for me if I could start with a couple of old ones. I know Michelle and I didn't part on the best terms, but I'd like to speak to her again. Do you think she'd be willing?"

"I can certainly ask her," Ed said. "Although I can't promise anything."

"Of course," I said, and gave him a piece of paper that I'd written my number down on before I left. "If she's willing, can you ask her to give me a call or drop me a text, please? There's no rush and no pressure, it would just be nice to hear from her, that's all."

"Sure, I'll give it to her," he said.

*****

I was quite pleased to find that Sinead still wasn't back when I got home, as I wasn't sure what I'd tell her if she asked where I'd gone. If I said I'd gone for a walk she would never have believed me, as exercise just wasn't my thing. As it happens, all three of them arrived home about half an hour after I did.

It was the first time I'd seen Mary up since her fall last week, and she looked a sorry state trying to use a Zimmer frame, especially as she didn't seem particularly sure why she was doing so. She appeared very frail as Eamon supported her into the house. Sinead walked behind, wheeling in the hand luggage sized case containing all Mary's things from the hospital.

"Hello, Mary," I said enthusiastically as she walked in. "It's good to see you up and about. Are you feeling better now?"

"Don't know what he sounds so happy about," she said grumpily.

"He's just welcoming you home," Eamon said.

"Home, when are you taking me home?" Mary asked.

"You are home Mum," Sinead answered. "This is your home."

"Is it? Since when?"

"Since forever," Sinead continued. Eamon and I glanced at each other; we all knew this was just a sign of things to come.

Happily, she did seem to settle as the evening wore on, and she appeared much happier once she'd eaten the spaghetti bolognese that Sinead had prepared for us.

"That was lovely, thank you," I said to her as I finished the last mouthful.

"Did you enjoy it, Mum?" Sinead asked.

"Yes, thank you," she said, although I doubted if she really knew what question she was answering. "Has the other lady had any?" she asked.

"No Mum, that lady was at the hospital, she doesn't live here with us."

"So, are we nearly ready to go out?" Mary continued.

"Not tonight," Eamon reassured her. "You need to rest tonight. We're going to take you back to Ireland for a few days tomorrow."

"Are you taking me home?" she asked.

"Yes," he answered. "Tomorrow we'll take you home."

The conversation continued in much this manner for the rest of the evening and, even though she was barely talking to me, trying to keep track of what she was saying was exhausting. Mary had always been a chatterbox, and she hadn't lost any of her exuberance for talking. Unfortunately, she had lost the ability to string coherent sentences together, which meant what she said made no sense to us and our replies were largely lost on her. It was a frustrating exercise all-round, although it didn't dampen Mary's enthusiasm for conversation.

"My feet are cold," said Mary. "Where are my slippers?"

"I think they're still in your case, Mum," Sinead replied.

"Yes, the case," Mary went on. "She only went and won it."

"Did she?" Sinead replied automatically, but given recent events, I picked up on the comment.

"Which case was that, Mary?" I asked.

"Betsy's case, she only went and won it."

"She's talking about Betsy Cohen," informed Eamon. "She was one of the partners in Mary's law firm."

"What case did she win, Mary?" I asked.

"She's not going to know that, is she?" Sinead said, but Mary was already replying.

"The murder case, she got that young lad off," she said, before looking at me intently. "Actually, he looked a lot like you."

Sinead shot me a startled look; she'd caught on to what I was doing.

"It can't have been me," I said. "I'm sitting here with you, aren't I?"

"Yes, I am," she said.

I wasn't quite sure what to add next, and neither, seemingly, did anybody else.

"See, I told you," she shouted suddenly, pointing at the window. I turned around sharply wondering what she was seeing, but it was dark, and the curtains were closed, so there was nothing and nobody there. I found myself wondering what she was seeing.

"Mary," Eamon asked. "Did you want to go up for a shower and get into your nightclothes?"

"Are you saying I smell?" she barked.

"No, but it is night-time, you need to get ready for bed."

"Do I?" she asked.

And with a bit of cajoling and a fair amount of encouragement, he managed to help her up the stairs.

"He can't keep doing that," I said to Sinead. "She either needs a room down here turned into a bedroom or he needs to have a stair lift put in for her."

"I have been telling him this, but Dad doesn't always see things that clearly until they happen. Once he realises how difficult it is, he'll have something done. He just can't foresee it, that's all."

"What do you think about what your mum said?"

"About Betsy's case?"

"Yeah, do you think she was seeing it?"

"I don't know, Gary. I don't know how we'd ever find out. I was impressed she remembered who Betsy was, though. It's just the rest of us she seems to have forgotten."

"It's a nice thought, though," I continued. "The other Gary from my video saw the lucid dream, managed to contact you or someone else in that other Worldline, they then got Betsy involved in the case and she managed to clear him. Buzzard did say he'd worked with Betsy at the meeting last Monday, maybe he helped her."

"There's a lot of assumptions in there, isn't there?"

"There is, but I think I take comfort from it. I think I managed to undo most of the damage."

"Apart from the fact Michelle is dead in that Worldline."

"Presumed dead," I corrected. "Either way, I don't think I'll be lucid dreaming again. Not now I know the impact."

"We still don't really know if any of this is real though, do we?" Sinead said. "That said, something changed in me when you told me you'd stabbed Michelle. It's as though I saw you in a different light. Things feel different now."

"Not too different, I hope."

"That's what I'm going to Ireland to find out. The thought of going away for a week without you would have seemed so unthinkable a couple of weeks ago, I'd have ached at the very idea of it. Now I'm quite looking forward to it, not because I don't want to be with you, but I want to know how it's going to make me feel."

"And if it doesn't make you 'ache', then what?"

Sinead smiled.

"One step at a time," she said. "I'm not going to leave you, but it may take me longer than it takes you to get over all of this."

"I'm never telling you about any of my dreams again," I said.

"In a weird way," she commented, "That's probably for the best. What do you intend to do whilst I'm away?"

"I haven't thought that far ahead," I admitted.

"And what are you going to eat?"

"I'll cope," I shrugged, although I hadn't thought of that either.

"Why don't you try cooking for yourself?"

"I don't think your dad would appreciate coming home to a burnt down kitchen."

"It's not that difficult," she said. "It might do you some good to learn how to cook. It would give you some confidence, and with Mum being unable to do it anymore, it might allow you to contribute more in the house."

"I'll think about it," I said, knowing I wouldn't.

With Mary being back home, Sinead and I slept in our own rooms that night. We were aware that she was largely oblivious to these things at this stage, but it seemed wrong to blatantly disregard her rules whilst she was under the roof. When she was in hospital, it was for Eamon to make the rules, but now she was home, her rules were now applied again.

It was quite late when they left the next morning. I expected them to be gone early, but it was nearly eleven o'clock before they left. Sinead said this was because their ferry wasn't until half past four that afternoon, and the drive was just under four hours. Eamon had been out back making calls for most of the morning, but when he came back in, he called me to one side.

"Gary," he whispered, "I need you to do me a couple of favours whilst we're away."

"Sure, what do you need?"

"I've called a couple of people this morning about making improvements to the house for Mary. Tomorrow morning someone will come over to give us an estimate on a stair lift for the staircase, as she can't really do the climb anymore. Then, on Thursday afternoon, a man will come over to measure up the garage. I want to convert it into an extra bedroom with an en-suite shower so that Mary doesn't need to go upstairs at all anymore. The conversion is the end goal, but it's probably going to take a lot longer, so I want the stair lift put in first."

"Do you want me to wait until you come back to give you the estimates, or do you want me to text them to you whilst you're away?"

"Send them to me, please," he said. "But don't send them to Sinead. She might start worrying about money if we start having loads of work done to the house."

"I think she'll just be glad you are getting things modified for Mary, to be honest," I added. "You should tell her. But I won't whilst you're away if you don't want me to."

"Ok, thanks. If the estimate for the stair lift is reasonable, I might ask you to phone the fellow back and book him for whenever he says he's next available to do it. If he wants a deposit let me know, and I'll transfer him the money online."

"Understood. I will do," I said.

Soon the bags were loaded up and the three of them were in the car ready to go. Sinead and I hugged and kissed before they left, but as they pulled away, I did sense a feeling of dread. I didn't know how Sinead was going to react to time alone, and I'd not been on my own for this long since I'd moved in here. Granted, I was always happier isolated and in my own little world, but I was anxious about being completely by myself for that period of time. It was moments like this I missed not having friends.

I walked back inside and sat down on the couch, wondering what to do now. I could hear a beeping noise coming from upstairs, not what I needed when I was in the house on my own. However, when I got up there, I realised it was my phone ringing. I just hadn't been able to distinguish what it was from downstairs. The number was one I didn't recognise, but as I was clearing the notification it rang again. Ordinarily, I'd ignore numbers I didn't recognise but, on this occasion, I decided to answer it.

"Hello," I said.

"Hello, is that Gary?" came a female voice on the other end of the line.

"Yeah, speaking," I confirmed.

"Hi, Gary, it's Michelle Peyton. Dad said you'd left him your number to give me. How are you?"

Worldlines

The story continues in:

The Futility of Vengeance

A 'MANY WORLDS' NOVEL

After the murder trial failed to bring Michelle Peyton's killer to justice, Gary Jackson attempts his own form of redemption. But will the knowledge he possesses about the dream world prove to be a help or a hindrance?

Meanwhile, the real perpetrator attempts to move on with his life. But a reunion with the woman of his dreams sets off numerous chains of events.

Which lines lead to justice? Which ones lead to happiness? Will any of them provide both? And can anyone avoid the ones that offer neither?

Available now from Amazon

About the author

Born in 1985, Adam Guest resides in his English birth town; Walsall, locates in the West Midlands, with his partner, Sarah, and their two children, Jacob and Jessica.

With a lifelong passion for writing, he first started planning the Many Worlds series back in 2014. Now, in the 2020's, the series will be brought to life.

Printed in Great Britain
by Amazon

21118434R00202